SM

P9-BJG-202

RELATIVELY DANGEROUS
BY
RODERIC JEFFRIES

DEAR MISS DEMEANOR
BY
JOAN HESS

CAUSE AND EFFECT
BY
RALPH McINERNY

Published for the
DETECTIVE BOOK CLUB ®
by Walter J. Black, Inc.
ROSLYN, NEW YORK

ALL RIGHTS RESERVED

No part of these books may be reproduced
or utilized in any form or by any means,
electronic or mechanical, including photo-
copying, recording or by any information
storage and retrieval system, without permission in writing from the Publisher.

RELATIVELY DANGEROUS
Copyright © 1987
by Roderic Jeffries

DEAR MISS DEMEANOR
Copyright © 1987
by Joan Hess

CAUSE AND EFFECT
Copyright © 1987
by Ralph McInerny

THE DETECTIVE BOOK CLUB ®
Printed in the United States of America

RELATIVELY DANGEROUS
BY
RODERIC JEFFRIES

Discovering the identity of the auto accident victim should have been simple, but each answer Alvarez gets raises a new . . . and uglier . . . question.

St. Martin's Press, Inc. Edition $13.95

DEAR MISS DEMEANOR
BY
JOAN HESS

Mr. Weiss was a petty tyrant who kept his faculty in line with cryptic threats. Although it was Miss Parchester's jar of peach compote that ended his reign, Claire Malloy believes it was another hand that added the fatal ingredient . . . cyanide.

St. Martin's Press, Inc. Edition $13.95

CAUSE AND EFFECT
BY
RALPH McINERNY

Agnes and Jacob learned, to their horror, that once begun their plan could not be stopped. It proceeded inexorably to its surprising, shocking conclusion.

Atheneum $15.95

RELATIVELY DANGEROUS

BY

RODERIC JEFFRIES

Published by special arrangement with St. Martin's Press, Inc.

CHAPTER 1

The lower slopes on either side of the deep, twisting valley were covered with pines; there was also the occasional evergreen oak standing proudly tall. The upper slopes were bare and on them grew only the occasional clump of weed grass, wild thyme, rock cistus, or thistle; in parts, their nearly sheer faces had been striated by the weather so that it looked as if in some past age they had been worked by man. Along the bed of the valley there ran a torrente, normally dry, but very occasionally carrying roaring flood water.

A road ran along the west side of the valley for a couple of kilometres; then, in a succession of sharp-angled bends, wound down to the bridge which spanned the torrente. This road was unfenced throughout its length, even though at a couple of points the drop beyond was as much as thirty metres. Nervous drivers stuck nervously to the middle of the road, preferring the risk of meeting an oncoming vehicle head-on rather than approaching too close to the dangerous edge. For some years there had been a plan to erect Armco barriers at the most dangerous spots, but this had low priority since few of the millions of tourists ventured so far away from the sand and the sea.

The Ford Fiesta rounded one very sharp bend with scrabbling tyres and raced down towards the next one; its speed in such circumstances was so dangerous that it suggested either mechanical trouble or an incapacitated driver. Near the second bend, violent braking made the tyres squeal and the car entered into an incipient skid and the back wheels slid within a metre of the edge of the road, just past the apex. A driver with even a vestigial sense of self-protection would have backed right off as he sent a brief prayer of thanks to the overworked St Christopher, but the driver of the Fiesta continued at the same ridiculous speed.

The side of the mountain came out in an uneven wedge shape and the left-hander started easily, but then tightened up to become fiercer than any of the previous bends. Because of this, there was a sign denoting a dangerous corner which, since few of the others had been so marked and none of them had been less than dangerous, should have been a double warning, but it went unheeded and the Fiesta entered the bend far too fast. Only as the bend tightened right up did the driver realize the extra danger and even then his reaction was incompetent; he braked harshly. There had been a light shower a couple of hours previously and where trees overhung the road this had still not quite dried; in addition, the surface was—near the occasional oak—littered with leaves which had been blown off in the brief, but fierce, wind which had come funnelling down the valley without warning. The car skidded and this time the driver's luck did not hold. The back of the Fiesta whipped round with neck-jarring speed and slid towards and then over the edge of the road; momentum carried the car forward past the point of balance and it fell.

The rock face was almost sheer for several metres, then there was a narrow ledge on which grew a few pine trees and grass; beyond the ledge was another and much longer drop, though not quite so sheer. The car landed on the ledge, rear-end first. The force sent the front end slamming down, crunching wheels and suspension. The doors flew open and the passenger was hurled out; he tumbled into a bush, arms and legs flailing. Momentum again took the car forward. It hesitated for a second on the edge of the ledge, then went over. This time the drop was over a dozen metres, a second one even more; a final fall brought it sideways on to a huge boulder. The car was crushed into a shapeless mass of twisted metal.

The violent, screeching noise had silenced both the

cicadas and the birds, most notably a couple of crossbills, but after a while the cicadas resumed their shrilling and the birds their calling. Hot sunshine reached down to the wreck.

CHAPTER 2

Alvarez reached over to his trousers, on the chair, and extracted from the pocket a handkerchief; he wiped the sweat from his face and neck. Considering it was still only the middle of May, the heat was unusual. Or perhaps the humidity was very high. In either case, the wise man did not overwork himself.

There was a call from downstairs. 'Enrique, are you awake?'

He stared up. The sunlight was being reflected up through the louvres of the closed shutters to form a pattern on the ceiling that took his mind back to his childhood, although he couldn't pin down the exact context of the memory . . .

'Enrique. Enrique.'

'All right,' he shouted back. Dolores was an admirable woman, a fine homemaker, and a wonderful cook, but she did fuss far too much. Fussing promoted ulcers.

After a while, he sat upright and swivelled his feet round until he could put them on the floor. He yawned and looked at his watch and was surprised to discover that the time was after five. Still, there wasn't much work in hand or, at least, work which need concern him too greatly. Times might have changed and parts of Palma have become centres of mugging, but Llueso remained reasonably calm and peaceful and only the occasional tourist suffered crime; since they were seldom on the island for more than a fortnight, their cases could soon be forgotten.

He stood, pulled on his trousers and shirt; his chin tickled and he scratched it to discover that he'd forgotten to shave that morning. He left the bedroom and went downstairs to the kitchen. 'Where's the coffee?' he asked, as he looked around.

Dolores said sharply: 'What's that?'

He belatedly realized that she was in one of her moods. Admirable woman that she was, she did have them. Jaime ought to have stopped this long ago, but he'd always been inclined to settle for an easy life rather than an authoritative one.

'Has the cat taken your tongue?'

'I just thought . . .'

'I know exactly what you thought. That I was here to slave for you. Coffee is to be ready exactly when you want it and never mind how busy I am. It is enough that you want your coffee now!' Her oval face, framed by jet black hair, was filled with haughty anger.

'There's no need to bother if you're too busy.'

She rested her hands on her hips. 'So now you wish to insult me by suggesting I'd let you leave the house without a mug of coffee and a slice of coca to last you until supper?'

'But you've just said . . .'

'Sit.'

He sat at the kitchen table. Perhaps Jaime wasn't really so much to blame. After all, how could any husband deal with a wife who was so illogical? He wondered if he should have asserted himself and left? But her coca was always as light as a fairy's footprint . . .

He arrived at the guardia building at a quarter to six and the cabo on duty looked up from a girlie magazine and said that Palma had repeatedly been trying to contact him by telephone. He climbed the stairs slowly. When he reached his office, he slumped down in the chair behind the desk and briefly looked at the morning's mail which was as yet unopened. He transferred his gaze to the window and the sun-splashed wall of the house on the other side of the street. He heard a girl singing and knew a sudden happiness that now girls could spend their youth singing instead of working all day in the fields so that in later life they were crippled from arthritis and rheumatism.

The telephone rang. Superior Chief Salas's secretary, a woman who spoke as if her mouth were full of overripe plums, informed him that the superior chief wished to speak to him.

Salas, typically, offered no friendly greeting, but immediately demanded to know where in the devil he'd been all afternoon and then, with Madrileño vulgarity, made it clear he was unconvinced by the answer. 'Then perhaps now you could manage to find the time to concentrate on your work? . . . Early yesterday afternoon there was a fatal accident on the Estemos road; a car went off at one of the corners. One man was thrown clear and he's now in the Clínica Bahía, the other died instantly. Neither man carried any means of identification. Find out who they are.'

'But, señor, surely the survivor in the clinic can say that?'

'Doubtless he could, if only he were not suffering from amnesia.'

'Oh! . . . And he had no papers on him?'

'The fact that you need to make inquiries surely tells you that he had none?'

'What about the car?'

'It was hired and the man who handled the hiring has returned to his home in Madrid because of illness in the family and the other staff can't find any record. Typical incompetence.'

'Where was the car hired?'

'At the airport.'

'Then it's possible the two men are foreigners?'

'Why do you imagine I've asked you to handle the matter rather than someone in whom I'd have greater confidence? I told you at the beginning that the injured man speaks English, but hardly any Spanish.'

'In fact, señor, you didn't mention that.'

'I know precisely what I said. Kindly concentrate. I want a full report on my desk by tomorrow morning at the latest. Is that clear?'

'I'll do my best.'

'I was hoping for a more forceful contribution.'

'Who do I speak to about the crash?'

'Gómez, B divisional HQ.' He cut the connection.

Alvarez opened the top left-hand drawer of the desk and brought out a small booklet in which were listed the telephone numbers of all departments of the guardia civil. He found the number, rang it, spoke to Gómez.

'The crash took place at just after three, yesterday, Wednesday, according to the smashed watch on the dead man's wrist. The car was travelling eastwards on the Estemos road and had just passed kilometre post thirty-seven.'

Alvarez visualized the area, so isolated and, in parts, even harsh that it could have been a continent removed from any tourist beach.

'They tried to take the tightest bend on that road far too fast and the car went over the edge. It hit a ledge which flipped open the doors and since the passenger wasn't wearing a seat-belt he was thrown clear, but the driver was belted in and he carried on all the way down. He never stood a chance.'

'What did the passenger do—climb back up to the road and call for help?'

'He was too confused to do anything constructive. We found him just wandering around half way between the road and the wreck.'

'If he didn't call you out, who did?'

'Another car came along and the driver stopped short of the bend for a leak. He saw something in the torrente glinting in the sun, walked round the bend to find out what it was, realized the crash could only just have happened and drove on to the nearest telephone, four kilometres away.'

'Why didn't he climb down to help the passenger?'

'He'd no idea that there was one. All he saw was the wrecked car. The passenger must have been hidden by the trees.'

'Wouldn't he have heard the car stop on the road?'

'Who knows? He can't speak Spanish and anyway was knocked silly.'

'He was lucky, then, that this other car stopped.'

'Right. Still, the hospital says his injuries aren't serious and he'll get over his confusion problems. I suppose that in the end he'd have got himself up to the road if no one had stopped.'

'And you haven't been able to identify either him or the driver?'

'After we'd got the driver out—and if I told you what that was like, you'd not want any supper—we searched him and the car. No papers of any sort.'

'And the same with the passenger?'

'Right again. And the only luggage was a backpack, the kind hikers use with an aluminium frame. That contained clothes and some tinned food, but nothing else.'

'Did you try to get a name out of the passenger even though he was so confused?'

'My oppo did, since he reckons he's learned a lot of English from the birds he's pulled on the beaches. Never got anywhere. Not learning the right kind of English, maybe.'

'It's funny, neither of them having any papers.'

'Not necessarily. Last week I stopped a car for crossing a solid line in the middle of a village at twice the speed limit and the driver, who was English, said he never carried any papers around with him because he didn't have to at home. I bloody near told him to clear off back there.'

'Even so, the backpack suggests a hiker. You'd expect him to carry means of identification around . . . I gather you've been on to a car hire firm at the airport?'

'Not me.'

'Who did get in touch with them?'

'I've no idea.'

'D'you know the name?'

'Worldwide Hire Cars.' Gómez's pronunciation of the English words was so poor that Alvarez had to ask three times for them to be repeated.

He thanked Gómez and rang off, phoned the car hire firm at the airport and spoke to a woman with a voice of honey and spice.

'I'm sorry, but I just can't answer you, Inspector. It's all very worrying and I've had the manager shouting down the phone, but Toni handled that hiring and when his mother was suddenly taken ill, he flew back to Madrid.'

'But somewhere there must be the usual record of the hiring?'

'Yes, of course. But as I said to the manager, I just can't find it. You see, I'm only relieving Toni and I don't know his system of filing.'

'Have you any idea when he'll be back?'

'As a matter of fact, he phoned an hour ago to say his mother's much better and he reckons to return early tomorrow.'

'Then I'll be along to have a word with him in the morning.'

He rang off, dialled the Clínica Bahía. A nurse told him that the unnamed patient's physical injuries were relatively minor and he was making a good recovery from them, but his mind was still very confused and his loss of memory complete. The prognosis? The doctors were slightly surprised that his mind should still be so confused—he didn't seem to have suffered any heavy blows to the head—but it was always very difficult to be certain about the brain; in the circumstances, they could offer no prognosis.

He replaced the receiver and relaxed. Toni was in Madrid, the car's passenger didn't know a thing. Even Salas, then, would have to agree that there was nothing more that could be done for the moment. His thoughts wandered. Hadn't

Dolores said that she was cooking lomo con col for supper . . .

CHAPTER 3

Terminal A was in chaos; long queues had formed at several check-in points, some of which were still not manned, the departure board had not been altered since the previous evening, the arrival board was not working at all, the public address system had hysterics, and the information desk was manned by an attractive woman who was too busy flirting over the telephone to monitor the VDU in front of her, which in any case was rolling so heavily that it was impossible to read, while the luggage handlers were having their second merienda of the morning so that all carousels in the arrival lounges were empty. A typical morning at Son San Juan airport.

Alvarez threaded his way through the press of people around the outer doors of the arrival hall and crossed to the line of booths which were occupied by representatives of various car hire firms. Above one of the middle ones was the name, in blue lettering on a white background, World-wide Car Hire.

A man, who was working at the desk, looked up. He noted Alvarez's less-than-smart appearance. 'Yes?' he asked in bored tones.

'Are you Toni Bibiloni?'

'And what if I am?'

'Inspector Alvarez, Cuerpo General de Policía.'

Bibiloni stood with studied elegance. He was dressed in lilac-coloured shirt and light green linen trousers. He was tall, slim, sleekly handsome, and very self-assured. 'You've come about the car that crashed?'

'That's right.' Alvarez's reaction was as immediate as it

was irrational—he disliked the man. 'Did the hirer pay by credit card or cash?'

'Cash.'

'Why isn't there any record of the hiring?'

'There is.'

'The person I spoke to yesterday . . .'

'Dear Tania,' said Bibiloni languidly. 'A simply charming person, but so inclined to muddle. She failed to look in the right place.'

Ten to one, thought Alvarez uncharitably, there was some sort of fiddle going on; probably Bibiloni diverted cash into his own pocket. It wouldn't be difficult, provided he'd got his hands on an extra supply of forms. If there were no queries, the cash stayed with him and there was no official record of the hiring; if there was, he simply 'found' the copy of the hiring contract and the money, carefully put on one side . . .

'Is there anything more?'

Alvarez jerked his thoughts back to the present. 'I'd like to have a look at it.'

'Presumably, you're referring to the copy of the hiring agreement?' Bibiloni turned, crossed to the desk, took a key from his pocket and unlocked one of the drawers, brought out a folder from which he extracted two carbon copies, one of which he handed over.

Alvarez read. Steven Thompson. Address on the island, Hotel Verde, Cala Oraña; passport number, C 229570 A; English driving licence number, 255038 ST16KD; date of hiring, 14th to 17th May. He looked up. 'Do you remember this hiring?'

'Of course.'

'Was he on his own?'

'Yes.'

'Had he flown from Britain?'

'I can't say.'

'He didn't mention where he'd come from?'

'No. Only that it was warmer here.'

'Which makes it sound as if he had come from Britain?'

'If you say so.'

'Did he mention why he was only going to be on the island for four days?'

'No.'

'What luggage did he have?'

'A small suitcase and one of those executive briefcases.'

'Then he might have been here on business?'

'Why not?'

'Did he speak Spanish well?'

'Since I am fluent in English, that is what we spoke; it's so much easier than listening to someone mispronouncing everything.'

Alvarez returned the copy of the hiring agreement. 'Make certain this doesn't disappear again until my inquiries are completed.'

Bibiloni shrugged his shoulders, but his expression was now watchful rather than supercilious.

Alvarez left and walked out through the west doors. The sky was cloudless and the sun was hot and by the time he reached his car he was sweating. Too much alcohol, too many cigarettes, and too much food; he must remember his resolution to cut back on all three, he thought, as he unlocked the driving door and sat, then hurriedly opened his window and turned on the fan because the interior of the ancient Seat 600 was like an oven. He picked up the pack of cigarettes on the front passenger seat and lit one, remembered his decision of only minutes before, decided that it would be a terrible waste to throw the cigarette away.

He drove on the autoroute until it came to an end, then continued along the Paseo Marítimo, the wide, elegant road which ringed the bay and gave a quick route to the west side of Palma and the succession of concrete jungles which had done so much to ruin what had once been one of the most beautiful bays in the Mediterranean.

Cala Oraña had originally been a small bay with a wide, curving beach that was backed by land of such poor quality that it had supported only scrub trees and undergrowth on which a few goats and hollow-ribbed sheep had browsed. It had escaped the first wave of development which had swept the island because the land had been left to two minors who were therefore unable to sell, even thought the price then offered had been very good. Their immediate loss became their ultimate gain. By the time both had attained their majority, the land they owned was worth many times its previous value because it was now one of the very last stretches of coastline undeveloped. They'd sold to a company whose directors had had more imagination and taste, if no less greed, than most of their competitors and the company had promoted an up-market development, aimed at attracting people who wanted to live or holiday within easy reach of Palma, but who were not prepared to suffer the sardine-ugliness of a Magalluf. Only two hotels and two appartment blocks were built and none of these was more than four floors high; on the rest of the land were medium to large luxurious villas, each in a plot of at least two thousand square metres. And, as an added bonus, all sewage pipes discharged into the next bay.

Hotel Verde was on the east side of the bay. Designed by a Brazilian architect, it was sharply modernistic in appearance, yet a certain restraint had made certain that it remained just in taste for a traditionalist; even the exterior green tiling, which had provided the pedestrian name, complemented rather than exaggerated. It was surrounded on three sides by a well-tended garden and on the fourth by the sand and the sea.

Parking was to the right of the main entrance and Alvarez drew in alongside a Mercedes 190E on tourist plates. He left his car, stared at the Mercedes and then at his 600 and sighed, climbed the steps up on to the patio and went through swing doors into a large foyer, cool and comfortable.

The reception desk was manned by two men, dressed in black coats and ties. He introduced himself to the elder and explained what he wanted. The receptionist had a word with the assistant manager, then showed Alvarez into the office behind the reception desk.

The assistant manager was tall for a Mallorquin, pale-faced, suggesting he seldom went out in the sun, and clearly somewhat harassed. He picked up a pencil and fiddled with it. 'You're trying to find out something about the unfortunate Señor Thompson? I'll see if I can trace his booking.' He swivelled his chair round to face a small desk-top computer and VDU. He tapped out a command on the keyboard and a string of names and dates, in vertical order, appeared on the screen. He leaned forward slightly to read, suggesting he needed glasses. 'He stayed here on the fourteenth, just for the one night.'

'How did he book?'

He deleted that list, entered another command and a second one appeared. He frowned. 'I wish the damned thing wouldn't get so muddled up.' He cleared the screen and summoned up a third list. 'Booked by telephone. There was no confirmatory letter, but then the call was only two days prior to the booking.'

'Have you any idea where he telephoned from?'

'None.'

'Did you meet him?'

'I didn't, no. In my job, I really only meet guests if they're complaining about something and the desk can't cool them down. Which is far too often.'

'Would it be possible to have a word with whoever booked him in and also to see the register?'

The assistant manager stood and went to the doorway and called in the younger receptionist, who brought with him a large cloth-bound book. This, opened, he passed over. Alvarez read the penultimate entry. Steven Thompson, British passport number C 229570 A, registered from the

14th to the 15th. 'Haven't you had more than one other guest since he was here?' he asked curiously.

'Good heavens, yes! That's the register for the independents; we naturally keep a separate one for the packages.' His tone said far more than his words. They would have chosen to cater solely for the independent traveller, but the world had changed and now even the luxury hotels had to accept bookings from package holiday operators. But those which were staffed by persons who still appreciated the difference between quality and quantity maintained what standards they could.

Alvarez spoke to the receptionist, handing back the register as he did so. 'Do you remember Señor Thompson?'

'I'm afraid I don't really. You see, it was change-over day and there's always trouble then.'

'D'you think any of the other staff would be likely to remember him?'

The assistant manager answered. 'The porter would have carried his bags . . . Who was on duty then?'

'Servero, I think,' said the receptionist.

'See if you can find him, will you, and ask him to come in here. But before you go . . . Inspector, would you like a drink?'

'A coñac would go down very well.'

'And I'll have my usual.'

The receptionist left and there was a short wait, then the porter, dressed in traditional waistcoat, entered the office, a tray in his hand. 'I was told to bring this along in a hurry,' he said, as he put the tray down on the desk. He was in his late fifties and had learned to perfection the art of insolent servility as found in most British hotels.

The assistant manager picked up the balloon glass of brandy and leaned across to pass it to Alvarez. 'The Inspector wants to ask you a few questions,' he said, just before he drank from the glass of still orangeade.

The porter's expression became wary.

'Do you remember Señor Thompson?' Alvarez said. 'He was here Monday night.'

'He was an independent,' said the assistant manager.

'Ah! You must be talking about the gentleman who arrived in a white Ford Fiesta.'

'He certainly was in a Fiesta,' said Alvarez, 'but I can't say what the colour was.'

'And his luggage was one small suitcase and a director's case.'

'That's right.'

'I've a very good memory,' said the porter complacently, apparently forgetting that initially he had appeared to be having difficulty in recalling the guest. 'Beautiful quality luggage. Not like most of them who come here; plastic for them.'

'You carried his luggage in?'

'That's right.'

'Will you tell me exactly what happened from the moment you met him?'

The porter, intent on proving just how excellent his memory really was, spoke at length. He'd carried the luggage in and across to the desk. The señor, allocated Room 34, had registered. He'd taken the key and had led the way up to the third floor and along the right-hand corridor to the end room. He'd unlocked the door and ushered the señor inside. He'd casually remarked that this was the nicest room in the hotel. It always made a guest feel doubly welcome to be singled out for special attention; or to think he had been.

'Was he talkative?'

'Very friendly, not like some of the people we get here.'

'Did you speak in Spanish or English?'

'English.'

'What did he talk about?'

'This and that. I asked him if he'd been to the island before.'

'Had he?'

'Several times . . . D'you mind telling me a bit more of what this is all about? I mean, he was a real gent—you can't mistake 'em, not if you've been in the job as long as I have—so what's the problem?'

'Unfortunately, he's been killed in a car crash and although we now know his name, we can't find any reference that will enable us to contact his next-of-kin.'

'There must be something written down in his papers.'

'We don't know for certain he was carrying any,' said Alvarez patiently.

'Then what d'you think was in his director's case?'

'We don't know because we haven't found it.'

'Then what about his wallet?'

'That was also missing . . . Did he comment on any of his previous visits? Did he suggest when they were or where he stayed?'

'Nothing like that.'

'D'you reckon he was deliberately avoiding any definite references?'

The porter, sharp but not particularly intelligent, was bewildered by the question and it had to be repeated in a different form before he answered: 'I wouldn't have said he was.'

'You learned nothing about his life?'

The porter scratched his neck. 'Only how much he liked sailing.'

'How d'you know that?'

'Because he talked about it and said as how it had been too squally for the past few days to take his boat out.'

'He talked about "his" boat?'

'That's what I've just said.'

'Anything more?'

'No.'

'If you should remember anything, get in touch, will you?'

'I've told you everything; I've a good memory.'

'Then thanks for all your help.'

The porter went over to the door, opened it, turned. 'I'll tell you one thing. He was a real gentleman.' He went out.

The assistant manager spoke drily. 'Obviously, the señor tipped him generously.'

Alvarez looked at his empty glass and wondered if the hotel would prove equally generous.

CHAPTER 4

Clínica Bahía, the smallest of the state hospitals in Palma, was situated on the eastern boundary of the city. It was an ugly slab of a building and inside little attempt had been made to brighten its image so that the gloomy reception area correctly set the scene. Plans either to replace or to modernize it were regularly updated, but never exercised. Yet despite this, the staff were efficient and cheerful and they usually managed to uplift a patient's morale.

Alvarez took the lift to the fourth floor and then walked along the right-hand corridor to the small recess in which was a desk for the nursing staff and, on either side of this, wash- and store-rooms. A young nurse was working at some papers and he explained what he wanted.

'Señor Higham? He's in Room 413.'

He spoke with sharp surprise. 'Then you have managed to find out his name?'

'I didn't because I don't speak any English and his Spanish sounds like Portuguese.' She grinned. 'But Dr Bauzá did post-graduate work in America and so he can speak English; he discovered the señor had recovered his memory.'

'Has it fully returned?'

'I couldn't say exactly, but I think it must have done because Dr Bauzá said he's making a good recovery and ought to be able to leave quite soon.'

'That's good . . . All right if I have a chat with him?'

'I don't see why not. But if he starts looking tired, you'll have to stop immediately.'

Most of the rooms on the floor contained four beds, but 413 had only two and the second one was empty. Higham was sitting up reading a paperback. A man in his middle forties, he had a round, plump face. A small, neat moustache, the same light brown as his hair, was set above a wide, cheerful mouth. The only visible signs that he had been in a car accident were the plaster on his right cheek and a bruise which stretched across his right chin.

Alvarez introduced himself, then said how delighted he was to find the other better.

'No more delighted than I am, I can assure you!' His voice was warm and tuneful. 'These last few days have been like . . . The nearest I can get to it is, it's been like having a spider's web throttling my brain. I've kept struggling to get my thoughts lined up straight, but they just wouldn't. Been rather frightening, really; a bit of me could still think and keep wondering if I'd gone round the twist. But, thank God, that's all over and done with and now I can think as straight as I ever could, which maybe isn't as straight as it ought to be . . .' He laughed, then became serious. 'Look, maybe you can tell me something. How's the other man, the driver? No one here seems to know. I've got this very hazy idea that he must have been badly hurt . . .'

'I am afraid that he died in the crash.'

'My God!' He fiddled with his moustache as he stared into the distance. 'I didn't realize things were that bad . . . I was lucky, then?'

'Very lucky. And almost certainly because you were not wearing your seat-belt so that you were thrown clear.'

'You never know, do you? Wear a belt and save your life; don't wear it and save your life.'

'Do you feel strong enough to answer a few questions?'

'I'm fine.'

Alvarez settled on the spare bed. 'We've had a bit of a problem because until this morning no one knew who either you or the driver was.'

'I don't follow. I mean, I wasn't sparking on all four cylinders, I know, but you've got my passport. And Steve must have had papers on him.'

'There were no papers of any sort on either of you.'

'But there must have been.'

'I'm afraid not. Where was your passport?'

'Everything like that was in my backpack. It was far too hot to wear a coat and papers and money aren't safe in a trouser pocket . . . You're not saying my money's gone as well?'

'We didn't find any.'

'You looked in the backpack?'

'It was thoroughly searched.'

'Christ! That just caps everything.'

'Was your money in cash?'

'Not very much. Most of it was in travellers' cheques . . . Then I did hear someone and it wasn't imagination!'

'How d'you mean?'

Higham shook his head, as if to clear it; he spoke quickly. 'The worst part was seeing what was going to happen and not being able to stop it. I tried to grab the wheel and steer us away, but it was no good. As we went over, I can remember thinking: So this is what it's like to crash. And then things got painful. And now they're still confused even though everything else is back to normal. I'm pretty certain I shouted for help for a while; nothing happened, so I picked myself up and stumbled around, but I kept falling over things . . . And it was when I was lying on the ground, too weak to move any more, that I thought I heard voices. I called out, but they didn't seem to hear me and in the end I kind of decided that the voices had only been in my mind. But if the money's gone, there probably was someone, wasn't there?'

'It certainly seems so,' he agreed, angered that there could be men who'd rob the dead and the injured and leave the injured to his fate. 'Do you have any idea whether Señor Thompson had much money on him?'

'He must have had a fair bit. After all, he gave me lunch at a restaurant that certainly wasn't cheap and there was still plenty left in his wallet when he'd finished paying.'

'Would you like to guess how much?'

'I wouldn't. I mean, I took care not to take too much interest.'

'Of course . . . You heard talking, which means two or more men. Did you understand anything they said or did the rhythm of their speech suggest what language they were talking?'

'No to both. Like I said, it was all so hazy I wasn't even certain I really was hearing 'em.'

'Señor, have you been long on the island?'

'Hardly any time at all. You see, I didn't leave England until . . .'

His job in England, a wages clerk, had been boring but safe. He'd married a little later than his pals, after he'd saved quite a bit of money—he'd always led a steady life although ever since he'd been a youngster he'd dreamed of adventure. Debbie had been considerably younger than he. At first, that hadn't mattered. Probably it never would have done if her sister hadn't married a man who knew all the dodges, especially how to work the more profitable VAT fiddles. Spent money like water. Debbie's sister had flaunted new clothes, jewellery, cars . . . Debbie had become as sour as hell and had nagged and nagged him to find another job where he'd make better money. Against his will, he'd moved. Things had worked out OK for a while, even though his income still fell far short of his brother-in-law's—but then cheap imports from the Far East had hit his new firm so hard that it had very nearly been bankrupted. Inevitably, there'd been redundancies and these had been based on the usual last in, first out. His redundancy money hadn't strained its brown envelope . . .

He'd hoped Debbie would understand; after all, if he hadn't moved, he'd still have a job. But she hadn't been willing to understand anything or to stand by him and she'd cleared out. Soon afterwards, he'd heard that she'd moved in with a friend of her brother-in-law who ran a Porsche and thought that a twenty-pound note was loose change.

Strangely, despite the bitter pain, his overriding emotion had been one of anger, directed not at her or her lover, but at himself. Why had he been such a bloody fool as to allow himself to be so trapped by conformity—since sixteen, all dreams ignored and all ambition directed towards a steady job with a pension, a house on mortgage, a worthwhile savings account—that he'd laid himself open to such hurt? And in his anger, he'd sworn an ending to all conformity. Draw a line through his past life and start again. Remember those dreams. Wander the world . . .

He'd sold the house and paid off the mortgage. He'd left that road in which he'd lived all those dead years without saying goodbye to anyone. He'd drifted through France, crossed the Pyrenees, taken months on the journey down to Valencia, where he'd spent the winter in the company of other, mostly much younger, drifters. In March, his feet had begun to itch once more. Someone had talked about standing on the north-west coast of Mallorca and watching the sun sink below the sea and discovering one's immortal soul. He didn't give a damn about his soul, but the mental image had triggered a desire. He'd crossed in the ferry, hitch-hiked to somewhere with a name like Son Ella, and had stood on a high cliff and watched the blood-red, oblate sun sink below the sea. It had been slightly eerie. No wonder ancient man had been scared at every sunset that the sun wouldn't reappear . . . 'I'm sorry. God knows why I'm going on and on like this. You probably won't believe me, but usually I don't bore other people with my problems.'

'Señor, I have not been bored. And perhaps it's good for you to speak about all these things.'

'Yes, but . . .' He stopped.

Alvarez smiled. 'But being an Englishman, you do not like to put your emotions on display?'

Higham looked embarrassed.

'Tell me, how did you come to meet Señor Thompson?'

'I was walking along the road, hot and tired, trying to thumb a lift. He stopped and when he heard I'd no definite objective, said he'd show me a part of the island tourists didn't usually see. We drove up into the mountains.'

'Then he knew the island well; perhaps had a house here?'

'He knew it well, yes. But from something he said, I'm pretty certain he didn't own any property here.'

'Did he mention friends and where they live?'

'No, he didn't. In fact, looking back, I'd say he was one of those types who's always interested in other people, but is careful never to talk about himself much.'

'I think he gave you lunch?'

'We stopped at a restaurant right up in the mountains that had a fantastic view. The place was obviously pretty pricey and I told him I just couldn't afford it. He said the meal was to be on him. Frankly, that had me thinking just for a second.'

'Thinking what?'

'Whether he was a queer and had me in his sights.'

'Do you think that was right?'

'No way. He was just one of those blokes who likes meeting people and hearing about them.'

'Did he drink a lot?'

'No. He mentioned that since early morning he'd had a migraine threatening and booze was one of the things which could bring on an attack. But that didn't stop him giving me a couple of drinks before the meal and ordering a good bottle of wine; so by the end, I was very cheerful, thank you . . .

'We hadn't long left the restaurant when he stopped the car. He was sick; God, how he was sick! When he'd begun to recover, I offered to drive, but he said the car was only insured for him and in any case he was OK. So he started up again. And then . . . He had another attack, much worse than the first and didn't stop in time. We started weaving all over the road and going like the clappers. I tried to grab the wheel, but he'd still got hold of it . . . And that's how we went over the edge.'

'A very frightening experience. Thank you, señor, for telling me.' Alvarez stood.

'D'you have to go, then?'

'Yes, I do.'

'D'you think . . . Is there any chance you could drop in again some time and have another chat? I mean, with no one but the doctor speaking English, I'm cut right off.'

'I certainly will call in if I can.'

'That's great. And if you do, I don't know if there'd be any chance of finding an English newspaper?'

'I will try.'

'That's a real pal . . . Just one more thing. D'you think there's much hope of recovering my cash?'

'Frankly, I'm afraid not.'

'If I could get my hands on those bastards . . . Still, at least I'll get a refund on the travellers' cheques.'

'Perhaps I can help you over that. Sometimes in order to claim one needs a note from the police to confirm that the loss has been reported to them.'

'That's a thought. D'you think you could let me have something?'

'Indeed.'

'Then thanks again.'

Alvarez said goodbye and left. On the ground floor there was a newsagent and in this he found a copy of the *Daily Mail*. He bought it, took the lift back up to the fourth floor and handed the paper to a nurse and asked her to give it to

Higham. Then he returned downstairs and left the building.
He was glad to escape. He loathed hospitals because they
reminded him that he was only mortal.

CHAPTER 5

After a slightly delayed siesta—since he'd returned late
from Palma—and a subsequent and essential cup of coffee,
Alvarez left the kitchen and went through to the front room
and the telephone. He reported to the superior chief.

'You've hardly made any progress,' complained Salas.

'On the contrary, señor,' he began, somewhat piqued,
'I've identified both men and determined the cause of the
accident . . .'

'Have you discovered who's the dead man's nearest relative and where he or she lives?'

'No . . .'

'Or the name and address of any friend who lives on the
island?'

'No . . .'

'Then you've attained little of any significance. Has it
occurred to you to send the number of the dead man's
passport to England to ask their help in tracing his next-of-
kin?'

'There hasn't been time, señor. I've only just returned
from making my inquiries. But it's my intention to get on
to England the moment I ring off now . . .'

'Inspector, if you could contrive actually to accomplish
one quarter of what you're always about to do, your crime
figures would be impressive instead of a disgrace.'

'Señor, my clear-up rate is quite good . . .'

'Only because you carefully forget to record, let alone
investigate, a large proportion of the crimes committed,'
snapped Salas, before he cut the connection.

Alvarez replaced the receiver. Sadly, Salas lacked the right attitude to command; praise, for him, was a dirty word. He returned to the dining-room, went over to the large sideboard, and opened the right-hand cupboard.

'What are you looking for?' demanded Dolores, startling him.

He looked at her as she stood in the doorway of the kitchen. 'I was just wondering if there was coñac for after the meal or whether I needed to go out to buy some.'

'There's half a bottle, which is far more than you two are going to drink this evening,' she said aggressively.

He wondered if he should go ahead and pour himself a drink now, which had been his original intention, quickly decided that that would hardly be politic since she was obviously in one of her more belligerent moods. 'That's all right, then.' He closed the cupboard door.

'You would be much healthier if you stopped drinking.'

'Yes, I suppose I might be.'

She glared at him, returned into the kitchen. A moment later, there was the ringing noise of something dropping on to the floor, followed by an angry expression of such vulgarity that he hastily assured himself he must have mistaken the words.

He looked at the clock. An hour before the meal. Just time, then, to go along to the guardia post and his office, there to phone through the details of the passport so that inquiries could be made in England. He stood. What right had Salas to imply that he did not show a keen initiative?

The next morning, Alvarez was preparing to leave the house —a little on the late side because he had slept through two calls from Dolores—when the undertaker from Fogufol rang. 'I've been on to Palma and they told me to talk to you because you're in charge.'

'In charge of what?'

'The car crash, of course. What am I to do with the stiff? Is there to be a funeral or isn't there?'

'Of course there is,' he replied testily. 'But until we can trace the next-of-kin, we don't know whether it's to be here or in England.'

'Are you saying I'm to keep him in store until I hear from you?'

'I'm saying exactly that.'

'You realize it's costing?'

'You'll be paid.'

'Just you remember that from now on you're responsible for seeing that it is.'

Alvarez replaced the receiver. No one could be prouder of being a Mallorquin than he, but that pride didn't blind him to the fact that for many of his countrymen money had become the most important part of life—or death.

In Palma, the litter-boxes and bins were emptied six times a week in late spring, summer, and early autumn, since in the heat anything perishable rotted very quickly. As the dustman lifted out the inner wire basket of one of the lamp-post boxes in Calle Arnoux, he saw among the paper and orange peel a wallet, between the two halves of which was a blue passport. He opened the passport. It belonged to Jack Higham.

Muriel Taylor looked at her reflection in the dressing-table mirror and initially was well satisfied, but then she noticed the curl of hair on the right-hand side. That blasted woman, she thought. The best hair salon in Palma and the head assistant couldn't trim properly. Archie had recently remarked that the country ran in spite of the people who worked in it, not because of them. He originally must have heard someone else say that.

She examined her face again. No one would ever guess from her appearance that she was closing up fast on forty.

Her skin had the purity and tautness of a twenty-year-old. Her eyes were an unusual blue; men were fascinated by them. Her nose was Grecian. A friend had once called her mouth Roman patrician. Truly cosmopolitan. Her teeth were white and regular and an advertisement for her dentist in Harley Street; she couldn't understand why so many of the British risked going to the local dentists who, for all she knew, still worked with treadle drills.

She left the stool and stood so that she could see herself in the full-length mirror. She had a near-perfect figure, hardly thickening anywhere, thanks to a rigorous diet, exercise, and will-power. She crossed to the longest of the built-in cupboards and slid back the right-hand door. Which dress to wear? Not too smart or it would be completely out of place. She chose a print frock which she had bought in Palma on a day when she was feeling dismal and needed to do something to buck herself up. She hadn't worn it again because once she'd cheered up she'd rightly decided it lacked chic, but today that would be an advantage. 'Oh, God, what a bloody bore!' she said aloud, thinking of the luncheon and all the pleased-to-meet-you women to whom she'd have to make the effort to be polite.

Not that she was a snob. Very far from it. She believed in valuing a person for himself, not because of his background. Not, of course, that that meant that she was indifferent to those backgrounds. She rightly demanded standards, even if she was broad-minded about them. She didn't hold that wealth was an essential. She knew one or two people whose incomes were as low as £25,000 a year yet who were perfectly pleasant. Schooling was important, but not an immutable criterion. Certainly the public schools —that was, Eton, Harrow, and Winchester—produced gentlemen, but the products of the bourgeois places, such as Sherborne, could often pass for same . . .

She slid the frock over her head and wriggled herself into it, zipped up the side, smoothed down the front, re-examined

herself in the mirror. On her, since she added considerable
ton, the frock wasn't nearly as *déclassé* as on the hanger. But
it would still suit its purpose because the other women
wouldn't be able to take offence. It was very important not
to shame them and thus incur their strange envies. The
Surbiton golf club secretary's wife, Archie had called them.
That also had to be a remark he had heard someone else
make . . .

She took off the dress and hung it up, put on the print
frock she had been wearing before. A neat little Cardin
number which suited her to perfection.

She left the bedroom and went down the wide, curving
staircase into the large hall. Many of the houses in the area
were little boxes, built for and by people without either
money or taste, but Ca'n Grande had been designed for
an Armenian, and one could say what one liked about
Armenians, the few educated ones had good taste and a
developed, if at times oily, sense of beauty. Archie said that
Ca'n Grande was like a spinnaker in a light breeze. She
rather liked the analogy, even though it was too fanciful to
be in really good taste. He was an amusing and comfortable
companion to have around the place, offering the same
devoted companionship as a bob-tailed sheepdog, but without all the mess of cast hairs. Of course, he wasn't particularly intelligent—which sometimes made her wonder why
he had not risen higher in the Navy—but he was properly
mannered. It was a pity that his elder brother had inherited
both title and estate.

One of the maids came into the hall. 'Good morning,
señora,' she said in broken English.

'Good morning, Catalina.' Muriel did not speak Spanish.
She was not the kind of person to go native.

'You wish breakfast?'

She nodded. When she'd bought the house and had agreed
to continue to employ the staff, she had encountered in them
a regrettable tendency towards familiarity, Mallorquins

having strange notions about equality. But she had soon taught them to show her due respect.

She went into the breakfast-room. The house was built on an outcrop of rock and the breakfast-room was to the south-east so that beyond the window was the patio and then, below, the sea. Few other homes on the island could boast so magnificent a view.

Catalina entered, carrying a tray. She carefully placed on the small circular table a silver teapot, milk jug, saccharine dispenser, toast rack with two slices of carefully triangulated toast, small bowl of Cooper's marmalade, and a large bowl containing oranges, tangerines, and very large white grapes.

'Thank you, Catalina.' She was invariably polite to her servants, even though she paid them. Only a parvenu was rude to staff.

She sat, spread the clean table napkin over her lap—serviette was for those who were ignorant or snobbishly unaware that napkin had by far the superior pedigree, being descended from Middle English—and helped herself to a piece of toast and marmalade. There was no butter. She had given up butter at breakfast because of the starving hordes in Africa.

She heard a car, looked at her watch and realized that this couldn't be Archie because she'd ordered him never to arrive before eleven o'clock. Then the car would be continuing on to the house which stood to the left of, and well below, Ca'n Grande. A Greek lived there. Greece might have joined the Common Market and he might be as rich as Crœsus, but she had nothing to do with him because he always belched after eating. She finished the first piece of toast, poured herself out some tea. She must make certain that Archie sat between her and the chairwoman at the luncheon. The chairwoman was a large, stout, and very earnest woman, filled with good works, whose husband had been something like a butcher. Archie was wonderful at dealing with butchers' widows. In fact, he was rather a dear.

If only he had some money, it would have been amusing to be married to him for a while ... . Good God! she thought, astounded. Hadn't her last marriage taught her anything? She finished her breakfast, furious because she had reminded herself of all the humiliation she had for years been so determined to forget.

She pressed the bell to tell Catalina to clear the table, opened the French window and stepped out on to the patio which ran round three sides of the house. The slightest of breezes ruffled the curls on her head as it brought the tang of the sea. She crossed to the swing seat, with wide overhead awning, and sat. A slight suntan was chic, a heavy one antipodean. In any case, too much sun stripped out the natural oils and replaced them with years. Several of her friends looked very much older than she.

There was the sound of another car approaching and this time it turned into the drive. If this was Archie, the time was eleven o'clock. There were moments when she wondered about his strict regard for time; was there, hidden away in his family tree, a rather serious mésalliance?

Catalina stepped out on to the patio. 'Señora, is Señor Wheeldon.'

'Tell him I am at home.'

Archibald Devreux Peregrine Wheeldon was large, cheerful, and boyishly handsome; the tight, curly hair which topped his oval face had been handed on through at least ten generations. His nose had been broken in a school boxing match and had not been properly set, the triangular scar to the right of his mouth marked where another 'gentleman' had kicked him in an inter-house rugger match. The two blemishes prevented his handsomeness being at all feminine. In deference to Muriel's wishes that he should dress decently and not like the average expatriate, he wore a silk shirt and square and a pair of fawn linen trousers with knife-edge creases.

'Good morning, Muriel.' He leaned over and kissed her

on the cheek, knowing better than to kiss her on the lips when they were in a situation where one of the servants might see them. 'You're looking lovelier than ever.'

He was not, she thought regretfully, an original lover, but he was sincere, which was a compensation.

He looked round for a chair and picked up one of the wrought-iron ones set about a very ornate wrought-iron table.

'You can't sit on that, Archie, it's far too uncomfortable: that's for people I don't want hanging about the place. Call Catalina and tell her to bring out one of the comfortable ones.'

'It's not worth bothering her . . .'

'She's paid to be bothered. In any case, she should have had the sense to put it out before you came.'

He went over to the small speaking grille on the wall of the house, pressed the call button, and spoke in fluent Spanish.

As he returned, Muriel said: 'Have you seen Genevieve since Saturday?'

'I don't think I have.'

'Tony says that she and Henry have had a row and he's gone back to England. I wonder if that's true.'

'I shouldn't think so.'

'She has seen rather a lot of Mark recently. Why, I can't imagine. Mark's so very swarthy.'

'His mother was Italian.'

'I would presume that she came from a long way south of Italy.'

'Wherever, he's a nice enough chap.'

'Archie, you're in one of your difficult moods.'

'No, I'm not.'

'Yes, you are. You're doing nothing but argue.'

Catalina came out of the house with an aluminium-framed patio chair which she found difficulty in carrying, because of its size and shape. He hurried over and took it from her;

she thanked him, smiled, returned to the house.

He set the chair down in front of the swing seat.

'What was she saying?' asked Muriel.

'That she hoped it would take my weight.'

'How dare she be so insolent!'

'Steady on, she was only joking.'

'My servants do not joke with my guests.'

'What do you mean, guest?'

'How else do you suggest I refer to you?'

'Forget it,' he said, with sudden, sad bitterness.

She said fretfully: 'You're not going to start that again, I hope. Not today of all days.'

'What's so special about today?'

'Have you forgotten? I've got to go to that beastly luncheon—you're coming with me—and be polite to all the people I normally take such trouble to avoid.'

'Some of them are very nice. You'd like them if you'd give yourself the chance.'

'That is very cruel of you.'

'Cruel?'

'Very, very cruel. What on earth has happened to upset you so terribly?'

'Nothing has.'

'Don't be ridiculous. You're being horribly prickly and that always means something has happened. Now, what is the matter?'

'It's just something I read in the *Bulletin*.'

'If you will not stick to *The Times* . . . What have you read?'

'They've identified the man who died in the car crash up in the mountains last Wednesday.'

'Why should that matter? Surely it's not anyone we know?'

'Steven Thompson.'

'Christ!'

He was surprised by her violent reaction.

'I need a drink.'

He opened his mouth to speak.

'And if you're going to start talking about the bloody yardarm, shut up.'

'I wasn't going to. I wanted to say that I didn't think you liked him or I wouldn't have told you so starkly.'

'God, you can be a bloody fool!'

He stared out to sea, an expression of bitterness furrowing his face. He couldn't think why she was so perturbed by the news; he only knew that he had cause enough.

CHAPTER 6

Robert Reading-Smith had been born plain Smith; he'd added the Reading when he'd made his first million. His father had been imprisoned in Reading jail.

He turned over on the bed and smacked the bare bottom of the woman by his side. 'Come on, move. You'll never get rich lying in bed all morning.'

'Suppose I don't want to?' she asked in a muffled voice.

'Then you're a fool.'

She rolled over on to her side. She was a natural blonde —normally this would not have been self-evident—and she had the soft, regular, svelte beauty made familiar by Hollywood.

He prodded her.

'That hurt!'

'You loved it.'

'I think you're a bit of a bastard.'

'So my mother told me.'

She giggled. Then wondered if she ought not to have done in case he had been telling the truth under the guise of a joke. She'd known him for six days, yet still couldn't begin to keep pace with him. He could be laughing and smiling one moment, coldly vicious the next, with no discernible reason for the change.

He rolled off the bed, crossed to the nearest window, unclipped the shutters and in turn swung them open and back until they were held by the wall catches. Sunshine flooded in.

She stared at the long scar just above his right hip. It was ridiculous, but that scar had come to mean so much. A person of tactless curiosity, the first time she'd seen it she'd asked him how it had happened. He'd answered with a long and involved story which he patently had not expected her to believe. Unable to take the hint, she'd asked again, that night. The second story had been no less lengthy or involved, but it had been totally different. Why was he so secretive about the scar's true origin? Over the next few days, she had allowed that scar to become both a symbol and an indicator. If he continued to conceal the truth, their relationship would be, for him, no more than passing; if he told her the truth, their relationship would have come to mean as much to him as to her . . . In eight days, her holiday ended. The flight back to cloud and rain, the dreary street in east Hounslow, the grotty semi, her dad forever rowing with her mum, her sister acting like a tart . . . 'Where did you get that scar?'

He turned and stared at her in a way that almost frightened her. 'A knife.'

'What d'you mean, a knife?' It was going to be another ridiculous story.

'Two heavies with knives tried to turn me into a soprano, one of 'em nearly succeeded.'

'But why?'

'I'd been smarter than them.'

She realized that this might, at last, be the truth. But she still couldn't be certain. Very wealthy people didn't usually get into that sort of trouble. Or had he been in some high-powered racket? That wasn't such an absurd thought.

He was smooth, but there was no missing the inner toughness. So had he finally told her the truth? Was she going to
be able to miss that plane? Would she never again have to
see 34, Grassington Crescent . . .

'We'll spend the day on the boat,' he said. He walked
past the bed and went through to the bathroom.

They'd been out on the motor-cruiser three times already.
Each time, she'd seen the envy on the faces of the people
who'd watched them sail. God, if only she could be certain
she'd see that envy week after week . . .

In the bathroom, he stood in the shower cabinet beyond
the marble-surrounded bath and enjoyed the tingling force
of the cold water. When he'd been young, he'd bathed in a
tin tub in front of the kitchen range; very D. H. Lawrence.
It was a memory which chuckled in his mind every time
one of the women ceased to be overawed by her surroundings
and began to visualize herself as mistress of them. Silly
bitches. Hadn't they learned that life was never so generous?

He turned off the shower, slid back the curtain, and
reached for a towel. They'd sail to Cala Noña, anchor, and
drink champagne. Cala Noña could only be reached by boat
and so was not besieged by hordes of tourists.

He returned to the bedroom. She was lying in a provocative pose, but he ignored her, crossed to one of the built-in
cupboards and brought out a clean shirt, pants, and trousers.

'Are you reckoning on spending all day in bed?' he asked,
as he pulled the shirt over his shoulders.

'What's the rush?'

'I told you, you'll never get rich lying in bed.' He pulled
on his pants, then his trousers.

'Come and kiss me.'

He left the bedroom and went out on to the landing. Casa
Resta was far larger than he needed—five bedrooms, each
with an en-suite bathroom, two with dressing-rooms—but
that was one reason why he'd bought it. It was obviously a
rich man's house. He crossed to the stairs and went down

and through to the kitchen. Rosa was emptying the washing-up machine. 'Is it OK for breakfast?' he asked, in a jumbled mixture of English and Spanish.

'Yes, señor. I bought some ensaimadas on my way here.'

'That's great. We'll be going out on the boat, so will you prepare a picnic lunch?'

He admired Rosa. She'd lived a hard life, but never moaned about it and was always smiling. And if she had any thoughts about the endless stream of women who warmed his bed, she kept them to herself and always showed respect to his current companion.

He left the kitchen, crossed the hall, entered the large sitting-room and went out on to the patio. The urbanización stretched up the lower slopes of a hill some six kilometres back from the sea and his house was at the highest level. Because of the steep slope, beyond the edge of the patio there was a sheer drop of five metres. The sea was clearly visible.

He sat at the bamboo and glass table, the sun hot on the left-hand side of his face. Many years ago, when schoolmasters had still freely turned to the cane, he'd received a thrashing for failing to learn a piece of poetry; ironically, he could still remember the lines which, when it had been important, he'd forgotten. 'I am monarch of all I survey . . .' That was how he felt on his patio, looking out over the other and smaller houses of the urbanización to the distant sea.

Rosa came out of the house, a tray in her hands. 'Is the señorita not ready?'

'She won't be long.'

'I will make some fresh coffee when she arrives.'

'Don't bother. She'll have it as she finds it.'

Rosa put the tray down and set everything out. Finally, she handed him a copy of the *Majorca Daily Bulletin*.

He pulled off a piece of one of the ensaimadas, buttered it, added jam, and ate. He read the headlines and leading article on the front page. More financial troubles back home, with the pound in retreat, the balance of payments adverse, and the gold and dollar reserves dropping. None of that affected him. He wasn't a fool, so he'd moved all his money out of Britain. He turned the page. He skimmed through several small items of news, came to an article headed 'Mystery victim identified'. The man killed in the crash on Wednesday afternoon was now known to have been Steven Thompson, an Englishman.

As Pat, dressed in cotton frock because he didn't like women dressed in jeans, stepped out on to the patio, she was shocked by his expression of fierce anger.

David Swinnerton had been a highly emotional, very shy man, who'd suffered from asthma from the age of five. The asthma had so interrupted his education that by the time he was eighteen he had possessed no paper qualifications and lacking these it had been very difficult to find a job, even at a time of relatively full employment; in the end, he'd worked in a local estate agent. Being an honest man, he'd disliked the work and had been thankful when one of the partners had suggested that perhaps, in view of his frequent illness, it would be best if he sought a less stressful occupation. He had immediately agreed and left. Thereafter, he'd stayed at home, writing poetry and keeping his widowed mother company.

His mother had died some years later, as the wind screamed up the valley and buffeted the slate-roofed house as if to demolish it into a funeral pyre. That night, he had written a memorial ode which for years afterwards had had the power to bring tears to his eyes.

Despite the very high level of death duties, he'd still inherited enough from his mother not to need to have to work. Six months later, he'd married. His few friends and acquaintances had, among themselves, expressed considerable surprise that he should ever have contemplated such a step, especially with Valerie Pope. She had no claims to beauty, was completely careless about appearances, and had firm opinions on most things which she seldom hesitated to express. What all of them had failed to understand was that he needed support as well as love and she needed to support as well as to love.

After several years of marriage, spent in the isolated farmhouse to the east of Snowdon, his asthma had suddenly worsened. He'd seen several specialists, the last of whom had put the situation very bluntly; if he wished to go on living, he must move to a better climate.

He and Valerie had consulted maps and read books, then applied for an extra allowance of foreign currency on medical grounds—it was one of those periods when the British were being denied the liberty of spending their own money abroad —and when this was reluctantly granted, they'd set off for the Mediterranean coast of Spain, the south of France being too expensive.

In Barcelona they'd met an Irishman—a bit of a rogue, but amusing—who'd told them that Nirvana was an island called Mallorca. They'd sailed there on the ferry. They'd arrived on an island which was not yet tainted by tourism, except in a few places, and where there was beauty around every corner. But not the solitude he needed. No matter how deserted a coast might appear to be, or how isolated a house among the almond trees, a closer examination would disclose other houses nearby and even a short acquaintance had shown that the Mallorquins were a gregarious people who believed everyone else to be the same. (Had he foreseen what would overtake so many of these beautiful coastlines he had admired, but regretfully discarded because of nearby houses, he would have fled the island.) So he'd turned his eyes to the mountains and in an old and incredibly decrepit Fiat, in parts literally held together with string, they'd climbed up into that harsh, often threatening world so alien to the soft, cultivated plains below.

They'd found the old house completely by chance. They'd

stopped for a picnic and had decided to have a short walk afterwards, looking at the wild flowers, and during this they'd suddenly come in sight of the house half way up a slope (shades of that home in Wales), little more than a ruin, backed by terraces whose walls were crumbling and whose land was neglected.

It had taken them two days to identify the owner and when they'd asked him how much he wanted for it, he'd stared at them in perplexity. Of what possible use was this abandoned, isolated place to two foreigners? No matter. He'd named a price that was, to him, astronomical. Translated into pounds, the sum had been so little that Swinnerton had immediately agreed. In the eyes of the owner, this had confirmed the fact that all foreigners were simple-minded.

Their currency allowance did not permit the purchase of a house, as cheap as that was, so Swinnerton had done something which had amazed him even as he did it, since never before had he knowingly and willingly broken the law. He'd returned to the UK, drawn fifteen hundred pounds in cash, stowed the banknotes in his suitcase, and told the hard-faced official at the airport that the only currency he was taking out of the country was the legal twenty-five pounds.

It had taken them six months to have the house rebuilt. The workers had come from Estruig, a village at the foot of the mountains, travelling to and fro in a vehicle that was half motorbike and half car. He'd paid them four pesetas an hour and they'd eaten lunch—a hunk of bread coated with olive oil and air-dried tomatoes—in their own time. They'd often sung as they'd worked, sad, wailing songs whose Moorish ancestry was unmistakable. They'd chatted to the Swinnertons in a jumbled mixture of Spanish and Mallorquin and laughed uproariously, but without the slightest meanness, when there'd been obvious misunderstandings. For the first time he could remember, he had not been frightened by people whom he did not know well.

When the house had been finished, the well had been
deepened. The foreman had said that the señor was lucky,
it was a good, sweet well that would flow all the year round
so that he would never be short of water. Coming from the
Welsh mountains, it had never occurred to either of them
that they might be. After the well had been lined with
sandstone blocks, and the manual pump installed and
tested, the men had repaired the walls of the terracing.
When he'd asked, somewhat diffidently as he remembered
conditions back home, if they'd mind very much clearing
the land at the same time, they had not replied that they
were builders, not gardeners, but had willingly cleared the
land. Then the Swinnertons had found two men willing to
work as gardeners, also paid four pesetas an hour, and in a
very short time the terraces had become filled with colour.

There had been no electricity and the distribution of
bottled gas had not yet become commonplace, so she had
had to learn to cook on a charcoal stove and the lights had
worked on poor quality paraffin. In the winter, which could
be cold at that altitude, with snow lying for several days,
they would have a log fire in the sitting-room and a brasero
under the dining-room table to roast their legs while leaving
their upper halves to chill.

Very happy, he'd written a great deal of poetry. At first,
he'd tried to get his work published, but his style was
emotional, his themes simple and understandable, and his
construction traditional, so that it was considered pedestrian
and only the occasional short poem was accepted by a
magazine which needed fillers. Soon, he'd ceased to bother
to send out his work. After all, every single piece was a love
poem addressed to Valerie and it was only her appreciation
that mattered.

They occasionally heard that the outside world was
changing, but thought that this didn't concern them. Perhaps the cost of some things was rising from time to time,
but their needs were simple . . .

The tourist industry expanded and prosperity flooded the island. Wages rose. Peasants who had eaten meat only during the winter when a pig was killed, now bought it at the butcher throughout the year; children grew up without ever discovering what it was like to be truly hungry; fincas increased in value from a 100,000 pesetas to 500,000, to a million, to five million; bicycles gave way to Mobylettes, Mobylettes to Seat 600s, Seat 600s to a bewildering choice of gleaming, luxurious cars; men left the land and worked in the bars, restaurants, hotels, discothèques, the women left their homes during the day and worked in the hotels and the homes of the thousands of foreigners . . .

The Swinnertons discovered a bitter truth: as Canute had known, it was impossible to slow down or stop the tides. He had never bothered to have his investments managed, naïvely assuming that what had been good in the past would be good in the future, and some of his shares had become virtually valueless and others hadn't appreciated as much as was necessary in times of inflation. As his income remained, at best, steady, prices and wages soared. Wine which had been ten pesetas a bottle rose to eighty. The gardeners demanded a hundred pesetas an hour, then a hundred and fifty; soon, it was two hundred . . . There came a time when the Swinnertons were finally forced to face the facts. If things continued in the same vein, before long they'd no longer be able to afford to live in their house. And when they couldn't and had to sell—for a price which would not reflect inflation because no Mallorquin would now live in such isolation and all those foreigners with money lived by the sea—they would be faced with moving into a tiny, noisy, stifling flat or returning to the UK.

At first, Valerie had thought it was the worry about their future which was making her husband look so drawn and had suddenly aged him, but initially she could not discuss the matter because he had tried to shield her from the facts and she did not want him to realize that she was just as

aware of them as he. Then, with icy certainty, she had
realized there must be something physically wrong with
him. He'd tried to evade any medical examination, but in
the end had been persuaded to see a specialist in Palma; the
specialist diagnosed cancer.

On the morning of the day he'd died, he had looked out
of the window and up the terracing and had whispered the
wish that he could be buried up there, among all the free
beauty instead of the confines of a cemetery. She had told
him he was being ridiculous to talk about burials, while
silently swearing to honour his wish.

The law on the island concerning burials was strict, as it
had to be with the heat in summer, and it did not permit a
burial away from an authorized cemetery. But he had died
in his own bed and it was not the custom for a doctor to
pursue a case if he was not specifically called in by the
patient, so that the doctor who had been treating him would
never on his own initiative call to find out how he was. In
any case, she would have defied a thousand laws in order
to carry out her unspoken deathbed promise. So somehow
she had managed to carry his emaciated body up to the
terrace with the twisted, tortured, centuries-old olive tree
which he had nicknamed the Laocöon, and there had buried
him.

By then, there was only one gardener—the younger of
the two—and he was simple-minded. He'd once asked how
the señor was and had then forgotten the subject. And
up on that terrace, David Swinnerton's body remained
undisturbed, amid the wild beauty he had so loved . . .

'Señora.'

The call cut across her sad, yet comforting thoughts. She
looked around and watched the gardener approach with his
shambling walk.

He came to a stop. 'Señora.'

She waited patiently. Tomás Mesquida so often had
trouble in expressing himself.

'I need . . .' He fiddled with his thick lips. 'I need more money.'

'I'm sorry, but I can't pay you any more.' Her Spanish was fairly fluent, though her accent was poor.

'My mother says I must have more or I stop.'

The foreigners had taught the Mallorquins to be avaricious and now money had become their god. To point out to Mesquida's mother that it would be very difficult for him to find another job and therefore it was surely better to continue to work here for a slightly lesser wage, would be a waste of words; she would never understand that something definite was better than the image of something more. Valerie turned, flinched at the stab of pain from her gouty foot, looked up at the twisted olive tree. If he left, the garden would quickly revert to a wilderness because she could no longer do the work.

Mesquida waited, then, when she remained silent, went over to his rusty Renault 4. He stood by the car for quite a while, as if expecting to be called back, opened the door, settled behind the wheel, drove off.

She turned and, limping slightly, went into the house. There was the sound of the old grandfather clock—one of the pieces they'd brought from Wales—striking the half hour. It reminded her that she was meeting the Attrays for coffee. Since her husband's death, she'd seen quite a bit of the few English residents who lived in, or near, Estruig, rightly judging that for her own mental sake she needed human contacts. In any case, she'd never been the natural recluse that he had.

She went upstairs to the bathroom to find there was no water. Slowly, and most of the time painfully, she returned downstairs and went out to the pump. It was becoming more and more of an effort to work it and normally each weekday Mesquida filled the tank on the roof. If he left her, she'd have to do it all herself . . . An electricity line had come within a kilometre of the house a couple of years before

and the electricity company had asked them if they wanted
to be connected. The estimate had come to two million
pesetas . . .

Twenty-five minutes later she left the house and went
down to the small stone shed in which she garaged the
ancient Seat 850 which was kept going by faith, hope, and
the charity of the garage who so often didn't fully charge
her for the work they'd done.

She drove down the often precipitous road to Estruig,
which was built on and around a small hill that stood a
kilometre away from the mountains. She parked in the main
square, crossed to the café, and looked for the Attrays, but
they were not there. She wasn't surprised. They were very
poor timekeepers. She sat at a table, newly vacated, and
picked up a copy of *El Día* which had been left on it.
She could read Spanish quite well. On the fourth page,
underneath a lurid description of a suicide, complete with
photograph, there was a short article which said that the
man who had died in the car crash near Fogufol had been
identified as Steven Thompson, an Englishman. Her expression became bitter.

CHAPTER 7

Mike Taylor replaced the telephone on its stand, turned,
rested his elbows on the bar. Whoever had said that life on
the island consisted of one long crisis was dead right. Not
very long ago, he'd been wondering how in hell they'd ever
pay for the alterations in the kitchen which the bloody
inspector had demanded be done before they received their
licence to open the restaurant (there was little doubt, but
no proof, that the inspector had been prompted by one or
more of the established restaurant owners), and no sooner
had that problem been solved than he was presented with

a fresh one. His work permit had just been refused. True, his lawyer said that they'd probably win the appeal, but there was bound to be delay. And unless they opened soon, they'd miss the main season which was when any tourist-based business had to make enough profit to last through the rest of the year. He looked through the nearest window at the bay. That view was worth a fortune. Diners with any souls would sit outside, in the shade of the palm trees, staring at so much beauty that they'd never notice whether the meat was tough—what meat in Mallorca wasn't?—and would feel impelled to order another bottle of wine . . .

'Well, is the maître d' satisfied?'

He turned to face Helen as she stood in the doorway of the kitchen. 'If you're interested, I'm thinking of committing suicide.'

'If you come to a decision, do it outside; so much easier to clean up the mess.'

'I'd die much happier if I knew I'd died a bloody nuisance.'

She left the doorway, went behind the bar, put her hands round the back of his neck and brought his head forward so that she could kiss him. 'What total disaster has occurred this time?'

'That call was from Ferrer. They've refused the work permit.'

'No.'

'Bloody yes.'

'Oh well, I suppose we shouldn't have expected it to go through first time. Stop worrying. Pablo will sort it all out.'

'Why are you always revoltingly optimistic?'

'It makes life more fun.'

'I suppose you do realize that if we don't get a work permit . . .'

'Relax. We will. I've complete faith in Pablo.'

'I don't suppose you know how he feels about you?'

'Someone told me that his nickname's Don Juan.'

'If he ever dares make a move in your direction, his nickname will become Doña Juana.'

She chuckled as she unclasped her hands and stepped back. 'I've nearly finished. When did the builders promise faithfully on the pain of excommunication to start work?'

'Yesterday.'

'Then there's just a chance, I suppose, they'll turn up tomorrow . . . As soon as I have finished, let's go for a swim?'

'Slacking?'

'That's right,' she said, happy to see that his black mood was beginning to lift.

He watched her return into the kitchen, lit a cigarette. A year ago he'd been bumming around the world, weighed down by the chip on his shoulder. In the tiny fishing village of Amozgat, in the south-west corner of Turkey, he'd fallen ill with some kind of intestinal infection so severe that he'd become convinced he was dying; a conviction which the villagers had obviously shared and which equally obviously had not caused them any concern beyond the problems that his death might raise vis-à-vis the authorities. On the third day, when death would have been welcome, Helen had appeared in the squalid, stinking room and had nursed him with a devotion which was extraordinary since they were strangers, she was not a trained nurse, and the side effects of his illness were highly unpleasant. Later, he'd learned that her presence in the village had been pure chance. She'd been travelling a hundred miles to the north, had stopped at a café for coffee, and had heard one of the other customers mention the name Amozgat. For some reason, still completely inexplicable, she had been overwhelmed by the certainty that she must visit this place whose name she had only just heard . . . But for that, he might have died and she would in all probability have returned to the man from whom she'd fled two months before . . .

All right, so fate moved in mysterious ways. But why in hell had it moved to turn down his work permit?

She returned to the restaurant. 'Let's go.'

They went out by the kitchen door, walked round the building, past the patio and the palm trees, across the road, and on to the sand. She took off her T-shirt and shorts to reveal a bikini; he was wearing trunks.

He was a much stronger swimmer than she and while she stayed within her depth—which, because the sea bed shelved so gradually was almost two hundred metres out— he continued on, enjoying the coolness of the water which had not yet warmed to tepid summer heat. Off the harbour, a large yacht was hoisting her spinnaker and as he watched the light wind began to balloon the multi-coloured sail. One day, when they were so successful that people came from as far away as Palma for a meal, he'd buy a yacht and name her *Helen*; she'd be the most beautiful craft afloat. He turned and, no longer employing a powerful crawl, swam slowly inshore. He thought how strange it was that now he should care so much for someone else when previously he'd been careful to care for nobody because experience had taught him that to care was to be rejected . . .

He reached her and they returned to shore. They stretched out on towels, rapidly drying in the hot sun. When the restaurant was a success, they'd shut up in the winter and he'd take her to Hongkong, Bali, Tonga . . .

'What are you thinking?' she asked.

'That when we're rich, I'm going to take you to all the glamorous places in the world.'

She reached out for his hand. 'I don't give a damn if it's Clacton-on-Sea, provided you're there.'

She was looking vulnerable, he thought, and he knew a fierce desire to protect her. Her character was a strange mixture of toughness and tenderness; no one could have been tougher than she in that Turkish fishing village, yet sentimentally she was weak.

They were silent for a while, then she said: 'I saw your stepmother when I was in the port earlier on. I wonder what she was doing in this part of the island?'

'Slumming. Did she deign to notice you?'

'She was on the other side of the road and I doubt she even saw me. She was with that friend of hers—what's his name?'

'The Honourable Archibald Wheeldon.'

'He's very handsome.'

'And wet.'

'Her clothes were really lovely; they must have cost a fortune.'

'She's no idea that one can buy a dress for less than five hundred guineas.'

'Mike, why do you two dislike each other so much?'

'I've told you before, it's traditional to dislike one's step-mother.'

'It's more than that. And it's such a pity.'

Such a pity the bitch didn't fall over the edge of her patio and break her neck. He could still remember, with bitter irony, the words his father had used when he'd first talked about his forthcoming second marriage. Beautiful, charming, generous, kind . . . His father had used words with such abandon and skill that people had accused him not merely of having kissed the Blarney Stone, but of having swallowed it whole. His father had got things very wrong with Muriel. She might be beautiful and charming—if she could be bothered—but she wasn't generous or kind . . .

He'd cleared out of her home just one step ahead of being told to clear out. That's when he'd begun his drifting which had ended in the village of Amozgat. It was funny—funny incredible—that not long ago he had managed to talk himself into believing Muriel would help him and Helen to buy the restaurant. It showed to what lengths self-deception could go. After all, in her eyes people who ran restaurants were on the butt end of the social scale. Yet he'd taken

Helen to see her and to ask for the loan—the loan, not the gift—of six million pesetas. She'd treated Helen with disdain and him with sardonic dislike; she'd said that she was very sorry, but she couldn't afford to help, certain that he knew full well she could have given him twice that amount without the slightest problem. Her contemptuous refusal had so infuriated him that he'd cursed the whole idea into oblivion. It had been Helen who had talked him round, stoutly declaring that somehow, somewhere, they'd find the six million . . . And they had!

'I suppose we ought to move,' she said.

'I suppose.'

'I could easily become as indolent as most of the foreigners out here.'

'You're far too intelligent.'

'For those few kind words, thank you. And next time you call me weak-minded for making a nonsense of my figures, I'll remind you of them.' She sat up. 'Come on, back to work.'

'They must have had a tyrant like you overseeing the building of the Pyramids.'

They returned to the restaurant and just before she went into the kitchen, he looked at his watch. 'I might find Carlos if I went along now.'

'Why not? And persuade him that once we're open, we want the vegetables picked much younger than they usually do.'

'I'll try, but you know what we're up against—if you don't grow it as big as it'll go, you're throwing away good money.'

He left and went round to the shed in which they kept the Vespino which he used when there was no need for the Citroën van. The Vespino proved difficult to start and as he pushed down the pedal for the fifth time, to no avail, he decided that the moment the restaurant proved successful, he'd buy a Volvo. He grinned. If he were to honour all his recent pledges, they'd have to start up a whole chain of restaurants . . .

Puerto Llueso lay to the east and it was appropriate that the first building he passed was a block of flats under construction, since for the past two years there had been an ever increasing rate of development. In one respect, this could be welcome. The more people, the more potential customers. But now the extent of building had reached the stage where it threatened to destroy the whole charm of the port, a charm largely based on sleepy smallness. Could not those responsible see that the development contained the seeds of destruction?

Ballester's finca lay between the port and Llueso, three-quarters of a kilometre back from the main road. Two years previously, he'd been left a little money and he'd used this to have a well drilled. He'd been very lucky. They'd struck flowing water that was sweet and not tainted by sea-water, as so much was now that more and more fresh water was extracted from existing sources to service the tourist industry and the natural water table was dropping. He was young, which was unusual since few young men now went into farming or horticulture because the work was so much harder and less well remunerated than were jobs in the tourist industry; even more unusually, he was ready and eager to learn new methods.

He was working a rotovator when Taylor arrived. He stopped this, crossed the brick-hard land, shook hands with traditional courtesy, talked about the weather. It was almost ten minutes before Taylor was able to introduce the subject of the vegetables. Ballester listened, thought, finally said that he thought it might be possible; then he added that the vegetables would, of course, have to cost a bit more . . .

Taylor returned to the port. He stopped at a newsagent to buy an English paper, but all these had been sold and he had to be content with the *Daily Bulletin*. He continued on

to one of the front cafés where prices were merely high and
not exorbitant and sat at one of the outside tables. He stared
across the road at the yachts in the harbour and he thought
about his earlier promise to himself . . .

A waiter asked him what he wanted. He replied in good
Spanish—he was a natural linguist—that he'd like a café
cortado. After the waiter had left, he began to read the
paper. On the second page, it stated that the Englishman
who'd been killed in the car crash near Fogufol had been
identified as Steven Thompson. His expression abruptly
changed.

CHAPTER 8

The Telex message arrived at ten-thirty on Monday morning. Reference the request for identification of the next-of-kin
of Steven Arnold Thompson, passport number C 229570
A. This passport was one of twenty-five which had been
stolen before issue some four years previously. An
examination of records showed no Steven Arnold
Thompson. It was, therefore, impossible to advise on
next-of-kin.

London added that they would be grateful if they were
informed should any details come to light as to how the
deceased had come into possession of this stolen passport
and they would in due course welcome the opportunity to
examine it.

'That,' said Alvarez to a passing fly, 'is not going to make
Salas's day.'

'I suppose I should have expected it,' said Salas over the
telephone.

'Señor . . .'

'It doesn't matter how simple a case is beforehand, the

moment you have anything to do with it, the complications start.'

'Señor, I really cannot be blamed . . .'

'How much do we know about the dead man?'

'Very little, I'm afraid.'

'Why?'

'Because the only person apart from the man who hired him the car and the porter at the hotel—and their evidence is virtually useless—who I've been able to find who knew him is Señor Higham. He's in hospital because he was in the crash . . .'

'To save time, please assume I have taken the trouble to acquaint myself with the basic facts of the case.'

'Yes, señor. Unfortunately, there's very little that Señor Higham could tell me. Señor Thompson—according to the three of them—flew in from somewhere where it was noticeably colder than here, he owned a boat, he was gregarious but yet a little secretive at the same time, and he suffered from migraine.'

'Are you suggesting that these details are of the greatest importance?'

'No, señor; I said they weren't. But I wanted to illustrate how little I've been able to find out.'

'Have no fear on that score.'

'But he said nothing personal . . .'

'Has it not occurred to you that he must have said more to the hitch-hiker than that.'

'I know it sounds reasonable . . .'

'Which is, no doubt, why you are so reluctant to accept the conclusion. Question him again and this time do so thoroughly.'

'You don't think . . .'

'Will you kindly obey my orders without arguing.'

'Yes, señor. I'll drive in to Palma tomorrow morning and . . .'

'You will drive in this morning.'

'But I have a great deal of work in hand.'

'I want this matter cleared up and cleared up quickly.' The line went dead.

Alvarez replaced the receiver. He'd planned a quiet day. But now he had to rush into Palma and question Higham again, when it was perfectly clear to anyone but a mule-headed superior chief that it would be a complete waste of time. He sighed.

The door banged open and a guard walked in, dropped a large brown envelope on to the desk, held out a sheet of paper. 'Sign this.'

'What is it?'

'It's come from Palma on the bus and they want a receipt. That's all I know.'

Alvarez signed and the guard left. He stared doubtfully at the envelope for several seconds—it was his experience that communications direct from Palma were seldom of a pleasant nature—finally opened it. Inside was a British passport and a wallet. He opened the passport. Jack Higham, accounts clerk, born in London on 21 October, 1941, residence England; height, 1.80 cms; signature a bit of a scrawl; photograph the usual stark, unflattering reproduction which left Higham's face almost expressionless.

He checked the wallet. No money, of course. No credit cards. A couple of stamps, a receipt from a hostal, a list of numbers with some crossed off, and a photograph of a woman who was laughing. The wife who had run off with another man because she couldn't take the bad times as well as the good? He replaced the photograph. If she were the wife, then the fact that Higham had kept it showed that his casual acceptance of all that had happened was a mask, concealing his true emotions. Poor sod, thought Alvarez, knowing what it was like to suffer.

He returned both wallet and passport to the brown envelope.

*

Higham was sitting in the armchair near the window, to the side of the settee. His colour was much better and the bruising on his chin had almost disappeared. Alvarez handed him the copy of the *Daily Mail* which he had just bought.

'That's really decent of you.'

He sat on the edge of the bed, produced the brown envelope and emptied out the wallet and passport. 'These were dropped into a litter-bin, here, in Palma.'

'Good God!'

'Im afraid all the money's gone. What happens is, the thief takes everything he wants, then drops the rest. That way, he gets rid of any incriminating evidence at virtually no risk to himself.' By leaning forward, Alvarez was able to pass them across. Higham flicked through the passport, then checked each compartment of the wallet.

'Have you spoken to the consul and asked him about the money?'

'Yes, I did; that is I phoned and spoke to someone who knew what I was talking about. She'll contact the bank who issued the travellers' cheques and tell them they've been stolen. One problem was, I couldn't say which ones I'd cashed.' He tapped the wallet. 'But I've a note of them here and I'll ring her again and give the numbers.'

'I hope the refund will come through quickly.'

'They always promise it will . . . You know, I've done a lot of thinking since I've been in here and I'm seeing things straighter. At my age, drifting around Europe won't change anything or get me anywhere; I've got too old for the dream. I need to return home and find another job; and perhaps meet someone . . .' He tailed off into silence and stared out through the window.

'I am very sorry that your visit to the island has been so unfortunate.'

'It has, hasn't it? But even so, I'm going to come back as soon as I can. It's so beautiful.'

'Then next time, I hope that nothing happens to spoil your pleasure.'

'I'll drink to that!' He smiled. 'One thing, I'll not try thumbing a lift.'

There was a short silence which Alvarez broke. 'Señor, I am sorry, but I have to ask you more questions. You see, because we did not know who Señor Thompson's next-of-kin was, we sent the number of his passport back to England and asked them to give us what information they could. They have reported that his passport was one which had been stolen, along with others, before it was issued.'

'Well, I'll be damned!'

'So now we are back to knowing almost nothing about him, but we need to trace his next-of-kin.'

'I don't see how I can help there.'

'Perhaps he said something which at the time seemed of no importance, and so you didn't bother to mention it when I spoke to you before, but which might help me now. For instance, where had he been driving from that morning?'

'I don't know.'

'And I think you told me, he didn't say where he was going?'

'He didn't, no.'

'Nor did he give you any hint of why he was on the island?'

'I'm not so certain about that. You see, there's something tickling my mind . . .' There was a longish silence before Higham continued: 'He mentioned something about having been driving around the island, seeing people. I asked him if he was on business. He laughed.'

'Did you understand why he should laugh at that question?'

'No. Your guess is as good as mine.'

'So either for some reason the question held an amusing connotation or it was the answer that did—the answer he didn't make.'

'It must have been something like that.'

'Did he ever mention the name of anyone on the island?'

'No.'

'Or any place?'

'No.'

'But he did tell you he'd visited the island before?'

'That's right.'

'Did he make any reference to the previous visits?'

'No.'

'Or talk about his home life?'

'Not a word.'

'So although he was a talkative man, he hardly told you anything about himself?'

'That sums it up.'

'D'you think he was being deliberately secretive?'

'I wouldn't like to say one way or the other.'

'You didn't gain any kind of an impression?'

'Look, you're asking me a whole load of questions I just can't answer.'

'No, of course not. But as I mentioned earlier, it's just that sometimes one can look back and realize one gained an impression, even though at the time one wasn't aware that one had.'

'Not this time.'

'So then it seems that maybe he'll remain a man with no background. All we shall ever know about him is that he flew in from somewhere, he'd been here before, perhaps was here on business, enjoyed sailing, suffered from migraine, and it was an attack of this which indirectly killed him.'

'In fact, not even that's certain.'

'How d'you mean?'

'Because . . . Well, I'm damned!' Higham's voice expressed his astonishment. 'It's funny how the memory works, isn't it? I've only this moment remembered that after he'd decided to take another pill—because the earlier one wasn't doing any good—and we'd driven off and he started feeling ill, he said no migraine had ever been like that before; his mouth and throat were burning as if he'd chewed half a dozen of the vicious little peppers which grow on the island and on top of that he didn't have any of the usual symptoms. He wondered if some of the food at the restaurant had been bad. But he'd only had steak and ice-cream . . . And then, like I said before, he was as sick as a dog, but would carry on driving. It's funny how life goes, isn't it? If he'd been more ill, he couldn't have gone on driving; if less ill, he'd have been able to keep control.'

Alvarez's mind flicked back over the years. If Juana-María had walked fractionally quicker or slower, the drunken Frenchman would not have pinned her to the wall with his car . . . He stood.

'You surely don't have to go yet awhile?'

'I am afraid so. It is still lonely for you?'

'And frustrating! There's a new night nurse who could be fun, but she doesn't understand a word of English.'

'I have heard that in such circumstances it is possible to communicate the essentials with signs.'

'I tried, but we don't seem to speak the same sign language.'

Alvarez smiled. 'How much longer will you have to stay here?'

'I'm feeling fit enough to leave now, but the quack says he still can't understand why I suffered a loss of memory at the beginning so he wants to make absolutely certain I didn't suffer any brain damage. I told him, only softening of the brain. He didn't see the joke and it took a hell of a long time trying to explain it . . . I guess the Spanish and English senses of humour aren't very similar.'

'That is very true . . . Señor, should you remember anything more, however unimportant it seems to you, will you get in touch with me?'

'Sure. But how do I get hold of you?'

'I will give you my home and office telephone numbers.

If you say my name, whoever answers will know to get hold of me if I'm around.' He wrote out the numbers, handed the piece of paper over, said goodbye and left.

The telephone rang at six-thirty that evening, just as Alvarez was wondering whether it really was too early to leave the office and return home.

'It's Cantallops here, Inspector.'

'Who?'

'The undertaker from Fogufol. You must remember—I rang you the other day.'

'Oh yes, of course.'

'I want to know if it's all right now to go ahead with the funeral?'

'There's no reason why not. What name are you going to use?'

'Thompson, of course. What are you on about?'

'He was travelling on a stolen passport so the odds probably are that that's not his real name. But then I don't suppose St Peter will keep the gates shut just because he's buried under the wrong name.'

'That's ridiculous.'

'I don't see why. Surely by then the name's quite unimportant?'

'It's ridiculous to say his name wasn't Thompson.'

'Why is it?'

'His son would have told me if it wasn't.'

'His son? Here, you'd better tell me what's been going on.'

'Nothing's been going on. Why do you people always suspect everybody and everything?'

'Because that's what we're paid for . . . But just for the moment, I'm not suspecting you of anything specific. All I want to know is, how come you've heard from the son?'

'There was this phone call. The son had just learned of the tragic death of his father and he wanted to know what arrangements there were for the funeral. I told him there weren't any. He said his father was to be decently and honourably buried.'

'When did you receive this call?'

'Saturday.'

'Why didn't you get on to me right away?'

'The money hadn't arrived then.'

'What are you talking about now?'

'Until I had the money, I couldn't go ahead and arrange the funeral, could I?'

'Depends what kind of a man you are . . . How much?'

There was a slight pause. 'Two hundred and fifty thousand pesetas.'

'Has the son ordered a gold coffin?'

'He asked me to prepare an honourable funeral.'

'How are you getting in touch with him to let him know the time of the honourable funeral?'

'I'm not. He said it was quite impossible for him to come over from England because of family problems . . . May I go ahead and arrange everything?'

'Yes. And then get back on to me with all the details.'

Alvarez replaced the receiver. He stared through the open window. Thompson had been travelling on a stolen passport and so it was reasonable to assume that Thompson was not his real name. The report of his death had been in the local papers, but was unlikely to have appeared in the British national papers. Then how had the son learned that he had died in the car accident?

CHAPTER 9

The present cemetery at Fogufol was three-quarters of a kilometre outside the village, reached by a narrow, twisting lane. From it, there was a view across the central plain of

the island and, especially after rain, the sea to the south-east
was clearly visible. The high surrounding stone walls had
been erected in the eighteenth century, the chapel and
room of remembrance in the late nineteenth. Originally, the
graves had been marked merely by single headstones, but
then the custom had arisen of spending on death more than
had ever been spent on life and headstones had become
large and elaborate, while those families with property had
erected mausoleums. The land was stone, making exca-
vation both difficult and costly, and therefore there were no
single graves; always, there was a shaft and excavated out
on either side of this were cubicles into which coffins could
be fitted.

The cemetery was, of course, for Catholics and the first
non-Catholic to die within the parish—a German botanist
—had presented the priest and the council with a problem.
The law said that the dead had to be buried within consecrated ground, the Church said that only a Catholic could
be buried within the cemetery. In the end it was decided
that just before he died, and even though he'd been alone
when he'd fallen fifteen metres on to his head, the German
had expressed the wish to become a Roman Catholic and
therefore it was in order to bury him within the cemetery.
Since then, the number of foreigners, many of them non-
Catholics, had risen very considerably and it had become
clear that since deaths must be expected, an elegant solution
for one must become an inelegant, not to say absurd, solution
for many. Eventually, it was decided to provide an area of
consecrated ground outside the actual cemetery where all
non-Catholics could be buried. A deep shaft, which accom-
modated six cubicles on either side, was blasted out of the
rock and above this was built a sandstone edifice which
resembled an old-fashioned steamer trunk; on the sides of
this were plaques on which, for a suitable fee, the names of
the deceased could be inscribed. When the last cubicle was
filled, the first one was emptied and the bones were taken

out and stored with the bones of those locals who had died well back in the past; in death there was no equality, in disintegration there was.

Religion raised one further question. Where was the burial ceremony to be held? The solution of the Fogufol priest, a traditionalist who viewed the spirit of œcumenicism in a less than happy light, was to ask that it be held under the archway of the entrance; after all, Moses had been allowed to view the Promised Land.

Alvarez parked next to the Citroën 2CV van, as battered as his 600, in front of a narrow flowerbed which ran the length of the cemetery wall. He walked slowly to the arched entrance to the cemetery. There were very few people present. The Anglican churchman was pacing backwards and forwards, a puzzled look on his ancient, lined, and toothy face; each time he reached the outer side of the archway, he came to a stop and stared up the path, seeking a press of people which never materialized. The undertaker and two assistants waited lethargically on one side, three men employed by the local council even more lethargically on the other. Taylor, his rugged face set in sullen lines, dressed in open shirt and cotton trousers, stood by the doorway into the chapel.

Cicadas shrilled, a hoopoe hooped, sheep bells clanged, and dogs barked. The clergyman cleared his throat as he looked at his watch. 'Perhaps we should begin the service.' He picked up a pile of printed sheets and handed these around; the council employees and the undertakers refused them. The clergyman announced the first hymn, la-di-dahed the tune, and then led the singing; it turned out to be a solo.

Alvarez studied the young man. He was casually dressed, as if he could not be bothered to offer the deceased any respect, yet his expression was unmistakably sad and, perhaps, resentful, in the sense that the living sometimes resented the fact that the dead had left them . . . The son had told Cantallops over the phone that he could not come to the funeral and this man's face was bronzed, whereas almost all newly arrived visitors from Britain were white, yet if the son did live in England there was still no obvious answer to the question, how had he learned of his father's death?

The clergyman announced that a last prayer would be said at the graveside and left. Taylor followed him. Alvarez returned to his car, opened both doors and sat, beads of sweat sliding down his cheeks and back to make him feel still more sticky and uncomfortable.

After a while, Taylor walked out of the archway and across to the Citroën van. As he opened the driving door, Alvarez called out. Taylor looked at him for a moment, climbed in behind the wheel, slammed the door shut. Alvarez crossed to the van as the starter engine engaged, but the engine refused to fire. 'One moment, please, señor.'

'What d'you want?'

'First, to know your name.'

'How the hell's that any of your business?'

'Cuerpo General de Policía.'

'So?'

'So I would like to know your name, please.'

'Where's your identity card?'

'My what?'

'Your card, proving you are a detective.'

Alvarez spoke with astonishment. 'Would I be here, on a day this hot, attending the funeral of a man I never knew, if I were not?'

'How do I know what anyone on this crazy island will do?'

'Your papers, please.'

'Look, I'm here for a funeral. That's all.'

'Of course. I would still like to see them.'

Taylor reached across to the locker and brought out of this a heavy-duty plastic envelope which, sullenly, he passed across.

Alvarez briefly checked the insurance papers, yearly

licence, and photostat copy of a Spanish driving licence. 'Your name is Michael Taylor and your address is Calle Llube, number fifteen, Puerto Llueso?'

'That's what written down.'

'Do you know that you should have with you your original licence and not a photostat copy?'

Taylor did not answer.

'Do you have a residencia?'

'Yes. And to save the question, it's at home.'

'You should carry that with you as well.'

'Look, if I did everything the law demands, I'd be schizophrenic.'

'Why have you come here this morning?'

'I'd have thought that was obvious, even to you.'

'Señor, I can quietly ask questions here, or I can demand that you come to the nearest guardia post where I'll ask them rather more loudly.'

Belatedly, Taylor realized that his sullenly provocative attitude was hardly a sensible one. 'I came to the funeral.'

'You knew Señor Thompson?'

'Yes.'

'Did you know him well?'

'No.'

'Yet you have come all the way from Puerto Llueso to attend his funeral?'

'I reckoned there ought to be someone here to see him buried.'

'Then you knew there would not be anyone else—how?'

Taylor shrugged his shoulders.

'Was it because you were aware that he was being buried under a false name?'

'I met him a couple of times and that's it. I've no idea what his private life was about.'

'When did you last speak to him?'

'I don't really remember.'

'How did you know the funeral was to be today?'

'Someone said it was.'

'Who?'

'I don't remember whom.'

Alvarez stared at the ground for several seconds, then looked up as he stepped back. 'Thank you for your help, señor.'

Taylor was clearly surprised, and relieved, at this sudden termination of the questioning. He engaged the starter again and this time the engine fired. He drove off, the engine emitting the typical high-pitched scream.

Alvarez returned to the 600. He sat, switched on the fan. Sweet Mary, but it was hot!

Dolores poured out a second cup of coffee for Alvarez, then went over to the doorway and shouted to Juan and Isabel that if they didn't get a move on, they'd be late for school. Safe from immediate chastisement, Juan replied that he didn't care.

'I don't know what's happening,' she grumbled, as she returned to the table. 'When I was young, I wouldn't have dreamt of speaking to my mother like that.'

'When we were young, things were very different.'

She recalled a life so hard that in comparison with the present it seemed as if her memory must be playing her false. Had there really been times when her parents simply could not properly feed the large family; had there been so much fear on the streets that only a fool ever said what was in his mind?

He spoke slowly. 'If only some of the things which were worthwhile had not been destroyed along with so much that was bad.' It might be utterly futile, but nothing could prevent his regretting the present lack of inner discipline and inner pride which together had kept a poor man's head held as high as a rich man's.

She was unconcerned with these aspects of past and present; not for her the problems which lay outside the family. 'No matter, I've no time to stand about and chatter, like a cluck hen. And you ought to have left for work half an hour ago.'

'Would you have me kill myself from overwork?'

She laughed scornfully, picked up a duster, left and went through to the dining-room. He drank the coffee and thought about Taylor. It was easy to mistake most emotions, but surely sorrow was difficult to misread. Taylor had been sorrowing. Then the relationship between himself and the dead man had surely been son and father and it had been he who had paid for the funeral . . .

Twenty-five minutes later, he telephoned Cantallops from the office.

'Where did the money come from?' said Cantallops. 'Where the hell d'you think?'

'Was it paid in cash, by cheque, or by bank draft?'

'I can't remember.'

'Then go and look.'

Cantallops swore, put the phone down. When he next spoke, he said: 'It was transferred direct into my account.'

'From which bank?'

'I don't know. You've more damn questions than a dog's got fleas.'

'Which, I can assure you, are no less irritating. Will you give me your authorization to find out from your bank where the money came from?'

'If I have to.'

CHAPTER 10

Calle Llube had, twenty years before, been the last road in Puerto Llueso; now there stretched beyond it one large urbanización, completed, and a second one under construction. It was a road of one-floor buildings, all with simple, bleak exteriors in which the only hint of beauty was in the window-boxes filled with flowers. However, behind their road fronts there was considerably more space and comfort than a casual observer would have thought; some had enclosed patios in which grew flowers and, occasionally, orange trees.

Alvarez stepped through the bead curtain of No. 15 and called out. A short, fat woman with an ugly but humorous face came into the room. He asked to speak to Taylor.

'He'll be at the restaurant.'

'But he does live here?'

'Rents the two rooms at the back.' She indicated with a quick wave of her pudgy hand the far side of the patio. 'Lives there with his woman.' She spoke with open disapproval. Had he been a Spaniard, let alone a Mallorquin, she would never have let him stay in her house with a woman who was not his wife.

'Where's the restaurant?'

'D'you know Las Cinco Palmeras?'

'Along the bay road?'

'That's it. Bought it and spent a fortune on it, by all accounts, but it's still not open.'

'Has he been with you for long?'

'Since last summer. Look, is something the matter?'

'It's only a question of papers.'

She was relieved—everyone had trouble with papers— since she liked the two of them, even though they weren't married.

He left, drove down to the front and then round the bay to the restaurant. He parked by the side of the patio and climbed out. Behind the buildings were marshland and farmland, some of it incredibly under the Philistine threat of development, which stretched to the encircling mountains; in front was the bay. The perfect site.

A few chairs and tables were stacked to one side of the nearest palm tree; the main door of the restaurant was shut and there was a notice in English and Spanish which stated that the restaurant would be opening at the end of the month. He walked round to the back. The battered Citroën van that he'd seen at the cemetery was parked near a shed. A woman was hanging up chequered tablecloths on a long line and when she saw him she dropped a tablecloth into the bucket and came across. 'Are you from the builders?' she asked in inaccurate, but understandable, Spanish.

'No, I'm not.'

'Blast!' Exasperation forced her into speaking English. 'I suppose that was much too much to ask for since it's only this morning they promised once again to come immediately.'

He said in English: 'We have a saying. A man waits for death and the builders and only death knows which will arrive first.'

'Oh, you understand! Then it's a good job I kept to ladylike language . . . Your saying suggests it's not only the foreigners who suffer.'

'That's right.'

'I know it shouldn't, but that cheers me up a bit . . . If you're not the builder, who are you and how can I help?'

He told her.

She said curiously: 'Mike should be back any moment. He just nipped into the port to buy some paint . . . Is something wrong?'

'I need to ask him a few questions.'

She was about to say something more when they heard the puttering of an approaching Vespino. 'That must be him now.'

Taylor entered the yard and braked the Vespino to a halt, cut the engine, drew the bike back up on its stand, picked out of the wire basket a four-litre tin of paint. It wasn't until he was a third of the way across that he recognized Alvarez; when he did, he came to a stop. Noting his expression, Helen's curiosity and perplexity changed to sharp concern.

'Good morning, señor.'

'What d'you want?' Taylor asked belligerently. 'To see
my driving licence because the law says a photostat copy
isn't good enough even though I couldn't have one if I didn't
have the original?'

'To ask you some questions concerning two hundred and
fifty thousand pesetas.'

He hunched his shoulders, as he might have done if
expecting to have to ward off a blow.

'Mike . . .' began Helen.

'Look, love, suppose you take the van and find the builders
and use all your charm to jerk them into some action?'

'But surely you phoned them only an hour ago . . .'

'Just go, eh?'

'No, I won't.' She walked forward until she could grip his
free hand in hers. She had no idea what was wrong, but
whatever was the trouble, she was going to share it.

'Perhaps it would be more pleasant if we sat down?'
suggested Alvarez.

Taylor looked as if he were obstinately going to refuse to
move, then suddenly changed his mind. After releasing
his hand, he led the way into the restaurant which was
reasonably cool, thanks to the open windows and the slight
sea breeze. The tables and chairs had been stacked to one
side, leaving three walls clear for painting, and after putting
the can down, using more force than was necessary because
violent action was one way in which he could release a little
of his bitter anger, he moved out one table and three chairs.
He sat, deliberately not waiting for them.

Helen, in an attempt to neutralize his all-too-evident
antagonism, said to Alvarez: 'Would you like a drink?'

'Thank you, I would very much. Do you have a coñac?'

She went through to the kitchen, to return with a tray on
which were three glasses, one with a drink in it, a bottle of
103, and a soda siphon. She put the tray on the table, turned
to Alvarez. 'I'm sorry, but we haven't any ice at the moment
—the wiring of the kitchen is one of the things we're waiting

to have done so neither of the refrigerators is working. It makes me wonder what on earth people did with food in the heat in the old days.'

'There was an ice factory in Llueso and each morning two mule carts brought ice down to the port for the ice-boxes.'

'You've lived here a long time?'

'Long enough to remember the ice-carts, señora, but I wasn't born at this end of the island.'

'When you first came to the port, it must have been quite small?'

'There were the few big houses on the front which belonged to the rich in Palma, one hotel, two or three shops, and many fishermen's cottages.'

'But no memento shops, or tourist bars, or discos . . . It must have been so lovely.'

'Lovely for the rich,' said Taylor. 'While the poor could always feast on the scenery.'

'Mike,' she said, worried.

'What you suggest is true, señor,' said Alvarez pacifically. 'There was much for the few, little for the many; now that has changed, but so has the life. Who can say which is the better?'

'The poor sods who didn't have anything then, but do now.'

'I suppose you are right. And yet . . .'

'Spiritually, so much has been lost?' she suggested.

'Crap!' Taylor said crudely.

'Mike, how can you be so certain that it's always better if the many benefit at the expense not only of the few, but also of the quality of life?'

'Because I've no time for an élitist society unless I'm one of the élite.' He finally poured out two brandies. 'Soda?' he asked Alvarez curtly.

'No, thank you.'

He added soda to his own drink. 'All right, we've sorted

out the problems of the world; now let's sort out yours. What's bugging you if it's not my bloody driving licence?'

'Did you pay two hundred and fifty thousand pesetas to Señor Cantallops for the funeral of Señor Thompson?'

Helen exclaimed: 'So that's why . . .' Abruptly, she stopped.

'No,' said Taylor loudly, 'I didn't.'

'Perhaps I should explain that I have spoken with the manager of the Banco de Bilbao in Foguful and with the manager of the Caja de Ahorros y Monte Piedad de Las Baleares here, in the port.'

'Then why in the hell ask?'

'Why did you pay for the funeral?'

'Is there any law to say I can't?'

'Of course not.'

'Then it's my business.'

'Señor Thompson was travelling on a false passport when he died. Now, I have to find out his true identity. Was he your father?'

Taylor drained his glass, poured himself another, and larger brandy, added soda, drank.

Alvarez produced a pack of cigarettes and offered it; Helen shook her head, Taylor ignored him. He lit a cigarette and waited with the timeless patience that marked his peasant background.

After a while, Taylor said: 'All right, he was my father. Steven Arthur Taylor. One of the Taylors of Chelton Cross, not that you'd get any of the present bunch willingly to acknowledge the fact.'

'Will you tell me about him?'

'Why not? It's amusing in a banana-skin kind of way and it can't hurt him any more.'

His family had been county, large landowners for generations; conscious of their position, yet equally conscious of the obligations this raised. It had become smart to sneer both at the squire and the subservient tenant, but when the system had been in the hands of honourable people it had worked well for both sides; better to touch a forelock than to starve in a town stew. (Taylor's tone expressed the dichotomy of emotions he felt; he admired the squires for what they'd done, held them in contempt for what they'd been.) But time had, as always, demanded change. When Steven Taylor was born, the land remained but the respect had to be earned and did not come as a by-product of the acres.

Steven Taylor had been a cuckoo in the respectable nest. People agreed that it was a mercy of providence that he had not been born the elder son since then he would have inherited the estate and to earn the respect of the staff and tenants it would have been necessary to conform, because they, being countrymen, were great traditionalists, yet from the beginning he had refused to conform. He was born five hours after an eminent gynæcologist had given it as a firm opinion that he wouldn't be for at least forty-eight hours. At his first prep school, the honours system had been in force; pupils were put on their honour not to cheat in their work and were not prevented from doing so by supervision, because this taught them to be true to themselves. When caught cheating, he had tried to explain to the headmaster that under such a system, anyone of intelligence was impelled to cheat because only a fool could ignore the advantages to be gained by so doing. The headmaster had been looking for repentance, not intelligence, and he had been so outraged that he had expelled Steven Taylor even though names from four previous generations of the family were on the Eton Scholarships board. His second prep school, chosen on the grounds that since it was only twenty years old its philosophy would be far more attuned to the sons of the middle class than those of the aristocracy and county, held that every pupil would commit every crime in the book unless prevented from doing so by either force or fear. The three years he'd spent there had taught him that survival called for an ability to think quickly, a gift for lying, and luck.

He went on to Eton, once more back in the mainstream of family tradition. At sixteen and a half, he was found in bed with one of the whores who worked from a house in Gleethorpe Road. The headmaster might, in view of his family history, have found some way of avoiding expelling him had he not, in answer to the question why had he done so degrading and socially dangerous a thing, replied that if degradation was a nineteen-year-old blonde, it was a difficult thing to resist, and honest fornication was surely far less physically dangerous than illegal homosexuality.

Australia no longer quietly received drop-outs from the wealthier families, so it became necessary for the family to decide what to do with him. In view of his known weaknesses —an eagerness to gamble, a disregard for convention, a tendency to lawlessness, the ability to concentrate on the ends and not the means, and an absence of any sense of shame—it was decided to use family influence to get him into a commodity broking firm.

The firm into which he was introduced had one rule that was absolute; no member might trade on his own behalf. At the age of twenty, he used some highly confidential information concerning frost damage in the Brazilian coffee plantations to set up a futures position which netted him half a million pounds. Unfortunately, he paid so much attention to his own affairs that he neglected the firm's and he lost them just under a million in sugar. The senior partner's final words on his departure were that, dishonest and incompetent, he was clearly far better suited to the stock market.

He spent the half million in just under seven years. He sampled everything life had to offer and frequently went back for more. His motto might have been: How could one possibly appreciate what was good without sampling what was evil?

When the last of the money was gone, he was faced with the problem of living. Lacking any sense of shame, he didn't hesitate to approach his elder brother and suggest he join the family trust which ran the land and the growing number of business interests. His brother, a sobersides, a roundhead, a pillar of the establishment, made it quite clear that in his view the father of the prodigal son had been guilty of a grave misjudgement.

Lacking any obvious means of gaining immediate and profitable employment, Steven Taylor accepted that he was left with only one course of action open to him, a course pioneered by the members of the aristocracy. To marry the daughter of a rich man. Even straits more desperate than those he now found himself in would not have persuaded him to marry the majority of such daughters, but Prudence was not only eligible, she was not noticeably spotty. Naturally, he was faced by considerable opposition from other indigent younger sons, but he had one asset none of them possessed, a golden tongue. Three weeks after coming to the decision, when her father was in Florida buying or selling some sort of property, he proposed and was accepted.

When her father returned home and heard about the marriage, he commented angrily on the insolent neck of penniless adventurers who were stupid enough to think he was a soft touch. Nothing more clearly illustrated Steven Taylor's subtlety of tongue (or perhaps it was the naïvety of property tycoons) than the fact that at the end of a two-hour interview, her father had agreed not only to the wedding, but also to continuing and even increasing Prudence's already very generous allowance.

The marriage had not lasted long. She was, even by the standards of her contemporaries, shallow-minded and to his chagrin he'd discovered that not even all her money compensated for her overriding ambition, to appear regularly in the more mindless upmarket social magazines. They parted soon after their son was born and she remarried, this

time to a man of substance—notable head of house at
Harrow, a first in Greats, one of the few Lloyds underwriters
who had never perfected a scheme to fleece his names, on
the invitation lists of all the best hostesses in London.
Strangely, the marriage soon bored her and after a while
she realized that this was because it was so bland and she
had been taught the taste of spice. In angry rebellion, she'd
emptied a bowl of rice crispies over her husband's head. He
never did understand why. Not long afterwards, she'd been
driving back to her flat in London when a drunken youth,
in a stolen Jaguar, had crashed head-on into her car and
killed her.

Steven Taylor had read about her death in a newspaper
and the article reminded him that he had a son.

Mike went to live with his father. Life changed abruptly
and then went on changing, with often heartbreaking
rapidity. One day they'd be rich, the next they'd be poor;
a large house in January, a terrace two up and two down in
July; a new Rover in February, a clapped-out Mini in
August. But far more bewildering than these swings were
those occasioned by his moves from one school to another,
from the private sector to the state one and then back again.
Each time he managed to make friends, it was only to be
wrenched away from them; each time he changed sectors,
he was jeered at by his peers and, until he learned to fight
ferociously, bullied because he came from an alien world.
School taught him that only the strong survive . . .

Then, without any warning, his father had married again.
He'd seen this as a betrayal, even though he was now
more than old enough to have realized that his father was
searching for security. Muriel was the attractive and very
wealthy widow of a much older husband who had originally
employed her as his private secretary and had then discovered that, unlike the previous ones, her price was not to
be computed solely in pounds.

For a time, life had stabilized. A large house near the

small village of Middle Cross, a few miles from Dover, a Philippine couple to run it, a Daimler and a Rover, holidays in exotic places which had not yet been overtaken by *hoi polloi* . . . Sometimes he wondered if his father and he would have settled down if Muriel had not been such a ridiculous snob who had deliberately set out to use her money to humiliate his father because his background was all that hers was not? But such a question was profitless. She was as she was and his father was as he was and life became too painful for him to stay any longer at Keene House . . .

'Did you often see or hear from your father after you left home?' Alvarez asked.

'Never.'

'But you must have had some contact with him?'

'I've just said, never.'

'I find that difficult to understand.'

'Lucky you! No bloody mixed-up feelings towards your own father? You can't see what it was like for me. He was my father, but it was he who was responsible for me having had to keep changing schools. Ever had a crowd of kids jeering at you simply because you speak with a different accent from them; and feeling so alone you wanted to die then and there? It was he who married Muriel and gave her the chance to humiliate him because she'd got the money and he hadn't.'

'You're saying that you hated him?'

'It's not so simple that one word can describe it. I loved him even as I was humiliated because he allowed himself to be humiliated by Muriel. I looked up to him, but . . .'

'But what?'

'Leave him alone,' said Helen fiercely. 'Can't you see how it hurts to talk about it?'

Alvarez changed the line of his questioning. 'But you did meet your father on this island?'

'Yes.'

'How often?'

'Twice.'

'Roughly when was this?'

Taylor shrugged his shoulders. 'Three or four months ago, then a month.'

'Didn't you see him at the beginning of last week?'

'I didn't even know he was back on the island.'

'How did he first learn you were living here?'

'Through Muriel; she lives on the island now.'

'You'd kept in touch with her?'

'When Helen and I decided to try to buy this restaurant, I was fool enough to go to her to borrow the money.'

'She refused?'

'Naturally.'

'Why d'you say that?'

'Imagine the blot on her social escutcheon if her stepson were to run a tourist restaurant.'

'She's so wrong,' said Helen.

'Of course she's bloody wrong,' he said bitterly. 'But she won't even consider heaven until she's convinced that only the right people are admitted.'

'Did you know that your father was travelling on a false passport?' Alvarez asked.

'I knew he'd changed his name.'

'Did this surprise you?'

'Nothing he did surprised me.'

'Why did he change his name?'

'I've no idea.'

'You didn't ask him?'

'No.'

'You weren't at all curious?'

'I've learned to mind my own business and leave other people to mind theirs.'

'He never gave even a hint of what the reason was?'

'No.'

Alvarez was certain that Taylor was lying, but equally certain that for the moment nothing would persuade him to

tell the truth. 'Thank you for all your help, señor. And I am
very sorry if it has been painful for you, but I promise you
that I had to ask the questions.'

Taylor made no reply, nor did he look up when Alvarez
stood. But Helen followed Alvarez out into the yard and his
car. 'He didn't mean to be rude,' she said earnestly, worried
that he had taken offence at the aggressive way in which
Taylor had spoken. 'It's just that he's had such a difficult
life and he normally hates talking about it. Today's the first
time I've heard some of the things he's just told you.'

'I understand.'

She studied him. 'Yes, you really do. Thank you.'

As he opened the car door and climbed in behind the
wheel, he thought how strange it was that she should think
it necessary to thank him for understanding that no man
could ever separate himself from his past.

Alvarez spoke to Superior Chief Salas over the telephone.
'His real name was Steven Arthur Taylor. He'd been married twice and was clearly a bit of a rogue, but by default
rather than intention.'

'What is that supposed to mean?'

'Well, that . . . What I'm trying to say is that I'm certain
he didn't have vicious motives, he just didn't find the same
dividing line between right and wrong that you and I do.'

'The practical difference escapes me. Send the information to London.'

'I've already done so.'

'You have?' Salas sounded surprised. 'Then the matter
can be closed and you can return all your energies to your
normal work.' He cut the connection.

Alvarez settled back in his chair and stared resentfully at
all the accumulated paperwork on his desk.

As so often happened, the line from England was clearer
than from Palma. Every word the Spanish-speaking chief

inspector said came through undistorted. 'About your message concerning Steven Thompson. You say that his real name was Steven Arthur Taylor and he was married to Muriel Taylor and used to live in Middle Cross, near Dover. You'll be interested to learn that, in fact, he died in a car crash in Kent roughly three years ago.'

CHAPTER 11

'I suppose,' said Superior Chief Salas, 'it is now your contention that Taylor died twice?'

'No, señor,' replied Alvarez.

'Not? But surely the idea appeals to your sense of the dramatic? And since when have you ever allowed your imagination to be constrained by impossibilities?' His anger finally surfaced. 'Goddamnit, why should I, of all people, be forced to suffer an inspector who is presented with a simple, straightforward car crash and within no more than ten days turns the incident into a second resurrection?'

'Señor, I don't see how I can be blamed for the fact that the Steven Taylor who died on this island appears also to have been the Steven Taylor who died in England.'

'Did you say "appears" to have died in England?'

'Yes . . .'

'Then you really do appreciate that it is impossible for the same man to have died twice?'

'Of course . . .'

'Experience suggests, Inspector, that in any case in which you are concerned the use of the words "of course" is irresponsible . . . In view of the fact that you accept that one or other of the reports of death must be inaccurate, what do you suggest doing?'

'We need to exhume the body of the man buried in Fogufol and Michael Taylor must be asked to identify it. If he

does identify the deceased as his father, we will know that
England made a mistake; if not, then the mistake is ours
and we will have to discover the true identity of the man
who died here.'

'Very well.'

'Shall I apply for permission for exhumation, or will you,
señor?'

'It will be best if I do. Otherwise, there's every chance
that the exhumation order will name Tutankhamen.'

A sectional ladder had been eased inside the mausoleum
and then down the shaft; two men, working with great
difficulty in the confined space, had coupled up the four
hooks of the rope sling to the coffin which had been eased
into the shaft and then hauled up by block and tackle.
Boards had been slid underneath the coffin, across the
mouth of the shaft, and it had been lowered on to these.
Four men lifted and eased it out into the open and the harsh
sunshine.

The undertaker and an assistant unscrewed the lid. The
undertaker said: 'We're ready when you are.'

Alvarez nodded.

They raised the lid. He looked down and swallowed
heavily. 'OK. Put it back on for the moment.'

He turned and walked back along the dirt track, round
the corner of the cemetery, to his parked Seat. Taylor was
standing by the passenger door. 'Are you ready?'

Taylor's face was heavy with strain; he was sweating
heavily and kept brushing the sweat away with the back of
his hand.

'Señor, it will be brief.'

'But not bloody brief enough.' He squared his shoulders.
'Let's get it over with, then.'

They walked down the dirt track to reach the coffin.
Alvarez motioned with his hand and the coffin lid was lifted
once again. Taylor stared down at the dead man for several

seconds, his face working, then he made a choking sound, turned away, and hurried over to the low drystone wall which marked the limit of the cemetery land.

Alvarez nodded and the coffin lid was replaced; the undertaker and the assistant prepared to screw it down, but he checked them. 'Hang on until I've had a word with him.'

He walked over to where Taylor stood, staring out over the land, and brought a small flask from his trouser pocket. 'This is brandy. Drink.'

Taylor took the flask, unscrewed the cap, raised the flask to his lips and drank. He passed it back.

'Was he your father?'

Taylor nodded.

'Thank you . . . I have to give one more order and then I'll drive you back.'

Taylor once more stared out, his gaze unfocused. Alvarez went back to the group of men and gave orders for the coffin to be returned to its tomb.

As Alvarez entered the guardia post on Monday morning, the duty cabo, seated behind the desk, looked up. 'There's someone waiting for you in your room; getting downright impatient. He's rung down twice to ask where the hell you've got to.'

'Who is it?'

'Borne.'

'Borne . . . Borne.' Alvarez thought for a moment, his brow furrowed. 'The name seems vaguely familiar, but I'm damned if I can think why . . .' Then a disturbing thought suddenly occurred to him. 'He's not the new comisario, is he?'

'Damned if I know, or care. But if he is your new boss, I reckon you'd better pull your finger right out.' The cabo looked at his watch. 'What time are you supposed to start work?'

'I was held up,' replied Alvarez defensively.

'Yeah. By oversleeping.'

He went up the stairs and along the corridor to his room. Inside, standing by the window, was a tall, thin man, with a long, narrow face whose sharp features expressed a strong measure of moral dyspepsia. He studied Alvarez, then said, in a voice which chilled: 'Are you the inspector?'

'Yes, señor.'

'I have been waiting here for the past twenty-two minutes. Are you not supposed to report for work by eight?'

'Indeed. And I left home well before then, but I didn't come straight here because I've an inquiry to pursue and since I couldn't find the man yesterday evening, I was hoping to do so first thing this morning.'

'You succeeded?'

'Regretfully, no. Once again, he was not at home.'

'I see.' The two words expressed disbelief, but also an acceptance of the fact that it would be almost impossible to prove Alvarez was lying. 'Hearing I had reason to come to this end of the island this morning, the superior chief suggested I spoke to you personally in the hopes that by so doing the investigation into the death of Señor Taylor might be dealt with with a little more efficiency than has hitherto been the case. When I expressed my surprise at the necessity for such a comment, he further remarked that whenever he knew you were handling a case of the slightest importance, he could never make up his mind whether he would prefer you to observe your usual level of incompetence, in which case nothing would get done, or to try to show some initiative, in which case there might well be total chaos. At the time, his words surprised me. Now they do not. Look at your desk.'

Alvarez perplexedly looked at it.

'I have never before seen such slovenly untidiness. Have you forgotten the maxim, *ex nihilo nihil fit*?'

'Er . . .'

'In future your desk will be tidy at all times and your

papers up-to-date and correctly filed. One more point; when you have occasion to pursue an investigation before reporting here in the morning, you will tell the duty guard so that he can inform anyone who inquires where you are. Is that clear?'

'Yes, señor.'

'I do not expect to have to refer to the matter again. Now, you fly to England tomorrow morning . . .'

'I what?'

'Kindly do not interrupt me. It is necessary for you to go because they stubbornly refuse to accept that it was Steven Taylor who died on this island last Wednesday week. Quite clearly, they are both unwilling and unable to accept that their own investigations of three years ago were incompetently handled. In consequence, you will now prepare a report on Taylor's death, detailing the facts in such a manner that they, despite their ludicrous pride, can no longer claim that they are right and we are wrong.' He looked at his watch. 'Thanks to your initial lateness, I am now going to have great difficulty in arriving on time for my appointment.' He walked over to the door, put his hand on the handle, stopped. 'It occurs to me that it would be best if I read through your report before you leave so that the necessary corrections can be made. Your plane takes off at eleven, which calls for you to check-in by ten . . . Be at my office at eight-thirty.'

'But . . .'

'Well?'

Alvarez realized that it would not be politic to point out that that would mean his leaving home at some quite ungodly hour. 'Nothing, señor.'

'It would clearly help you more closely to emulate *justum et tenacem propositi virum*.'

'Yes, señor.'

The comisario opened the door and left.

*

The main CID room at Brackleigh Divisional HQ was very large and it contained a dozen desks; at the far end, a space was partitioned off to form the detective-sergeant's room. Detective-Sergeant Wallace, a round, cheerful man, with the beginning of a double chin, finished reading the report which Alvarez had translated into English. He leaned back in his chair. 'I've got to admit that that seems definite. The son identified the father. So that presents us with the interesting question: Who did we bury?' He reached over for a folder and read one of the loose pages inside. 'How much do you know about our end of things?'

'Very little, señor.'

'Let's cut out this señor talk. I'm Ian and you're . . .?'

'Enrique.'

'Right . . . I'll fill you in. When your initial request about tracing the next-of-kin of Steven Thompson came in, we shunted it to the passport people. As you know, they came back with the news that the passport had been pinched some four years back. That rang the alarm bells and we asked you for further details. You then identified Steven Thompson as Steven Arthur Taylor, late of Keene House, Middle Cross. Because he'd been travelling on a stolen passport, we put his name through the computer and that came up with the information that he'd one conviction for fraud and was dead.'

He turned over a page, read for a while. 'His style of fraud wasn't original, but he was extraordinarily successful at it. I gather that basically it's a simple scheme and if the operator is very careful, not even illegal. He buys a load of shares which are quoted very low and sets out to sell them for considerably more than he paid for them. Obviously, this calls for a seller with the gift of the gab and a buyer who's either a natural sucker or else has a streak of larceny in his make-up and who, when presented with a share he's told he can buy cheaply only because someone else is being tricked into selling before discovering it's worth many times

its quoted price, rushes to buy . . . Taylor only ran into
trouble when he let his tongue run too far ahead of the facts
—drunk on his own verbosity. The judge at the trial—
which was quite some time ago now—was an old fool who
was gullible enough to believe Taylor's fervent promises to
reform and so handed out a suspended sentence instead of
sending him to jail . . .

'This brings us to a little over three years ago. Word
reached us that he was back to his old tricks and had
overstepped the line again. We started making inquiries and
eventually discovered it was true and the papers were sent
to the DPP for his decision on whether to prosecute; the
point at issue was, were Taylor's actions just legal or had
they slipped into being illegal? It was a very abstruse point,
the kind that makes a lawyer break open a celebratory bottle
of champagne. Things were at that stage when he was
involved in a car crash which killed him.

'Obviously, when someone under investigation has a car
crash and his body is so badly burned that it is not immediately recognizable, we need to be convinced that it is his
body . . . What did we have here? The car was his. It had
skidded off a wet road, gone through a stone parapet and
crashed below, bursting into flames. The road wasn't a busy
one and it was several minutes before another car came
along. The driver of this raced off to the nearest house to
raise the alarm and while he was away the burning car
exploded.

'When it was possible, the wreck was examined. The body
had fallen on to its left-hand side and because part was
pressed against solid metal, we had a section of clothing and
flesh which escaped burning. This gave us points to check
with the wife. When he'd left the house, he'd been wearing
a sports coat which she described in some detail and a blue
shirt; the section of unburned coat matched her description
and the shirt was blue. She told us he'd a crescent-shaped
scar on his left leg, a few inches above the knee; the corpse

showed signs of a crescent-shaped scar above the left knee. He'd worn dentures; we contacted his dentist who identified the dentures from the corpse as his. There was an autopsy. The deceased had not been murdered, he had died from a massive coronary thrombosis. Finally, there was not one person recently reported missing who could possibly have been the dead man.'

'That would normally seem conclusive,' said Alvarez.

'You can say that again. But now you tell us that he died in Majorca almost a fortnight ago, identified by his son, so that the corpse in the car was not his. Which raises the sixty-four thousand dollar question, how and where did he find a dead man, near enough his own age and build to be passed off as him (the evidence about the scar shows his wife was an accomplice—which in turn suggests why she sold up and left the country soon afterwards), who died a natural death and whose disappearance created no disturbance?'

'An undertaker?'

'I'd say that that's it in one. What's more, it would need to be a busy undertaker in order to provide the wide choice there would have to be for him to find a suitable candidate. And even then, it would still take time for the exact combination to turn up, which explains why he didn't fake his death when he first realized we were on to him, but waited until the last moment. He couldn't do anything else.'

They were silent for a moment, thinking about what had just been said. Wallace was the first to speak. 'I seem to remember that your report mentioned he might have been on the island on business. Was he working the same old game with the expats there?'

'I haven't been able to find out exactly what he was doing. Even his own son did not . . . That is, I believed the son when he said he did not know what his father was doing on the island, but now I begin to wonder.'

'He may have known, or guessed, but been too ashamed to speak?'

'That must be very possible. The son's relationship with his father was obviously a very stormy one, but there was still natural love. A son would always want to defend his father's reputation.'

CHAPTER 12

Brackleigh was a market town set among well-wooded countryside, some eight miles back from the coast. Not on any direct road route to London, its railway a branch line with a poor service, it had never become a commuters' town and had thereby escaped much of the sad development which had scarred so many other towns in the county.

The undertaker's premises were to the west of, and on the edge of, the town, a very convenient location since both churches were also to the west, while the crematorium was three miles further out. Wallace led the way into the reception area. A middle-aged woman asked them in a hushed voice how she could help them and Wallace said he'd like a word with Mr Gates, if free. A moment or two later, she escorted them through the Hall of Loving Care, where half a dozen coffins in different styles were tastefully on view, and into a large office.

Gates was tall, broad-shouldered, slim-waisted. He had a wide, rubbery face, an air of solicitude, and a voice with treacly undertones. He was dressed in black coat, stiff collar and black tie, and striped trousers. He shook hands with a firm, but moist grip. 'Good afternoon, gentlemen. I am delighted to make your acquaintances. Miss Carol, would you be kind enough to provide two chairs?'

She had already set one chair in front of the desk and

now she put a second one alongside it. She left, without a word.

'Miss Carol,' said Gates, as he returned round the desk and sat, 'informed me that you wished to ask me certain questions. I shall be delighted to assist in any way I can.'

'Fine,' said Wallace, who'd taken an instinctive and immediate dislike to the undertaker, but was trying not to show this. 'I think I'm right in saying that your firm conducted the funeral of Steven Arthur Taylor, of Keene House, Middle Cross, three years ago last March?'

'Who did you say?' asked Gates, inclining his head as if to hear more clearly, although previously he had shown no signs of deafness.

'Steven Arthur Taylor.'

'I do not immediately recognize the name as one of our passed-ons, but you will, I know, understand that we conduct so many laying-to-rests that it is not possible for me to remember all the names.'

'But you'll keep records?'

'Since the day this firm was founded the name of every passed-on has been recorded in the Book of Loving Remembrance.'

'Then will you check?'

Gates gestured with his plump, very white, smooth right hand. 'Naturally, I am eager to accede to your request. But will you first acquaint me with the reason for it? If you will excuse the little conceit, I regard myself as the guardian of the memories of those whose layings-at-rest I have conducted and I would not like to think that I have in any way betrayed that guardianship.'

Wallace said: 'My companion is Inspector Alvarez, from Majorca.'

'From Mallorca? . . . Please pardon my small correction, but I endeavour always to refer to a country or town in the same style as do the inhabitants; a subtle compliment to them . . . Mallorca. An island of beauty and charm. But no doubt you are well aware of its many virtues?'

'I've never been there. Inspector Alvarez has been investigating an accident in which a man died. His name was Steven Arthur Taylor.'

Gates rested his elbows on the desk, joined the tips of his fingers together to form a triangle, brushed the tips of his middle fingers backwards and forwards across the hairs which grew out of his nostrils. 'Forgive me, but I fear I have become confused. Did you not previously ask me whether we had laid to rest Mr Steven Arthur Taylor three years ago last March?'

'Yes.'

'Then I do not understand.'

'I'm wondering if you buried a man who wasn't dead.'

'Sergeant, surely you cannot begin to believe that we, or any other member of our honourable profession, could possibly lay to rest someone in whom the breath of life still lingers? Such a happening belongs only to the lowest and most disagreeable fiction.'

'That's good news for anyone in a coma, only it's not what I'm talking about. But before we go any further, suppose you check if you did handle his funeral?'

Gates, his expression pained, used the intercom to ask for the Book of Loving Remembrance to be brought in. A moment later, Miss Carol carried in a large, leather-bound ledger and carefully laid this on the desk. She left, again without a word. Gates put on a pair of spectacles and opened the ledger. After a while, he looked up. 'Steven Arthur Taylor, who had resided at Keene House, Middle Cross, was laid to rest on the sixteenth of March, three years ago.'

'Then how come he was buried a fortnight ago in Majorca?'

Gates sat back and interlocked his fingers across his lower chest. 'That is quite impossible.'

'It is what happened,' said Alvarez.

'No, señor. It cannot be what happened.'

'His body was exhumed and his son identified it.'

'Then I can only suggest . . .'

'Come off it,' said Wallace crudely. 'Where's your body buried?'

'Are you referring to Steven Arthur Taylor who passed on three years ago last March?'

'I'm referring to the man you buried, who most certainly wasn't Steven Arthur Taylor. Which cemetery is his grave in?'

'He was not laid to rest in a cemetery. His family wished him to be welcomed by the divine flame.'

'What's that mean—cremated?'

Gates inclined his head.

'How very convenient.'

'For those who do not subscribe to tradition . . .'

'For those who don't want an exhumation.'

'All the proper certificates were presented.'

'I'm sure they were.'

Gates's expression was blandly patient, but he could not quite hide the sharp watchfulness of his deep brown eyes.

'What other male funerals did you carry out during the previous week?'

'I do not think I am at liberty to answer that. As the guardian . . .'

'Then I'll get a warrant.'

Gates sighed. 'I fear, Sergeant, that you are not of a sympathetic nature.'

'In this case, you're right, I'm not. Now, do I get the names, or do I get a warrant?'

Gates leaned forward, adjusted his spectacles, read, and then slowly and reverently named ten people.

'Which of those was in his forties and died from coronary thrombosis?'

'I cannot possibly answer.'

'You must have seen the death certificates.'

'Of course. But I never record such details since when one has passed on, one's mortal . . .'

'Give me the names again, this time with the dates of the funerals. I'll check 'em out.' Wallace wrote down the list. 'Which were buried and which cremated?'

Gates provided these further details, then said very earnestly: 'Sergeant, may I ask that if you insist on disturbing their memories, that at least you conduct your inquiries with all due decorum?'

Wallace arrived at the hotel at which Alvarez was staying at six-thirty that evening and suggested they had a drink at a country pub he knew and liked. During the drive, Alvarez stared at the lush, green pastures and heavy crops and mentally compared them with those at home where, unless there was water for irrigation, pastures were burned off by the sun and crops were light. Then he stared up at the cloud-covered sky which had been threatening rain for hours and he ceased to envy the farmers whose lands promised such wealth.

The Five Legged Horse stood on crossroads, opposite what had once been the village shop, but was now a private house. The pub, reputedly an old smugglers' cottage— history, however, did not record any period of great smuggling activity in the area—had been modernized several years previously, but this had been done with taste and a happy lack of plastics, chrome, and humorous drawings.

'What'll it be, then?' asked Wallace.

Alvarez would have liked a brandy, but knew from experience that the size of an English tot would have shamed even a Basque, while its cost would be beyond disbelief.

'A lager, if they have one,' he answered, choosing to be safe.

They sat at one of the small, round tables. Wallace opened a bag of crisps and pushed this across, raised his glass. 'The first today and all the sweeter for that.' He drank, put the glass down, helped himself to a couple of crisps, munched those as he brought a sheet of paper from the breast pocket of his sports coat. 'I got one of my DCs to check out the death certificates; here's the result.'

Alvarez read down the list. 'The only real possibility is this man of forty-nine who was also cremated.'

'Right.'

'But is there any way of being certain?'

'I'd say we can be certain. The question is: Can we ever prove it? I suppose we might be able to trace out the evidence of the money Gates was paid to work the switch, but I doubt it. If you want my opinion, he's so bloody fly that only an insecticide will ever fix him.' Wallace contained a belch. 'Excuse me. Indigestion. The missus says it's because I eat too much fried food. I tell her, if the canteen didn't fry the food, we wouldn't be able to eat it.' He reached down to a pocket and brought out a small pack of tablets, one of which he swallowed. 'I've never read the instructions, in case they say, not to be taken with alcohol!'

Wallace's actions and his words recalled a scene for Alvarez. He remembered Higham's description of the meal in the restaurant up in the mountains and how Taylor had hardly drunk anything because to do so might be to trigger off the attack of migraine which the pill was meant to prevent . . . And how the subsequent violent illness had, according to himself, resembled no other attack of migraine he had ever endured . . .

'Is something up?'

'I think, Ian,' he replied slowly, 'that perhaps I have been investigating a murder without, until now, recognizing that fact.'

CHAPTER 13

'Let me try to understand,' said Superior Chief Salas wearily. 'You now claim that three years ago Steven Taylor faked his own death in England by bribing an undertaker to provide a body which he could substitute for his own in a faked car crash in order to escape arrest for fraud?'

'Yes, señor.'

'And you go on to say that Steven Taylor's real death, two weeks ago, was not accidental, but was murder—yet once again, you can prove nothing?'

'At the moment, no, but it does seem possible . . .'

'For you, is anything impossible?'

'What I've done is put two and two together . . .'

'And inevitably arrived at several solutions, none of which is four.'

Alvarez doggedly continued. 'We know that when Steven Taylor was over here, he was probably engaged in some kind of business. What could be more likely than that it was similar to what he'd done in England before his "death"—in other words, a swindling scheme? There are many wealthy foreigners who live here and by all accounts he could talk so persuasively that he could encourage even a rich man to part with money. When one swindles, one breeds bitterness and anger. Someone he swindled was determined to get his own back.'

'Did this someone arrange the car crash?'

'No, señor, what he surely did was to substitute a capsule containing poison for one containing the drug which Taylor took whenever he felt a migraine threatening. The fact that the initial symptoms of the poisoning caused him to crash was pure chance.'

'And you have reached this conclusion solely on the grounds that he was sick after the meal?'

'He ate and drank very little, then suffered symptoms that were unlike those he'd ever suffered before. Señor, I wish to investigate further.'

'How?'

'I would like to find out where he lived after his faked death and who he has defrauded on this island. May I have your permission to proceed?'

'Why bother to ask?' demanded Salas, with a fresh rush of anger. 'You never have in the past.'

Alvarez drove round the side of Las Cinco Palmeras and parked in the yard. Two cats watched him climb out of the car and then scurried away. The sun beat down and he remembered the cool, moist green of Kent.

Helen stepped out of the back door of the kitchen, hand raised to shield her eyes. When she identified her caller, her expression tightened. 'Mike's not here.'

She was a fighter, he thought admiringly. 'Do you know when he will be back, señora?'

'It's señorita and you damn well know it is.'

'I hoped you would accept that as a compliment, not as any intended insult.'

The answer surprised and bewildered her because there could be no mistaking the sincerity with which he had spoken. Then she remembered that on his previous visit he had shown himself to be very sympathetic and her manner changed. 'I'm sorry, but I really don't know when he will. You see, he's gone to try and find the builders.'

'They still have not done the work?'

She shook her head.

'Do you know their name?'

'It's Ribas. Someone told Mike that they were the most reliable people around. If they are, all I can say is, God help anyone employing one of the others.'

'I will have a word with Javier. I will tell him that if he doesn't start, I will investigate all the work he's recently done for which no proper licence was ever issued. He will arrive here immediately.'

She smiled. 'You really are a most extraordinary detective. Blackmailing a builder! You're either one of the nicest men I know, or one of the nastiest.'

'Am I permitted to ask which?'

'You may ask, but you certainly won't get an answer. Now, let's go inside and have a drink. And this time I can even offer you ice. Mike managed to persuade an electrician to come here and do a lash-up job and get one of the refrigerators running.'

They went inside. Since Alvarez's last visit, the painting had been finished and the tables and chairs were now set out. She pointed to the nearest table. 'Grab a seat. And what would you like to drink?'

She went into the kitchen, returned with a tray on which were two glasses, already frosting. 'Brandy, ice, and no soda, for you.' She handed him one glass, raised her own. 'To long, sunny days with few shadows.'

They chatted. She told him about the difficulties they had encountered in buying and altering the restaurant, trying to give it more character than it had had, and then spoke excitedly about the future.

They heard the shrill scream of the Citroën van's engine. When this was cut off, there was the slam of a door, then the stamp of approaching feet. Taylor shouted: 'Helen!'

'In the main room.'

'The bastards say . . .' He stopped abruptly as he entered and saw Alvarez. 'So it's your bloody car that's in the way.'

'Mike, the Inspector's promised to help us,' she said, trying to lessen the impact of his boorish words.

'Doing what?'

'He says he'll have a word with Ribas and persuade him to start on the work right away.'

Taylor turned and went into the kitchen. They heard the chink of ice being dropped into a glass. Helen's expression was once again worried and her previous vivacity was gone. 'Please,' she said in a low voice, 'remember it's all been so difficult for him. He's not really trying to be rude.'

Taylor returned, slumped down on the nearer of the two free chairs at the table. 'What d'you want this time—apart from free booze?'

'To tell you something and ask you something.'

'What's the news? My work permit's still at the bottom of the pile?'

'On Wednesday I flew to England and went to Brackleigh.'

Taylor's expression tightened.

'While I was there, I learned certain facts. First, your father's funeral three years ago was faked.'

'You knew that before you went.'

'Second, I learned why it was faked.'

Taylor drank, put the glass down with so much force that a few drops of liquid spurted up and spilled out on to the table. 'In this bloody world, you run and you run and still you get hit by what you're running from.'

'What d'you mean?' asked Helen, with sharp worry.

'Ask him, not me.'

She faced Alvarez. 'Why did Mike's father fake his own death?'

Alvarez hesitated.

'Are you suddenly suffering scruples?' asked Taylor violently. 'Don't bother. Have fun. Throw the family's dirty linen high into the air.'

'Señor, I would prefer to discuss the matter with you alone and then you can decide what to say to the señora.'

'D'you get an extra kick out of hypocrisy?'

'Mike!' Now there was anger as well as worry in her voice.

'What's the matter? Haven't you realized that this is other people's fun day?'

Alvarez said: 'Señor, I am here because what I have learned suggests that your father was poisoned before his death.'

'Now you're being bloody crazy.'

'Why should anyone want to poison him?' she asked.

'Because such person had been tricked out of money.'

Taylor ran his fingers through his rebellious mop of hair. He picked up his glass and drained it, abruptly stood, went through to the kitchen, returned with a bottle of brandy, one-third full, and a rubber tray of ice cubes. He sat, refilled his own glass, pushed the bottle across the table, pressed four ice cubes out of the tray into his glass. He drank heavily, then said: 'You've got to understand something. If at the beginning life hadn't kicked him so hard . . .' He stopped, slammed his clenched fist down on the table. 'Who the bloody hell am I trying to flannel? If a man's honest, he stays honest, however unfairly life treats him.'

'Can you be so sure of that?' asked Alvarez.

'What's a copper's philosophy? Call no man honest until he is dead; until then he is at best lucky? . . . Just for once, I'm going to indulge in the painful luxury of seeing things as they really are, not as I'd like them to be. Father was a man who couldn't see that there's always a distinction between right and wrong, even if the base for that distinction can shift; for him, right was what he wanted . . . I don't know what his scheme was, but it was something to do with shares. For a time, he made a lot of money and it was one of our "rich" periods, then things went wrong and he ended up in court on a charge of fraud. They found him guilty.'

She drew in her breath sharply.

He faced her. 'So now the skeleton's out of the cupboard and stalking the land and the dirty linen's flying high. If I were you, I'd start walking.'

'You damned fool,' she said, as she reached over and gripped his hand.

He drained his glass and, using his free hand, refilled it.

'D'you want to learn what hell really is? It's not the traditional pit of flames, it's not merely Sartre's other people,
it's a crowd of little bastards of your own age circling you
and shouting that your father's a thief. D'you want to know
what abject, humiliating betrayal is? It's standing in the
middle of that circle and hating your father and wishing to
God you could be given the chance of denying him . . .

'He was sentenced two days after he was found guilty.
The judge said he'd needed that time to consider the matter.
He decided not to jail Father because he saw in him a sense
of real remorse and the desire for redemption . . . I can still
remember Father laughing and boasting about how he'd
softened up the old fool of a judge with his superb eloquence;
laughing, when I'd been suffering hell because of him . . .
We left that district, which meant I changed schools. No
one ever found out at the new one what had happened and
for once some of the boys were friendly to me even though
I was a newcomer, arriving in the middle of the term. So
life ought to have been a whole lot happier. But every time
I looked at Father, I remembered how I'd have denied him
if only I'd been given the opportunity . . .

'Then he met Muriel. As I said, he saw things not as they
were, but as he wanted them to be. Before he married her,
he saw her as a loving wife whose money would screen him
from ever again risking imprisonment. He couldn't see her
as the bitch she really was.

'There was never any mistaking his background, even
though he never tried to impress; even when he stepped out
of the dock a convicted, but freed, criminal, he was one of
the upper crust. And when they were together, this became
even more obvious; as did the fact that her background was
totally different. And because she's an arrant snob, she
pretty soon came to hate him for something over which he'd
no control. And d'you know how she set out to get her own
back? By making him plead with her for every penny she
gave him. Then, she could despise him.

'I couldn't stand seeing him humiliated, so I cleared out. Just before I went, I told him he'd got to do the same. He laughed and said he would, all in good time. I soon learned what that really meant. He'd worked out a new scheme for making money and was determined to get this going and so become financially independent before he broke away from her. I told him to forget it—look at last time. He said it wasn't the same and the idea was cast-iron. Soft brass, more like. Things went wrong and the police got on his trail again and it became clear that the moment they'd collected enough evidence, they'd arrest him for fraud. And this time, not even he could be bloody optimistic enough to believe the judge would give him a second chance. It would be jail. And so he thought up a way of escape. And because, with his help, she'd been impersonating the landed gentry—large house and God knows how many acres, cherry brandy stirrup cup for the hunt—the thought of what people would say if he was publicly branded a convicted criminal was enough to give her hysterics. She agreed to finance his plan.'

There was a long silence, which Alvarez broke. 'Thank you for telling me all that.'

Taylor shrugged his broad shoulders.

'Where has your father been living in the past three years?'

'I don't know.'

'You really do not have any idea?'

'Look, I cleared out because I couldn't stand what was going on. It was a complete break.'

'When you saw him here, he didn't mention anywhere?'

'Not specifically. But on one occasion he talked about getting the train into Barcelona, so I suppose if he had a place, it was near there.'

'How near?'

'I've told you all he ever said; and if he'd ever said any more, I bloody wouldn't pass it on.'

'Why not?'

'Haven't you understood what I've been saying?'

'Yes, señor, I have. But have you, for your part, understood that if he was murdered, it is necessary to find the murderer? Can you tell me whether he was carrying out some business on this island?'

'No, I can't.' He poured himself a third drink. 'All right, you'd have to be stupid not to be able to guess. He'd some scheme or other going on.'

'A scheme that was connected with shares?'

'What d'you think?' Taylor stared into space. 'And you know something really comic? He'd finally hit the jackpot. He told me that when he gave us the money to buy this place. He'd made so much that he was going to retire and imitate an honest man. He'd made it, just in time to die . . . according to you, to be murdered.'

He'd been murdered, thought Alvarez, because he had been about to retire a dishonest man, not an honest one.

Alvarez stared at the list of figures which the meteorological office in Palma had just provided over the telephone. On May 14 Steven Taylor had flown in to Mallorca and that day the weather had, along the Mediterranean coast, been sharply layered as it often was at that time of the year. From the French border to just south of Barcelona, there had been strong winds and the temperature had been cool (relatively speaking); from just south of Barcelona to Alicante, the winds had been light and the temperature warm; further south still, there had been virtually no wind and the temperature had been hot. These conditions had been holding for several days. Taylor had told the man in Worldwide Car Hire, at Palma airport, that he had just come from somewhere noticeably colder; he had told the porter at Hotel Verde that recently there had been too much wind for him to sail his boat; he had told his son that he had caught a train to Barcelona. Put those facts together and there was good reason for saying that he had been living on the coast between Barcelona and the French border.

It was going to be necessary to telephone Salas. Alvarez sighed, leaned over and opened the bottom right-hand drawer of his desk. He brought out the bottle of brandy and a glass.

CHAPTER 14

The moving walkway carried Alvarez from the airport to the station, from which a train left within five minutes. On arrival at Sants, the more westerly of Barcelona's stations, he inquired when the next train for Figueras left, and from which station, and was told that the TALGO would be departing from there in twenty minutes.

He enjoyed train travel. One didn't take off and land, so that there was no need to shut one's eyes and pray, believing, yet very conscious that there were times when the Almighty slipped up. He stared out at the green, rolling, and in parts wooded countryside, and thought that here one could buy very many more hectares of fertile land for the same money as on the island. Perhaps after he'd retired, he could move to the Peninsula and buy the finca he had always longed to own, could till the land, plant the seed, harvest the crop . . . But he knew he was deceiving himself. He would never be truly happy away from the island.

The train drew into Figueras and he alighted. He'd been promised that someone from the municipal police would meet him, but there was not a uniform in sight so he crossed to a seat, near a board which showed the make-up of the next train to Barcelona, and let the drowsy warmth engulf him . . .

'Inspector Alvarez?'

He awoke with a jerk, stood, and shook hands with a man much younger than himself who spoke in Catalán, yet

seemed to have some difficulty in understanding his Mallorquín. They walked down the platform and left by one of the
unmanned exits, crossed to a car which was parked under
the shade of a tree. They drove to the police HQ, an old
four-storey building not far from the Dalí museum. There,
he spoke to a man who had checked with the town hall and
the Ministry of the Interior. 'Sorry, but there's no house
been purchased by a Steven Arthur Thompson and no one
of that name's taken out a residencia or permanencia.'

'Blast!'

'Don't forget, despite the amnesty, there are still one hell
of a lot of foreigners living in the area who ought to have
papers, but don't.'

'You wouldn't have a list of 'em?'

The man laughed. 'I don't know exactly what you had in
mind . . .?'

He looked at his watch. 'A drink and then lunch.'

Along the coast, a number of developments specifically
aimed at yachtsmen had been built and of these, Corleon,
set around canals, was perhaps the best. Spain's answer to
Port Grimaud. Unfortunately, its initial success had proved
to be far in excess of expectations, with predictable results.
More canals were dredged, the density of housing was
increased and finally, on the outskirts of the urbanización,
dozens of rabbit hutches were built, specifically aimed at
the French holiday market, while large and ugly blocks of
appartments began to line the beach.

Alvarez parked the borrowed car and climbed out. The
sun shone out of a cloudless sky, but a sea breeze prevented
the heat from building up. He looked across the raised
pavement at the estate agent and sighed. When he'd said
that he intended questioning all the estate agents in Corleon
to find out if any one of them had sold a house to Steven
Thompson, which for some reason had not been registered,
he had been regarded with amusement. Having gained a

rough idea of the number of estate agents there were, he understood the reason for that amusement.

Two hours later, he used a handkerchief to wipe the sweat from his forehead and neck; it might not be as hot as on the island, but it was still too warm to spend the day walking from one office to another, asking the same questions, receiving the same answers . . . And if he failed to find any trace of Steven Thompson here, there were many more developments up and down the coast . . . Across the wide road was a café, with tables and chairs set outside under the shade of an awning. He waited for a French registered Mercedes to drive past at twice the speed that was reasonable, crossed and gratefully sat. He ordered a coffee and coñac.

Had he made too many assumptions, he wondered, as he drank and watched with appreciation the scantily clad women go by—it was difficult to remember that there'd been a time when even men in bathing trunks had been supposed to wear guards over their knees. When told that Steven Taylor enjoyed sailing and owned a boat, he'd assumed this to be a sailing boat which probably required a berth; but 'sailing' could mean a power boat, which could be moved by trailer so that Taylor might well live inland. He'd assumed . . . A young lady, wearing a see-through blouse and no brassière, went past and the sharp sunlight picked out the curves of her flesh. He watched her cross to the far side of the road and enter a large supermarket. That gave him an idea.

He finished the coffee and coñac, paid the bill, which was high enough to make it clear that few locals ever drank there, left and crossed the road to the supermarket. He asked the cashier at the one till which was operating if the owner was around and she answered that if Agueda wasn't downstairs, she'd be upstairs, in tones which suggested that Agueda kept a suspicious eye on everything at all times.

Agueda was checking through a display of beach accessories.

'From Llueso? My mother was born not ten kilometres from there and many's the time I've been there before I was married! Tell me, how much has it changed?' She was a large, heavily-boned woman who deliberately dressed to emphasize her size rather than to conceal it. She used a great deal of make-up and her mouth was a most unusual colour. She wore so much jewellery that most people assumed it to be imitation, but in fact it was all genuine.

They went down to the ground floor and through to the office which lay behind the bread counter. She offered him a drink. 'Well, what is it you want exactly?' she asked, as she handed him two glasses and a bottle.

'I'm trying to find out more about a foreigner who died on the island recently; I don't have an address, but there's reason to believe he lived here.'

'You must have asked at the town hall in Figueras?'

'I have, but no luck; and the same goes for the estate agents. So I'm wondering if he rents a place, in which case it could prove difficult to track him down. But I reckoned there's just the chance you could have come across him.'

'Most of the foreigners come here to shop,' she agreed complacently, fingering one of her rings as she spoke. 'What's the name?'

'Steven Thompson.'

She repeated the names, her heavy accent distorting them. She shook her head. 'I don't know anyone by that name.'

'Ah well, it was just an off-chance,' he said philosophically. 'Tomorrow morning, I'll see if any of the banks have changed money for him.'

'Here, fill your glass again. But leave mine as it is.'

He gave himself a generous drink, happy to make the most of the chance to enjoy the Carlos I brandy.

'What was that first name again?'

'Steven. It's possible it was usually shortened to Steve.'

'Steve . . . Steve . . . I've heard that before. I wonder if . . . When did this man die?'

'A fortnight ago last Wednesday.'

'You know, that could be about the time.'

'What could?'

'When the woman lost her man.' She continued with all the enthusiasm and irrelevancies of a born gossip. Charlotte Benbury was always called Charlie, which was confusing because an Englishman had told her that Charlie was a man's name. Still, when one stopped to think about it, Spain wasn't always that logical. A man was called José-María, but María was a woman's name. And it was better to be called a woman's name than Jesus. Agueda snorted. As a good communist—as she gesticulated to emphasize her standing, one of the diamonds on the largest ring caught the light and flashed out ice-cold sparks of colour—she had only contempt for people so conditioned by superstition . . . To get back to Charlie? Well, she was English. And men clearly found her very attractive. But then any man under the age of ninety was interested in only one thing, so none of them could see that she was a bitch . . .

'Why d'you say that?' he asked.

'Because that's what she is.'

She wasn't a prude by any means, but there were limits. When Charlie's man had been alive, they'd been like a honeymoon couple, even though he was a good bit older than she. Then he'd died and what had happened? Had she mourned her lost love? Had she hell! Within something like three days, she'd reappeared and started going about with Pierre, the Frenchman, who boasted that during the summer season he never bedded the same woman two nights running. When the two of them had walked into the supermarket, arms about each other's waists, she'd wondered why God —not that she believed in such a superstition—had not struck her dead.

'What happened to the first man?'

'Someone said he'd been killed in a car crash.'

'D'you know where?'

'Can't say. And if you want my opinion, it's a great pity she wasn't with him at the time.'

'The young do things differently these days,' he said pacifically.

'The men don't,' she replied with crushing contempt.

'Is she still living here?'

'I saw her only yesterday. The bitch.'

There was possibly, he thought, more than a touch of jealousy in her outrage; perhaps her youth had been conventionally dull. 'D'you know where she lives?'

'Somewhere in Servas. I don't know the number, but it's the biggest house around, on the water, and there's a huge yacht tied up. Masses of money. D'you think she'll get all that?'

'How would I know?'

'It'd be just like a fool man to have left her everything so that now she can waste it on that Pierre.'

'Lucky Pierre.'

She was not amused.

He found the house quite easily. It was a long U-shaped bungalow, built on two plots, and it fronted one of the main canals so that a yacht, fully rigged, could berth there. To the left was a hard tennis court and to the right a swimming pool, partially concealed from the road by a row of cupressus. The property was ringed by a high chain-link fence and both the small and the large gates were secured with heavy locks. At regular intervals there was a notice which said in Spanish, English, and German, that the house was protected by alarms and guard dogs.

He pressed the button of the speaker, to the side of the smaller gate. 'Who is it?' asked a woman in Catalán, her voice sounding harsh and tinny.

He identified himself and said he'd like a word with the señorita.

'You can come on in; the dog's shut up in the kennel.' There was a sharp click from the lock of the gate.

As he walked through the gateway, a dog began to bark and he saw to the side of the house an enclosure in which, standing very stiff-legged, was a large, woolly, black dog whose teeth, even at a distance, struck him as exceedingly dangerous.

A middle-aged woman in an apron opened the front door and showed him into a very large sitting-room, tastefully furnished with good quality Spanish furniture; through one of the picture windows, he could look across the sloping garden to a schooner. Money might not buy happiness, but it helped one to enjoy one's misery . . .

'Good evening. You wish to speak?' asked a woman in laboured Castilian.

He turned. Agueda had referred to Charlotte Benbury as being very attractive, but she had also named her bitch so that he had subconsciously been expecting her character to flavour her looks. Far from it. She was of such pure, stunning beauty that for a moment she shocked; tall, shapely, a round face topped by a cascade of honey-coloured hair, eyes more blue than the summer Mediterranean, a mouth shaped by Cupid, peaches-and-double-cream complexion . . . He saw both innocence and experience, cool purity and fervid passion . . . 'I am sorry, I was admiring the yacht,' he said in English, trying to explain away his gaucherie. 'May I have a word with you?'

'Thank goodness, you speak English!' She smiled.

A man would run ten miles in the July heat for such a smile . . . 'Señorita, as your maid probably told you, I have very recently arrived from Mallorca where I have been investigating the death of Señor Thompson, whose real name was Taylor.'

She bit her lower lip, hesitated, moved to her right to sit in an armchair.

'You knew him?'

She nodded.

'He lived here?'

She nodded again.

'I am sorry to have to pursue a subject which must be painful—' Perhaps!—'but because of certain facts surrounding his death, I must. You will have been told that he was in a car which crashed; did you also know that his passenger was lucky enough to be thrown clear before the car reached the bottom of the cliff and so lived?'

'All I care is that Steve was killed.' Her tone was flat, her expression blank.

'The passenger suffered some injuries and for a while lost his memory. When this returned, he told us certain facts which have subsequently raised very serious questions.'

She was staring into the far distance, almost as if bored.

He spoke more starkly than he would otherwise have done, determined to force her to understand that the past could not be as readily dismissed as she would have it. 'What the passenger told us makes it seem certain that the crash occurred because Señor Taylor had been poisoned.'

'What?' She swung round to face him, her expression now strained. 'That's impossible.'

'It is the truth.'

She began to pluck at a fold in her linen print frock.

'Did the señor suffer from migraine attacks?'

'Yes.'

'Did he know when an attack was impending?'

'Sometimes. Not always.' She spoke in a nervous, staccato manner.

'Have you any idea what triggered an attack?'

'Chocolate, cheese.'

'What about wine?'

'He thought it did. But he liked it so much . . .' She failed to finish the sentence.

'What did he do if he believed an attack was starting?'

'He'd take medicine.'

'Would there be any of it in this house?'

'Maybe.'

'You've been too busy with other matters to discover what he's left?' he said, which heavy sarcasm.

She looked at him with sudden alarm. So, he thought, she wasn't completely indifferent to other people's opinions. 'Did you know that Señor Thompson's real name was Taylor?

She made no reply.

'Did you?'

'Yes.'

'Do you know why he lived under a false name?'

'What's it matter now?'

'Because it probably explains why he was poisoned. Did he ever tell you he'd faked his own death in England in order to escape being arrested for fraud?'

After a while, she nodded.

'That fraud was in connection with share dealings. Since he lived here, did he deal in shares?'

'I . . .' She stopped.

'Do you want to help, or don't you? Does it matter at all to you that he was poisoned?'

'Of course it does.'

'Then had he been dealing in shares?'

'Yes.'

'How?'

'I don't know. I asked him once what it was he was doing and he refused to explain. He said it was much safer for me not to know.'

'Didn't you ever gain any hint?'

'No.'

'It's almost impossible to run any kind of a business without records. Did he keep them?'

'I suppose so.'

'Why are you uncertain?'

'He often used to work in the study, but if I went in there I never looked at what he was doing.'

'Are you saying you weren't in the least bit curious?'

'He was insistent that I never learned anything.'

'Because if something went wrong, you wouldn't be inculpated?'

'Yes.'

And you repay his love by offering yourself to Pierre only days after his death, he wanted to say, but didn't. Are all his papers still in the study?'

'I haven't touched anything.'

'Then I want your permission to look through them.'

For a while she made no comment, then she stood and it was obvious that this was the answer.

The large room was both library and study. Two of the walls were lined with shelves filled with books, there was a small desk, and an old-fashioned, free-standing safe.

The drawers of the desk contained nothing of interest. He asked her for the keys of the safe and she left, returned with them. On the top shelf of the safe there was a jewellery case and a considerable amount of money in pounds, dollars, and pesetas; on the bottom shelf were several files. He lifted out the files and put them on the desk.

It soon became obvious that Steven Taylor had been a systematic man. Each file covered a geographical region and one was for Mallorca. This contained papers listing the names and addresses of Archie Wheeldon/Muriel Taylor, Robert Reading-Smith, and Valerie Swinnerton. Against each name was a figure, two hundred thousand, four hundred thousand, forty thousand and a company's name.

'Do you know what Yabra Consolidated is?'

She shook her head.

'Would you know if Señor Taylor left a will?'

'Yes, he did.'

'Where is it?'

'In one of the files.'

He looked through those he had not examined and found two wills, one in Spanish, one in English, that were essentially the same. Taylor had named only one beneficiary, his son.

'Do you know the terms of his wills?'

She nodded.

'You're not mentioned. So his son now owns this house and all its contents.'

'No. Steve bought it in my name. That's why I put it up for sale, not him.'

'When was this?'

'I don't know. Maybe a couple of months ago.'

'Why are you trying to sell?'

'Steve told me to.'

'What was his reason for wanting to move?'

'He was worried?'

'About what?'

'Someone had threatened him.'

'Who?'

'He wouldn't say.'

'Have you any idea how much his son stands to inherit?'

'No.'

'Where is his money held?'

'I don't know.'

'You must.'

'I don't. I've an account with the Banque de Crédit Agricole in Berne and he paid money into that when it was needed. He never said where that money came from.'

'Then how will his son learn the extent of his inheritance?'

'I suppose he's told Mike where he kept his capital.'

'You've met Mike?'

'No. But Steve often talked about him.'

He checked through all the files again, seeking a reference to bank accounts, but there was none. He replaced the files in the safe, locked it, handed her the keys. 'Where will I find the medicine?'

She led the way into a bedroom that was nearly as large as the sitting-room and also faced the canal. The furniture was a strangely harmonious mixture of modern and antique so that the Spanish bed with barley-sugar headboard and footboard did not seem at all out of place in company with the superbly inlaid, serpentine dressing-table whose delicate elegance suggested it was French. To the side of a heart-shaped mirror on the dressing-table was a framed photograph. It was a poor photograph because flat lighting had stripped away all subtlety; nevertheless it was possible to discern in it all the features of the dead man he had seen in the coffin, even though many of those features had been attacked by decay. The frame was antique embossed silver. How, he wondered, could she leave that photograph there when she shared the bed with Pierre?

She opened the small top left-hand drawer of the dressing-table and brought out a medicine bottle and handed this to him. He unscrewed the lid. Inside were a number of capsules, half red and half white. 'I'd like to take these.'

'I don't want them.'

He pocketed the bottle. He was glad that now he could leave.

As he sat behind the wheel of his car, he saw that she was still standing in the front doorway of the house. What were her real emotions? Worry and shame, not because of what she'd done, but because he might have learned of what she'd done? He knew a sudden, sharp anger that anyone so beautiful could at heart be so rotten . . . But that, surely, was to ignore completely the question of what kind of a man Taylor had been? Might he not have been swindling her out of love, as he had swindled others out of money? Might she

not have discovered this and that was why she had been so
ready to throw herself into the arms of another man? . . .
Yet if that were so, could she really have been so hypocritical
as to keep the photo on the dressing-table instead of ripping
it out of the frame? He swore. He knew precisely what he
was doing. Searching for what was not there because he was
far too sentimental; inventing the most ridiculous excuses
rather than admit that there could be evil in beauty.

CHAPTER 15

Alvarez sat in his office and stared through the window.
The day was already pulsatingly hot; there had been no rain
for weeks and wells were beginning to empty and in another
month only those which tapped underground streams or
lakes would not be dry; on unirrigated land, all growth
would shrivel to a uniform brown and it would seem as if
the earth itself were dying . . .

Reluctantly, he jerked his thoughts back to the present
and for a while he considered all the work he should be
doing. Then he rang the Institute of Forensic Anatomy and
spoke to Professor Fortunato's secretary. Were the results
of the post mortem on Señor Steven Taylor yet to hand?
Frostily, she replied that since the exhumation had taken
place as recently as the previous Saturday morning, they
were hardly likely to be.

He telephoned Detective-Sergeant Wallace at Divisional
HQ in Brackleigh. Was Yabra Consolidated the name of
shares and, if it was, what were they worth?

'You must have a funny idea of the kind of money we
make, Enrique, to ask me! The only thing I can tell you
about shares is, they're dangerous. A mate of mine decided
to go for British Telecom and when they started to rise his
wife persuaded him to sell because she wanted a new settee.

After he'd sold 'em they continued to rise and she went for him all ends up for losing so much money by selling. Nearly caused a divorce, that did!'

'But you perhaps know someone who can tell me the answers?'

'Sure. A mate works for a stockbroker in the City and his bonus each year almost makes my entire salary look silly. I'll chat him up and then get back on to you. By the way, what's the weather like?'

'Sunny and much too hot.'

'It's stair-rodding here and bloody cold. Can't you dig up a case that needs me along to give a hand?'

After saying goodbye, Alvarez slumped back in the chair. Apart from sending the capsules he had brought back from Corleon to Palma for testing, there really was nothing more he could do. Nothing more, that was, other than to make a start on clearing up the backlog of work on his desk . . .

'You're looking tired,' said Dolores, as she looked across the luncheon table at Alvarez.

'And old,' said Juan. Isabel giggled.

She swung round. 'How dare you say such a thing!'

'But he's becoming bald.'

'Another word from you and I'll wash your mouth out with kitchen soap.'

Juan felt aggrieved because he had only spoken the truth, and all his life he'd been instructed to do that, but he knew better than to argue with his mother when her voice held that sharp tone.

'You can go outside and play,' she said.

He reluctantly stood—he was certain the grown-ups were going to talk about something interesting—and left, followed by his sister.

'You're looking tired,' said Dolores, for the second time.

Alvarez ran his forefinger along the line of his hair and persuaded himself that it had not receded.

'You need a really good siesta.'

Jaime passed the bottle of brandy across. 'This'll help you sleep.'

Dolores pursed her lips, but for once kept quiet. After all, her husband might just be right.

Alvarez drank the last of the coffee, checked the time. 'I'd better be moving.'

Dolores, already beginning to prepare the supper, looked up from the chopping-board. 'Be back on time. I'm making frito Mallorquín.'

'I'll be back before time,' he promised. Her frito Mallorquín was the best on the island. Not a trace of greasiness.

He left the house, drove to the main square, and was lucky enough to find a newly vacated parking space against the central, raised portion. Practically all the tables set out in front of the two cafés were occupied. The tourists would be paying one price for their drinks, the foreign residents less, and Mallorquins, if any, less still. Which was just. Let the visitors pay for at least some of the damage they caused . . .

He walked down one of the narrow roads and reached the guardia building, went up to his room and sat, waiting to phone until he'd regained his breath.

Wallace spoke with cheerful surprise. 'You've pulled a right one out of the bag this time, Enrique!'

'I'm afraid I don't quite understand.'

'Then pin back your ears and prepare to listen to a modern fairy story . . . When you first mentioned Yabra Consolidated, the name seemed to ring a bell, but I was damned if I could think why. Then this pal of mine who works in a stockbroker's office told me what's what and I remembered all the press hullabaloo. Yabra Consolidated is the name of an Australian mining company. The Australians are great gamblers and one of the things which really attracts the punters is stocks and shares. Not surprisingly, this brings the worms out of the woodwork and they set up very doubtful, or downright bogus, companies, flog the shares and get rich, leave the punters to become poor. The mining sector's the worst. There've been three companies in the past twelve months who've been caught salting land or faking assays to promote a good launch of shares.

'Yabra Consolidated was formed five years ago to prospect for gold, uranium, and diamonds. As my pal said, that combination of aims would have taxed even a large and established company and so it ought to have warned the punters, but it didn't. The shares were fully subscribed at a dollar each. A year ago, they stood at two cents and that, apparently, was an overvaluation.

'Then, recently, the impossible happened. Gold was discovered on land over which the company has mineral rights and the shares shot up and up until right now they're standing at five dollars.'

'But that's . . .' Alvarez stopped.

'Yeah, I know. Backside about face.'

'I was sure Taylor had persuaded people to pay money for shares he knew to be worthless. Instead of which . . .'

'Instead of which, it sounds as if he was hoist with his own petard.' Wallace chuckled. 'Can you imagine his feelings when he discovered that instead of swindling his victims, he'd made them rich?'

'But from all accounts, he had made a great deal of money for himself shortly before he died.'

'Then either he talked himself into keeping some of the shares or else he heard they'd unexpectedly come good and he was in time to buy them back before the news became general.'

And that, thought Alvarez, would be quite enough to make a seller think of murder. He started to thank the other, when Wallace checked him.

'Hang on. There's another piece of news which should interest you. One of my blokes has told me that not very

long ago he had a private detective try to pump him about
Steven Taylor.'

'In what connection?'

'It wasn't all that clear, but it seemed as if this man had
been employed to discover if Taylor had any sort of a
record.'

'Why should he have been suspected?'

'I can't answer. If you're interested, I'll find out as much
as I can.'

'Will you? And especially the client's name.'

'Leave it with me . . . By the way, how's the weather
now?'

'Still too hot.'

'We haven't seen the sun in days. Why in hell can't you
be having rain just once when I'm talking to you?'

The chemist shop was in the same narrow road as the
guardia post, but nearer to the square. A married couple,
both of whom were qualified pharmacists, ran it and Alvarez
went through and spoke to the husband who was checking
stock in the room beyond the shop.

'So how are things with you?' asked the husband.

'I can't complain.'

'Then you're the only one who can't, with IVA doubling
prices . . . Francisca saw Dolores the other day and said she
thought Dolores wasn't looking too fit; could that be right?'

For a while, they spoke about general matters of interest.
Although about ten thousand people lived in and around
Llueso, so few of them or their ancestors had ever lived
anywhere else that relationships were extensive and complex. It was relatively rare for two locals to meet and not to
have at least one distant cousin in common. Finally, Alvarez
brought the conversation round to the reason for his present
visit. He produced the medicine bottle Charlotte had given
him. 'What can you tell me about the contents?'

'Is this an official question?'

'At the moment it's unofficial, but it's likely to go official very soon.'

'Have you any idea what the capsules are for?'

'They're said to be for an impending migraine attack.'

The husband crossed to a small desk, brought down three fat books from a shelf, searched through these, frequently referring back to the capsules. At the end of five minutes, he said: 'As far as I can tell, they're what the label says they are. Of course, it'll take an analysis to be certain, but on visual identification these capsules contain a drug that is put out for migraine sufferers to help ward off attacks.'

'How long would one take to work after swallowing?'

'I don't know that I'd like to say—you'll have to ask the manufacturer. All that's certain is that they'll be fairly fast because if they're to stop an attack consolidating, they've got to be.'

'Something like a quarter of an hour?'

'I doubt it's that quick, but as I said, you'll have to ask the manufacturer.'

Taylor had taken one capsule earlier in the morning and then a second one just before—or was it with?—the meal at the restaurant because the first one hadn't worked. It looked, then, as if it was probably the earlier one which had contained the poison. 'Would it be difficult to substitute a foreign substance for the drug in one of the capsules?'

'Nothing easier. They're made in halves. All you'd have to do would be to separate the two, empty out the contents and put in whatever you wanted . . . Are you saying that that's what was done?'

'It looks like it.'

'So then what happened?'

'The driver of a car crashed and was killed.'

The husband whistled.

CHAPTER 16

El Granero was a part of the island which Alvarez seldom visited. First, it lay to the west of Palma, near concrete-jungle land, secondly, it was a development unashamedly pitched at the rich, thirdly and most importantly, Granero meant granary, a name which reached back to the time when one half of the island's grain had been grown there, and the contrast between past and present was too bitter.

He drove past houses set in large gardens which raised his scorn for so much wasted land, came in sight of Ca'n Grande and suddenly all scorn was gone and he knew only a wistful wonder that anyone could be so lucky as to own and live in anywhere so beautiful. The rock, suddenly breaking out of the rich soil, stretched out into the small bay and the house seemed to flow upwards from the rock, as if built by nature, not man.

It grew in size as he approached, not simply because he was nearer to it, but because the graceful lines helped to conceal until the last moment exactly how large it was. He parked, by the side of a bed filled with magnificent roses in full bloom, and walked up to the heavy wooden door which had the deep rich patina which came only from regular hard polishing. He rang the bell and the maid answered it, then led him through a hall and a wide passage out on to the patio. She said she'd call the señora.

He looked out at the sea, spread below, and he thought that here was somewhere which rivalled even his beloved Llueso bay . . .

'You wish to speak to me?'

He turned and saw a woman who almost managed to conceal her age with elegance; her expression and tone of voice denoted bored indifference. 'Yes, señora.'

'In what connection?'

'Señor Taylor.'

'I fail to see that the subject of my late husband can be of any concern to you.'

'Not even,' he said, choosing to be objectionable, 'when he died twice?'

She walked over to the swing chair and settled in the shade of the awning.

He moved a chair and sat. 'Your husband was supposed to have died three years ago, in England, but in fact he died here, on this island, almost three weeks ago.'

She gave no indication that she had heard him.

'Can you tell me what he was doing on this island?'

'No, I cannot.'

'Then full inquiries into his supposed death will have to be made in England; how he faked it, whom he bribed, and where the money for that bribe came from.'

'Are you trying to blackmail me?'

'Señora, I am a member of the Cuerpo General de Policía.'

'What's the significance of that? You're asking twice as much?'

'The suggestion is insulting.'

The lift of her eyebrows suggested that she was surprised he believed himself capable of being insulted.

He struggled to keep his temper in check as he thought that it was small wonder the British had been booted out of their Empire. 'Did you see your husband three weeks ago?'

'I did not.'

'Are you quite certain?'

'I am not in the habit of lying. Or, I might add, of being called a liar.'

'Can you explain why your name and address were written down in one of his business files?'

'I wouldn't bother to try.'

'I believe it was because in the last few months he sold you certain shares.'

'If you can believe that, you can believe anything.'

'Did you buy shares from him?'

'I have already indicated that I most certainly did not.'

'Did he offer to sell you some?'

'He was not that much of a fool.'

The maid stepped out on to the patio. 'Señor Wheeldon, señora.'

'You can ask him to come through.' She turned back to Alvarez. 'Is there anything more before you go?'

'Yes, señora.'

'How very boring.' She looked towards the house and as Wheeldon appeared, she called out: 'Archie, will you tell Catalina to bring out the drinks trolley?'

Wheeldon briefly returned into the house, then crossed the patio. ''Morning, Muriel.' He looked at Alvarez as he waited for the introduction.

'He's from the police.'

'The police, eh?' Wheeldon looked round for a patio chair, brought one across. He grinned as he sat. 'What have you been up to, old girl? Robbing a bank?'

'Don't be so bloody stupid.'

'Here, I was only having a little joke.'

'That's all I need to make my day!'

'You mean something really is wrong?'

'Señor,' said Alvarez, 'I am investigating the circumstances of Señor Steven Taylor's death.'

'But he died three years back, in England. What's that to do with you now?'

'Señor Taylor died three weeks ago, on this island.'

Wheeldon said to Muriel: 'I say, what the devil's he getting at? You've told me yourself that your husband died before you came out here.'

She said, with cold fury: 'He was Steven Thompson.'

He stared at her, slack-jawed. 'But you said . . .'

'Will you stop saying the same thing over and over again. The English police made a mistake in identification.'

'But . . . but dammit, you must have discovered that he wasn't really dead?' Only after he'd finished speaking did he realize the implications of what he'd just said.

The maid, wheeling a cocktail trolley, came out on to the patio. She positioned it close to Muriel's chair and checked that the brake was on. 'Is some crisps, señora. 'And . . .'

'That's all.'

The maid returned into the house.

'I want a whisky,' Muriel said.

Wheeldon stood, opened the two top flaps of the trolley and these, through a system of counterweights, brought up a shelf on which were several bottles, an insulated ice container, and half a dozen glasses. He poured out a whisky on the rocks and passed her the glass. He looked at Alvarez. 'He doesn't want anything,' Muriel said. Innate courtesy made him ask Alvarez: 'Are you quite certain you won't have something?'

'Thank you, I'd like a coñac, please, with ice but no soda.'

She became still angrier.

Wheeldon poured himself a pink gin, sat.

'Señor,' said Alvarez, 'did you meet Señor Thompson, or Taylor, when he was on this island?'

Wheeldon cleared his throat. 'As a matter of fact, I did, yes.'

'Where did this happen?'

'At some party or other; I can't remember exactly which.'

'And when was this?'

'The first time? I suppose it was three or four months ago.'

'You've seen him since then?'

'I . . . Well, as a matter of fact, I have, yes.'

'You saw him again?' she said sharply.

'Look, I'd no idea he was your husband. You never said anything.'

'Of course I damn well didn't.'

'But why not?'

'God Almighty, that has to be the year's stupidest question.'

'Señor,' said Alvarez, 'did you buy shares from him?'

She said, her voice filled with scorn: 'Not even Archie could be that soft.'

Wheeldon spoke uneasily. 'I . . . The thing is . . .'

'Christ! You're not trying to say you actually did?'

'He made it sound so promising.'

'Of course he did. And you believed him? It's a wonder he didn't sell you a slice of moon cheese at the same time.'

'I'm not quite as thick as you seem to think.'

'Impossible.'

'I doubled my money.'

She laughed scornfully.

'I'm telling you, I literally doubled my money. What's more, if you like I can prove it.' He stood, crossed to the cocktail trolley and poured himself a second pink gin.

'How much did you pay for the shares, señor?' Alvarez asked.

'It was the equivalent of five cents, Australian,' he answered, as he sat.

'How many did you buy?'

'Two hundred thousand.'

'And what did you sell them for?'

'Ten cents clear.'

'You made ten thousand Australian dollars?' she said, her voice high from astonishment.

'Yes, I did.'

'Señor,' said Alvarez, 'how much would your holding be worth now?'

Wheeldon picked up his glass and drank quickly.

Muriel looked at Alvarez, then at Wheeldon. 'How much, Archie?'

'I don't know.'

'What's the name of the shares?'

'I've forgotten.'

'Yabra Consolidated,' said Alvarez.

'What? You bought Yabra Consolidated at five cents?'

'Yes.'

'And then sold them at ten? When they're now worth over five dollars?'

'How was I to know . . .?'

'D'you realize how much you've lost?'

'I haven't lost anything. I told you, I've doubled my money.'

'Christ! you've got a mind that walks one inch high. Your holding's now worth a million dollars. But you sold it for ten thousand. You gave him practically a million!'

'I didn't give him anything. He bought them from me . . .'

'You call it buying, when he knew they were worth fifty times what he was paying for them?'

'Maybe he didn't.'

'You can really think he'd offer you a profit if he didn't know they were worth five dollars? My late husband may have been many things, but he was nobody's fool. He'd sized you up as God's gift to a con-man from the moment he first met you. Don't you have the wit to understand anything? When you bought those shares at five cents, they wouldn't have been worth half that. Then they shot up and he must have been absolutely shocked to discover that for once in his worthless life he'd sold something that was increasing in value. So what did he do? Rushed out here to offer you twice as much as you'd paid, quite certain you'd jump at the chance of a hundred per cent profit and never have the nous to stand back and wonder why a man like him should willingly let you make money. You were so blind greedy, you threw a million dollars down the bloody drain.'

He was so angrily humiliated that he answered back. 'And were you so very clever? What did you call me when I suggested you bought some of the shares? So naïve I thought Carey Street was a good address? The shares were worthless and always would be? So how much did you throw down the bloody drain? You could have bought a million shares and they'd be worth fifty million dollars now. So you've lost fifty million compared to my million. So who's the bigger fool?'

'How . . . how can you be so cruel and vicious?'

He was immediately contrite. 'I'm terribly sorry, Muriel, old girl. I was upset and didn't realize what I was saying . . .'

Only a complete idiot, thought Alvarez, would have apologized after forcing her on the defensive.

'If I had bought them,' she said sharply, determined to salvage her pride, 'I'd have known a damn sight better than to sell them back to him before I'd checked out why he wanted to buy.'

'I . . . I suppose you would.' Wheeldon stared down at his glass.

Alvarez said: 'Señor, when did you next meet Señor Taylor?'

'It was about three weeks ago.'

'Why did he come and see you this time? Was it still in connection with the Yabra Consolidated shares?'

'I don't remember.' He went over to the cocktail cabinet and poured himself a third pink gin.

She said: 'You must remember.' Her tone was sharp and clearly his earlier remarks had really hurt and now she was determined to gain revenge for his presumption. 'So if you don't want to talk about it, it must be embarrassing. I wonder what Steven said on his last visit that could so disturb you?' She paused, as if thinking. 'It surely can't be . . .?'

He looked appealingly at her.

'You know, Steven was always ridiculously proud of his ability to talk people into behaving like fools and the greater the challenge, the prouder he felt . . . Which means, of course, that originally he couldn't gain much satisfaction out of conning you.'

'Muriel, old girl . . .'

'I think he returned because he knew that by then you would have discovered how he'd conned you out of a fortune and you'd be sick with anger. Now, to sell more shares to someone in that state would really be a challenge. Right?'

'I was only trying . . .'

'Your motto—always trying? What went on in your mind? Did you manage to see yourself as a financier, making and destroying financial empires with a brief nod of the head?'

'Why won't you understand?'

'But I do, perfectly. I understand you just as thoroughly as I understood my late, but unlamented, husband.'

'Señor,' said Alvarez, 'did you buy some more shares from him?'

He looked at Alvarez with astonishment, as if he had forgotten the detective was also present.

'Well, did you?' she said mockingly.

'He . . . he said it was a red-hot tip which he was telling me about because in the circumstances he wanted to help me. Don't you see how I . . .'

'Help? What genius, to use that word after he'd swindled you out of a million dollars! But I don't suppose that even now you've appreciated the full irony of it . . . How much did he take you for this time?'

'I invested five hundred pounds.'

'Invested. How words change their meanings . . . And you handed it over without a whimper; the sacrificial lamb, running to its slaughter. He must have laughed himself nearly sick.'

Alvarez knew pity, but also contempt, for Wheeldon; no man should allow himself to be the butt of such vicious contempt at the hands of a woman, however much he loved her. He stood.

She looked up. 'Are you leaving? You're probably right. It looks as if the entertainment's over for the day.'

CHAPTER 17

Cala del Día—which in this context could loosely be translated as 'beach for the daytime—' was now the name given to a large area which included the urbanización and the complex of shops, cafés, and restaurants which served it, but originally it had pertained only to a very narrow strip of land which ran along the edge of a cliff. The name adumbrated Mallorquin humour; there was no beach, since the cliff plunged into the sea, and at night time, lacking any form of guard, it had been all too easy for a walker to tumble over the edge, especially on a fiesta.

Alvarez reached the foot of the urbanización and began the steep, zigzagging drive upwards. It was odd, he mused, how much the foreigners were prepared to pay for a view. To build on a slope cost up to fifty per cent more than on the level, especially if one demanded a large patio with pool. Yet all over the island there were developments along the lower slopes of hills and mountains. He modified his thoughts. He should be applauding his countrymen's business acumen rather than wondering at the gullibility of the foreigners. After all, such rocky slopes were otherwise valueless.

The road ended at Casa Resta, which stood on a fold of the mountain and therefore had views both to the east and the south; because of the steepness of the slope at this point, the outside of the foundations had had to be built up several metres. It was a large house, with a typically formless jumble of different roof levels; not much artistic talent would have been needed to make it far more visually appealing.

He rang the front-door bell. Rosa opened the door and

told him that the señor was down in the village, but would almost certainly be coming back soon—did he want to wait? She took him through the house to the patio. 'Feel like some coffee?'

'Mallorquin style?'

'What d'you think?'

As she went inside, he walked to the edge of the patio, just beyond the end of the swimming pool. At Ca'n Grande, one had the illusion of floating above the sea, here, the many houses in the urbanización below precluded any such fanciful thoughts; Ca'n Grande said there could be beauty in wealth, Casa Resta, only vulgarity.

Rosa returned to the patio with a tray on which were two cups of coffee, milk, sugar, and one balloon glass well filled with brandy. She set everything out on the patio table, sat. 'You can always hear him coming back.'

'He's the kind of man who wouldn't like to find you here?'

'Sometimes he'd laugh, sometimes he'd shout his head off. You just can't tell where you are with him. But he's a foreigner, so what d'you expect? Have anything to do with them?'

'Too much. I live in Llueso and sometimes I think half the population's foreign.'

'You're from Llueso? Then maybe you know my cousin from Playa Nueva?' She said that her cousin was a very cunning man who had made a fortune building houses on what had been a swamp. Almost all the houses were damp and the buyers were forever complaining. Wasn't it incredible that anyone could be so stupid as not to know that a house built on a swamp was going to be damp?

Alvarez returned the conversation to Reading-Smith. What kind of a man was he? A strange man. One minute he'd be friendly, the next he'd kick up hell. And if something refused to work, like the washing-machine or the toaster . . . She wondered if it was when he feared he was being made a fool of. But to think that of a machine! . . . There was, of course, something else which raised his temper. When he was getting fed up with whichever woman was living in the house. If he started shouting that the house was filthy and the housekeeping bills ridiculous, she knew that the current woman was on the way out. She often thought about the women. Had they no shame? Just because the señor was rich beyond the dreams of ordinary people, was that a reason for any woman to sell herself? But then, they were always foreigners. Mostly English. But there had been that French-woman who'd walked around the house naked. Not naked in a bathing costume; naked naked . . .

They heard the growl of an approaching high-powered car, its engine note rising and falling as it took the sharp bends.

'That's him.' She collected everything up.

'What's his woman situation at the moment?'

'A new one who'll be around for a while yet.' She picked up the tray. 'I remember our priest warning us that a special part of hell is reserved for fornicators. His place must have been booked a long time back.'

Soon after Rosa had returned into the house, Reading-Smith walked out on to the patio. There was no mistaking his essential toughness. It was in the cragginess of his face, the set of his mouth, the way he shook hands, and the tone of voice which made every statement a challenge.

'You're the police?'

'Yes, señor.'

'What d'you want?'

'To ask some questions concerning Señor Thompson.'

'Why?'

'I am investigating his death.'

'Does that mean it wasn't an accident?'

'Probably not.'

'I can't help you.'

'I think that perhaps you may be able to.'

Reading-Smith hesitated a moment, as if deliberating whether to throw Alvarez out, then said: 'It's like a bloody oven out here. We'll go inside.'

The sitting-room was air-conditioned and initially struck cold. Reading-Smith went over to an armchair, sat, hooked one leg over an arm. 'All right, let's hear how in the hell I'm supposed to be able to help.'

'Did you know that the señor's name was really Steven Taylor and his wife, Señora Muriel Taylor, lives in El Granero?'

'He was the husband of that stupid bitch? ... Hang on. Her husband died years ago, back in England.'

'His death in England was faked.'

'Really?'

'Did you buy some shares from him?'

'If I want shares, I get my stockbroker to buy 'em, not a confidence trickster.'

'Why do you call him that?'

'If you've an ounce of intelligence, it stuck out a mile.'

'And you have many ounces of intelligence?'

'You've a quick tongue in your head, haven't you?'

'I don't know; but I doubt it is as quick as yours or the señor's. I've been told several times that his was very quick and very clever.'

'So?'

'I believe he persuaded you to buy four hundred thousand shares in an Australian mining company called Yabra Consolidated.'

'Believe what you bloody like.'

'You paid five cents when they were probably only worth two cents.'

'I'd have had to act like a bloody fool to do that.'

'Or to have listened too hard to his clever tongue ... And when you'd realized what you'd done, your pride was very badly hurt. Which is why, when he returned and offered to buy back the shares at ten cents each, you immediately sold them without stopping to wonder at the reason for his making such an offer.'

Reading-Smith leaned forward and opened a silver cigarette case, helped himself to a cigarette, lit it.

'Later, you learned that the shares had increased greatly in value and your holding would have been worth two million Australian dollars.'

'So bloody what?' he shouted. He came to his feet and stood square to Alvarez.

The far door opened and a woman, wearing a string bikini, jet black hair falling down to her shoulders, stepped inside.

Reading-Smith swung round. 'What d'you bloody want?'

'I thought you called me.'

'I didn't. So get lost.'

'Bob, love, I really did think . . .'

He crossed the floor in five long strides, gripped her shoulders, swung her round, pushed her through the doorway, and slammed the door shut. He turned back. 'Have you finished?'

Clearly, the interruption—and brief physical action—had enabled him to regain his self-control and there was no longer a chance of needling him into angrily blurting out something he would later regret. Alvarez said: 'I've just one more question, señor.'

'You sound like my lawyer.' He returned to the chair.

'What did Señor Taylor want when he came here for the last time, roughly three weeks ago?'

He stubbed out the cigarette.

'Was it to sell you more shares?' Alvarez had been expecting a bitter denial, since otherwise this would have been to admit to having been made a fool a second time, but instead Reading-Smith said softly: 'That's right. He talked me into buying another five hundred quids' worth.'

Alvarez couldn't make head or tail of so ready an admission. He said goodbye and left.

As he settled behind the wheel of his car, he reflected that Steven Taylor's golden tongue and lack of any moral principles would surely have taken him right to the top in politics.

Alvarez braked the Seat to a stop on the hard shoulder, checked the dog-eared map of the island, and confirmed that although the straight line distance to Estruig was not very far, much of the journey was in the mountains and therefore would take at least an hour. From Estruig to Llueso, either by the shorter route over the mountains or the longer one returning to the plain, would take another hour which meant that if he visited Señora Swinnerton, he could not be expected to be home until well after eight . . . On the other hand, Comisario Borne was the kind of man who, if he discovered that one of his inspectors could have completed his work in one day, but hadn't . . . Regretfully, he decided to drive to Estruig.

Although he would not have liked to live up in the mountains—one had to be born among them to want to do that—he loved them, not least because they had not been despoiled in the name of tourism. The address he had was too indeterminate to locate Ca Na Muña unaided, but luckily he came across a man driving a mule cart, who'd been working in one of the fields in the small valley, and was directed along a dirt track which wound its way up an ever increasing slope until it came to a stop in front of a house. He climbed out of the car. What or who had originally driven a man to built his home here, where even a subsistence level of life called for endless toil? How many generations had it taken to build the terrace walls and carry up enough soil from the valley? And what kind of foreigner had chosen to live here, virtually cut off from all other human contact?

He climbed stone steps to the narrow level in front of the house, knocked on the door. There was a shout from further up the mountain and when he crossed to the side of the house and looked up he saw a woman who, laboriously and with an ungainly action, was descending more stone steps.

· She reached the level. 'I'm sorry to keep you waiting like this,' she said breathlessly. She suddenly flinched.

'Is something wrong, señora?'

'It's just my leg. The beastly gout keeps plucking at me.'

He wondered why, if she suffered from gout, she had ever climbed up the terracing? He explained who he was.

'Do come on in and have a drink; it's such fun having someone to talk to! I'm afraid I've only wine, but at least there's plenty of that. And in case you're thinking that if I suffer from gout, I shouldn't drink, I'm happy to say that that myth was exploded some time ago!' She led the way to the front door. 'Mind how you go because the doorways are all so low; although you obviously don't have to be as careful as my husband did, but then he was tall and would walk around with his mind fixed on something else.'

The room they entered was both entrance hall and sitting-room. 'Which do you prefer, red or white?'

'I would like some red, please, señora.'

After she had gone through an arched doorway, he looked round the room. There was no missing the shabbiness. The covers of the two armchairs were frayed, the oblong carpet was faded and part threadbare, one of the two small wooden tables had a leg propped up by a wedge of newspaper, one curtain was missing, several floor tiles were cracked, and the walls and ceiling needed redecorating. Yet nowhere was there any sign of dirt or dust. It was the shabbiness of financial strain, not of sluttishness.

She returned with two glass tumblers and a litre bottle of wine. She filled the glasses and handed him one. 'David used to say that the vino corriente here was death to educated palates, but it didn't really matter because these days only expense-account businessmen and head waiters could afford to have one. I don't know enough about it to have an opinion, but his tastes certainly changed. After we'd been living here for a couple of years, he bought himself a special birthday treat of a very expensive bottle of Château Latour. He didn't enjoy it nearly as much as he'd expected and was quite happy to return to the usual Soldepeñas ... But I'm quite certain you haven't come here to hear me go on and on rambling away, have you?'

'Señora, I am investigating the death of Señor Steven Taylor.'

'So you mentioned earlier, but I'm certain I've never met anyone with that name so I don't really see how I can help.'

'About three years ago he changed his name to Steven Thompson.'

'D'you mean the man who was killed in a car crash on the island? Good heavens! I was so sorry to read about that. So often the nicest people die before their time ... He whom the gods favour dies young. So true and so sad ... Now, what about Mr Thompson; or Mr Taylor, as you say his name really was?'

'Three years ago he was about to be arrested for fraud by the English police and so he faked his own death to escape —which was why he changed his name.'

'This island really does attract the most extraordinary people! David always said that the interesting foreigners who came to live here all had something to hide; being rather outspoken to me, he added that the uninteresting ones were far too boring ever to have done anything. I'd certainly never have guessed that Mr Taylor could have been like that because he was so friendly and amusing. Living on one's own, humour is one of the things one misses most. It's almost impossible to be funny with oneself.'

'Where did you meet him?'

'At a cocktail-party.' She chuckled as she looked down at the faded and patched print dress she was wearing. 'I know I hardly look like cocktail-party material at the moment, but I promise you that I can smarten up!'

'Did he sell you some shares?'

'How on earth did you know that?' She laughed again. 'Perhaps one ought to say that I persuaded him to sell them to me. You see, he'd stayed on after the party because he had a sudden attack of migraine and was hoping it would go before he needed to drive back and I'd stayed on because the Galbraiths had invited me to supper. He started talking to them about some shares which were absolutely bound to increase in value. He was very enthusiastic and obviously hoping the Galbraiths would buy some, but they're very rich and so they'll never do anything that isn't their idea in the first place. Anyway, I was thrilled because of the chance to make a little money and towards the end of the evening I buttonholed him and told him he must sell me some of the shares.'

'Forty thousand, I think?'

'Now tell me, how in the wide world did you discover that as well?'

'I had to search through his private papers and I found a note of the number of shares two or three people had bought.'

'And here was I beginning to think you must be clairvoyant!' She refilled her glass, passed the bottle across to him. 'You shouldn't have explained. Wasn't it Sherlock Holmes who said something to the effect that the brilliance of a deduction could never survive an explanation?'

'I'm afraid I don't know; I have never read any of the stories, only seen them on the television.'

'Not the same thing at all. The subtlety is lost. Especially, I imagine, in translation.'

'Señora, about two months later, you sold the shares back to him, didn't you?'

'That's correct. He turned up here and asked me if I'd like to sell them. He explained how the shares had risen in value and he wanted me to enjoy the profit. It was so kind of him.'

'And he bought them back at ten cents?'

'Indeed, and didn't charge any commission so that it was all profit. In two months, I more than doubled my money. It made me feel very guilty that originally, after I'd given him my cheque, I began to worry in case he wasn't quite honest. You see, I'd never met him before that night and if I'd lost all the money . . . It would have been quite terrible.'

He cleared his throat. 'Señora, I'm sorry, but I think you have to understand that when he sold you those shares they were probably really only worth two cents each.'

'He had to make a little money for all his trouble, didn't he? And he knew they were going to increase in value.'

'At the time he sold them to you, he did not expect them ever to increase in value.'

'Isn't that rather a nasty thing to say?'

'I'm afraid it's the truth. He was a swindler who was intent on swindling you.'

'How can you possibly say that when he more than doubled my money for me?'

'That only happened because unexpectedly the shares shot right up in value. And when he bought them back from you, he should have paid you five dollars a share, not ten cents.'

She was silent for a while, then she said quite firmly: 'I don't care, I shall remember him as someone who made me laugh and who helped me make some money.'

The contrast between her attitude towards events and those of Muriel Taylor, Wheeldon, and Reading-Smith, could hardly have been greater. He knew a sense of warm thankfulness that not everyone put money before all else. 'Señora, I wish there were more people who think like you,' he said impulsively.

'That's very kind of you. You really are the nicest possible detective!'

He felt slightly embarrassed and said hurriedly: 'I am afraid I have to ask you one more thing.'

'Don't worry. Talking with you is a real pleasure.'

'Did Señor Taylor come here about three weeks ago?'

'As a matter of fact, yes, he did.'

'That was to persuade you to buy some more shares?'

'It's funny you should say that because I told him I wanted to, but he wouldn't let me. No, he came to give me another thousand pounds.'

'He gave you money?'

'You sound surprised? I tell you, whatever his past is, he was a nice man. He said that when he'd sold the shares they'd done even better than he'd expected and he felt he owed me the extra.'

He now understood why she had repeatedly said that her money had been more than doubled. He thought he also understood the sequence of events. Taylor had originally met her at a cocktail-party given by very wealthy people and so he had imagined her to be, at the very least, reasonably well off; that she had not been expensively dressed would not have counted for much because a certain kind of rich woman was often eccentric in some matters. But when he had first visited her in her house he had immediately realized that far from being wealthy, she was poor. So he had later given her the money he had just swindled out of Wheeldon and Reading-Smith (the third act of swindling, by which he had proved to himself that he really was the best), enjoying to the full the role of Robin Hood . . .

A quarter of an hour and another glass of wine later, he said he must leave. She hoped he'd come again and he replied that he certainly would if he could think of an excuse that would fool his superior chief.

He was outside, about to go down the stone steps to his car, when she said: 'I wish you had come here a few years ago.'

'Why, señora?'

'Because then we were both alive and well and the whole of the garden was a mass of colour. David used to say that one of the few things created by man that was truly beautiful was the garden. He wrote a lovely poem about that.'

'There is still a lot of colour.'

She looked up, shading her eyes from the sun with her hand. 'But it's not like it used to be. And my gardener's finally left so now the weeds will grow unchecked and the only flowers which will survive will be those which don't need watering and don't mind being crowded . . . But I shouldn't really talk like that. David loved a cultivated garden, but he believed that a natural one, even with all its weeds, was still beautiful.' She tilted her head back as she looked even higher. 'Do you know why I shall remember Mr Taylor for the nice things he did, not the nasty?'

It was clearly a rhetorical question.

'Because the money he made me helped to make certain I can live here just a little longer.'

He finally said goodbye and left. As he drove away, he felt both uplifted and saddened; uplifted because she had proved that there were still those who were untouched by avarice, saddened because she had shown that old age was a time when one had to search too hard to find compensation for living.

CHAPTER 18

As Alvarez left his parked car and walked towards the nearer back door of Las Cinco Palmeras, something began to bother him. Only as he knocked on the door of the kitchen did he identify what that something was—the silence.

'Who is it?' Helen called out.

'Enrique Alvarez, señora.'

'Come on in.'

She was wearing damp, stained overalls over a T-shirt. 'You don't by any chance know anything about plumbing, do you?'

'I regret not.'

'I've been trying to make a tap work and can't. Soon, I shall assault it with the biggest hammer I can find.'

'But why are the builders not here? I saw Javier and he promised to start work just as soon as he could. I will go now and see him and tell him that if he doesn't come immediately . . .'

She brushed some hair away from her forehead. 'Don't waste your time.' Her tone was suddenly bitter.

'I can promise you . . .'

'He turned up and said he'd start the moment his bill was paid.'

'But I thought . . .'

'So did I. But Mike, the silly fool, never told me the truth because he was trying to protect me from the worry. Practically all the money Mike's father gave him for the repairs ᵥas paid out for the funeral.'

'Oh!' There was really nothing more he could find to say immediately. Then he struggled to reintroduce a note of optimism. 'Perhaps if he spoke to one of the other and smaller builders, he could persuade them to do the work now, but wait to be paid until you are open and making money?'

'Mike thought of that right away. He's seen every local firm and not one of them will do it. The trouble seems to be, quite a few foreigners haven't been paying their bills once their houses are finished because they've learned how slow the law moves and how difficult it is to recover a debt. One or two are even boasting about how clever they are in not paying—God, what I could do to them! . . . When you arrived, I was trying to see if I could do some of the work. I've discovered I can't . . . Anyway, that's enough of that.

What's brought you here this time—not more trouble, please.'

'I hope it won't be that,' he answered uncomfortably, 'but I have to speak to the señor.'

'He went off to see someone who might lend us the money in return for a stake in the restaurant. The trouble is, this person wants such a large stake. I suppose you can't really blame him because it's good business. But I'm always so stupid I hope people will help in the same way that I'd try to help them.'

He wished he had the money to offer and so drive away from her blue eyes the worry that filled them.

They heard the whine of the approaching Citroën van.

'Go and sit out in the front,' she said, making a determined attempt to lighten her mood, 'and I'll send Mike out with a drink.'

'There's no need for that.'

'We've plenty of alcohol, if nothing else.'

He went through the restaurant and sat at the nearest table, in the shade of a palm tree. A couple of minutes later Taylor, a glass in each hand, came out. 'What the hell is it this time?' His manner suggested that the meeting with the possible backer had not been successful.

'I have just returned from Corleon—did you know that that is where your father lived?'

'I told you last time, I'd no idea where he was.'

'With him lived a friend; a very beautiful young lady.'

'He always did have good taste.'

'The house and large yacht were bought in her name and so now are hers.'

'That ought to help dry a few of her tears.'

'But did you know that under his will, you are his sole beneficiary?'

'How the hell could I?'

'He must have discussed the matter with you.'

'Maybe he must, but he bloody didn't.'

'Nevertheless, as his only child, you must have expected this?'

'I expected nothing.'

'Where are his assets?'

'How would I know?'

'You father must have told someone so that they could be distributed according to his will after his death.'

'Like as not, he didn't have any to worry about.'

'Why do you say that? A man doesn't usually spend all his money and so leave himself without any reserves.'

'My old man didn't know about "usually". He subscribed to Barnum's philosophy—there's a sucker born every minute. So when he needed money, he went out and found a sucker.'

'He gave you the money to buy this restaurant and to meet the cost of the original repairs?'

'Where's the problem? Obviously, he'd just found a sucker.'

'In fact, he'd found at least three. He sold them Australian mining shares at five cents when they were probably only worth two.'

'That's my father.'

'He bought them back at ten cents because by then they stood at around five dollars. He made about three million dollars.'

Taylor stared at Alvarez for several seconds, then laughed. 'So the old bastard really did find El Dorado!'

'Where do you think all that money is?'

'The answer remains, I've no idea.'

'Are you certain of that?'

'What are you trying to get at?' Taylor's expression sharpened. 'Last time you were here, you were talking about the possibility my father was poisoned.'

'That is correct.'

'Was he?'

'The results of the post mortem aren't yet through.'

'But you're behaving as if they were. You're bloody

wondering if I murdered him for the three million dollars, aren't you?'

'I have to investigate that possibility.'

'It hasn't occurred to your sweeping intelligence that if I had, I wouldn't now be tearing out my hair trying to find the money to pay the builders?'

'Perhaps the safest way of concealing new wealth would be to give the appearance of remaining hard up.'

'You've a mind like a bloody sewer. He was my father.'

'Sadly, sons murder fathers. And as you have told me, the relationship between the two of you was less than close.'

They heard the sounds of Helen's coming out of the restaurant and turned to watch her approach. 'I wondered if you were ready for another drink?'

Taylor said bitterly: 'Remember telling me what a wonderful man the Inspector was: so kind and thoughtful and not at all like a policeman?'

'What on earth's the matter?'

'Your wonderfully kind and thoughtful inspector has just accused me of murdering my own father.'

'No, señor, I did not say that,' objected Alvarez quietly. 'I said that I have to investigate the possibility that you did; if indeed he was murdered. That means establishing whether you had a motive—and you had. But in this, you are not alone. There are four other people who also had one.'

'Who?'

'The three whom he tricked out of a great deal of money and Señorita Benbury, who may well know where the fortune is held and is determined to get hold of it for herself.'

CHAPTER 19

Alvarez was pouring himself a second brandy when the telephone rang. Juan said he'd answer it and ran out of the dining-room into the front room. Dolores said from the kitchen doorway: 'When you've finished drinking, the meal's ready.'

'Give it a quarter of an hour,' replied Jaime.

'You are not going to eat?'

'Of course I am. What . . .'

'Then your drinking's finished.' She returned into the kitchen.

'Women!' he muttered, as he looked at his empty glass and the bottle. 'I've a good mind to . . .' He did not specify what. It wasn't that he was afraid of incurring Dolores's wrath—no Mallorquin husband could ever be so weak—but experience had taught him that her standards of cooking varied according to her humour and he greatly enjoyed his food.

Juan returned. 'The call's for you, Uncle.'

'Who is it?' asked Alvarez.

'Someone who talks very fast.'

Off-hand, he couldn't think of anyone who spoke particularly quickly.

He carried his glass through to the front room, drank just before he said: 'Yes?'

'This is Borne speaking.'

'Who is it?'

'I said, this is Comisario Borne.'

'I'm sorry, Comisario. It's just that my nephew—who isn't really my nephew—said that the caller spoke very fast, not that it was you, and I was wondering who it could be and then you said Borne and I have a friend who's name is rather like that, but he doesn't live in Palma and you don't sound like him and I was a bit confused.'

'Clearly. I am ringing to inform you that a telex has just arrived from England. It reads: Re Steven Taylor stop Private investigator identified as Raymond Barton stop Retained on eighteenth April to investigate Steven Thompson who was described as fraudulently selling shares in Mallorca stop Through unidentified police contacts Barton finally identified Thompson as Steven Taylor stop Transmitted to client full details of Taylor's criminal record and supposed death stop Client's name Reading-Smith address Casa Resta Cala del Día stop Hope it's stair-rodding with you stop Ian Wallace . . . Do you understand the meaning of that last sentence?'

'I think, señor, that Detective-Sergeant Wallace is hoping that it's raining here because the weather in England is so bad.'

'Were I his senior officer, I would point out that that is not a subject for an official message. Does the information assist you?'

'To be frank, señor, I'm not quite certain. I'll have to sit back and think about it.'

'Then will you please do that. Have you received a report on the post mortem?'

'Not yet.'

'Has it occurred to you to point out to the Institute that the matter is of very considerable urgency?'

'Yes. But I don't think that that had much effect.'

'You do realize, do you, that it is essential before any real progress can be made in this case to know for certain whether or not we are dealing with a murder?'

'Yes, señor.'

'Superior Chief Salas asked me this afternoon whether I thought you had yet grasped that fact. I had to reply that it was very difficult, if not impossible, to give a definite opinion.'

'Señor, I have been doing my best.'

'Possibly. Superior Chief Salas further remarked that most regretfully you always seem concerned more with irrelevancies than those matters which are pertinent.'

'I'm afraid he doesn't seem to understand that I like to get to know as much about the background of all the people in a case as possible.'

'It is very seldom an advantage to undertake a disorganized approach. Concentrate, Inspector; concentrate on the points which matter and ignore those which do not.'

'Yes, señor.'

Borne said a distant good night, rang off. Alvarez sighed as he replaced the receiver. Life was so simple for superiors. They demanded information and issued orders and then did not have to concern themselves about the means . . .

'Enrique, are you coming?' Dolores called out. 'It's getting cold.'

He drained the glass. He thought that he now understood why Reading-Smith had so readily admitted that he'd been conned into buying a second load of shares, when his character suggested his reaction would have been one of angry denial.

Alvarez rang the Institute of Forensic Pathology at midday and spoke to Professor Fortunato's secretary.

'As a matter of fact, Inspector, I was just about to get in touch with you to tell you that the post mortem has been completed and it is established—not that, of course, there was ever any real doubt—that actual death was due to injuries received in the crash. There are no obvious signs of poisoning and further and more detailed tests are to be carried out.'

Alvarez thanked the secretary, then rang the forensic laboratory.

'In the sample listed "Corleon", the content of all the capsules was correct; in the sample listed "deceased", the content of two capsules was the poison colchicine.'

'What exactly is that?'

'It's a vegetable poison which comes from the Meadow Saffron and is a cytotoxin, or cell poison. Each of the capsules contained approximately eight milligrammes of the poison, together with neutral binders, which is generally held to be a less than fatal dose for an adult in good health —not that one can ever be dogmatic on that score.'

'Would it be easy to get hold of the stuff?'

'Nothing easier, if you live somewhere where the plant grows wild. I was on holiday once and saw a field almost carpeted with them. I can remember looking at the colourful picture and wondering just how many people that one field could kill . . . Virtually every part of the plant contains colchicine, although the flowers, seeds, and corms contain the greatest concentration.'

'How soon would it start to work after swallowing?'

'Very difficult to say because that depends on so many variables—how long since the last meal, what did that consist of, how susceptible is the victim . . . But say between three and six hours after ingestion, remembering that any figure can be wrong.'

'What are the symptoms?'

'They're very similar to those of arsenical poisoning, which is why it's sometimes called vegetable arsenic. One's throat and mouth begin to burn and there's tremendous thirst, but when one goes to drink there's considerable trouble in swallowing. Pretty soon, one's suffering violent nausea and vomiting. These symptoms can last as long as twenty-four hours before the really serious ones start— agonizing colics, paralysis of the central nervous system, growing difficulty in breathing. It can take up to another twenty-four hours to die. So if you've someone you really dislike, feed him some!'

'I just hope there's no Meadow Saffron growing round our way.'

The assistant laughed. 'I can name another dozen plants just as deadly, or even more so. And actually, it's got its good side as well as its bad. For quite a time now, tests have been carried out using therapeutic doses in some cases of arthritis and I believe there have been some very encouraging results.'

'I'll stick to aspirins.'

'Watch it. Take too many of them and you're in trouble.'

Alvarez rang off. At last they were certain. Someone had tried to murder Steven Taylor and although he had not died from the poison, his death was directly attributable to it.

CHAPTER 20

Alvarez left his car, walked up to the front door of Casa Resta, and knocked. Rosa opened the door. 'You again!'

'Is the señor in?'

'He and his woman are out for the day on the boat; I had to prepare the picnic lunch for them.'

'Damn!'

'But you might just catch him if you hurry because they're not long gone and they were buying some rolls on the way.'

'What's the name of his boat?'

'It's something like . . .' She stopped and thought, frowning heavily. 'I can't remember, except it's an English name. But you can't mistake which one it is because it's almost at the end of the breakwater and it's the biggest there.'

'Sail or motor?'

'Motor, I suppose. I mean, it must be, seeing it's not got a real mast.'

He returned to his car and drove down to the village and the port. There was no bay to offer natural protection from heavy seas and winds and so two curving breakwaters had been built; these were wide and they provided moorings on their inboard sides. Rosa had not said whether the boat was tied up to the port or starboard arm, but cars could only drive along the starboard one and this was clearly where the larger boats berthed. Alvarez parked two-thirds of the way along, then walked past several yachts and motor-cruisers of increasing size, a surprising number of which flew the British flag, suggesting to him that despite all their hypocritical claims, the British were no less astute at avoiding their tax claims than the Continentals.

He approached the largest boat present and the fact that this was Reading-Smith's was confirmed when a bikini-clad figure came out of the accommodation and walked for'd. If that were really possible, Vera's costume was even skimpier than the one she had been wearing when he had seen her up at the house.

There was a small gangplank, rigged with a single set of ropes, and because the stern of the boat rode high it tilted upwards at a steep angle. He stepped on to it, gripped the top rope very tightly with his left hand, and tried not to think about the gap that was opening up either side of his feet. It was absolutely ridiculous, but even now his altophobia was flooding his mind with fear.

He reached the head of the gangplank and thankfully stepped on to the deck to realize that Reading-Smith was now standing immediately outside the accommodation and had obviously been watching his ascent. Vera, by his side, was giggling.

'I'll give you a piece of free advice,' Reading-Smith said boisterously. 'Don't think of serving before the mast.'

He had never done so.

'What's it this time? And you'd better be bloody quick because we're sailing in five minutes.'

'I have some more questions.'

'If you got paid by the dozen, you'd be rich. Questions about what?'

'Señor Taylor's death.'

'I suppose you want a drink? After your dangerous climb, I'd say it was a bloody necessity!' He turned and went into the accommodation, followed by Vera.

The saloon was twenty feet long and almost the width of the boat. Aft, there were several easy chairs and two bulkhead settees, amidships a table and dining chairs, and for'd a small bar, complete with bar stools. Reading-Smith went behind the bar and opened a bottle of champagne; Vera settled on one of the aluminium-legged stools.

'All right, what are the questions?' Reading-Smith filled a tulip-shaped glass and handed it to Vera.

'First of all, señor, I must tell you that now we know for certain that Señor Taylor was poisoned before the crash. The poison was administered by substituting it for the contents of at least three capsules he was in the habit of taking to counter a threatened migraine. The amount of poison he swallowed was not sufficient to make him so ill he could no longer drive and, despite being very sick, he would not let his companion take the wheel. As a result, and due to a fresh attack of nausea, he misjudged his driving and the car crashed and he was killed. Because the sequence of events stems directly from the giving of the poison, his death was murder.'

As Reading-Smith passed Alvarez a glass, he said: 'All very interesting, but what's it to do with me?'

'It's now my duty to discover whether it was you who filled the capsules with poison.'

'Why the hell should I have done that?'

'You see yourself as a clever and sharp businessman, don't you?'

'Do I?'

'But Señor Taylor proved that you are neither.'

'Any more compliments?'

'Do be careful,' murmured Vera.

He swung round. 'Why don't you just shut up?'

'But you can't talk like that to a policeman . . .'

'On my own boat, I'll talk how I bloody well like.'

'You must have wanted to murder Señor Taylor,' said Alvarez, 'when he made a fool of you for the third time?'

'That's a bloody lie.'

'Do you remember telling me that you'd never buy shares from anyone other than your stockbroker? Yet you bought a large number of shares from him.'

'You don't understand.'

'That he had a golden tongue? Oh, yes, señor, I have
understood that from the beginning. But you didn't—and
that surprises me. After all, I am a simple islander while
you are a clever and successful businessman and, I'd have
thought, far too clever to be caught.' Alvarez's tone changed
as he set out to goad Reading-Smith. 'But then I remind
myself that the smarter a man believes himself, the easier it
is to catch him. Which is why Señor Taylor was able to
persuade you to sell him back the shares at a fiftieth of their
true value. He could judge exactly how best to persuade
you. You'd be so eager to cover up your own stupidity,
especially from yourself, that you'd rush to have him buy
them back because for you, to be clever is to make money
and he was offering you the chance to make some; it would
only be later that you'd stop to wonder why he was offering
you such a chance. And when you worked out the answer,
you must have been very, very angry.'

Reading-Smith drained his glass, refilled it.

'Bob . . .' Vera began.

'Clear out.'

She was frightened by the expression on his face. She slid
off the stool and hurried out of the saloon by way of the
for'd starboard door.

Alvarez said: 'Perhaps the most incredible fact is that you
let him make a fool of you a third time!'

'Like bloody hell I did.'

'Didn't you? Despite everything, he was still able to
persuade you to buy more shares from him.'

'You think I bought 'em because he was still taking me
for a sucker?'

'Naturally.'

'You're so bloody wrong . . .' He stopped.

'Yes?'

He struggled to contain his anger.

'Señor, were you going to say that you let him sell you
more shares not because you were still a fool, but because

then he was in your house long enough for you to substitute poison for the contents of some of the capsules in the medicine bottle?'

'No.'

'You had the motive for his murder. Every time you thought about how he'd been laughing at you, you must have hated him a bit more. Someone of your character would have to get his own back.'

'But not by murdering him,' Reading-Smith shouted.

'To a naturally violent person, that's the obvious solution.'

'I . . .'

'Yes?'

He angrily shook his head.

'What alerted you to the fact that he might have a criminal record? His professionalism? You were convinced that only a true professional could have swindled you so easily?'

'What's it matter?'

'It should matter to you. That is, if you don't wish to be arrested for murder.'

'I didn't poison him.'

'Prove it.'

'How the hell can I prove a bloody negative?'

'By telling me the truth.'

Because the admission would portray himself in so nasty a light, Reading-Smith tried desperately to find a way out of making it, but even through his anger it became obvious that it was his only way of escaping arrest.

He spoke quickly, his voice thick. Yes, he'd determined to get his own back on the smart bastard—but not by committing murder. He'd hired a private detective in England to find out about Steven Thompson, a professional swindler who'd worked a racket with shares. Eventually, the detective had discovered that Thompson's real name was Taylor and that he'd had one conviction and was facing a second one when he'd conveniently 'died' in a car crash.

RELATIVELY DANGEROUS   155

This had given Reading-Smith the handle he'd been seeking. There was now an extradition agreement between Spain and Britain. Unfortunately, it was not retrospective because Spanish law did not permit this and so there could be no extradition for a crime committed before the passing of the act, but the Spaniards had a genius for attaining a desired result by devious means if the direct one proved impossible; they'd introduced a further law which gave the authorities the right to expel any foreigner whose habits were likely to bring the country into disrepute. Under this law, Taylor could be expelled; once expelled, he'd either have to return to the UK and face arrest or move to another country— where the extradition laws would probably catch him. So obviously what was necessary was to provoke Taylor into committing an act which would render him liable to arrest, and extradition (now the act was in force) or to expulsion. It had been quite a problem . . . Until, incredibly, blinded by his own pride, he'd turned up again, offering to sell more shares. The next move became obvious. Buy the shares, prove they were worthless and Taylor must have known they were, introduce the evidence which showed that Taylor was a professional swindler, and the authorities wouldn't, at the very least, hesitate to expel him. Then warn the British police to keep their eyes open . . .

'And you'd have had the satisfaction of knowing he was spending the next few years in jail,' said Alvarez contemptuously.

Alvarez entered the tall, ancient building that was the town hall in Mentaña and spoke to a clerk who referred him to a second man who referred him to a third. The last, having no one else to whom he could reasonably send Alvarez, reluctantly agreed to consult the property books.

'Señor the Honourable Archibald Wheeldon . . .' He stumbled over the pronunciations. '. . . lives in Calle General Castillo Martínez, fifteen.'

'Is that here, in Mentaña?'

He replied with indignation that everyone knew that Calle General Castillo Martínez was in Mentaña; had not the General been born only two streets away from where they now were? And hadn't the Caudillo himself said that if only he'd had two more generals with the fire and dash of Castillo, he'd have won the Civil War within six months . . .

Alvarez left. The way was not steep, nevertheless by the time he reached the famous road he was breathing very heavily and sweating profusely. He remembered his recent, and second, promise to cut back on eating, drinking, and smoking, and assured himself that tomorrow he really would honour that promise.

No. 15, one in a long line of terrace houses, of different roof levels, which directly fronted the narrow road, was in obvious need of decoration and at least some light repairs; the paint on the shutters was peeling off and patches of rendering had fallen. He knocked on the front door, since a foreigner lived there, and waited. After a time, the door was opened. 'Good morning,' said Wheeldon. Then he hastily corrected his Spanish to, 'Good afternoon.'

'Good afternoon, señor,' replied Alvarez in English. 'May I have a word with you?'

Wheeldon looked perplexed until he identified his caller and then his manner became nervous. 'Aren't you the detective chappie who was at Muriel's . . . that is, at Señora Taylor's?'

'That's right.'

'Nice to see you again,' he said with patent insincerity.

They went through one room, used as a hall, into a second one which was filled with large, heavy, and rather uncomfortable local furniture.

'What can I get you? A cup of coffee? Or is it not too early for a drink?'

'On this island, señor, we have a saying—it can never be too early for a drink, only too late.'

'That's rather good. I must try and remember it. So what would you like?'

After he'd served the drinks, Wheeldon sat, then said: 'Are you busy? I don't suppose there's much crime here, of course . . .'

'These days there is, sadly, a growing amount.'

'Bit difficult to understand that. I mean, everyone's so sleepy . . . Oh! Please don't misunderstand me. Much of the charm is . . .' Again, he tailed off into silence, finally aware of the fact that it would be better if he did not try to explain.

'I have received the results of the post mortem on Señor Taylor.'

'Really? Nasty thought. I mean, knowing what they do to the body . . . I was sorry he died in that crash. Cheerful kind of a chap with a fund of amusing stories. Of course, he did have a bit of a history which makes him . . . Not that I knew all about that at the time.'

'He was poisoned.'

'My God!'

'He crashed as a direct result of the poisoning, so now I am investigating a case of murder.'

'I suppose you must be.'

'I need to know who had a motive for the murder.'

'Yes, I can see that, but why come here? I mean, I hardly knew the man.'

'You bought shares from him and then sold them back to him.'

'Yes, but . . . Look, I made money doing that.'

'Not nearly as much as you should have done.'

Wheeldon gesticulated with his hands, as if trying to suggest that that was of small account.

'He should have paid you a million Australian dollars, shouldn't he?

'Yes, but . . .'

'That offers a very strong motive.'

'For killing him? Can't you understand, I couldn't ever do such a thing.'

'Why not?'

'Why not? But you've got to know, why not.'

'Have I?'

Miserably, he tried to explain, leaving out any personal details because a gentleman did not discuss such matters— nevertheless, it was easy to fill in the omissions. He was in love with Muriel. She could be difficult, she could embarrass, but he loved her. And as far as he was concerned, her money was of no account because a gentleman did not marry for money and remain a gentleman. Unfortunately, she had not been born to money—which was not to suggest for one second that she had married the first time because of it— and so she saw it as a status symbol and a measure of . . . well, worth as a person. And unfortunately, like others in her position, she suspected people of being friendly because of her money, not in spite of it. Her second marriage hadn't helped. With his golden tongue, Steven Taylor had silenced her suspicions and reservations long enough to persuade her to marry him, but afterwards, when things had gone wrong, all her prejudices had been reinforced. So when he, Wheeldon, had fallen in love with her, she had . . . Well, even though they were good friends, she would not marry him because he didn't have much money. Unfortunately, he was old-fashioned enough to want to be married. Taylor had turned up—of course, at the time he'd had no idea that Taylor was her 'dead' husband—and had talked about shares that were bound to rise in value and it had all sounded so attractive that he'd done something he'd never done before and that was to risk a part of his very limited capital because he'd believed that if only he could make some money, Muriel would then be able to realize that he loved her for herself. When Taylor had offered him twice what he'd paid, he'd naturally jumped at the chance of a hundred per cent profit. A few more deals like that . . . He'd read in

a paper about the spectacular rise of the shares and had
learned that he'd parted with the fortune he was so desperate
to obtain . . .

'So what were your feelings towards Señor Taylor?'

'I . . . Well, I . . .'

'You must have hated him?'

'I suppose so.'

'Sufficiently to wish him dead?'

'Of course not.'

'Why not? He'd deprived you of what you'd most wanted.'

'My God, you can't think like that! I couldn't ever get so
worked-up as a Mallorquin would . . .' He stopped.

'That is very true. An islander has a violent argument
and before he thinks what he's doing, he pulls out a knife
and uses it. But poisoning is not a hot-blooded act, it is a
cold-blooded one.'

'That's not what I'm trying to say. I'd never think of
murder just because I'd been swindled.'

'Not even the third time?'

'What d'you mean, the third time?'

'Señor Taylor sold you more shares.'

'Yes, but they . . . they may rise in value just as Yabra
Consolidated did.'

'Have you checked that they are worth at least as much
as you paid for them?'

Wheeldon shook his head.

'Why not?'

'I . . . Well, the truth is, if they turn out to be worth a lot
less, it'll make me look such a fool.'

'I'd prefer to say, too trusting.'

'You must believe me.'

Alvarez stood. 'I do,' he said sadly.

CHAPTER 21

Alvarez walked into the chemist shop and spoke to the husband, who had just finished serving a customer. The husband led the way into the stock room.

'I want to find out something. I gather colchicine is a pretty potent poison?'

'That's right.'

'But even so, it's used therapeutically?'

'Lots of poisons are; maybe they all could be if we knew enough about 'em—natural, not manmade poisons, that is. I've heard it claimed that that's one more proof that the universe is totally symmetrical; there's always a plus to balance a minus. Frankly, that sort of stuff leaves me cold, but it is a hard fact that a poison like colchicine can cure as well as kill.'

'What's it used for medically?'

'As far as I know, just the treatment of arthritis. I read not so long ago that its use is being extended and there have been promising results in cases of rheumatoid arthritis.'

'Extended from what?'

'From its traditional field, which is gout.'

Friday morning brought the first clouds for days, but as the sun rose higher these were slowly burned away and by eleven the sky was once again clear and the sun shone with burning brilliance. Alvarez parked in front of the stone stairs which led up to Ca Na Muña, turned off the engine, stepped out. One by one, the cicadas, which had been disturbed by his arrival, resumed their shrilling; overhead, but not immediately locatable, came the sharp cry, twice repeated, of a raptor; a branch of a tree, moving in the very light breeze, scraped against something with a soft, rhythmic sound; the air was heady with the scent of wild thyme.

Valerie came out of the house, her movements slightly easier than when he had last seen her, and she met him at the head of the steps. 'Hullo again. I hope you've come for a long chat?'

'Señora, I fear that I have to ask you more questions.'

'Why be sorry? I told you last time, I'm delighted to have someone to talk to. Now, come on in and we'll have a glass of wine.'

'Perhaps we should have the questions first.'

'Good heavens, no! You'll be able to ask much nicer ones and I'll be able to answer them much more wisely if we have a drink beforehand.'

He followed her into the coolness of the house. A newspaper was on the floor by the side of one of the chairs and she bent down and picked this up. 'I went into the village yesterday and met some friends and they gave me this copy of the *Daily Telegraph*. I rather wish they hadn't. Britain's become a dreadful place because of all the crime.'

'There's crime on this island. Señor Taylor was poisoned.'

'Was he? Oh dear! What a horrid way to die.'

'He didn't die from poisoning, but because of it; that's what caused him to crash.'

'I suppose there is a difference?'

'Yes, although it remains a murder.'

'I know it's wanting to bury my head in the sand, but can't we talk about something nicer?'

'I'm afraid not. That's what I have come to discuss.'

'Oh dear! . . . Anyway, let me get the drinks first. Would you still prefer red wine?'

She went out into the kitchen, returned with two tumblers of wine, one of which she handed to him. 'This is a different wine which I bought yesterday in the village; the woman in the shop told me it was much nicer than the one I usually have.' She smiled. 'Perhaps she couldn't sell it to anyone else, so decided to unload it on a fool foreigner.'

'Señora, I have just been to the town hall in Estruig. I asked them for the date on which Señor Swinnerton died. They could find no record of the señor's death. I then asked them to check burials. There was no record of the señor's burial. Yet I distinctly remember your telling me that he died in this house. In such a case, it was necessary to notify the town hall in Estruig and for the burial to take place in Estruig cemetery.'

There was a silence.

'Why did you not notify the authorities of the señor's death?'

'What does it matter now?'

'Where is he buried?'

She gave no answer.

'Last time I was here, you walked down from the terraces above and you were moving with difficulty because of pain from gout. Crippled to such an extent, you would surely only have climbed up if there were some very important reason to do so.' He waited, but she remained silent. 'Señora, is your husband buried up on one of the terraces?'

She seemed to shiver; seen in profile, her heavy face held an expression of sad resignation. She said in a low, distant voice, 'He knew he was dying, but thought I didn't. For as long as he could he pretended that he was feeling better and I pretended that I believed him . . .

'Then he became too weak to move. He lay on the settee in the other room because the window's so low and he could look out at the mountains he loved so much. Towards the end, he wasn't fully conscious and quite often he asked why it was so hot. I tried to explain that we weren't in Wales, but he couldn't understand. Once or twice, he thought I was his mother . . .

'On the last day his mind suddenly cleared and he knew that I knew. He told me that our marriage had always been so happy that he'd dreaded the bill—he was so certain that happiness always had to be paid for. He talked about the

garden and how he hoped there really was a life after death
so that he could keep the picture of the garden together with
the picture of me. He told me how he wished he could be
buried amid the garden and not in a cemetery, hemmed in
by walls and frowned on by tombs which had been built to
impress. He was talking about the beauty all around here
only seconds before he died . . .

'I knew that I had to give him what he had most wanted.'
Tears were trickling down her furrowed cheeks, but her
voice held steady. 'I buried him on one of the terraces, near
the twisted olive tree he called the Laocöon, I don't care
how wrong that was.'

'Señora, nothing that so strong a love does can be truly
wrong.'

'Do you . . . Do you really believe that?'

'Yes.'

'Thank God . . . It's all become so difficult since David
died. You see, he never understood how to manage the
money we had and so there wasn't much left and no matter
how hard I tried, because everything had become so expensive I had to keep using a little of the capital. One day I
discovered that very soon I wouldn't be able to afford to
live here any longer. That would mean leaving David and
I couldn't bear to think of doing that . . .

'I went to the cocktail-party where I met Mr Thompson
and he talked about how easy it was to make money if you
knew what you were doing . . . I thought that if I could
make some money, perhaps I could stay here until I died
and then I would have kept faith with David. So I asked
Mr Thompson to sell me some shares. And the next time I
saw him, he said that they had gone up until they were
worth twice as much and he strongly advised me to sell and
take the profit before they went down again, as he expected
them to do. The extra money meant that I could stay here
a little longer and look after David. I told Mr Thompson
how grateful I was and he said that it was helping people

like me which made his life so worthwhile.

'I was in Estruig one day and in a newspaper I read about the shares. They were worth fifty times what he'd paid me. If he'd given me the proper price, I would have had enough money not only to be certain I could go on living here until I died, but also to employ a gardener again so that David was surrounded by his favourite flowers . . .

'Mr Thompson came to the house. I begged him to give me the extra money and explained why I needed it. He said . . .'

'What did he say, señora?'

'That a promise to someone who was dead was meaningless.'

'A man like him could never understand.'

'He gave me another thousand pounds . . . He made it seem he was doing me a favour instead of having cheated me. I couldn't bear it . . . I kept thinking of David . . .'

'So you poisoned him?'

She opened her mouth to speak, said nothing.

He thought he understood her sequence of emotions. She was a woman of peace and love and was shocked and horrified by what she'd done. She believed in forgiveness and redemption, but only after expiation. So having poisoned Taylor, she wanted to expiate her sin, which meant she should now confess and suffer the penalties the law decreed. But imprisonment would mean deserting David . . .

He had to be certain of the details. 'You suffer from gout and one treatment is to take therapeutic doses of colchicine. You knew that this was a poison and it was dangerous to take more than the prescribed dose. You had learned that Steven Taylor suffered from migraine and had seen the capsules he always carried around with him, so you got hold of the bottle, extracted some of the capsules, emptied these and refilled them with as much of your ground-up pills as you could get into them. Sooner or later, he would swallow one of these poisoned pills and, you hoped, would die.'

'No,' she said fiercely.

He looked at her with pity. 'Where are the pills you take to alleviate your gout?'

'I don't have any.'

'If necessary, I will search this house.'

'All right, I do take some. But I didn't do as you've just said.'

'Will you get them for me, please.'

She stood, left. He heard her slowly climbing the stairs, which led out of the next room, then crossing overhead, her footsteps loud because the floor was bare concrete. When she returned, she handed him a bottle half-full of small round green pills.

'Do you have any more of these?'

'No.'

'Then I'll only take a few.'

'Aren't . . . aren't you arresting me?'

'Since you deny having substituted some of these pills for the contents of the capsules, I have to prove that that is what you did—at the moment, I have no such proof. Indeed, it's not even certain that these pills contain colchicine.'

'But you'll find the proof?'

'I'm afraid I probably will, señora.'

'And then you'll arrest me?'

Being a coward, he was glad that now it would be the superior chief and not he who would initiate the actual arrest.

CHAPTER 22

On Tuesday, a south wind brought the heat and the sand of the Sahara; everything in the open became covered in fine sand and the temperature rose above a hundred so that even the foreigners left their homes shuttered throughout the day. Villages appeared to be deserted.

At breakfast, Dolores had asked Alvarez to drive on from the port—when he'd finished his work there—to Playa Nueva to buy some cold smoked pork from the German shop and he remembered this as he passed the petrol station on his way back to Llueso. He swore, stopped the car on the hard shoulder, and looked at his watch. Nearly half twelve. If he now drove over to Playa Nueva he would not be home much before a quarter past one and for the past hour he'd been looking forward with ever increasing impatience to the first iced brandy. On the other hand, if he didn't get the pork, Dolores would not be best pleased . . .

He waited for two cars to pass, made a U-turn. Once more in the port, he cut through the back streets to the front, where he turned right. The bay was at its most beautiful, perhaps because the hard sun and burning air were exaggerating contrasts. David Swinnerton had wanted to remain among the beauty of the mountains, he would choose the bay . . .

The blast of a horn jerked his thoughts back to the present and he realized that the car had wandered out into the centre of the road. He pulled in to the side and a builder's van swept by; as it passed, he read the name on the side: Javier Ribas. Builders and property developers were the modern plutocrats, making so much money that they didn't know how to hide it all from the tax people . . . The van's right-hand blinker flashed and it turned off the road. Gone to Las Cinco Palmeras, he thought. Then did that mean the young couple had found the money? He hoped they had. Helen was someone who deserved to succeed.

He didn't consciously make the decision, yet he braked and also turned right. The yard behind the restaurant was, despite the heat, filled with energetic movement. Near the kitchen door, a concrete mixer was turning and a man was shovelling the last of a pile of sand into it; beyond, a second man was working at a plumber's bench which had been

placed up against the building, to take advantage of the
shade. The lorry had turned and was now backing. It came
to a stop, the driver shouted to the man by the concrete
mixer who unclipped the tail-board, the hydraulic ram
slowly raised the loading bay and sand began to spill.

Alvarez left his car and walked round to the door of the
kitchen. It looked as if every fixture inside had been ripped
out or was being ripped out . . .

'It's a horrible mess, but it's wonderful!'

He turned to face a smiling Helen.

'The builder's promised by all the saints in every calendar
that the work will be finished in time for the inspector to
pass it by the end of the month. So we'll be able to open on
time after all . . . You must have a drink to celebrate.'

'I wish I could, but I'm on my way to Playa Nueva . . .'

'You can't find the time to wish us luck?'

'Señora, when you speak like that I will be honoured and
my cousin will just have to go without her smoked pork.'

'Great. So let's go round to the front and try to get away
from the worst of the racket.'

As they walked round the building, she said: 'If you want
to see a change in someone, look at Mike. There's none of
that surly bad temper now. Of course, it was really all
frustration.'

They reached the palm trees. She pointed at the several
tables and chairs. 'They're new. I set them out to see what
they look like. We could have made do with the old ones,
but they were beginning to look shabby and the British
worry more about that sort of thing than the food . . . Sit
down and I'll get the drinks. Are you still drinking brandy
or would you prefer something else?'

'A coñac would be fine, thank you.'

She left and went into the restaurant through the main
doorway. He stared at the bay, enjoying the view of which
he never grew tired . . . He heard the shrill whine of the
van before he saw it turn on to the track and come down,

to pass out of sight. Helen returned with a tray on which were two glasses. 'I think the señor has just arrived,' he said.

'I love it when you call him the señor; it sounds so very grand.' She chuckled as she sat. 'I told him yesterday that at night he ought to wear tails to give us a little touch of class. His reply was interesting but unrepeatable!' She passed one glass across. 'And speaking of the devil . . .'

Taylor came up to the table. 'Drinking again?'

'I fear so,' replied Alvarez.

'I told him he had to stay and celebrate,' said Helen.

'Quite right. And since two's a celebration, but three's an orgy, I'll join you. Just get myself a drink.' He went back into the restaurant. When he returned, he raised his glass. 'To our opening day. May it not be completely shambolic.'

'Why should it be?' she asked with mock indignation.

'Because, my darling cook, as I've tried to explain before, we are by the dictates of local custom obliged to offer free food and drink to all potential customers. And if there's a hungrier and thirstier man than a Mallorquin on a free tuck-in, it's a Britisher.'

'You'll have to make certain that there's never too much around at any one moment.'

'Easier said than done, especially with some of the free-loading Brits who live here. They can smell out an unopened bottle at half a kilometre.'

Alvarez said: 'The señora tells me that Javier has promised the work will be completed before the end of the month?'

'He has. And I've made it very clear that unless this promise is a damned sight more reliable than all his previous ones, I'll personally shoot him.'

'I'm very glad you managed to sort out your problems.'

'We didn't,' said Helen. 'It was . . .'

Taylor cut in. 'I was lucky enough to meet an old friend who loaned us the money.'

'And you were always trying to say that you'd been born under an evil star.'

'Maybe that star's regressed.'

'Will you put that down in writing and sign it? . . . Mike, when you say it was an old friend who lent you . . .'

He cut in a second time. 'In this case, I literally did bump into him. I was rushing to buy some washers, tripped, and all but sent him flying. Took us a second or two to recognize each other, then it was a case of commemorating the reunion at the nearest bar. He wanted to know what I was doing out here and I told him and being down in the dumps, I filled in most of the sordid details. He said his father had died a year or so back and left him a fortune and why shouldn't he lend me the money for as long as I needed at nil interest? . . . I know one shouldn't borrow from friends, but I just didn't have the courage to turn it down.'

'Who would, in such circumstances?' said Alvarez. He wished Taylor's interruptions had been more subtle and that Helen had not allowed her puzzled surprise to be so obvious. Then, he would not have started asking himself questions.

There were times when Alvarez wondered how he could be such a fool as not to leave well alone when he had the chance? If he'd reached a solution that seemed obviously correct, why worry about one small conflicting detail that was probably totally immaterial? What did it really matter if Taylor had given Helen a different version of events? He might have wanted to avoid admitting to her that he had borrowed the money from a friend. And yet it was somewhat difficult really to believe that . . . He sighed as he drove back to Puerto Llueso.

He parked in the square, close to the Caja de Ahorros y Monte de Piedad de Las Baleares, went inside, and asked to speak to the manager.

The manager said: 'You want to know about a large

cheque he may have received in the past few days?'

'That's right.'

'Could it be bad?'

'I doubt it.'

'Then why . . .?' The manager waited, but Alvarez said nothing. 'All right, I'll find out.' He used the internal telephone to speak to someone, replaced the receiver. 'It won't be a moment.' He cleared his throat. 'You wouldn't like to tell me what this is all about?'

'I'm not certain.'

'He's not been banking very long with us.'

'I don't suppose he has.'

'He's bought Las Cinco Palmeras, round the bay.'

'I know.'

'He's modernizing it and hopes to open quite soon.'

'Yes.'

'There was a problem about money for repairs and alterations.'

'I know.'

'Goddamn it, Enrique, you're being closer than a bloody oyster!'

'An oyster without a pearl.'

A man in his twenties, with a neatly trimmed, very dark beard, entered and put a sheet of paper down on the desk. The manager read what was written. 'Is that all we know?'

'At the moment. The cheque went to head office in the usual bag.'

The manager spoke to Alvarez. 'Last Saturday, he paid in a cheque for seven hundred thousand.'

'Who drew the cheque?'

'I can't answer. As you've just heard, it's gone to head office for clearing.'

'Will you find out?'

The manager nodded at the cashier, who dialled the main branch in Palma. He spoke briefly, replaced the receiver. 'They'll get back on to us.'

'Thanks.'

The cashier left. The manager asked how Alvarez's family was and for several minutes they chatted amiably. Then, the expected call came through.

'The cheque was on the Banco de Bilbao in Corleon and was signed by Señorita Benbury,' said the manager.

CHAPTER 23

Alvarez walked into the supermarket in Corleon and asked one of the two cashiers where Agueda was; he was directed through to the bread counter. There, he waited until the last customer had been served with a barra, then said: 'D'you remember me?'

Agueda was dressed even more flamboyantly than before and her fingers sparkled with jewellery; her make-up was less than subtle. 'Of course—the detective from Llueso who enjoys a good brandy. Let's go through to the office and see what we can find.' She called over an assistant—there was now another customer wanting bread—and came round the counter. 'So how's the tourist trade on the island this summer? Down a bit on last year?'

Speaking rapidly and commenting sarcastically on government policy, the greed of shop assistants, and the iniquities of IVA, she led the way into the office. She produced a bottle of Carlos I and two glasses, pushed the bottle across. 'I always leave the man to pour.'

He half filled the glasses, passed her one.

She drank, put her glass down on the desk. 'Now you can tell me what's brought you back here?'

'I'm trying to tie up a few loose threads.'

'It's a long way to come just to do that.'

'My boss is a very tidy-minded man . . . I wanted to have a word with Señorita Benbury, but when I went to her house

I couldn't get an answer. The maid wasn't in and the
dog seems to have gone. Is she not living there any
more?'

'I haven't heard she's left.'

'When did you last see her?'

She opened a drawer and brought out a box of cigars; she
lit a match for both of them. 'It must have been the end of
last week.'

'Was she on her own?'

'Pierre was with her, as usual.'

'She's still thick with him, then?'

'It's a funny thing about that.' She drew on the cigar,
exhaled slowly and with pleasure. 'Like I told you before,
she began by throwing herself at him. But recently, damned
if it didn't look as if the boot's on the other foot.'

'How sure of that are you?'

'I don't reckon to have lived forty-one years without
knowing who's doing the chasing.'

He thought it was probably more than forty-one years.
'Perhaps she's got fed up with him. Or else she's decided to
play hard-to-get.'

'After what's happened?'

'Then what's the answer?'

'She's a bitch.'

'Whatever she is, I need a word with her.'

'One flutter of her eyelids and you can't keep away?'

'Maybe Pierre can say where she is now—where's he
live?'

'Right at the back of the urbanización in a grotty little
bungalow, although if you listened to him you'd think he
owned the biggest house on the main canal. But at this time
of the day, he'll be in a bar.'

'Any particular one?'

She shrugged her shoulders. 'Wherever the most foreign
women are . . .'

*

Alvarez found Pierre Lifar in El Pescador, a large bar on the front road whose walls were decorated with many of the implements which the fishermen had used before the tourists had arrived and destroyed their trade. He had expected Lifar to be an Adonis, but found him to be a medium-sized man, knottily built, with a rugged face that spoke of strong living, strikingly blue eyes, and his only ostentation an unbuttoned shirt which displayed his hairy chest.

'I'm Pierre Lifar. So who are you?' He spoke Spanish fluently, rolling his R's with Gallic freedom.

'Inspector Alvarez, from Mallorca, of the Cuerpo General de Policía.'

'We've all got our problems.'

'Indeed. Shall we sit outside?'

'Is that an order?'

'A request, señor. You will have a drink?'

'I'll have a Ricard, even though my mother taught me to be beware of policemen who offered me drinks.'

Alvarez carried the glasses out to one of the tables which was in the shade of an overhead awning.

Lifar added water to his drink. 'What d'you want from me?'

'I need to speak to Señorita Benbury and I'm told you know where she is.'

'Then you've been told wrongly.'

'But you are very friendly with her?'

'And if I am?'

'Then you can probably tell me where I can find her.'

'I probably can't.' He sipped the milky liquid, put the glass down. 'What's your angle? Something to do with the car crash?'

'That's right.'

'Why? It's history.'

'Not yet. Señor Thompson was poisoned.'

'Christ!' Lifar stared at him in open-mouthed astonishment. 'Is that on the level?'

'He was poisoned with colchicine. This did not directly kill him, but because it seriously affected him, he crashed and was killed.'

'Are you suggesting Charlie knew anything about all that?'

'If you're asking me if I suspect her of having administered the poison, I know for certain she did not.'

'Then how does she come into it?'

'It is what happened after the accident that now interests me.'

'I don't understand.'

'There is no need for you to.'

'You're bloody sharp, aren't you?'

'Just rather sad.'

'What the hell . . .?' He drank, bewildered and irritated.

'I need to know about your relationship with the señorita.'

'That's my business.'

'It is also mine.'

They stared at each other with silent hostility. Lifar, who had begun by despising the shambling inspector, realized that he was dealing with a far more determined character than he had imagined. He also remembered that he had not applied for a residencia, being unable to bring into the country the minimum amount of money that was necessary. 'What d'you want to hear about?'

'Everything.'

He spoke with surly resentment. He hated having to admit to a defeat and by referring to it he was reminding himself of the possibility that from the beginning she had been using him while all the time he'd believed he had been going to use her.

He'd marked her out the first time he'd seen her—which was hardly surprising since she was extravagantly beautiful. He'd been surprised that she could appear to be so in love with a man noticeably older than herself, but had been satisfied that this could only work in his favour; certain women initially were attracted by older men, but it was an attraction which seldom, if ever, managed to meet the determined challenge of someone young, vigorous, and irresistible, and then their passion was all the greater. So when her man was killed in a car crash, he'd been about to go after her when she'd thrown herself at him like crazy. Only . . .

'Only she wouldn't hop into bed with you?'

'I got all I wanted,' he answered defensively.

'You're lying.'

'How the hell would you know?'

Alvarez stared at the passing traffic for a time, then said: 'Did you know she's left?'

'Left where?'

'Corleon.'

'Who says she has?'

'So she just used you until the last moment, then cleared off without a word.'

Lifar finished his drink.

CHAPTER 24

As always, Alvarez was reluctant to enter a hospital, but he told himself he was being stupid and walked across to the reception and inquiry desk in the Clínica Bahía with what he hoped was an air of resolution. He told the middle-aged woman he wanted a word with someone in accounts and she directed him down the right-hand corridor.

Several patients were waiting to pay their accounts, or give the details of their medical insurances, but he was able to attract the attention of a man who took him through to the office behind the general area.

'You're inquiring about Señor Higham's account—what exactly is it that you want to know?'

'Whether he made any phone calls while he was here.
You'd have a record of them, wouldn't you?'

'Yes, of course. They go on the bill.'

'Would anyone here know where he was calling?'

'Our only record is the number of pulses.'

'They should be enough. Can you find out the details?'

It took less than two minutes to turn up the details of the
account.

'Señor Higham made three calls and they added up to
seventy-one pulses.'

'You don't have the number for each call?'

'No, only the total.'

'What rates were they at?'

'One at full, one at normal, one at cheap.'

'If they were all local calls, they must have been long
ones?'

The man smiled. 'Interminable, I'd say.'

'Thanks very much . . . There's one last thing. D'you
mind if I telephone the British consulate?'

He spoke to the assistant consul and asked if Señor
Higham had requested anyone in the consulate to help
expedite the repayment of his stolen travellers' cheques?
There had been no such request. To the best of anyone's
memory, there had been no communication of any sort from
Señor Higham.

Alvarez left the hospital and walked back to his car. He
sat behind the wheel, lowered the windows, and switched
on the fan to try and clear the heat. He knew exactly
what Superior Chief Salas was going to say. An intelligent
detective would have realized the truth long ago . . .

For several days after the crash, it had been impossible
to know who the two victims were—their papers had been
stolen, one of them was dead, the other was suffering from
loss of memory. The doctors had been puzzled by that loss
of memory because there had been no obvious head injuries
serious enough to account for it; but what doctor could

ever speak too dogmatically about the human brain?

Some days after the car accident, Higham's passport and wallet had been thrown into a street refuse container. This was a normal way of getting rid of incriminating evidence. But why had not the thief, or thieves, taken the opportunity to dispose of Thompson's things at the same time?

Back in the UK, Higham's wife had left him and he'd no relatives to whom he'd be able to turn for comfort or help. It was his first visit to the island. So whom had he been phoning from the Clínica Bahía? How had he paid his account in cash when all his money had been stolen and he'd not called on the consulate to help him gain a refund on the travellers' cheques?

There could be little doubt that Charlotte Benbury had been very much in love with Taylor. Yet within days of his death, she had thrown herself at Pierre Lifar. Only a bitch could act like that. Yet when he, Alvarez, had met her, he'd been sufficiently surprised and shocked that she should have acted as she had to begin constructing excuses for her; one might be shocked by the actions of a bitch, but surely seldom surprised, so somewhere within him there must have been doubt. A bitch would not have kept the photograph of the dead man on the dressing-table in her bedroom. Yet a woman who had loved deeply would surely have had a much better photograph than the one he had seen?

How had Charlotte known that Mike Taylor was so desperate for money? Why should she send him seven hundred thousand pesetas when she had never met him and might, such was human nature, easily be jealously resentful of him? And why had he tried to hide the fact that it was she who had given it to him when on the face of things there was no reason to do so?

Steven Taylor had been a man of charm and a golden tongue, with an inability to understand normal moral values. He'd made money by swindling people, been caught and convicted, yet by luck had escaped a prison sentence.

Even his conviction had not taught him discretion and later, after an impossible second marriage, he'd resumed his swindling ways. Disaster had threatened. The police were gathering the evidence to arrest him again and now he could be quite certain that he would be imprisoned. So he'd planned his 'death', successfully blackmailing his wife into financing it because his arrest and conviction would have shrivelled her snobbish soul.

Reborn in the name of Thompson, he'd resumed his old ways. He'd met Charlotte and had fallen wildly in love with her and, despite the difference in their ages, she had fallen equally in love with him.

He'd travelled to the island, possibly when temporarily short of funds and hoping against all the probabilities to get some more money out of his wife, and had met, in addition to her, his son and three potential victims. He'd set up a swindle and had sold shares in Yabra Consolidated to Wheeldon, Reading-Smith, and Valerie. Only this time, irony had played a hand. Instead of the shares being value-less, they'd suddenly become valuable. Inevitably, he'd set out to retrieve them and because of his golden tongue and a self-confidence that nothing seemed capable of denting, he'd succeeded. But for once his choice of victims had in part been bad. Reading-Smith was a self-made millionaire, contemptuous of any standards but those he set himself, ruthlessly convinced that his wealth set him apart from ordinary mankind. A man of his nature could never suffer being swindled without becoming determined to get his own back. Instinct had told him something about Thompson, a private detective had filled in the details. So when Thompson had returned, driven on by an inflated ego to sell him more shares, he'd bought them. And then made it clear that Thompson had just landed himself in trouble.

Thompson had considered the situation and very rapidly come to the conclusion that the only practical thing was for Charlotte and him to sell up and move out of Spain. Once they were in another country, living under different names, they should be safe.

Just as he'd misjudged the kind of man Reading-Smith was, so he'd misjudged the intensity of Valerie's emotions which, at times, had a trace of madness about them. And when she'd pleaded with him to give her the rest of the money that her shares had made, he'd not understood that it was love which drove her, not cupidity. Had he done so, he might have been warned. Then again, perhaps he would just have laughed.

On the Wednesday, he'd given Higham a lift. He was not only a good talker, but also a good listener (in his 'job', it was often just as important to listen as to talk) and by the time they'd stopped for lunch, he'd learned a lot about Higham's life. An attack of migraine had been threatening all day and he'd taken a second capsule, but it was the first one which had contained the poison. He'd drunk very little, leaving Higham to finish a bottle of wine on top of the pre-lunch drinks. By the end of the meal, Higham wasn't drunk, but neither was he sober.

They'd driven away from the restaurant. Almost immediately, Thompson had suffered the initial symptoms of colchicine poisoning. One attack had been followed by another and this second one had left him too ill to continue driving. So he'd changed places with Higham. By chance, he'd not fastened his seat-belt; feeling too ill to bother, probably.

Higham had never before driven on roads such as that one, with its acute bends, sharp, winding ascents and descents, and unguarded edges, and at a time when he'd needed all his wits they'd been befuddled by alcohol. He'd been going far too fast for the corner, had not braked in time, but had braked too violently when he did; he had failed to correct the ensuing skid. The car had gone over the edge. Thompson, unbelted, had been thrown clear; Higham, belted, had stayed with the car for the whole of the fall and had been killed.

Shock can do strange things to the system. It can even, to some extent, counter the effects of poisoning for a brief while. Thompson, injured though not seriously, overcame the poisoning which in any case could never have been fatal because Valerie had been unable to pack a sufficient amount of crushed pills into any one capsule, and began to think clearly enough to realize that if he was delayed on the island for any length of time, Reading-Smith would probably succeed in amassing sufficient evidence to ensure he was arrested. He also realized that now fate, and not design, had given him the chance to 'die' a second time and so escape that possibility. And he had a fortune waiting so that never again would he have to put himself at risk (always supposing he could forgo the pleasure of proving to himself just once more how brilliant he was).

Higham's wife had left him, he'd no immediate family alive, and no one in the UK expected, or particularly wanted, to hear from him, so he offered a perfect false identity. But somehow, the passports had to be switched . . .

Previously it had not been difficult for an expert to lift a photograph from one passport and paste it on to another, but the impressed strip of clear plastic had been expressly designed to prevent that and because of this there was no way in which, in his present circumstances, he could make the alteration. Yet if only there were time, there'd be no difficulty. In every major city there were men skilled enough to unbind a passport, swap pages, and then rebind it so that only the most detailed examination—and certainly not the normally casual one of an immigration official—would disclose what had happened. But even if not badly injured, he needed hospital treatment and the moment he entered into official hands, he'd have to declare his identity . . . Then he thought up a plan by which he could gain time.

He had gathered up the two passports, the wallets, and all the papers, and had hidden them near the scene of the crash. Then he had waited to be found and taken to hospital.

In hospital he'd simulated loss of memory. The doctors had
been slightly surprised, but not suspicious; why should
they be, when it was in his own interests, apparently, to
remember who he was? He'd telephoned Charlotte, told her
where everything was hidden and who to contact in Palma.
She'd flown over from Barcelona, collected the passports,
etc., paid to have the page switched, destroyed the remains of
Thompson's passport. She'd dumped the passport of
Higham, now bearing Thompson's photo, in a litter-bin,
together with the emptied wallet. She'd returned to Corleon.

As Higham, he'd regained his memory. His passport confirmed his identity. He'd repeated all that Higham had told
him in the car, giving it as the story of his own life. His one
fear, of course, was that by ill chance someone on the island
who knew him as Thompson would find him in the hospital
under the name of Higham, but he was a gambler and correctly reckoned the odds were all in his favour. And the deception only had to remain good until he was fit enough to be
discharged from hospital, whereupon he would vanish . . .

In the event, his gamble would have failed but for one
factor—ironically, a factor which he had never taken into
consideration; that was, the complex relationship which
existed between his son and himself. If called upon to
describe this, he probably would present it in much simpler
terms from those Mike had employed; but then he saw the
world as a much simpler place. Mike had both loved and
hated him and because of the hate he had known guilt and
remorse. It was the remorse which had made Mike lie when
called upon to identify the exhumed body—realizing that
his father was not dead but had made yet another switch
with a dead man. Correctly assuming that this must be
because he had again been swindling people and was in
trouble in consequence, he had made the false identification
in the hope of expiating at least a part of his guilt . . .

Perhaps the truth would never have surfaced had
Charlotte not been so in love. Because, knowing how close

to death he'd come, so luminous with relief that he'd escaped, she'd recognized that she could never convincingly simulate enough grief and thus the only alternative, if the fiction of his death was to be supported, was to act the part of a bitch . . .

Alvarez used a handkerchief to mop the sweat from his forehead. Did Steven Taylor even now appreciate why Charlotte made him the luckiest dead man alive?

Alvarez came to a halt in front of Ca Na Muña. He switched off the engine, pulled the handbrake hard on, and put the car into reverse gear as an added precaution. He climbed out.

Valerie stepped into the doorway of the house and stood there as he climbed the stone steps. She was looking old and rather feeble. 'I suppose you've come to arrest me? If I can have a few minutes to pack . . .'

'Señora, I am not here to do that,' he answered, as he crossed the narrow level.

'Why not?'

'Because Steven Taylor is still alive. The man who died was Señor Higham, a hitch-hiker who was actually driving at the time of the crash. Afterwards, Steven Taylor changed identities in order to disappear. While you can clearly still be charged with administering the poison with intent to murder, it would be necessary for a successful prosecution for him to come back and give evidence against you. I am quite certain he will never do that.'

She turned and looked up at the olive tree she called the Laocöon. 'He's still alive?' she said in a low, toneless voice.

What was her overriding emotion? Thankfulness that after all she had not murdered, or bitterness that the man who had robbed her of her chance of honouring her promise to her husband was still alive? Alvarez found he could not answer the question.

THE END

DEAR MISS DEMEANOR

BY

JOAN HESS

Published by special arrangement with St. Martin's Press, Inc.

Dear Miss Demeanor,
  How far should a girl go on the first date?

Dear Reader,
  On the first date, a girl should go as far as Okie's Hamburger Mecca. She should then order french fries. If she paces herself well, the final fry will be consumed five minutes before curfew. Once on the front porch, she may shyly allow masculine lips to be brushed across her cheek before fleeing inside to telephone Miss Demeanor with all the juicy details.

Dear Miss Demeanor,
  My old lady won't put out. Should I dump her and find someone else?

Dear Reader,
  A proper lady will put out the garbage, put out the cat, or, with adequate equipment, put out a forest fire. That is what you meant, isn't it? Perhaps the lady in question lacks asbestos boots.

Dear Miss Demeanor,
  If a married man is seen with a woman at the Xanadu Motel, should someone tell his wife?

Dear Reader,
  Let us presume it was his wife. In any case, what were you doing at the Xanadu Motel?

"O"N"E"

Caron and Inez skittered into the Book Depot like bumper cars gone berserk. Caron's cheeks were scarlet, either from the exertion or, as I suspected, some new bout of outraged indignation. With fourteen-year-olds, indignation is a daily affair. With my daughter, it approaches an hourly schedule.

Caron is all red hair, freckles, and frowns. As an enfant terrible, her imaginary friends were all mischievous imps who knocked over lamps and terrorized the cat. Inez is quite the opposite; she may have been an imaginary friend. Her pale, blurred face hardly ever flushes, and her eyes are too deeply hidden by thick lenses to flash with fury, unbridled or otherwise. She did, however, shove back her stringy brown bangs with a gesture that neared irritation.

I eyed them with an instinctive wariness. "What's up?"

Caron slammed her books down. "You must Do Something, Mother!"

"You really must, Mrs. Malloy," Inez added over Caron's shoulder. She had not yet learned to speak in capital letters, but it was only a matter of time. Caron is an excellent tutor in the delicate art of adolescent melodrama.

"What must I do?" I asked mildly.

"It is absolutely Terrible!" Caron said, beginning to stomp up and down the bookshop aisles. "The situation is absurd, absurd,

absurd! Poor Miss Parchester would never Dream of doing what—what they said she did. She is a Lady!"

Inez bobbled her head earnestly. "That's right, Mrs. Malloy. Miss Parchester is above reproach."

It was, as usual, mystifying. I raised an eyebrow, but as I opened my mouth to protest that I personally had not accused Miss Parchester of anything, a deafening roar shattered the relative tranquillity. A two-hundred-pound woodpecker tearing through the roof. A locomotive coming down the aisle. An ocean liner docking in the living room. Or, foregoing whimsy, a jackhammer a few yards from the door of my bookstore.

I buried my face in my hands as the noise continued to pulsate through every inch of my body. Caron and Inez gaped at each other, by necessity speechless. Just as I thought my head would explode, the roar stopped.

"The street crew," I said, rubbing my temples.

Caron went to the door and peered out. "What on earth is going on, Mother?"

"Powers that be have decided to take up the railroad tracks in the middle of the street, since the last train went through Farberville twenty years ago. Although I cannot fault the sentiment, the noise is driving me crazy! Didn't you see the—"

"I am too worried about Miss Parchester to concern myself with street crews," Caron interrupted. "You have to do something, Mother, before she has a Nervous Breakdown." Inez punctuated the sentiment with a sniffle.

I looked out the window as I formulated a response to their incomprehensible demand. The jackhammer man was rubbing his hands together as he studied his instrument. The gloat on his face brought to mind images of satanic Spanish inquisitors positioning their racks. Caron was right. I did have to do something.

I shooed the girls outside, locked the door, and hung a flyspecked sign on the doorknob. Until Thurber Street was once again a peaceful path to the campus, the Book Depot was closed.

A week or two without an income was cheaper than a hearing aid or a trip to the butterfly farm. There were a few minor matters, such as overdue rent, groceries, Caron's allowance, and payments to the great plastic factory (I never left home without it), but I wouldn't make any money until the crew left. My clientele was too genteel to climb over sawhorses to seek literature. Or semipornographic paperback thrillers, for that matter. Somewhere in Farberville a banker sighed; I felt the icy breeze on the back of my neck, but there wasn't much to do about it.

We walked up the hill. Caron and I live in an upstairs apartment across from the Farber College campus. Although I never before considered it an especially serene location, it was a cemetery in comparison to the construction site in front of the Book Depot. The sorority girls next door produced squeals, but never machine-gun fire.

I took two aspirin, made a cup of tea, and went into the living room. "Who's Miss Parchester?"

Caron's lower lip began to inch forward. "She *was* the journalism teacher at the high school, before He told her that she was fired. I had her for Journalism I, and when Rosie got mononucleosis, Miss Parchester let me take over the column."

"What column?" I asked. Inevitably, it took a while to elicit coherence from Caron, but I was used to it. Motherhood has been with me for fourteen years, although it has crystallized in the last three. Razor-sharp edges and all. The dreaded developmental stage called the terrible twos has nothing over the traumatic teens.

"The Miss Demeanor column," Inez said weakly. I had to search the room for her; she was invisible on the upholstery, like a transparent plastic cover.

"Misdemeanor?" I said. "Is this some sort of legal advice to potential juvenile delinquents? Are you really qualified to——"

"Miss Demeanor!" Caron enunciated the consonants with little sputters of irritation. "An advice column about manners and proper behavior. The students write letters about dating, eating in restaurants, and so on."

My jaw dropped in spite of my efforts to control it. "And you're giving advice about proper behavior? When did you turn into Farberville's Emily Post?"

"When Rosie got mono, Mother; I explained that already. I was Rosie's freshman assistant. Freshmen aren't allowed to be on the newspaper staff, but Miss Parchester thought I could handle Rosie's column until she comes back to school." Caron fluffed her curls and shot me a beatific smile. "Mono can last as long as six months."

"So you're writing the column? You're in charge of etiquette at Farberville High School?"

"I *was* doing the column, but now the *Falcon Crier* has been canceled for the rest of the year. That's why you have to Do Something." The smile vanished as her chin began to quiver, and tears welled in her eyes. I was not impressed, but Inez hurried over to pat the tragic figure's tremulous shoulder.

"It is unjust, Mrs. Malloy," she said in a low voice. "Miss Parchester has been accused of embezzling money from the journalism accounts. I think she's just on some kind of leave, but *he* said that she couldn't even come to school until the account was audited and the money replaced. Poor Miss Parchester was distraught."

"I'm sure she was," I said. "Who's this ominous 'he' you keep mentioning?"

Caron and Inez widened their eyes at each other. "Mr. Weiss," they whispered in awed sibilance.

"Who is Mr. Weiss?" My patience was beginning to evaporate. I had a perfectly wonderful mystery novel in the bedroom. The water in the teapot was still hot. I could put myself to bed and bliss.

Caron gulped at my irreverence. "Mr. Weiss is the principal of Farberville High School, Mother."

"Oh," I said wisely, then proceeded to reiterate the bare outlines of their story, which took no time at all. Accounts short, teacher dismissed, newspaper production halted. Career in journalism thwarted in its infancy. "There's not one thing I can do about any of this, girls. I'm not a CPA, and I doubt my opinion will affect Mr. Weiss's decisions. If Miss Parchester would like a discount on paperback romances while she does a prison term, I could—"

"Mother!"

"Mrs. Malloy!"

The squeaks were almost worse than the jackhammer. "Let's be reasonable," I continued. "This is a high school problem. Surely the proper authorities can resolve this, and if Miss Parchester is as innocent as you say, then she will be back shortly, as will the newspaper and all its columns."

"You have to help," Caron said. "You have to investigate and find out who really took the money. Mr. Weiss won't do anything; he thinks Miss Parchester is a thief. By the time he hires a new teacher, Rosie will be over her mono and I won't get to write the Miss Demeanor column until I'm a senior. That'll be years from now. Eons."

"I am a bookseller, not a private eye. I have no idea how to find bugs in the accounts, nor am I in a position to find out who might be behind the heinous crime. I'm sorry about the column, but there is no way *I* can help Miss Parchester, Miss Demeanor, or the *Falcon Crier*."

Caron had recovered nicely from her semihysterical state. Slyly smiling, she said, "I told Miss Dort that you would substitute for Miss Parchester. You can snoop around between classes."

I will not elaborate on my unseemly reaction to this astounding announcement. Inez was sent home (she left briskly and gratefully), and Caron and I verbally explored the ramifications of volunteering others without prior permission, among other things. My voice might have peaked upon occasion, but for the most part I kept my temper under admirable restraint. Caron ran through her repertoire of postpubescent poses, including contrite child (ha!), defender of truth, unjustly accused victim, etc.

I had reached a new plateau of rhetorical sarcasm when the telephone rang. Stabbing my finger at Caron to keep her in place, I grabbed the receiver. "What?"

"Mrs. Malloy?" quavered an unfamiliar voice. "This is Emily Parchester. I was wondering—well, hoping—or should I say, praying—that you might be able to visit me for a cup of tea this afternoon? I realize you must be terribly busy, and I would never dream of imposing on a stranger, but I really have nowhere else to turn."

I glared at Caron as I struggled for decorum. "Miss Parchester—from the high school?"

"Formerly of the high school," she said with quiet dignity. A hiccup rather destroyed the effect. "Would you be so kind as to come to my house, Miss Malloy? I must talk to you."

I made a noise that she interpreted as agreement. After she had given me her address and a time, she bleated out a lengthy promise of gratitude and finally hung up. It took me several minutes to uncurl my fingers in order to replace the receiver—and remind myself of the legal repercussions of child abuse.

"Miss Parchester has invited me to a tea party," I told Caron when I could trust myself. "She has some wild idea that I can salvage her reputation and restore her to her position at the high school. Wherever would she get such an idea?"

Caron shrugged modestly. "I told her how you had solved those murders, and convinced her that you would help her. She's a poor old spinster, Mother, and she's all alone in the world. No one at the high school cares about her. If she loses her job, she'll just sit home by herself until she dies." My daughter, the compassionate columnist.

"In that you face the same fate, you'd better clean up your room so that your body will be discovered at some point during decomposition. Then you may clean the bathroom, finish the dishes, and begin your homework. I'm going to a tea party."

"I don't have any homework."

"Do it anyway." I closed the door with more energy than necessary and went down the stairs. To tea. All I needed was a hat and white gloves. Or a mad hatter and a dormouse.

Miss Parchester lived in a white-shingled house in the oldest section of Farberville. At one time, the cream of society sipped iced tea on the wide verandas, and carriages rolled down the tree-lined streets on their way to the charity balls in vanished hotels.

The ancient elm trees were still there, but most of the houses had been subdivided into apartments for Farber students and transient waiters. Bustled ladies had been replaced with T-shirt-clad students armed with frisbees and beer. Subcompacts filled the carriage houses.

My battered hatchback felt no shame. I mentally straightened my hat and pulled on gloves, then went up the brick sidewalk and stopped to read the names taped on the row of black metal mailboxes. Miss Parchester lived in 1-A. Wonderful. As I hesitated, considering a brisk retreat and another discussion with Caron, a pigtailed college girl bounced through the door, sized me up with undue arrogance, and informed me that Miss Parchester lived in the first apartment on the left.

I managed an insincere nod of thanks and went inside to do my distasteful duty. Tea, sympathy, and firmness, I reminded myself in a determined voice. I was neither detective nor substitute teacher. I was a widow who needed to earn a living in order to support a treacherous, locquacious teenager until she could be tucked away in a college dormitory. Preferably at the University of Fairbanks, or Iceland Polytech.

Before my knuckles reached the door, it flew open. A tiny woman with thin white hair looked up at me as if I had just arrived in a chariot drawn by angels. She wore a black dress and a sensible, handmade cardigan. Her feet were covered by shabby pink slippers, a strange combination.

"Mrs. Malloy? How terribly kind of you to come so promptly."

"Miss Parchester, I want to thank you for offering tea, but I want you to realize——"

"Yes, of course," she said, "please come in. Caron——such a sweet child——has told me so much about you. Although she's only a freshman, she shows surprising talent, don't you think?"

She chattered in that vein as she put me on a brocade sofa, then shuffled down a dark hallway. I looked around curiously. The room was oddly shaped, and at last I deduced it had been divided to create another apartment. The ceiling was high, with an elaborate molding and elegant cornices. The windows, too, were high, but shades let in only a dull yellow light. The furniture would have given an antique dealer a stroke on the spot, if he could have seen it without the teetery piles of bleached newspapers, magazines, ancient composition books, and dust. It smelled of camphor——and dust.

Miss Parchester shuffled back in with a tray. Once I was supplied with tea and one of "mother's sugar cookies," she said, "I do so enjoy tea in the afternoon, Mrs. Malloy. The youth of today seem to prefer those vile carbonated drinks, but tea is so refreshing."

So was scotch, but I didn't mention it. "I'm afraid Caron has given you the wrong impression——"

"The tea service belonged to my great-grandmother," she continued blithely, "and has been in the family for nearly a century. My mother used to serve tea to the Judge every afternoon on the veranda, even though he might have preferred a gentleman's drink."

The woman was clearly a teacher, and a pro. I ceded to the inevitable and politely murmured, "The judge?"

"My father, Judge Amos Parchester. He served three terms on the state Supreme Court, although you're too young to have heard of him. His decisions are still noted to this day. He was an ardent defender of constitutional rights, Mrs. Malloy."

"Indeed?" What else could I say?

"Which is why I chose a career in journalism, as you must have guessed. It was, of course, unthinkable for a lady to work for a newspaper, so I chose to instruct our youth. I've taught for forty years at Farberville High School." She hiccuped on the final word, and gave me a bleary look of apology.

Miss Parchester had been nipping at the elderberry wine, I realized uneasily. The afternoon had been veering downhill, but this was more than anyone should have to put up with. I put down my teacup and said, "We need to discuss whatever non-sense Caron told you about me, Miss Parchester. I am not a detective. I am not an accountant. There is no way that I can——"

"I have never been more humiliated in my life than I was this morning, when Mr. Weiss came into my room," she said, dabbing at her cheek with a wispy handkerchief. "He accused me of being a common thief, of stealing money from the department accounts! Judge Parchester is surely rolling in his grave, and poor mama—bless her soul—must be. . . ."

"I cannot help you," I repeated, trying to sound steadfast.

"There must be some error in the books," she said. The flow from her watery blue eyes increased until the handkerchief was sodden. She daintily wrung it into the cup in her lap, tucked it in her cuff, and then continued, "Mr. Weiss refused to allow me to search for a discrepancy, although it must be a simple error on my part. If only you could check the deposit slips to see if they correspond with the entries, then we could determine if I indeed am responsible for this distressing situation. I had planned to retire this spring, you know, so that I could enjoy whatever pleasures I could find within the limits of my teacher retirement fund and what little I've saved. I had hoped to take up watercolor painting, or perhaps take a short bus tour."

In the far corner of my brain, a violin began to play. Visions of pathetically inept landscapes flashed across my eyes. A short bus trip. Miss Parchester sitting in the mausoleum, gradually disappearing under a layer of dust. Drinking from a cracked wine goblet and talking to the judge. The judge answering. A string quartet took up the melody.

I found myself agreeing to check the deposit slips. "But," I added in desperation, "I am not qualified to substitute for you. I have no teaching credentials, and the only thing I've done with a newspaper is read it."

"Miss Dort feels that your literary background is adequate," Miss Parchester said, taking a slug of what I suspected was not straight Lipton. "You do have a degree in English, don't you, dear? The students are quite capable of handling the production of the newspaper; some of them have worked on the staff for two years."

I shook my head. "I cannot—"

"Of course, you can. As the Judge used to say, a healthy attitude can overcome a mountain. You'll be a splendid teacher, Mrs. Malloy."

The teacup was removed from my numb fingers. Somehow or other, I was congratulated for my endeavor, tidied up, and left on the doorstep to ponder the situation—which was clearly out of control. The jackhammer had done it, I told myself morosely as I returned to my car. Brain damage.

I drove home and climbed the stairs, still bewildered by preceding events. Caron looked up as I opened the door, the receiver in her treacherous hands.

"She just came in, Miss Dort," she chirped.

Miss Dort's name had been popping up like a dandelion in recent conversations, but I had no idea who she was.

"Hello," I said, eyeing the liquor cabinet in the kitchen. If Miss Parchester could indulge before five o'clock, then surely I deserved to do the same.

"Mrs. Malloy, this is Bernice Dort at the high school. I'm the vice-principal in charge of administrative services," said a brisk and somehow brittle voice. "I have been informed that you are willing to substitute for Miss Parchester until a permanent replacement can be found—or until the problem is resolved."

I would not have selected the word "willing." Bulldozed, coerced, emotionally blackmailed—but not "willing." I realized I was staring blankly at the receiver and managed to say, "Something like that, yes."

"I shall assume that you are aware substitute teachers receive thirty-eight dollars a day, and that you are familiar with both the standard state and federal withholdings and the obligatory contribution to the teacher retirement fund. Were you certified, Mrs. Malloy, you would receive forty-three dollars a day."

I did a bit of multiplication in my head. "I taught two undergraduate sections of English literature," I suggested tentatively. It would surely take me a week to solve Miss Parchester's problems, which would appease Visa and keep Lean Cuisines in the freezer. The hypothetical banker's breath on my neck seemed warmer.

"I was speaking of the secondary education certification block, not the amateurish attempts of graduate students to earn their assistantships. The fact that you lack proper credentials does pose a problem for me, Mrs. Malloy. It certainly would have been more expedient had you previously filled out an application at the administration office, but I may be able to slip through a backdated STA111. It will entail extra paperwork."

I wondered if I owed her an apology for the extra paperwork.

I wondered if Caron could be boarded with an Eskimo family. I wondered if the jackhammer was all that bad.

"Mrs. Malloy, are you there?"

"Yes, Mrs. Dort, I am here. If the STA111 is too much trouble, I'll be glad to step aside. I'm sure that there are plenty of qualified substitutes—"

"No, there are not. On an average, we require twelve to fifteen substitutes each academic week, and we are always desperate to fill the gaps so that the educational process can continue with minimal disruption. I fear we must both accept the necessity of a little extra work. Now, I'll need your social security number for the W-8, your date of birth, your academic record, and two personal references—anyone who can confirm that you're not an axe-murderer," Miss Dort said.

I produced the information, listening to the sound of an efficient and officious pen scratching on the other end of the line. When we reached the point of two character references, I drew an embarrassing blank.

"Anyone, Mrs. Malloy," Miss Dort prompted me. "Anyone who knows you well enough to attest to your moral standing in the community."

Miss Parchester? Inez? The jackhammer operator who should have worn a black, hooded cape? I could almost hear Miss Dort's mind questioning my moral standing.

"Peter Rosen," I sputtered. "He's the head of the CID."

"The CID? May I presume that is a government agency of some sort?"

"The Criminal Investigation Department of the local police force," I said. "He's a personal friend of mine, and will certainly vouch for me."

"How fascinating." Miss Dort wasn't fascinated. "I'll need one more name, Mrs. Malloy. There surely is at least one more person who can attest to your character, isn't there?"

I finally remembered the name of the sociology professor who lived downstairs and repeated it grimly. If he were asked about me, I hoped he could figure out who I was. Her forms filled, Mrs. Dort assured me that she would stay at school until midnight to process my paperwork, and told me to report to her office at seven-thirty the next morning.

I replaced the receiver and went to find Caron. The door to the bathroom was locked, and I could hear water gushing into the tub. Apparently the sound was loud enough to muffle my comments, in that I received no reply. If the child had any sense, she would remain in the sanctuary of a bubble bath until her toes turned to prunes. I made a face at the door, then went into the kitchen for a much-needed medicinal dose of scotch and a few more aspirins.

Farberville High School is, no doubt, a perfectly lovely place. Caron and approximately five hundred other students attended daily without much uproar. All sorts of dedicated teachers appeared to do their best to instill knowledge in adolescent heads. As far as I knew, no serious crime riddled the campus or precipitated armed guards in the hallways to protect teachers. I had gone to such an institution myself, although it had been a few years. It hadn't been all that bad. The Book Depot was closed until the street was repaired; I really had nothing of any great importance to do in the interim. The money would hardly finance a shopping spree in Paris, but it would very definitely come in handy should Caron and I decide to indulge in madcap, extravagant activities such as eating.

"It's only for a few days," I reminded the ceiling. Why, then, did it have the same ring as life without parole?

A knock at the door saved me from further schizophrenic conversation with the architecture. I found a smiling Peter Rosen on the landing, a bottle of wine tucked under his arm. He put the wine down and spent a few minutes greeting me with great charm.

"What's only for a few days?" he asked, turning on his inno-

cent smile. At one time in our past the smile had enraged me—
but so had his presence. The effect was quite the opposite now.
For the most part.

"You wouldn't believe it," I said. While I took the wine to the
kitchen, I told him the identity of the newest substitute teacher
at the high school, although I omitted any references to the absurd investigation. Peter does not approve of amateur involvement in piddly little puzzles—on principle. This I knew from
experience.

"I was going to suggest we have dinner tomorrow night," he
said, putting on a show of disappointment that would not have
passed muster in a kindergarten pageant. "But I suppose you'll be
home grading papers and devising lesson plans. Perhaps Caron
will be my escort."

When he wished, the man could be as funny as sleet.

"T"W"O"

The high school resembled a collection of yellow blocks abandoned on a moth-eaten shag carpet. No ivy or any such traditional nonsense; just jean-clad students exchanging insults and displaying anatomy as they streamed into one of the four double doors. I felt like a first-grader on the first day of school. I did not hold Caron's hand, however; she could not have survived the humiliation.

I was escorted to the central office, introduced to a pimply boy behind the counter, and warned to wait until Miss Dort appeared. Caron then squealed a greeting to Inez and disappeared into the human tidal wave. My pimply baby-sitter eyed me incuriously, picked up a stack of manila envelopes and left. People of all sizes wandered in and out, ignoring me.

I read a poster that warned against smoking on campus, drinking alcoholic beverages on campus, running in the hallways, missing classes without excuse, and a variety of things I hadn't known teenagers were aware of. I then scanned the list of honor graduates from the previous year, the school calendar for the next year, and everything else tacked on the bulletin board. When in doubt, read the directions.

A rabbity little man with oversized glasses scurried into the office. "Are you the new juvenile parole officer?" he gasped, looking thoroughly dismayed. "I haven't done the seven-one-four

forms yet, but I do have the nine-thirties from the spring semester."

"I am not the new parole officer," I said gravely.

"Oh, my goodness no!" He disappeared through a door behind
the counter. I heard a series of breathless disclaimers drifting out,
as though he needed further reassurance of my identity—or lack
thereof.

I was edging toward the nearest exit when a tall, unsmiling
woman swept into the office. A gray bun was pinned to the top
of her head like a mushroom cap, and pastel blue glasses swung
on a cord around her neck. There was a hint of a mustache on
her decidedly stiff upper lip.

"Mrs. Malloy? I'm Bernice Dort. Sorry to be late, but Mr.
Eugenia has made a muddle of his first quarter grades and someone had to explain it again. And again. It's merely a matter of
recording grades, according to the code in the manual, on both
the computer card and the reporting form, but Mr. Eugenia
seems unable to follow the simplest instructions."

"I'm beginning to wonder if I ought to fill in for Miss
Parchester," I said, continuing to retreat. An elbow caught me in
the back before I reached the doorway.

"Humph!" A large, red-faced man pushed past me to confront
Miss Dort. His silver hair had been clipped with military precision, and nary a hair dared to take a tangential angle. His face
was florid, and his bulk encased in a severe blue suit and dark tie.
"I want Immerman in my office, Bernice—and I want him now.
That boy has gone too far! Perkins called this morning to tell me
that Immerman had demanded reinstatement of his eligibility!"

"Oh, how dreadful, Mr. Weiss. Immerman has indeed gone
too far. I shall have Mr. Finley send him to the office immediately," Miss Dort agreed in a frigid voice. "Mr. Weiss, this is
Mrs. Malloy. She's subbing for Miss Parchester until central admin can locate a certified teacher for the journalism department."

Mr. Weiss stopped in midstep, as if an invisible choke collar had been tightened around his neck. Two small, hard eyes bored into me. His mouth curled slightly in what I presumed was meant to be a smile of welcome, but the message was lost.

I fluttered a hand. "Hello."

"Malloy. Aren't you the woman who runs the Book Depot?" he barked in accusation. "Weren't you involved in some sort of police investigation?"

Caron and Inez had every right to be awed. Although I was nearly forty, I felt a rush of heat to my cheeks and had to pinch myself to hold back a whimper. "That's correct," I said. "I assisted the police with a problem involving the Farber College faculty."

"And now you've decided to be a substitute teacher?" he continued, still staring at me as if I tripped into his office under a beanie with a propeller on the top.

Miss Dort cleared her throat. "Mrs. Malloy has offered to help out, Mr. Weiss. You know how difficult it can be to find a substitute six weeks into the semester, so we'll simply have to make do with what we can get. Now, if you'll excuse us, I'll take Mrs. Malloy down to the journalism room and get her settled. Her paperwork is on your desk, although I've already sent the triplicates to central admin."

Mr. Weiss gave her a tight nod. "Then get Immerman in here. Tell his first period teacher that he'll be in my office during class."

Miss Dort seemed on the verge of a heel-clicking salute, but she instead bobbed her head curtly and picked up her clipboard. Thus armed, she led me out of the office and into the battle arena. We marched down several miles of hallway as she rattled off names, departments, and other bits of meaningless information. Students leaped out of our path, and conversations were revived only in our wake.

We then descended into the bowels of the building. A bell jangled shrilly as we reached the bottom step; seconds later students scuttled through doorways like cockroaches caught in the light.

Miss Dort pointed at a scarred door. "That is the old teachers' lounge, Mrs. Malloy. The new one is on the second floor in the west wing; you may find the distance inconvenient. Most of the teachers in the basement still congregate in the old room, but you may use whichever you prefer."

I suspected I would prefer the one with a well-stocked bar. Nineteen minutes had passed since Caron dragged me through the door. Nineteen incredibly long minutes. Seven hours remained in the school day. This scheme was insane. I would personally buy Miss Parchester a pad of watercolor paper and a bus ticket to wherever she desired to go. Caron could accompany her as a porter.

"This," Miss Dort announced as she opened a door, "is the journalism department."

The room resembled the interior of a cave. The air was foul, reminding me of the miasma of a very old garbage can. Miss Dort snorted, switched on a light and gave me a stony look meant to impede flight.

"You do not have a homeroom class, so you will not have to deal with the attendance reports until your first class arrives in seven minutes. Miss Parchester's daily unit delineations will be in a dark-blue spiral notebook, and her rosters in a small black book. Good luck, and keep in mind the faculty motto: TAKE NO PRISONERS." The woman actually started for the door.

"Wait a minute!" I yelped. "What am I supposed to do about—"

"I have to make the daily announcements, Mrs. Malloy. Homeroom will be over in six and one half minutes, and I must remind the students about the variations in the bus route on snow days." She sailed out the door before I could argue.

I did not sink to the floor and burst into tears, although the idea crossed my mind. On the other hand, I did not linger to explore the murky corners of Carlsbad Cavern. I figured I had over five minutes of free time, so I bolted for the teachers' lounge—which had to be more enlightening than any book of daily unit delineations.

The lounge was decorated in early American garage sale. The several sofas were covered with tattered plaid variations that would have convulsed a Scotsman; the formica-topped table was covered with nicks, scratches and stains. There were two rest rooms along one wall, and between them a tiny kitchenette with a refrigerator, soda machine, and—saints be praised—a gurgling coffee pot. A variety of cups hung on a peg board; not one of them said "Malloy" in decorative swirls, or even "Parchester."

The situation was dire enough to permit certain emergency measures, including petty theft. I took down a cup, poured myself a medicinal dose of caffeine and slumped down on a mauve-and-green sofa to brood. Four minutes at the most. Then, if I remembered my high school experiences with any accuracy, students would converge on my cave, their little faces bright with eagerness to learn, their little eyes shining with innocence. Presumably, I would have to greet them and do something to restrain them for fifty minutes or so. Others would follow. Between moments of imparting wisdom, I was supposed to audit the books and expose an embezzler.

In the midst of my gloomy mental diatribe, a woman in a bright yellow dress came into the lounge. She was young, pretty, and slightly flustered by my presence. "Hello, I'm Paula Hart," she said with a warm smile. "Beginning typing and office machines."

"Claire Malloy. Intermediate confusion and advanced despair," I said. My smile lacked her radiance, but she probably knew what daily unit delineations were.

"Are you subbing for Miss Parchester? This whole thing is just unbelievable, and I feel just dreadful about it. Poor Emily would never do such a thing. She must be terribly upset." Miss Hart went into the kitchenette and returned with a cup decorated with pink hearts. "I'm in the room right across from you, Mrs. Malloy. If you need anything, feel free to ask."

I opened my mouth to ask the definition of a delineation when a thirty-year-old Robert Redford walked into the lounge. He was wearing a gray sweatsuit, but it in no way diminished the effect. Longish blond hair, cornflower blue eyes, dimples, compact and well-shaped body. The whole thing, living and breathing. And smiling solely for Paula Hart, who radiated right back. They had no need for physical contact; the space between them shimmered with unspoken messages.

Young love was nice if one liked that sort of thing, but I was more concerned with my personal problems. Before I could suggest they unlock eyes and make constructive comments about my classes, the bell rang. The sound of tromping feet competed with screeches of glee. Locker doors banged open and slammed closed. The war was on, and I couldn't do battle in the lounge.

"Bye," I said as I headed into disaster. Neither of them seemed visibly distressed by my departure—if they noticed.

The journalism room was, as I had feared, filled with students. I went to the desk, dug through the mess until I found a black book, and then tossed it at a pudgy girl with waist-length black hair and a semblance of intelligence.

"Tell everyone to sit down and then take roll," I commanded coolly. If I could only find the other book, I suspected I could discover who they were and why they were there.

The girl goggled briefly but began shouting names above the roar. Eventually the students sat down to eye me in a disconcertingly carnivorous way. I squared my shoulders and reminded myself that they were simply unpolished versions of the species.

We quickly established that they were Beginning Features, and I was a substitute with no interest in their future. They agreed to hold down the noise; I agreed to leave them alone until I found the daily unit delineation book. My pudgy aide at last produced it from a cardboard box beside the desk.

Since we were all content with the present arrangement, I left them to whisper while I scanned the book. Second period was to be Intro to Photo, and third was gloriously free, followed by a reasonable lunch break. Fourth period was *Falcon Crier,* which I presumed had something to do with the newspaper, fifth was Photo II, and sixth was something called "Falconnaire." If I was alive at that point, I could go home.

The whispering grew a bit louder. I turned a motherly frown on them, and the noise obediently abated. Pleased with my success, I wandered around the room, discovering a coat closet filled with old newspapers, boxes of curled photographs, a quantity of dried rubber cement bottles, and a small, inky hole that proved to be a darkroom in all senses of the word. It also proved to be the source of the garbage can aroma. I now knew the confines of my domain, for better or worse.

I was sitting at the desk with an old newspaper when a box on the wall above my head began to crackle. After a moment of what sounded like cellophane being crumpled, a voice emerged.

"Mrs. Malloy, I have neither your attendance list for first period, nor your blue slips. I must have them at the beginning of each period." Miss Dort, or Frosty the Snowman.

I gazed at the box. "So?"

"So I must have them, Mrs. Malloy."

Good heavens, the thing worked both ways. I wondered if she could see me from her mountaintop aerie as well. "I'll send them to the office," I called with a compliant expression, just in case. The box squawked in reply, then fell silent.

Pudge waved a paper at me and left the room. Hoping she knew what she was up to, I returned to an article on the chances of a district championship in football, complete with photographs of neckless boys squinting into the sun, but nevertheless optimistic.

On the last page, I found a photograph of Robert Redford himself. The caption below informed me that this was the new assistant coach, Jerry Finley. He thought the chances for a championship were good if the boys worked hard during practice, perfected their passing game, and gave the team their personal best. He was delighted to be at Farberville High and proud of the Falcons. His hobbies included water-skiing and Chinese cooking. When not on the gridiron, he would be found teaching general science and drivers' ed, or supervising study hall in the cafeteria.

Or dimpling at Miss Hart, I amended to myself.

The bell rang, and the class departed with the stealth of a buffalo herd. Their replacements looked remarkably similiar. I tossed the attendance book to a weedy boy with glasses, made the same announcement about immediate goals, and even managed to send my attendance slip to the office before the box crackled at me.

I spent the period rummaging through Miss Parchester's desk for anything that might contain accounts. I found a year's supply of scented tissues, worn pencils, blue slips whose purpose escaped me, and other teaching paraphenalia. When the bell rang, I went down the hall to the teachers' lounge to drown my sorrows in coffee.

As I opened the door, I heard a furious voice saying, "Mr. Pitts, you are a despicable example of humanity. I have told you repeatedly that you must not—must not—enter the lounge for any reason other than maintenance. I shall have to report you to Mr. Weiss!"

The speaker was a grim-faced woman with hair the color of concrete. On one side of her stood a diminutive sort with bluish hair, on the other a lanky woman whose shoulders barely supported her head. All three wore long dark dresses, cardigans, and stubby heels. They also wore disapproving frowns. Despite minor variations, they were remarkably similar, as if they were standard issue from some prehistoric teachers' college; I had had them or remarkable facsimiles throughout my formative years. Many of said years had been spent cringing when confronted with steely stares and tight-lipped smiles.

The object of their scorn was a man with a broom. His thin black hair glittered in the light from years of accumulated lubrication. He wore dirty khaki pants, a gray undershirt that might have been white in decades past, and scuffed cowboy boots. His lower lip hung in moist and petulant resignation, but his eyes flittered to me as if to share some secret amusement. Having nothing in common with lizards, I eased behind the three women and slipped into the kitchenette.

"Well, Mr. Pitts," the woman boomed on, "it is obvious that you have been rummaging in the refrigerator once again. Stealing food, contaminating the lunches of others, and generally behaving like a scavenger. I am disgusted by the idea of your filthy fingers in my food! Disgusted, Mr. Pitts! Have you nothing to say in your defense?"

"I didn't even open the refrigerator," he growled. "I ain't been in here since yesterday evening when I cleaned. You don't have no reason to report me, Mrs. P."

"My coffee cup is missing, Mr. Pitts. The evidence is clear."

Oh, dear. I stuck my head out the door and pasted on an angelic smile. "I'm afraid I may be the cup culprit. I was in earlier and borrowed one of them."

Three sets of eyes turned to stare at me. The middle woman said, "We do not borrow cups from each other. It is unhygienic." On either side of her, heads nodded emphatically.

"I'm sorry, but there were no extra cups. I'll wash it out immediately and return it to you," I said, trying to sound composed in the face of such unanimous condemnation.

"There is no detergent," the woman said. "I'll have to take it to the chemistry room and rinse it out with alcohol." She held out her hand.

I meekly gave her the cup and babbled further apology as the three marched out of the room. Once they were gone, I sank down on a sofa and lectured myself on the ephemerality of the situation.

"Who're you supposed to be?" the lizard snickered.

"I'm the substitute for Miss Parchester in the journalism room."

"I'm Pitts, the custodian. I used to be a janitor, but they changed my title. Didn't pay any more money, though. Just changed the title to custodian 'cause it sounds more professional. I had hopes of being a building maintenance engineer, but Weiss wouldn't go for it."

"How thrilling for you," I said, closing my eyes to avoid looking at him. I immediately became aware of an odor that topped anything in the journalism room. Decidedly more organic, and wafting from the custodian's person. I decided to risk everything and steal another cup; coffee held squarely under my nose might provide some degree of masking.

Pitts leered at me as I went into the kitchen and randomly grabbed a cup. "You stole Mrs. P.'s cup awhile ago, didn't you?" he called. "She was gonna have my hide, but she's always trying to get something on me. I'm beginning to think she doesn't like me—ha, ha."

I couldn't bring myself to join in the merriment, so I settled for a vague smile. I returned to the sofa and tried to look pensive. Pitts watched me for a few minutes, then picked up a bucket and ambled into the ladies room, his motives unknown.

The lounge door opened once more. A man and woman came in, laughing uproariously at some private joke. The man was dressed in tweeds, complete with leather elbow patches. His light brown hair was stylishly trim and his goatee tidy. My late husband had been a college professor, and I was familiar with the pose. I wryly noted the stem of a pipe poking out of his coat pocket.

The woman had no aspirations to the academic role. Her black hair tumbled down to her shoulders, and her makeup was more than adequate for a theater stage or a dark alley. She wore a red dress and spike heels. She was dressed for a gala night on the town. At eleven-thirty in the morning, no less.

The two filled coffee cups (I hadn't stolen theirs, apparently) and came in to study me.

"*Cogito, ergo sum* Sherwood Timmons," the man said with a deep bow. "Or I think that's who I am. Who might you be?"

"Claire Malloy, for Miss Parchester."

The woman's smile vanished. "I'm Evelyn West, French. In case you missed it, Sherwood's Latin—and other dead languages. We're all so upset about Emily's forced vacation. Weiss was rash to assume her errors were intentional."

"Anything Weiss does must be taken *cum grano salis,*" Sherwood added as he sat down across from me. "So you're our newest of our little gang, Claire. How are you doing with the *profanum vulgus?*"

Evelyn kicked him, albeit lightly. "Sherwood has a very bad habit of thinking himself amusing when he lapses into Latin. I've tried to convince him that he's merely insufferable, but he continues to torment us." She added something in French. Although I do not speak the language, the essential profanity of it was unmissable. He laughed, she laughed, we all laughed. Even Pitts, who had slithered out of the ladies room, made a croaking noise.

"Hiya, Mr. Timmons, Miz West," he added in an obsequious voice. "Say, Mrs. P. is mad at me again, but I didn't do nothing. Could you see if you could maybe stop her before she goes to Mr. Weiss?"

"Part of the reason she's upset is that you did precisely nothing last night, including clean the classroom floors, empty the trashcans, or wipe down the chalkboards. It's beginning to disturb even me, Pitts, and I vowed on my grandmother's grave that I would be kind to children and dumb animals."

"*Quis custodiet ipsos custodes?*" Sherwood murmured.

Pitts smirked. "I like that, Mr. Timmons. What does it mean?"

"Who will guard the guards themselves. In your case, Arm Pitts, it loosely refers to who might be induced to clean the unclean."

Pitts snatched up his tools of the trade. "That ain't funny, Mr. Timmons. It's not easy to keep this place clean, you know. The students aren't the only dirty people around here. Some of the teachers ain't too sanitary—especially in their personal lives." He stomped out of the lounge, muttering to himself.

"Arm Pitts?" I inquired, wrinkling my nose.

Evelyn began to fan the air with a magazine. "Rather hard to miss the allusion, even in Latin. Pitts is a horrid, filthy man; no one can begin to fathom why Weiss allows him to keep the job. The supply room is around the corner from the lounge, and rumor has it that Pitts has enough hooch to open a retail liquor store. The cigarette smoke is thick enough to permeate the walls. Who knows what he peddles to some of our less innocent students while Weiss conveniently looks the other way."

"Tell me about Mr. Weiss," I suggested. If for no other reason, I needed to know the enemy.

"Herbert Weiss," Sherwood said, "is a martinet of the worst ilk. The man has the charm of a veritable *anguis in herba.*"

"Sherwood," Evelyn began ominously, "you——"

"A snake in the grass," he translated, a pitying smile twitching the tip of his goatee. "In any case, Farberville High has survived more than ten years of his reign of terror, but this year he has become noticeably *non compos mentis*—to the *maximus.*"

"That's true," Evelyn added. "I've been here four years, and I have noticed a change for the worse this fall. In the past, Weiss has remained behind his office door, doing God knows what but at least avoiding the staff. Now he roams the hall like Hamlet's daddy, peering into classrooms, interfering with established procedure, and generally paying attention to things he has never before bothered with."

"Perhaps he's up for a promotion," I said. "Often that produces an attempt at efficiency."

"We've toyed with that theory," Sherwood said. "Of course, that means we'd have Miss Dort as the captain of our ship. In any case, I shall escape through my muse."

"Sherwood is writing the definitive work on parallels between the primitive forest deities and the Bible," Evelyn said. "If he can get it published, he hopes to scurry into an ivy tower and teach those who strive for a modicum of academic pretentions."

The author stiffened. "I've had some interest shown by several university presses. My manuscript is well over a thousand pages now, but I hope to complete it for formal submission before the end of this semester. It is, and I speak modestly, *sui generis*. In a class by itself."

When Sherwood the infant had lisped his first word, it hadn't been modestly. However, I found the two amusing and civilized, especially in comparison to the others. I inquired about the woman whose coffee cup I had stolen.

"So you've met the Furies on your travels," Sherwood said gleefully. "Alecto, Tisiphone and Megaera apply their stings to those who have escaped public retribution. Guardians of the FHS code of morality, our dear Eumenides."

"They don't like Sherwood," Evelyn said with a shrug. "They suspect him of saying rude things, but none of them understands Latin. They're right, of course."

On that note, the Furies trooped into the lounge in a precise vee formation. The coffee cup was presumably sterile, its owner assured that my germs would not mingle with her own. But from their expressions (cold and leery), they were not sure that I wouldn't pull another vile prank in the immediate future.

Evelyn said, "This is Claire Malloy, who is subbing for Emily. Claire, this is Mrs. Platchett, chairman of the business department. On her left, Miss Bagby, who teaches sophomore biology, and on her right, Miss Zuckerman, who teaches business."

I stood up in an attempt to elicit forgiveness. "I'm pleased to meet you, and I'm truly sorry about using the coffee cup."

Mrs. Platchett remained unmoved by my gesture. "As Mae can tell you, certain microbes can cause great distress for those of us with delicate constitutions, although the carrier can remain unaffected. Will you be able to bring a cup from home, or shall I use our little lounge fund to purchase one for you?"

"I'll bring one tomorrow." It seemed time for a new subject. "So you teach with Paula Hart? I met her here during the homeroom period."

"Miss Hart's class was unusually rowdy this morning," Mrs. Platchett said in an icy voice. "I should have realized she was remiss in her homeroom obligations. It is hardly surprising to learn she was not even there."

The thin woman flared her nostrils in sympathy. "I noticed the noise across the hall, Alexandria, but I assumed Miss Hart was doing her inept best to control the class. It is often impossible to teach over the uproarious laughter from her room."

Typing wasn't all that much fun, but I didn't point that out. Nor did I mention the lovers' tryst that was obviously scheduled in advance for optimum privacy.

Sherwood stood up and straightened his tie. "Pitts said you were on his case, Alexandria. Did you follow through or was it an idle threat?"

"I shall presume, Mr. Timmons, that you are asking if I spoke to Mr. Weiss about Pitts's shameful neglect of the basement classrooms. I did, although Mr. Weiss seemed unimpressed. He did agree to have a word with the man, but I doubt we shall see a substantial improvement in the future."

Evelyn joined Sherwood in the doorway. "The only word that might help would be 'fired.' In the meantime, I have a portable vacuum cleaner that I'll gladly share."

Sherwood bowed. "In any case, ladies, *carpe diem*. Or to translate loosely in accordance with the current debasement of the English language, have a nice day." With a wink, he strolled out of the lounge.

"T"H"R"E"E"

For the next fifty minutes, I huddled on the mauve-and-green sofa, trying to provoke appendicitis or something equally time-consuming. The best I could do was a sneeze, hardly worthy of hospitalization.

The Furies took plastic containers from the refrigerator and settled around the formica table. Mrs. Platchett opened hers warily, as if suspecting it had been booby-trapped to explode.

"It seems to be untouched," she sniffed after a lengthy examination. "If Pitts has been poking in it, he left no fingerprints."

The diminutive one gave the contents of her container the same careful scrutiny. "Mine appears intact, also, but I doubt that carrot sticks and broccoli spears might take fingerprints. The idea is enough to induce nausea, Alexandria. I'm not at all sure I can eat today."

"Nonsense, Tessa! You must eat, and you know it. Your doctor was most precise in the dietary orders." Mrs. Platchett picked up a sandwich, and they all began to chew the precise number of times for optimum digestibility. Termites do the same thing, I understand, but more quietly.

Paula Hart came by and offered to share her salad with me. Preferring to remain the martyr to the very end—and unsure if lettuce took fingerprints—I declined, and she left to munch greens in more congenial surroundings, or to peel grapes for the assistant coach with the dimples. Chomping steadily, the Furies failed to acknowledge her brief appearance.

I finally decided to return to the cave to sulk without sound effects. As I rose, Miss Dort darted into the lounge. "Here you are, Mrs. Malloy. I went by the journalism room, but you were not there."

I certainly couldn't argue with that. "I was on my way there," I said. "The daily unit delineation book is more thrilling than a gothic romance, and I wanted to settle down with it for a few minutes before the next class."

Miss Dort perched her glasses on her nose to peer at me. "Indeed, Mrs. Malloy. I wanted to remind you to turn in your blue slips with your attendance slips each period. They are vital." She went into the kitchenette and came out with a square plastic box. "So sorry I can't eat with you ladies today. The paperwork is piled sky-high on my desk, and of course I must prepare for the arrival of the auditors from the state Department of Education."

Mrs. Platchett washed down a masticated mouthful. "Bernice, I want you to realize how distressed I am by this sordid affair. Emily is quite innocent; she would never touch a penny of the school's money. The idea is preposterous."

The one I thought was Mae Bagby nodded. "Emily Parchester has served the students of Farberville High School for forty years, and her reputation remained unblemished until yesterday."

The third Fury, who had dozed off, opened her eyes to add her support. "Her father was Judge Amos Parchester of the state Supreme Court, Bernice. That bears comment."

Miss Dort could read the storm signals as well as I. "The auditors will see," she murmured as she started out the door. She halted and looked at me over her shoulder. "Teachers meeting this afternoon, three-thirty in the cafetorium."

"What?" I sputtered. I had other plans for that time. I fully intended to be on the heels of the last student out the door. If I was agile enough, I might be on his toes.

Three heads swiveled to stare at me. "We always have a teachers meeting the third Thursday of the month," Mrs. Platchett informed me coldly. "It is a tradition that has survived for a very long time at Farberville High School." And no whippersnapper was going to disrupt it if she had any say in the matter.

I did not care if she had ridden a brontosaurus to the first meeting. I cared about escape, a hot bath, and a world populated by adults with minimal interest in education. I opened my mouth to protest, but Miss Dort had sailed away to her paperwork, smug in the knowledge that I was neatly trapped. I rather wished I knew a Latin expletive; my Anglo-Saxon ones would have caused a three-cornered swoon.

The bell rang in the middle of my decorous growl. I ambled down the hallway in time to shoo a few stragglers into the cave, then forced myself to follow them. My darling daughter was perched on the desk like a leprechaun on a toadstool.

"How's it going, Mother?" she chirped.

I pushed her off the desk and pointed at a girl with frizzy hair. "You, what's your name?"

"Bambi McQueen, Mrs. Malloy."

"On your birth certificate?"

"Yes, ma'am. I'm the student editor for the *Falcon Crier,* and your fourth-period aide."

I tossed the roster book to her. "Take role, send in the attendance slip and the little blue things, and then tell everybody what to do."

"But, Mrs. Malloy, if the newspaper isn't going to come out next week, then I don't know what to tell everybody. Should we just read or something, or should we go ahead and do assignments for the paper anyway?"

I glared at Caron as I spoke to the cervine whiner. "I don't care what you do, Bambi. I hope not to be here more than a few days; thus I have no interest in your academic progress, the next issue of the newspaper, or your interim activities. Think of something to amuse yourselves."

The candor perplexed her. She chewed on her lower lip for a long minute, gauging the potential limits. "Maybe some of us should go to the printer's to let him know that the newspaper won't come out as scheduled?" she suggested.

I flipped a hand. "By all means, let us not keep the poor man in suspense."

Bambi and ten eager volunteers dashed for the door. When we were alone, Caron flopped down in a desk. "That was dumb, Mother. They just wanted to leave the campus; they could have called the printer. Seniors!"

"They may drive to the West Coast, for all I care. I have to devise a way to avoid a barbaric tradition known as a teachers meeting—this afternoon after school."

"What about Miss Parchester? Have you figured out who framed her yet?"

"I have been here slightly more than five hours. For some inexplicable reason, students keep appearing in the room in droves, expecting to be supervised if not regaled with mature insights. An opportunity to figure out who, if anyone, framed Miss Parchester has not yet arisen. I need an excuse to avoid the teachers meeting."

"Have you met Mr. Weiss or any of the teachers?" Caron said without a flicker of sympathy for my plight. The child knew nothing of meetings; her day would come. Of death, taxes, and committees, I preferred the first two.

I ran through the list of those I had encountered during the morning. When I mentioned Miss Hart and her coach, Caron interrupted with a noisy sigh.

"Aren't they the cutest couple? Miss Hart used to date Mr. Timmons, but he wouldn't marry her so she could have babies.

When she saw Coach Finley, it was love at first sight, and now everyone except Mr. Timmons knows that they're secretly engaged." More sighs.

"How do you know all this?"

"This is a school, not a monastery, Mother. Do you want to hear what Mr. Timmons said when he found out that Miss Hart was dating Coach Finley? It was in Latin, but it was still dirty."

"No, I don't. This zoo may be a microcosm of society, but I have no desire to delve into its social interactions." I sat down behind the desk and produced a few sighs of my own. "I suppose I'll have to stay after school for this silly meeting. You can go home and cook dinner."

"But what about the newspaper—and Miss Parchester?"

There was that. I shrugged and said, "The accounts are not here; Miss Dort must have them in her office. Even if I had some idea of what to do with them—and I don't—I haven't seen them. I don't know the procedure for depositing money or writing checks to pay bills."

Caron gathered up her books and purse. "Ask Miss Hart. She's the cheerleader and drill-team sponsor, the business club sponsor and the senior class advisor, so she deals with oodles of club accounts. I'm going to the library, Mother." She left with the briskness of a Dort.

I picked up a copy of the *Falcon Crier* from the previous month and flipped through the pages. Miss Demeanor was on the second page, which was dated October 22.

Dear Miss Demeanor,
My boyfriend wants to take me to a fancy French restaurant for our one-month anniversary. He wants to order champagne, but the waiter probably won't serve us. What should we do—walk out?

Dear Reader,
Miss Demeanor must sympathize. Coq au vin does not go well

with coke au cola. However, Miss Demeanor prefers to cater to her stomach before she caters to her sense of injustice. Eat, pay the bill, and then walk out. That will show 'em.

Dear Miss Demeanor,
    Two boys have asked me to the homecoming dance next week, and I don't know which one to say yes to. One of them has pimples, but he also has a neat car. The other one is really foxy, but he barfed on my dress at the September Mixer. I'm not sure I'd feel safe with him anywhere near. Besides, I have a really nifty new dress. What do you think?

Dear Reader,
    How much did the dress cost? How much did the neat car cost? How much will the dry cleaners cost? If you can't figure it out, sign up for general math.

Dear Miss Demeanor,
    The reason I was at the Xanadu Motel was because I was following the married man. His wife has brown hair, but the woman he was with didn't. What do you think about that?

Dear Reader,
    Nothing at all. Why should I? For that matter, why should you? There are at least three people more qualified than either of us to ponder the situation.

    Puzzled, I folded the *Falcon Crier* and stuffed it into Miss Parchester's middle drawer. The first two letters sounded like typical adolescent stuff, but the third had an edge that neared nastiness. I wondered why Miss Demeanor had bothered with it. I wondered where the Xanadu Motel was, and who would want to go there. I then dismissed the muddle to wonder if there were any way to disappear at three-thirty without risking the wrath of Bernice Dort.
    The bell rang once again, and shortly thereafter the room swelled with Photo II, a.k.a. the newspaper photographers. We exchanged the necessary courtesies and they managed to talk among themselves until the class was over. Ho hum. Teaching wasn't all that hard.

My last (thank God) class was the mysterious "Falconnaire." Although I was less than frantic for an explanation, I was mildly curious. Once the dozen or so students were seated, I asked them.

"The Falconnaire is the yearbook," said a blond girl with the body of a lingerie model. Her blouse did little to discourage the comparison; buttons were nearly bursting out all over. She made no effort to hide a broad yawn as she added, "I don't think we can do anything until they find a replacement for our embezzling teacher."

"What's your name?" I said peevishly. Now I was going to have to withstand the compulsion to yawn for fifty minutes.

"Cheryl Anne Weiss," she said. When I failed to react with any visible astonishment, she produced a pout of superiority. "My father happens to be the principal of Farberville High School."

"That's right," grunted a hulking form in the back of the room. "Cheryl Anne's daddy is the king of this dump. She's kinda like a princess."

I tried a stern, teacherish frown. "What's your name—Prince Albert?"

"Theodore Immerman, ma'am; everybody calls me Thud. I'm in charge of the sports section of the yearbook, if there is a yearbook. Are you gonna take Parchester's place and tell us what to do, or just take the rest of the money?" Smirk, smirk.

"Why are you so sure Miss Parchester is guilty, Mr. Immerman? Isn't it possible that there was a simple error on someone's part?"

His massive shoulders rose like snowy Alps. "I don't know, ma'am. I just know she had the checkbook, and now the money is gone. I sure as hell didn't write myself any bonuses."

The class tittered nervously, but Thud seemed pleased with his little joke. It was, I decided, in keeping with his intellectual capacity. A girl in the front row murmured that they could continue to organize the layout of the sophomore pictures, even though Miss Parchester was not available to supervise them.

I rewarded her with the roster, instructed the class to busy themselves with the layout of said pictures, and went to the cabinet to find more copies of the *Falcon Crier*. The Miss Demeanor column was quite clever for a postpubescent mind, although I wasn't sure if the ailing Rosie had written the examples before her quarantine, or if my daughter had done so. The coq au vin was a bit startling; the only chicken Caron had eaten at my dining-room table arrived in a cardboard bucket, an original recipe but not of mine.

Before I could dig out a copy of the newspaper, an argument broke out on one side of the room. Cheryl Anne Weiss was not happy with darling Thud, nor he with her.

"I can't do it!" the blond girl squealed. Her ponytail swung around her head to flop across her eyes, and she swung it back with a practiced hand and an equally practiced scowl.

"You said you could, dammit!" Thud thundered. "You swore that he wouldn't yank my eligibility!"

"He won't listen to me, Thud. I tried as hard as I could, but now I don't know what to do. I'll think of something else."

I slammed the cabinet door to get their attention. "Excuse me for disturbing you, but the discussion will have to be postponed until after class. I left my whistle at home."

Thud's simian brow sank until his eyes were barely visible, and his lips crept out. Cheryl Anne, on the other hand, gave him an impertinent sneer and flounced back to her desk. The ponytail and other things wiggled with disdain. The rest of the students resumed their whispers, feigning no interest whatsoever in the argument.

I decided to forego the newspaper and spent the rest of the period preventing a holocaust in the cave. Thud and Cheryl Anne exchanged numerous dark looks and made numerous inarticulate and threatening noises, but restrained themselves from further verbal combat. I kept the maternal frown on full power until the bell finally rang and I could send them away. As the two met in the doorway, they resumed their argument. I could hear them all the way down the hall, but I didn't care. It was three-twenty-five.

The cafetorium was at the far end of the first floor. I found a seat toward the rear, smiled vaguely at those around me, and prepared for utter tedium. Other teachers looked equally excited. The Furies marched in and took possession of the front row; Miss Hart and Coach Finley slipped in to sit in the row behind me. Evelyn and Sherwood joined me seconds later, looking like naughty children who had come straight from the cookie jar. Sherwood bowed slightly and gave me a broad wink.

Mr. Weiss strode to the front of the room, with Miss Dort on his tailwind. He snapped at her to take attendance (to whom would she send it?) and glowered until she made her way from "Aaron" to a final "Zuckerman." All were present.

"This will be short and to the point," he barked. "Item one: the schedule for Homecoming activities is on the mimeograph Miss Dort will distribute, along with the names of dance chaperones and stadium-concession supervisors. There will be no changes, tradeoffs, or excuses. If your name is there, be there. Thirty minutes early."

Miss Dort snapped to attention and passed out the pale purple mimeographs, eyeing us challengingly. When she arrived in the rear, she curled her lips at me. "You'll cover for Parchester at the dance, Mrs. Malloy," she whispered with the expression of a barracuda swimming alongside a cellulitic snorkler. I managed a nod.

Mr. Weiss tapped his foot until Miss Dort finished her chore and scurried back to his side. "Item two: the auditors will be here next week to examine every club ledger, along with the journalism account and our general accounts. I want records in my office tomorrow morning before home room. I want copies of expenditures for the previous year. I want a list of deposits and checks for this semester—in duplicate. Your books had better balance to the last cent. No excuses."

A groan went down the rows, and a particularly unhappy one from Miss Hart behind me. According to Caron, she had oodles of accounts. No hot date that night. From Sherwood Timmons came a barely audible, "*Quem Deus vult perdere, prius dementat*—those whom the Gods wish to destroy, they first make mad. The man's a veritable draconian these days."

"Any questions?" Mr. Weiss said, looking over our heads.

Paula Hart raised her hand. "Mr. Weiss, the seniors are frantic to know what will happen with the yearbook. Several of the girls actually burst into tears in my room because they're so worried they won't have a memento of their final year."

To my surprise, Mr. Weiss did not roar at the insubordination. He located Miss Hart in the corner and smiled with all the sincerity of an airport missionary. "I have not reached a decision about the Falconnaire. The seniors would be concerned, naturally." He tugged on his chin, then glanced at Miss Dort. "Tell the substitute—ah, the Malloy woman—to get on with the yearbook, Bernice. Miss Hart and I wouldn't want our senior class to be disappointed, would we?"

"Wait a minute," the Malloy woman yelped. "I have no idea how to 'get on' with the yearbook. I don't make books; I sell them. They come ready made."

"The Falconnaire staff can handle it," Miss Dort said firmly.

Paula Hart tapped me on the shoulder. "I'll help whenever I can, Mrs. Malloy, and I'm sure Coach Finley will, too." Jerry nodded without enthusiasm.

In the front of the room, Mr. Weiss's expression turned to stone. "Coach Finley may find himself occupied with other matters, Miss Hart. I received certain information today from Farber College that may shed a new light on Coach Finley's career at our school."

That earned a collective gasp, followed by furtive looks and whispers. Sherwood murmured, "Has Weiss made a *lapsus lingua*, do you think?" His comment earned a kick from Evelyn. "A slip of the tongue," he translated in a wounded tone as he rubbed his shin.

Jerry stood up, his hands on his hips like a playground combatant. His blue eyes were circles of slate, his dimples tucked away for the moment. "What's that supposed to mean, Mr. Weiss?"

"That means, Mr. Assistant Coach Finley, that you and I shall have a long conversation as soon as the auditors are gone."

"As long as I have your attention, Mr. Weiss," Jerry continued tightly, "what about Immerman's eligibility? He said you refused to consider a temporary suspension of the rule until midsemester grades are in. That means he can't play in the Homecoming game. Our policy says that—"

"I am aware of our school policy. I do not need a first year assistant coach to explain it to me, nor do I care to engage in an argument about my decisions. Immerman is no longer eligible to participate in extracurricular activities, in that his grades are below one point two five. Is that clear?"

"As clear as mud, Mr. Weiss!" Our gray-clad hero stormed out of the room without a parting glance for Miss Hart, who seemed on the verge of a collapse. Beside me, Evelyn looked grim, but Sherwood Timmons was battling not to snicker too loudly. I considered a kick, but opted for a glower.

"*Dum spiro, spero,*" he said, shrugging. "While I breathe, I hope."

"Shut up, Sherwood," Evelyn hissed. She looked back at Paula Hart. "Don't worry about it, honey. Once the auditors arrive, Weiss will forget all about this. But in the meantime, keep Jerry away from him."

Paula's eyes filled with tears, but she bravely held them back. "Jerry doesn't deserve to be abused, and it's not fair," she said in true pioneer-woman fashion.

Miss Dort cleared her throat. "One final item, please! Today I noticed a marked increase in the flow of students in the hallways during class, especially from the basement. Any student who leaves your room for any reason must have a blue slip with the current date, room of origin, destination, and your signature. Is that clear?"

Oh, dear. How slipshod some teacher must be to allow students to roam the hallways without blue slips. I slumped down and stared at my ankles, which are trim and appealing. When those around me began to shuffle, I presumed it was safe and stood up.

Evelyn accompanied me to the sunless labyrinth of the basement. "By the way, Claire," she said as I turned toward the cave door, "on Fridays we have a potluck lunch in the lounge. The Furies, Paula and Jerry, the Latin pedant, and whoever else drops by. Sherwood considers it a prime opportunity to needle any and all of the aforementioned, but you mustn't pay any attention to him."

"I haven't yet," I said. "I understand from the gossip that he and Paula used to—to, ah . . ."

She laughed. "For almost three years, Sherwood had a jewel, and he knew it. She did his tax returns, balanced his personal checkbook and that of the Latin Club, edited and typed his manuscript, and did almost everything a devoted wife would do for her hubby. All in hopes, I'm afraid, that he would marry her so that she could quit teaching and start reproducing in a vine-covered cottage."

"Then Jerry showed up?" I said encouragingly. I will admit to a flicker of shame for encouraging gossip. A teensy flicker. Curiosity snuffed it.

"He strolled into the first staff meeting of the year in his saggy gray sweats, his blond hair flopping in his eyes and his boyish grin just a shade shy. Paula melted; she hasn't recovered since."

"Was Sherwood devastated by the loss of free labor?" I was now utterly shameless, and I scolded myself without mercy as I panted for further details.

"More irritated than devastated, I believe. He does sulk whenever the lovebirds coo too loudly in the lounge, but other than that, he seems to have recovered. He may think he can persuade me to take over her duties."

"Is that possible?" Pant, pant.

"As the kids would say, no way. I was married once upon a time, to a tool salesman from Toledo. During the first trimester of newly wedded bliss, I had the opportunity to meet two of his other wives. And I thought bigamy was reserved for Mormons!" Laughing, she waved and clicked away down the hall.

I picked up a bundle of old *Falcon Criers* and started for the stairs and a dose of scotch. As I passed the teachers lounge, I heard loud voices from its interior.

"Jerry," Paula said with surprising vehemence, "there's nothing he can do to you. Even if he does fire you, there are lots of coaching jobs in other schools. It'll be okay."

"He's a damn tyrant. How in the hell did he ever get hold of my transcript, anyway? I'm doing a good job with the team. Fred thinks I'm a good assistant coach, and so do the boys. We have a chance at the district title, Paula. Fred's talking about retiring at the end of the school year, which means I could take over the head coach position. We could afford to get married!"

"Oh, Jerry," she sighed.

Conversation halted. Anyone with an ounce of scrupulosity would have tiptoed away, and allowed the two to do whatever they were doing in private. I edged closer to the door.

Jerry came up for air. "Somebody ought to do something about Weiss. Maybe I'm the somebody."

"What can you do? He already knows about your past, and he's probably told Miss Dort. She'll tell the Furies, and they'll broadcast it to God." Paula was trying to sound stern and sensible.

"I'll think of something." Jerry merely sounded angry.

Wincing, I opted to retreat before the door opened and my nose was creased. I turned around and ran into Sherwood Timmons, who was wiggling his eyebrows like venetian blinds.

"Trouble in paradise?" he murmured, noticeably undistressed. "Could there be some bone of contention between the two?"

"I have no idea. I came by to see if I left a folder in the lounge."

"And were prevented ingress by our Echo and Narcissus? Did you catch them in *flagrante delicto*?"

Evelyn had the right idea—and the right shoes—to deal with Sherwood. I gave him a quick frown and went around the corner to go upstairs, but he followed like a faithful old dog. Or a slobbering old bloodhound. I gave up and stopped.

"Yes, Mr. Timmons? Was there something else?"

He backed me into a corner, close enough for me to smell a hint of wintergreen on his breath. "Would you be interested in a peek at the journalism accounts, Mrs. Malloy?"

We had found the darkest corner of the basement, which was no sunlit meadow to begin with. I dared not glance at the ceiling, due to a phobia of bats and other rabid creatures, including men in goatees.

I put a finger on his chest to remove him from my face. "Why would I be interested in a peek at the journalism accounts, Mr. Timmons? I'm a substitute teacher, not a CPA."

He leaned forward and propped an arm on the wall above me. "Ah, but in reality you are a bookseller—not a substitute teacher. It's rather obvious why you've come to Farberville High School, my dear literary peddler. Your reputation precedes you."

"What reputation might that be?"

"As our local amateur sleuth, dear woman. I'm sure all your activities were *pro bono publico*—"

"If you say one more syllable in Latin, I will yank off your goatee to use as a mascara brush. I will then apply my foot to your *gluteus maximus*."

"My apologies; I shall do my utmost to restrain myself. Now, about your purpose for infiltrating our little school, Mrs. Malloy. May I call you Claire? It's obvious that you're on an undercover mission to expose the financial diddlings."

"It is? Perhaps I'm here to help out until a replacement can be found for Miss Parchester. Civic responsibility, a commitment to education of our youth, that sort of thing."

He chuckled at my silly attempt. "You're here to snoop around and discover our closet embezzler, Claire. You need not be ashamed. In truth, it's quite admirable. That's why I offered to help you get your lovely hands on the journalism accounts."

As a Mata Hari, I was not good. As a loser in the skirmish of wits, I could at least struggle for a graceful concession. "Where are the journalism ledgers? When I couldn't find them in the journalism room, I presumed Miss Dort locked them away in the office for the auditors."

Sherwood put a hand in his pocket and pulled out a key. "She did, but that needn't stop us. Shall we say tonight at midnight? The two of us, tiptoeing through the darkened hallways lit only by shafts of moonlight, our hearts pounding wildly yet in unison as we approach our shadowy destination?"

A door opened across the hall. Pitts smirked and said, "I'm supposed to fumigate the offices tonight, kids. Try a motel, or the backseat of a car." The door closed with a soft squeak.

"Do you think he heard the entire conversation?" I gulped.

Sherwood took my elbow to steer me up the stairs to the land of the living. "Pitts has an ear to every wall and a finger in every cesspool. Luckily, he is too much the resident troglodyte to use the information wisely."

"Well, we can't get into the office tonight," I said, relieved. My conscience (a.k.a. duty to Miss Parchester) prodded me to add, "I suppose we could try tomorrow night. Midnight seems overly furtive; shall we say ten o'clock?"

Sherwood agreed, although he looked vaguely disappointed by my more prosaic suggestion. In the parking lot, he hopped into a red sports car and roared away in a cloud of dust. I chugged home, left my purse on the living room floor, and headed for the nectar of the gods. And I don't mean apricot juice.

"F"O"U"R"

I felt obliged to appear the next day at dear old FHS. Miss
Parchester had telephoned the previous evening; I had admitted
failure and defeat, rather hoping she would tell me to forget the
silly scheme. She had wished me luck.

The cave was hardly home sweet home, but the aroma was
familiar. When the homeroom bell emptied the hall, I took my
personalized coffee cup (I had scratched an *M* on the bottom,
as in "mindless") to the lounge, left a box of saltines and a package of cream cheese in the refrigerator (I hate potlucks), and
filled my cup (I need caffeine). All this was accomplished in semi-
solitude. A mute Fury came and went, but the lounge lovebirds
apparently had found another place to wish each other good
morning.

I returned to the cave in time to greet the first class. They
chattered, I read, and the bell rang. The second-period class came
on schedule. I had just counted noses and settled them down
when the door opened, and Miss Parchester tiptoed in. She wore
a baggy blue coat, a plastic rain scarf, and galoshes. She had an
umbrella in one hand, but it may have had more sinister applica-
tions than protection from the elements. For the record, the sky
had been blue and cloudless when I went underground earlier.

"I thought I'd drop by to see if I might help you in any way,"
she murmured apologetically. "You mentioned that the Falcon-

naire would be published as scheduled. Perhaps I can offer a few words of advice."

"Ah, thank you, Miss Parchester," I said. "But are you sure you ought to be here? Mr. Weiss might be upset if he knew you. . . ."

She clasped her hands over her bosom as her eyes began to fill with tears. The umbrella swished past my nose with only an inch to spare. "I so wanted to visit, Mrs. Malloy, if only to see my dear students for a brief moment."

Her dear students were gaping like guppies, their eyes unblinking and their little mouths opening and closing silently. I took her elbow and escorted her into the darkroom. "I'm not sure this is wise, Miss Parchester. I appreciate your offer to help with the yearbook, but I don't want you to jeopardize the situation. It really might be better for you to slip away before anyone else notices you."

She gazed up at me. Her breath would have pickled a cucumber at one hundred feet, and her eyes were etched with fine red lines. I realized she had tied one on since breakfast, no doubt with her blessed mother and the Judge in attendance. Her sorrowful smile was interrupted by a hiccup.

"Oh, dear." She covered her mouth with her hand. "I must have sipped my tea too quickly in my haste to visit you."

"Oh, dear," I echoed weakly. "Let me bring you a cup of coffee from the lounge, Miss Parchester. Black coffee, I think."

She caught my arm in a birdlike claw. "I much prefer"—hic—"tea, dear. Coffee does stain one's dentures. You're much too young to worry about that, but we senior citizens must be careful."

I was aging rapidly; gray hairs were popping out each second I remained in the darkroom with the tipsy trespasser. "One cup of coffee won't do any permanent damage. Trust me. Now, if you'll promise to sit on this stool—"

"You're too kind," she said, shifting from manic to maudlin with amazing ease. "It's been so dreadful these last few days. Everyone must think I'm a common criminal, a petty thief with no conscience. I am beginning to wonder if I might have made an error—although I must assure you it was done in innocence. I—" She broke off with a helpless quiver.

"I'm sure any error was unintentional, Miss Parchester. Please let me bring you a cup of coffee. Please."

She shook her head as she dug through her purse for a hand-kerchief. We were seconds away from a deluge that was apt to result in a forty-day cruise. Black coffee, in quantity. Immediately. I opened the door, but again the claw stopped me.

"I shall go to the lounge on my way out of the building," she said. "I brought a jar of my brandied peach compote for Mr. Weiss. He is terribly fond of it, and I thought he might enjoy it even if—if—it was brought by a common thief!" She squared her shoulders, lifted her chin, gave me a jaunty wave, and weaved through the door. A hiccup sufficed for a farewell.

The guppies and I watched her coattail disappear around the corner. I frowned warningly, and they began to whisper among themselves. Miss Parchester's brief appearance would not remain a secret, nor would her condition. The peach compote was not the only thing with a slug of brandy in it.

Thirty minutes later the bell rang. I went down the hall to the teachers lounge, aware that I was apt to find Miss Parchester snoring on a sofa. The room was empty. I refilled my coffee cup and sat down on the mauve-and-green to think of a way to salvage the poor woman's reputation.

Evelyn came out of the ladies room. "That room is filthier every day. Pitts is impossible; I wish Weiss would do something about finding a replacement."

"Did you happen to see Miss Parchester in here earlier?" I waited to hear whether the woman in question was asleep in a stall in the ladies room—or worse.

"Oh, my God, is she in the building? Weiss will have a tantrum if he finds out. He's in a foul mood today, and——"

A thin young woman rushed into the lounge. She pulled a tissue from her pocket and began to wipe furiously at her dripping eyes. Small, muffled sobs came from under the tissue. I stared at the display of misery, unsure how to offer comfort or aid. Before I could decide, the woman crammed the tissue in her pocket and flew out the door.

"My student teacher," Evelyn explained. "She is no match for the French II class. They get her every day at about this time."

"And she wants to be a teacher?"

"When she grows up. I didn't see poor Miss Parchester, so we can hope she left before Weiss spotted her. Are you ready for our weekly potluck free-for-all?"

I admitted that my preparations had extended only to a stop at the grocery store on my way to school. A brief stop, at that.

Evelyn shook her finger at me. "The Furies live for the whoosh of the Tupperware containers on Friday, Claire. Our little luncheons are a major part of their social activities—those and chaperoning the school dances. What a life."

"I'm supposed to be chaperone!" I buried my face in my hands. "Miss Dort informed me that I was to appear in Miss Parchester's place. I tried to block it out."

"Don't worry about it. All you have to do is keep the kiddies sober and celibate, the band from undressing or eating their instruments, and the roof from collapsing. Don't forget earplugs— and shin guards, in case one of the sophomore boys asks you to dance."

"Asks me to dance? I trust you're making a little joke, Evelyn. I would no more dance with a sophomore boy than I would balance a desk on my nose while chanting the Koran."

"They make book on it in the boys' bathroom. I believe it's some sort of primitive rite of passage. I was worth ten dollars.

The Furies, on the other hand, run into larger sums, thus far unclaimed."

"I don't intend to be a substitute for more than a few days. Miss Dort is searching for a certified teacher to replace me. I may take out an ad in the *New York Times*." I sank back in the bilious plaid. "Tell me about the Furies, Evelyn. I can't seem to keep them straight."

"Only Bernice can do that. They are equally drab, tedious, and morally superior. They kept Paula in tears for months, but she finally learned to stand up to them or simply ignore them."

"Why are they so hard on her?"

"She has made two very serious breaches of conduct in the lounge. For one thing, she has committed the sin of being young and pretty. The girls all adore her, and the boys can barely breathe when she bends over someone's typewriter in the classroom. Her second sin is to encourage Jerry to come in the lounge."

"He's a teacher, isn't he? Why shouldn't he come in the lounge with the rest of us?"

"He is also a coach. Coaches do not come into the lounge; they loiter in their offices or on the fields. It's an unwritten law that coaches and principals avoid the lounge. Coaches are inclined to smell of physical exertion, and principals are the topic of many conversations. Weiss has been lurking in here since the beginning of the semester, mostly in order to glower at Jerry and Paula."

"I thought Sherwood——"

"Herbert Weiss is a notorious lecher, despite a vague presence known as Mrs. Herbert Weiss. She materializes each year for fifteen minutes at the faculty Christmas party, where she smiles politely at everyone, and then vanishes until the following December. I doubt she has any effect on her husband or daughter."

"Does every male in the building have his eye on Paula?" I asked. "It sounds ominously competitive."

"As far as I know, Weiss and Sherwood are the primary contenders for the maiden's hand. To their regret, it is not available for warm, suggestive squeezes."

The door opened before I could elicit any more details of the idle, but nevertheless interesting, gossip. Sherwood Timmons had a bottle of champagne in his hand.

"I thought we might celebrate the arrival of blessed Friday," he announced as he went into the kitchenette and put the bottle in the refrigerator. "What is this? Could Emily Parchester have been sneaking around the basement this very morning, brandied peach compote bulging in her purse?"

"She came by to see me," I called. I did not elaborate, but it wasn't necessary.

Sherwood stuck his head out the door with an impish grin. "I heard she was a bit *non compos mentis,* but her compote—*sic itur ad astra* . . . her pathway to the stars."

"If Pitts hasn't been pawing in it," Evelyn said. "I think we ought to use the lounge fund to buy a padlock for the refrigerator."

"That would merely delay him," Sherwood said. The refrigerator door closed, and water ran in the sink. "The man could pick it with his teeth if motivation were strong enough."

While I pondered the wisdom of a diet, the door opened again. The Furies stalked in and took places on a sofa across from me. Miss Dort came in seconds later and continued into the ladies room. Mr. Weiss was next, followed by Jerry and Paula Hart.

Large, black clouds rolled in from the hallway. Lightning crackled invisibly, and thunder crashed soundlessly. The air was thick with odorless ozone. What air there was. I wondered if they really went through this every Friday, and for what reason. Fun, it clearly wasn't.

Evelyn stood up. "Well, shall we eat?"

Herbert Weiss stared at Jerry, who returned the gaze with ill-disguised anger. Paula tugged at her coach's hand and whispered

something in his ear, but he brushed her aside. Sherwood smiled
to himself. The Furies wiggled on the sofa and tried to look
uninterested.

"Shall we eat?" Evelyn repeated, a hostess to the bitter end.
"Claire, will you help me bring things to the table?"

I strolled into the kitchenette where I had to grab a drawer
handle to keep myself upright. "Why are we doing this?" I
hissed. "This is not my idea of a gala party."

Evelyn shrugged and began to pull plastic bowls and boxes out
of the refrigerator. She piled them in my arms, balanced a stack
of napkins on top, and sent me into the lion's den. She followed
with paper plates, the champagne, and someone's saltines.

With the high spirits of a funeral cortege, we assembled
around the table. Jerry sat down next to Paula at one end; the
Furies formed a row across one side, impenetrably grim. The rest
of us scattered about to act as buffers. Plastic lids whooshed
loudly in the silence.

Mrs. Platchett examined a tidy formation of deviled eggs. "I
see no sign that Pitts has been foraging today. It is safe to eat."

"Alcoholic beverages are not permitted on campus," Weiss
snarled, pointing at the offending bottle.

Sherwood gave him a disdainful smile. "Are we reduced to
following petty rules, Mr. Weiss? I presumed we were all above
such things, but if you wish to insist. . . ?"

"Do whatever you want, Timmons. Perhaps we can have a
discussion about your manuscript one of these days, if you're not
too busy doing research at the college library."

"*Ars longa, vita brevis,*" Sherwood snapped. It was menacing, in
an obscure way. He did not offer a translation, and for once
Evelyn did not prompt him to do so.

Weiss disappeared into the kitchenette. The soda machine rattled briefly, followed by a popping sound as a bottle was decapi-
tated. He then called, "Has Miss Parchester been in the building,

Bernice? I told her quite firmly that she was not to come back until the auditors have completed their investigation."

"I'll telephone to remind her," Miss Dort said. She picked up her clipboard and scribbled a note.

The Furies looked as though they were on the edge of a rebuttal. Mrs. Platchett eyed the doorway with a frown, and on both sides of her her cohorts flared their nostrils and tightened their lips. Tessa Zuckerman (I thought) actually opened her mouth for a fleeting moment, then closed it with an unhappy sigh. Her complexion seemed excessively gray, as though she were inflated with fog.

Weiss came to the doorway with the jar of compote in his hand. He took a fork to pull out a dripping piece of yellow fruit, and with a greedy look, plopped it in his mouth. "I suppose I'll overlook her presence in the building this one time, since she did leave a little something for me. I may regret Miss Parchester's absence in the future; her compote is remarkable. Is there any way we might persuade her to share the recipe, Bernice?"

"I shall inquire when I speak to her." Miss Dort picked up the clipboard and scribbled yet another note.

"Exactly how much money is missing from the journalism account?" Sherwood asked, giving me a conspiratorial wink. "Enough for riotous living in some singles' condominium for silver-haired swingers?"

"The amount is hardly the issue, Timmons. The funds belong to the students, and the embezzlement is all the more serious because it threatens their trust," Weiss said through a mouthful of yellow goop. "In any case, I am aware of the gossip this situation has generated, and I want the entire faculty to put a stop to it. It is an administrative concern."

"I am confident Emily will be found innocent of any wrongdoing," Mrs. Platchett said. "Then the school can return to its normal routine, and the journalism students can once again have valuable experience in preparation for their careers. Emily quite inspires them, as you well know."

I sensed an aspersion on the substitute's ability to inspire said students. "We're working industriously on the yearbook," I said, taking a deviled egg with a devil-may-care look. "We hope to complete the sophomore layout next week." Whatever that was.

"But we have no newspaper over which to chuckle," Sherwood said. "I was finding the Miss Demeanor column quite compelling, if not exactly Pulitzer material. Just as it was becoming most interesting, it was cut off in its prime. Of course, *humanum est errare,* but in the Xanadu Motel? One wonders if something might be astir within our little community. . . ."

"The insinuation of a tawdry scandal is inappropriate for a school newspaper," Miss Dort sniffed. "Mr. Weiss and I both agree that impressionable adolescents should not be exposed to that sort of thing. As faculty advisor, Miss Parchester had an obligation to forbid the publication of such filth. She refused to comply with the numerous memos I sent regarding the situation, citing some nonsense about freedom of the press. This is a school, not a democracy; the students have whatever rights we choose to allow them."

Weiss gave her an approving smile as he shoveled in the last of the peach compote. The smile died suddenly. He clutched his abdomen and doubled up as the contents of his stomach disgorged on the carpet. His scalp turned red, his face white. "Bernice," he managed to croak. "My God! Help me!"

"Herbert? What's—what's the matter?" she answered, shoving back her chair to run across the room and clasp his arm. She looked wildly at us over his back. "Do something to help him! Get a doctor!"

"I don't need a doctor," Weiss said abruptly, his voice weak but more normal than it had been seconds ago. He yanked his arm free and stood up, a handkerchief already in hand to wipe his chin. "I'm fine now. I don't know what came over me, but I certainly will not permit it to happen again. Have Pitts get in here immediately, and call the carpet cleaning service to make— reservations."

"Reservations?" Miss Dort said. She picked up her clipboard and began to write in precise little scratches, although without her usual briskness. "Carpet service—reservations. Why don't you lie down on the sofa for a few minutes, Mr. Weiss? You look rather pale."

He nodded and stretched out on the mauve-and-green. Miss Dort left the lounge, presumably to fetch the despicable Pitts, and returned within a minute or two. The rest of us toyed with our lunches, our earlier enthusiasm dampened by the increasingly pervasive stench. Even the Furies seemed to find it difficult to pick up the cadence of sound nutritional practices.

"Damn doctors shouldn't be allowed to teach," Weiss said suddenly, his finger poking holes in the air. "Think they're too damn good for the rest of us."

"I'll make a note of it," Miss Dort said, her voice noncommital despite the bizarre words coming from the principal. She stared defiantly at us, daring us to offer an editorial. No one moved.

"Bunch of copycats," Weiss said. He jerked up and glared at us through wide, glazed eyes. Suddenly they bulged like balloons as he clasped his throat. Burbling wildly, he clawed the air. His hands froze, and he slowly rolled off the sofa to sprawl on the rug.

Miss Dort scrambled to her feet and shrieked something about an ambulance as she ran out of the lounge. Paula grabbed Jerry, while Sherwood and Evelyn went over to touch the unmoving shoulder with timid fingers. Mrs. Platchett clasped her bosom.

"Oh, my goodness," she announced whitely.

The Fury on her left sighed, but the third stole the show. "Oh, dear," she whooshed as she toppled out of her chair. The ensuing thud was fainter and more ladylike than the previous one, but it sounded painful and seemed to bring us out of our collective shock and into action, albeit chaotic and ineffectual.

Ambulance attendants dashed in a few minutes later. The fainted Fury was on a sofa, attended by her sisters. Mr. Weiss was still facedown on the stained carpet; there hadn't been much reason to worry about his comfort. The rest of us were standing about, wringing our hands both literally and figuratively, while muttering inanities about heart attacks and/or strokes. How sudden they were, etc.

Miss Dort came in behind the attendants, and behind her was the rabbity little man I'd seen in the main office.

"Oh, this is terrible!" he sputtered. "I just cannot believe— believe that—that this sort of tragedy—absolute tragedy— could—"

"Shut up, Chips," Miss Dort said absently, intent on the body on the floor. "What was it—a heart attack?"

One of the attendants stood up and studied us with a masked expression. "No, it wasn't a heart attack. You'd better call the police."

"Why?" Miss Dort countered. Her fingers tightened around the clipboard, which was pressed against her chest like a shield.

"The guy was poisoned, lady."

Miss Dort blanched, took a step backward, and slowly collapsed in the doorway. The clipboard clattered down beside her.

The room was beginning to resemble the forest scene after Mount St. Helen's eruption. I glared at the ambulance attendants. "I will call the police. In the meantime, why don't you occupy yourselves with the lady on the floor or the one on the sofa? You do have some paramedical training, don't you?"

Grumbling, they split up to deal with the supine figures. I went upstairs to the office, shoved past the pimply Cerberus, and snatched up the telephone. The number was familiar; seconds later Peter Rosen came on the line.

"So glad you called," he said with an audible smile. "There's a wonderfully terrible movie at the drive-in theater, something about a giant asparagus attacking a major metropolitan area. We may end up parked beside your students, but I thought it——"

I interrupted and told him what had happened. He then interrupted and told me that he and his squad would be there shortly. I tried to interrupt with a question or two, but it didn't work. I was speaking to a dial tone.

A keen-eared secretary came out of her room to goggle at me. I told her to announce on the intercom that all students should go to fourth-period classrooms and remain there until further notice, and told her which teachers would have to wait in the lounge for the CID. She nodded, I shrugged, and we both marched off to our respective duties.

Miss Dort and the Fury were still unconscious, but everyone else looked fairly chipper. Evelyn and Sherwood huddled in one corner, watching the attendants wave vials under noses. Jerry and Paula cuddled in a second corner to whisper. The two conscious Furies hovered about, pale but determined, although I wasn't at all sure what they were determined to do.

Mr. Weiss hadn't produced any motion that I could see. I muttered something about the police being on the way, then perched on an arm of a mustard-and-red sofa. When the door opened, I assumed that Peter and his minions had broken all speed records to rescue me. How wrong I was.

Pitts slithered in, a bucket in one hand and a mop in the other. His reptilian eyes were bright. "Well, I'll be a bullfrog's bottom. I heard that Weiss had dropped dead in the lounge, but I didn't think it was true. I'll be a bullfrog's bottom on a hot summer night!"

From her corner, Evelyn snapped, "Get out of here, Pitts! Go mop a hallway or something."

He scratched his head with the mop handle. "What'd he kick off from? And what's wrong with them two?"

Peter came in before Pitts could suffer the same fate of the soda bottle—decapitation. He glanced at me, then began to order everyone about with cold authority. Miss Dort was revived in time to accompany the group to a vacant classroom next to the lounge; the Fury refused to cooperate and was rolled away on a gurney. She looked extremely ill.

Then we sat. A bell rang, but no footsteps tromped down the hall. I told Miss Dort what I had arranged with the secretary, and was rewarded with a pinched frown. It had seemed quite efficient to me. I hadn't even had a clipboard.

Sherwood wiggled his eyebrows at me, no doubt intending to look conspiratorial. "So our *summum bonum* was poisoned. Have you identified the murderer, Claire, or are you waiting for a more propitious moment for a denouement?"

Before I could respond, Paula Hart stumbled to her feet and dashed out of the room. A uniformed officer returned her without comment, and she sank down in a desk to sniffle bravely. Jerry went over to pat her shoulder.

Sherwood murmured, "I'm surprised you have tears for such things, my dear. After all, Weiss was about to dismiss and disgrace your beloved, which would have complicated the daily allotment of stolen kisses in the lounge. Now, you and your *particeps criminis* are free to indulge yourselves."

Jerry growled. "Look, Timmons, Paula and I had nothing to do with this. Weiss and I might have had hard feelings, but I sure as hell didn't poison him."

We all exchanged uneasy looks.

Sherwood clapped his hands with the glee of an infant beholding a popsicle. "The brandied peach compote! How utterly fascinating! Miss Parchester has more strength of character than I had credited her with."

Now Evelyn, Miss Dort, Paula, Jerry, and the two Furies all growled, sounding like a pack of wild dogs converging on a wounded animal. Sherwood smiled at them, but his goatee trembled and his eyes flickered in my direction.

Pitts, who had managed to include himself in the group, chortled. "I saw that yellow slime on the floor. Is that what killed the old man? Miss Parchester was here earlier; I saw her sneak into the lounge, and she had a funny look on her puss."

She probably did look rather peculiar, but I saw no point in discussing her condition with the lizard. "Mr. Pitts," I said, "you were not a witness to the unpleasantness in the lounge, so there really is no reason for you to be here. I'll speak to Lieutenant Rosen about allowing you to leave." For Mongolia, on a train.

"I saw plenty of interesting stuff. I know who went in the lounge—and why. Mr. Fancy Lieutenant Rosen will be pretty damn eager to talk to me."

Mr. Fancy himself came into the classroom. "We have not finished with the lounge. I'll need a room from which to conduct my investigation."

Miss Dort fluttered her clipboard. "I'll see to it at once, Lieutenant. However, what shall I do about the students and other faculty? The bus schedule will require modification, and—"

"Don't do anything," Peter said hastily. "Is there someone who can take charge upstairs for the remainder of the school day?"

"Mr. Chippendale is the dean, but I doubt he could manage," Miss Dort said, shaking her head. "And who will notify Mrs. Weiss and poor little Cheryl Anne?"

Peter beckoned to the officer in the doorway, and told him to locate Mr. Chippendale. Paula Hart mentioned that Cheryl Anne was in the typing room at the end of the hall and left to tell her the news before the gossip spread. Once bureaucratic details were under control, Peter gazed around the room at his collection of witnesses.

"Cyanide, I think," he said conversationally, as though running through the menu for a dinner party, "although we'll have to run tests to be sure. I would guess it was introduced in that yellowish substance on the floor. Would anyone care to tell me where it came from?"

We all stared at the floor. The linoleum hadn't seen a mop in at least a decade.

Pitts waggled his mop. "I can tell you exactly where the goop came from, sir. Miss Emily Parchester brought a jar of brandied peach compote this morning, 'cause she knows how much Weiss liked it. I think you got yourself a murderer, sir."

Peter looked at me. "Is that true, Mrs. Malloy?"

Presumably I was the very same Mrs. Malloy with whom he shared bottles of wine and moments of ecstasy on an occasional basis. He seemed to have forgotten. I stared at him and said, "She did leave a jar of compote in the kitchenette, but she did not lace it with cyanide, Lieutenant."

"That will have to be determined," he said. He paused as a gurney squeaked past the closed door on its journey to the morgue. "I'll need to take statements from each of you. Will Miss Parchester's address and telephone number be available in the main office?"

Mrs. Platchett rose like a missile head. "Emily Parchester did not leave a jar of poisoned compote in the lounge, Lieutenant. Her father was Judge Amos Parchester of the state Supreme Court, and her mother came from a very old Farberville family."

"The Borgias were an old family, too," Sherwood commented. "That hardly kept the children from——"

"Who are you?" Peter said. His teeth glinted, wolf-style. His molasses-colored eyes were flecked with yellow flints.

I might have melted, but Sherwood merely bobbed his head. "Sherwood Timmons, at your service. I was speaking in jest; *nemine contradicente* when I say that we all have faith in Miss Parchester's unflagging innocence."

Evelyn once again overlooked his verbal transgression. "Emily is hardly the sort to do such a thing, Lieutenant. She's a harmless old lady who taught journalism for forty years, until unfortunate circumstances forced her to retire."

"The journalism teacher," Peter said. He turned back to me. "She was here earlier today, with the compote. Weiss was fond of the stuff."

"The jar was left in the kitchenette for over half an hour," I retorted. "Anyone could have put cyanide in it."

"But why?" he countered.

I tried not to glance at Jerry, who had been thundering threats the previous afternoon, or at Sherwood, who might have been muttering them in Latin. "I have no idea, Lieutenant Rosen."

Paula Hart had been there, too. "Jerry didn't mean what he said," she offered tremulously. She clutched his hand and held it to her cheek as she stared defiantly at Peter.

"What didn't he mean?"

"He was only kidding when he said someone ought to take care of Mr. Weiss," she said. The girl was a veritable wealth of helpful information. "Jerry didn't poison the compote."

The coach's face matched his gray sweats. "That's right, Lieutenant, I was just blowing off steam."

Peter was unmoved by the sincerity glowing on the young faces. "Let's discuss it in private," he suggested with a smile. His teeth—or should I say fangs—glistened in the subsequent silence.

From the *Falcon Crier,* October 29

Dear Miss Demeanor,
   Do you think it's undignified for juniors to throw eggs and toilet paper at houses on Halloween and basically act like children? I think it's immature, gross and utterly disgusting.

Dear Reader,
   Miss Demeanor senses an underlying trepidation in your letter.

She wonders if you're worried that no one will throw an egg at you or decorate your lawn with white steamers. Have no fear: Miss Demeanor has your address.

Dear Miss Demeanor,
    I'm a sophomore with a terrible problem. You see, this boy wants me to go steady, but we both have braces. I read somewhere that the braces can get locked. I would absolutely die if that happened.

Dear Reader,
    Miss Demeanor wonders where in the annals of history going steady got locked with kissing. Sophomores have no business kissing, anyway. Take advantage of your lowly status to perfect hand-shaking and meaningful looks. Then, Miss Demeanor suggests that you search for a boy whose father is an orthodontist, for financial as well as utilitarian concerns.

Dear Miss Demeanor,
    How's this for a trick-or-treat surprise? I call somebody's wife and tell her that her husband has a standing reservation at the Xanadu Motel every Thursday afternoon. Do you think she'd get a kick out of that?

Dear Reader,
    Although Miss Demeanor promised to answer every letter in her box, she must admit this motel business is becoming a bit tedious. This is clearly adult stuff. The only person who's getting a kick out of it is you, Reader. If you call somebody's wife, you're likely to get another kick—in the rear. Can we just drop it, please?

"F"I"V"E"

The afternoon did not skip by; it trudged in lead-lined snow-shoes. At the end of the last period, the students were sent away. Several hundred of them found a reason to parade down the basement hallway, all very casual and distracted by meaningful inner dialogue. Adolescents respond to violence much the same way moths do to a candle, or iron filings to a magnet. It is not endearing.

We were not sent away. Peter set up shop in the lounge at the formica table, and each of us was called in to make a statement. My name was the last on his list, which fooled me not at all, and it was almost four o'clock before I was beckoned into his parlor.

I glanced at the chalked silhouette on the carpet and the circular stain of dampness. "Did you arrive at any brilliant deductions in the last four hours? I would have offered suggestions, but I was having too much fun in that dusty room counting flowers on the wall and cracks in the ceiling."

He grinned at me. His curly black hair and three-piece suit gave him the appearance of either an executive or a Mafia hit man. He's clearly a New Yorker, from the jutting nose to the jarring accent, but I had grown accustomed to his face, among other things. He has talents that are best left unspecified. At the moment, we were lovers, although it was much like making goulash with dynamite and nitroglycerine. Too much personality, and usually not in tune. However, we did certain things very well, and legal entwining was occasionally discussed. I was the one who shied away. I have tried marriage; the results were not distasteful, but I have learned to enjoy my unwedded solitude.

"I deduced," Peter said wryly, "that this place rivals any afternoon soap opera for intrigues, gossip, and back-stabbing, to put it mildly. Do these people actually teach?"

"It does boggle the mind, doesn't it?" I said, sitting on the mauve-and-green monster. "I've felt as if I had been airlifted into Peyton Place the last two days. What have you learned thus far?"

"This is an official investigation, Claire," he said. The grin inverted itself into a frown. "I know that you haven't paid any attention to that niggling little detail in the past, but this time I want you to stay out of it."

"As long as Miss Parchester is out of it," I said with a lofty expression. It never failed to irritate him.

"Emily Parchester is very much in it, for the moment. She did sneak into the building with a jar of peach compote, knowing that Weiss was especially fond of it. She, on the other hand, was not at all fond of him. The compote was laced with cyanide, possibly from inception. It's not easy to overlook the coincidence, Claire."

"It seems fairly easy to jump to conclusions, however. If you'd ever met her, you'd realize she's a harmless little old lady, not some character out of *Arsenic and Old Lace*. She's going to paint watercolors and ride in buses when she retires, for God's sake."

"Let's hope she hasn't already climbed aboard, then, since we don't seem able to find her. The uniformed officers have questioned her neighbors, but no one claims to have seen her since yesterday evening, when she discretely put a sack of liquor bottles in a garbage can. A large sack. We would very much like to discuss her recipe for peach compote."

"The entire Farberville police force can't find one old lady?" I laughed merrily. "Perhaps she's gone underground to escape the dragnet." I watch old shows on television when I can't sleep.

Very old shows, I suspect, since all the characters are either black, white, or gray.

"We'll find her," he said, unamused by my cleverness. "We should have a report from the medical examiner's office within twenty-four hours, but we're operating on the premise that the poison was in the damned yellow goop. It reeked of bitter almonds, as did Weiss's mouth. The symptoms were consistent with cyanide poisoning: nausea, cramps, mental confusion, and death within minutes. It's a painful poison, but it is reasonably easy to get one's hands on . . . and inexpensive for someone on a tight budget."

"You don't need to question her—just hook her up to the electric chair and throw the switch! You obviously think she's the culprit, simply because she brought the compote to school. It was sitting in the kitchenette for half an hour. Anyone could have added the cyanide."

"That's what *we'll* investigate. Now, I need a full statement from you so that we can get out of this place before dark."

A minion named Jorgeson appeared to write down my words of wisdom. I reiterated my movements for the last two days, from homeroom to sixth period. Without a whimper, I might add. Jorgeson rewarded my conciseness with a smile, I signed the silly thing, and we left the building together.

Always a gentleman, Peter walked me to my car. "I guess I can't take you to see *The Massachusetts Asparagus Massacre* at the drive-in tonight. After a break for hamburgers, we're going to search the entire building for anything with cyanide in it. I suspect we'll still be there when the homeroom bell rings Monday morning."

"I presumed you'd be on a stakeout at Miss Parchester's house." I gazed up with a sweet smile. "*Carpe diem,* Peter."

I drove out of the parking lot in a skimpy mist of dust, since I valued my shocks more than my desire for a grand exit. When I arrived home, I found Caron and Inez on the sofa, salivating for details.

"Oh, Mother," Caron sighed, "were you really there at the Fateful Moment? Did he clutch his throat and accuse Miss Parchester?"

Inez clutched her throat. "My sister was in Typing II when Miss Hart came in to break the ghastly news to Cheryl Anne. It was awful, Mrs. Malloy. Cheryl Anne turned white. Miss Hart was white, too, and crying, then all the girls started crying. None of them could finish the time test. Cheryl Anne had to go to the nurse's office to lie down."

"Did they find Miss Parchester?" Caron demanded. "Did she admit that she nursed a Secret Hatred of Mr. Weiss?"

"Did the police really discover her cowering in the basement?" whispered Inez.

I considered ignoring Tweedledee and Tweedledum, and taking a cup of tea to bed. On the other hand, the two were apt to be better informed than I; FHS was not a monastery, as I well knew. It was a radio station, complete with news bulletins and in-depth commentaries.

Once I was armed with tea, I returned to the living room. "So the popular theory is that Miss Parchester did it?"

Caron shook her head. "That's what the seniors think. The juniors think Coach Finley did it Out of Love, the sophomores are backing Mr. Timmons, and the—" She broke off with a funny expression. She has a variety of them, but this one was unfamiliar.

"And?" I prompted. I took a long drink, just in case.

Inez shot me her version of a funny expression. It was noticeably baleful, but tempered with sympathy—for Caron. "Some of the freshmen think you did it, Mrs. Malloy. Caron and I told them in no uncertain terms that you didn't, of course."

"Thank you, Inez. Why do the freshmen harbor such ideas?"

"Because you were so upset about the Falconnaire. Everybody

heard that you were livid in the teachers meeting, and snarled all sorts of threats at Mr. Weiss."

"And then poisoned him to avoid having to supervise work on the yearbook? Don't the freshmen find that a bit extreme?" I told myself that the question was absurd; I knew from personal experience that freshmen did indeed find things a bit extreme, including such things as life.

Caron sniffed. "Inez and I tried to tell them, Mother. I mean, the idea is preposterous. If the police will just find Miss Parchester, they can make her confess and clear your name." Not to mention other people who were saddled with the same name through no fault of their own.

The telephone rang. I went to answer it while I toyed with my defense. To my astonishment, Miss Emily Parchester was on the line.

"Mrs. Malloy, I was hoping you might be able to visit me sometime in the next day or two. I am quite curious about your progress in the mysterious case."

Mysterious was a mild description. I turned my back on the audience on the sofa and whispered, "Where are you?"

"I am at a country establishment, taking a rest for a few days while I try to keep this troublesome situation from disturbing me. I have experienced some difficulty in sleeping, and felt fresh air and the presence of a well-trained staff might soothe me. Have you made any progress?"

Nothing beyond being the freshman class's candidate for murderer, I thought bleakly. "There have been a few developments. Have the police not contacted you to discuss them?"

"Then the auditors are certain I was remiss in my accounts? Oh, Mrs. Malloy, whatever shall I do? The Judge must be roll-ing—"

"In his grave, on a rotisserie. Where is this establishment, Miss Parchester? I do think I'll come by for a visit today. Immediately."

She gave me directions, and I hung up. Caron and Inez were
both flipping through magazines, competing for the title of Miss
Nonchalance. I wondered what Caron found so fascinating in
Bookseller's Monthly Digest, but I didn't ask. Instead, I said, "I'm
going out for an hour or so, girls. Can you feed yourselves without burning down the kitchen?"

"Who was that on the telephone, Mother?"

"My Avon lady. The winter mascara has just arrived, and it
may be my color. I'll see you later."

"What shall I tell Peter if he calls?" she continued, her lips
pursed in great innocence as she adjusted an invisible halo.

"Tell him that I'll test 'Tarnished Copper' first."

Miss Parchester's so-called establishment was several miles out
of town. The name was vaguely familiar, and I recalled its reputation when I stopped in front of a ten-foot-high iron gate. A
chain-link fence topped with concertina wire disappeared into
the woods in both directions, creating a formidable enclave designed to keep out hikers and stray dogs. Happy Meadows Home
was not an ordinary country inn; it catered not to vacationers,
but to inmates.

A guard appeared at my window, his eyes hidden behind reflective sunglasses. "You got business here?"

I checked my lipstick in the twin reflections. "I have come to
see Miss Emily Parchester."

"You got permission from the office?"

"I was not aware I needed permission from the office," I said,
mimicking his surly tone. "Is this a prison, and is Miss Parchester
locked away somewhere in solitary confinement? For that matter,
where are the happy meadows—and your supervisor?"

"I'll have to call the office, lady. No one's supposed to go in
unless they got business." He went into a gatehouse and reappeared after several minutes. "You can talk to her medical ad-

visor, but before you go in, I'll have to search your car and your person."

"Don't be silly," I said as I rolled up the car window. When the gate remained closed, I gave up and allowed the officious goon to search my car and purse, although I rebelled when he made a move toward my person. It has never been searched thus far—at least not for weapons or whatever he feared I had stashed under my unmentionables.

He ran a professional eye over my body, shrugged, and unlocked the gate. Wishing I had concealed a submachine gun on my person, I drove along a winding road to the front of a stately white house. No bars that I could see, but the goon at the gate did discourage trespassers. Once inside, I stopped at the reception desk and asked for Miss Parchester's room number.

I ended up in a claustrophobic room with a pale young man in a white coat. All he lacked was an oversized net and a hunchbacked, lisping lab assistant. "You wish to see Emily Parchester? This is highly irregular. Are you a family member or merely a friend?"

"I'm her attorney. She called me to discuss matters that are confidential." When he paled further, I went for the jugular. "The matters concern her incarceration in a certain establishment."

"Her stay is voluntary."

"That remains to be determined, perhaps through the auspices of our legal system. Now, if I may see my client. . . ?"

I was told that she was on the terrace, having tea. Feeling like a red-haired Joyce Davenport, I sailed out of the room and minutes later found myself with a porcelain teacup in one hand and a mushy cucumber sandwich in the other.

Miss Parchester beamed at me. "I am absolutely thrilled by your little visit, Mrs. Malloy. Although this establishment is restful, it does get a teeny bit boring. Now, what can I do to assist your investigation?"

"I still haven't found the accounts," I told her, suddenly remembering my appointment for that evening with Sherwood Timmons. It was out of the question now; I hoped he would realize the police might notice the two of us creeping down the hall. "Things are rather complicated at the moment, and I don't know when I'll be able to try to analyze the deposit slips."

"I'm sure you'll do your best. You're so kind to take on this burden for me; I don't know what I'd do without you. I've been so fortunate."

Without me, she wouldn't have visited the journalism room and dropped off her little gift in the lounge. She wouldn't have been accused of murder. She wouldn't have a policeman in the bushes beside her house or a supercilious lieutenant determined to arrest her at the first opportunity. I decided not to tell her how fortunate she was until I had cleared her name, along with the Judge's and dear mamma's.

"You're more than welcome," I murmured. "I was curious about the brandied peach compote, Miss Parchester. Did you use your normal recipe?"

"I used Aunt Eulalie's recipe, dear. It's been in the family for years and years. The Judge always spoke highly of it."

"And you didn't add anything to it?" I continued, inwardly wincing at the necessity of grilling an old lady, even if it was for her own good.

"No, I followed the recipe religiously." The faded blue eyes narrowed. "Was there something wrong with it? A funny taste or peculiar odor? The peaches were a few days old, and of course they're not as fresh as they were when one bought them directly from the farmer who came to the house in his wagon, but——"

I interrupted to tell her as gently as I could about the lethal consequences of the compote. Her teacup shattered on the flag-

stone surface as she turned ashen. A cucumber sandwich fell unnoticed in her lap, and then tumbled onto her fuzzy pink slipper.

"Surely you speak in jest, Mrs. Malloy! I've made hundreds of
gallons of my special peach compote in my life, and no one has
ever accused me—accused me of—of poisoning—murdering
someone with—with—oh, dear!"

She stood up, looking frail and ill. The cucumber sandwich
was smashed to a white circle as she fled inside, leaving me alone
on the terrace.

I popped the last bite of sandwich in my mouth and started for my
car. A grim matron stopped me at the front door.

"You're the one who upset us, aren't you? Who are you and what
did you say to us? We're beyond coherence, and I cannot get a word
out of us. We are likely to have a relapse at any moment, just when
we're beginning to become nicely dried out and calm."

"I told us that a certain police detective thought we might
have poisoned our boss with peach compote," I explained politely. "If we have any sense at all, we'll keep us out of sight until
this thing is cleared up. We hope that we won't have to tell
anyone that we're at Happy Meadows, but we have a low pain
threshold, and they may force us to talk."

I left her to ponder the pronouns and went to my car. When I
arrived at home, it was blessedly still. I learned from a scrawled
note that Caron and Inez had gone out, destination unspecified. I
heated a Lean Cuisine, painted my toenails, ate, and tried to
watch television, which wasn't easy under the best of circumstances. I was staring at a blank screen when the doorbell rang.

Peter came in, his face lined with fatigue. I gave him a glass of
wine and sat down beside him. "Did we—I mean you, find any
cyanide in the building?"

"We found cyanide compounds in the journalism darkroom, in
the custodian's supply closet, in the secretary's desk to kill
roaches, and in both the biology and chemistry labs. We also

found a jar of rat poison in the girls' locker room and another in the band room. And another in the art room."

"Lots of cyanide."

"There is enough cyanide in the high school to kill off the entire student body and most of Farberville," Peter said, sighing. "We still have a few other rooms to search, and we'll probably find an adequate supply for the state. I thought poisons were supposed to be kept away from children."

"I'm very sorry the murderer didn't use some obscure South American tree sap." I toyed with an errant curl above his ear. It never failed to distract him, and I wanted to ease him in to a more pliable frame of mind. "Have you found Miss Parchester yet?"

"No, she hasn't come home. One of the neighbors saw her leave in a van, but had no idea what kind of van it was. We have an officer waiting at her apartment."

I tucked my feet under me and tried to look mildly sympathetic, as opposed to extremely curious. I did not ask if the van driver had reflective lenses and the warmth of a drill sergeant. "Did you learn anything of interest in the statements?"

"With a few exceptions, everyone seemed eager to assist us. Now I am well-informed of the bell schedule and the morning class times, the procedure with blue slips, the absentee reports, the alternate bus routes on snow days, and I know more than anyone should about computerized personal grade records. I also heard about Miss Parchester's little problem with the journalism accounts."

"All a misunderstanding."

"Isn't it interesting how you were available to substitute in the midst of the crisis? One would almost be inclined to think that your presence was along the lines of calling in the Mounties. . . ."

"As a member of the community and a concerned parent, I was merely helping out by agreeing to substitute," I said. Lied, actually—but only because he was looking so damned smug. "The students must have supervision. The perpetuity of the physical structure demands it."

"And you weren't trying to delve into the accounts?"

Ah, the burden of a reputation for brilliant deduction. I considered my next move as I refilled our wine glasses. I opted to delve into his accounts—of the crime.

"Miss Parchester left the journalism room at ten o'clock, and presumably put the jar in the refrigerator in the lounge," I commented in a conversational tone. "The jar was unattended for the next half hour, until I arrived. After that, no one came into the lounge."

"That's the time period we're interested in," Peter said. "The French teacher—ah, Evelyn West, said that she went into the lounge toward the end of second period for a cup of coffee. She saw the jar in the refrigerator, but did not realize that it was the infamous compote until later. That was at ten-fifteen or so."

"She didn't see anyone while she was there?"

"Her student teacher came in for a few seconds, but did not enter the kitchenette. Apparently, she comes in to cry on a regular basis." He gave me a puzzled look. "Does that make sense to you?"

"No, but I've witnessed it. Who else came to the lounge?"

"Bernice Dort, the vice-principal, came by for a soda, and our victim came in with her. Mrs. West says that they were unaware of her presence in the ladies room, but refused to elaborate. Miss Dort confirms the time."

"No one else came into the lounge?"

"According to the statements, no. You arrived at the beginning of the third period at about ten-thirty, right? You and Mrs. West were there until everyone arrived for the potluck, and no one else could have slipped into the kitchen to spike the compote."

I wrinkled my nose and tried to remember. "I think that's accurate," I admitted. "But what about the period from ten to ten-fifteen? Was anyone in the lounge then?"

Peter downed the last drop of wine and stood up. "No one has admitted being there, except for the custodian, who says he came in to clean the rest rooms."

"And he has cyanide in his closet! Pitts is the murderer, Peter;

I'm sure of it! He's the slimiest specimen of reptile I've ever seen, and he slinks around the building like a mongrel."

"But he doesn't have a motive."

"Yes, he does. Weiss was getting static from the teachers in the basement. Pitts hasn't been cleaning the classrooms for quite some time, and the teachers were beginning to get tired of the dirt. I know Miss Platchett was in Weiss's office earlier to demand that Pitts be terminated, preferably with extreme prejudice."

"That's not much of a motive," he pointed out. "Did Weiss agree to fire him?"

"It didn't sound like it, from the report I overheard. But that doesn't mean that Pitts might not be eager to prevent Weiss from taking drastic measures at a later date."

"By poisoning all the teachers in the lounge?"

"Maybe not. Miss Parchester wouldn't have risked it, either. Her dearest friends and staunchest supporters were likely to nibble the compote. She's hardly a Borgia sort."

I earned a gaze that blew straight from the North Pole. "I wouldn't know," he murmured, "since I haven't been able to locate the woman for a statement. No one seems to know where she is. Her friends don't know, her neighbors don't know, and her brother in Boise, Idaho, doesn't know."

"Well, don't look at me." Not like that, anyway. "You'd best run along and let me do some work on the yearbook layout. We teachers are a dedicated lot."

"As much as I'd like to stay and discuss the whereabouts of the elusive Miss Parchester, I wouldn't want to interfere with your obvious dedication. I'm going back to the high school to see if Jorgeson has found another gallon or two of cynaide in the home-economics room."

We parted amiably, if a shade warily. Corpses have always had that effect on our relationship.

"S" "I" "X"

Nothing much happened over the weekend. Peter called Sunday evening to say the CID was making little progress, but they had confiscated enough poison from the school to wipe out the country, if not the continent. The lab results were not yet in, so they had no theories as to the origin and composition of the cyanide compound. All of the teachers and staff had been questioned again, as had a few students who admitted they'd been in the halls during the second period. I mentioned that I hadn't been questioned again and was informed that I was not a suspect—or a particularly important witness. What charm the man possessed. The freshman class took me more seriously than he did, even if they overestimated the depth of my desire to avoid the yearbook.

Peter was not especially amused when I asked if he had found Miss Parchester, and his response does not bear repeating. Nor does mine when he inquired about my progress on the layout. The conversation ended on a slightly testy note when he reiterated his order about interference in the official investigation and I laughed. The man requires deflation to keep his head from exploding. It falls in the category of public service.

His little jibe did, however, remind me of earlier questions about the school newspaper's most infamous columnist. Said columnist was doing homework on her bed, a bag of potato chips within reach should malnutrition threaten to impair her intellectual skills. The radio blared in one ear, and the telephone receiver was affixed to the other.

I suggested she turn off, hang up, and cease stuffing potato chips in her mouth. After a nominal amount of dissension, we achieved an ambiance more conducive to conversation, albeit temporary and at great personal sacrifice on one party's part.

"When did you take over the Miss Demeanor column?" I asked.

"Last week. That's what makes all this So Irritating, Mother. If you don't do something about this mess, I'll never get to actually write the column. Bambi said—"

"So you didn't write any of the previous columns?"

"I intended to do the next one, but then Miss Parchester Absolutely Ruined Things by getting herself accused of embezzlement. This whole mess is incredible." And her mother's fault, although the sentiment remained unspoken.

"I'm sure Mr. Weiss agreed with you, as do his widow and daughter."

"I wouldn't be too sure about Cheryl Anne," Caron sniffed. "She hated her father because of what he did to Thud. Inez's sister said that Thud told one of the junior varsity linebackers that he wished he could meet Weiss in a dark alley some night."

"Does this have something to do with eligibility?" I remembered the discussion in the teachers' meeting, but not with any clarity. It hadn't made much sense.

"Thud's furious," Caron said solemnly. "So is Cheryl Anne. In fact, she's reputedly livid."

"What precisely is he ineligible to do? Produce an intelligible remark? Walk and count at the same time? Marry Cheryl Anne?"

Her expression resembled that of a martyr facing slings and arrows from a herd of drooling tribesmen. "Football, Mother. Thud is a big football jock, the captain of the team and all that, and plans to get a college scholarship for next year. Mr. Weiss pulled his eligibility, which means he won't get to play in the Homecoming game."

"Merely because he's flunking all his classes? How unkind of Mr. Weiss. After all, what's a mere education when it interferes with football?"

"It's our Homecoming game, Mother. If Starley City wins, it will be too humiliating for words. The dance will be a wake. Cheryl Anne is this year's Homecoming queen—naturally—and she's told everyone she'll literally die if the team loses on the most important night of her life." She eyed the telephone. "I really do need to work on my algebra. Big test on Wednesday."

"Your devotion to your education is admirable, but it will have to wait another minute or two. Has anyone suggested that Cheryl Anne or Thud might have—done something drastic because of the ineligibility problem and the impending ruination of Cheryl Anne's life?"

"It sounds rather farfetched, Mother, but I could call Inez and ask her if her sister's heard anything," Caron said with a flicker of enthusiasm. "Inez's sister hears Absolutely Everything. She's a cheerleader."

Caron was right; it did seem farfetched to poison daddy to ensure a football victory and subsequent festive celebration. Daddy's demise wouldn't guarantee that the eligibility would be reinstated, nor would Thud's presence on the field guarantee a victory. Neither of the two had access to the lounge, although it seemed as if cyanide in some form or other was accessible to all. I put the theory (which wasn't much good, anyway) aside and went on to a more promising line before my daughter commenced a full-scale rebellion.

"I need to speak to the girl who wrote the column before she caught mononucleosis," I said, raising one eyebrow sternly in case she made a grab for the telephone.

Caron produced the information. I razed her dreams by telling her to stay off the telephone until I was finished, then ducked out the door before her lower lip could extend far enough to endanger me.

Rosie's mother was reluctant to allow me to speak to her, but I finally persuaded her that I was not a girlfriend with a weekly gossip report. Rosie came on the line with a timid, "Yes?"

I gave her a hasty explanation of my current position at the high school, then asked how she chose the letters to answer in her column.

"There's a box in the main office," she told me. "I emptied the box every week and answered all the letters. I made a pledge in the first issue, so it was vital to my journalistic integrity."

I had rather hoped Caron would mellow with age, but it seemed we might have a few more years of tribulation if this was the norm. "I found your column very amusing, Rosie. Some of it rather puzzled me, though. What did you think about the Xanadu Motel letters?"

"I thought somebody was bonkers, but I felt obligated to answer as best I could. It was vital to my—"

"Of course it was," I said quickly. "Did you have any idea who wrote those letters? Any clues from the handwriting?"

"The letters were confidential, Mrs. Malloy," she said, sounding scandalized. "Even if I had been able to guess the identity of the correspondents, I would never divulge the names. That would compromise my—"

"Indeed," I said. I wished her a speedy recovery and a good night's rest, then retreated to my bedroom. There wasn't any reason to link the peculiar letters in the *Falcon Crier* with Weiss's murder, or even with the accusations against Miss Parchester. It was just a nagging detail, a petty and obscure campaign being waged by an anonymous general against an equally anonymous enemy. Who, according to the letters, spent many a Thursday afternoon at the Xanadu indulging in activities that required little speculation. After a few minutes of idle thought, I dismissed it and spent the rest of the night dreaming of bell schedules, lounge visitors armed with lethal jars, and the prevalence of Tupperware.

Monday morning arrived. I arrived at dear old FHS and scurried down to the cavern just as the bell shrieked its warning to dilatory debutantes and lingering lockerites. As I stepped through the door, the intercom box crackled to life for the daily homeroom announcements. Miss Dort rattled off a brief acknowledgment of our beloved principal's sad demise and extended all of our collective sympathy to the bereaved family. School would be closed the following day so that we could, if we desired, evince the above-mentioned sympathy by our appearance at the funeral. Date and location were announced.

She then swung into a more familiar routine of club meetings, unsigned tardy slips, and illicit behavior in halls and rest rooms between classes, all of which made her tidy little world go round.

I went to the teachers' lounge for a shot of caffeine. As I entered, Evelyn caught me by the arm and pulled me back into the hallway. "I need your help," she whispered. "We're going to get Pitts. The filthy slime has gone too far, and I'm going to expose his nastiness once and for all. Now that Weiss is no longer around to protect him, Pitts will get exactly what he deserves."

It was mystifying, but certainly more interesting than Miss Dort's announcements or the watery coffee in the lounge. Evelyn was flushed with anger; her dark eyes sparkled with an expectancy that bordered on mayhem. Once I had nodded my acquiescence to whatever she had in mind, she hurried into her classroom and returned with her student teacher. The quivering girl was told to go into the ladies room in the lounge and make a production of checking her lipstick and hair in the mirror.

"Is Pitts in the ladies room?" I asked.

"Worse. I'll show you where the beast is—and what he's doing."

She led the way around the corner into the dark area of the hallway where I'd had the conversation with the Latin pedant.

We entered the custodian's door and tiptoed through a labyrinth of paper towels, murky mops and buckets, odoriferous boxes of disinfectants, and the other paraphernalia necessary to combat youthful slovenliness.

Beyond the storage room was Pitts's private domain, a dismal room with a chair, a coffee table, and a sagging cot covered with a tattered blanket. Yellowed pinup girls gaped over their exposed anatomies, pretending astonishment at having been snapped in such undignified poses. The calendars below were from former decades, but I supposed Pitts hadn't noticed.

In one corner was Pitts himself. He failed to notice our entrance, in that he had one eye and all of his attention glued to a hole in the wall. Evelyn glanced back at me to confirm my perspicacity as a witness, then crossed the room and tapped his shoulder.

He spun around, his lips shining moistly in the dim light. "Why, Miz West! What're you all doing in here?"

"The more important question is: What are you doing, Mr. Pitts?"

"Nothing. Gitting ready to mop the hall like I always do on Monday morning. Then I got to repair a broken window in Mr. Weiss's office and see about the thermostat in the girls' gym. Don't want those girls to get cold in them skimpy gym suits, do we?"

"Imagine all that work. Wouldn't it be more entertaining to peek at the women teachers in the ladies room?"

"Now, Miz West," he began in an awful whine, "I don't know why you'd say something like that. I wouldn't never—"

Evelyn brushed him aside with one finger and put her eye to the hole. "What a delightful view, Pitts. I'd always presumed you received your jollies smoking dope with the sophomore boys, but now I see you've branched out into visual amusements as well. I am going upstairs to report this to Miss Dort, the superintendent of schools, the head of custodial maintenance, the school board, and anyone else who will listen."

"Now, Miz West——"

"You will be dismissed, Pitts, and it will be a day of celebration for the entire school. A holiday, with dancing in the halls, followed by a touching ceremony in which you will be literally booted through the back door, never to be seen here again."

"I didn't make this hole. I jest found it and was trying to see where it went is all I was doing, Miz West. That's the honest-to-gawd truth—I swear it." He ducked his head and shuffled his feet in a cloud of dust. I waited to see if he actually tugged his forelock in classic obsequiousness, although it would have had to be unglued first. He settled for the expression of a basset hound put outside on a cold night.

Evelyn gave him a cold look as she joined me in the doorway. We left the room and made our way back to the hall, Pitts's sputters and whines drifting after us like a breeze from a chicken house.

"Brava," I murmured. It had been impressive.

She was shaking with anger, but her expression held a hint of satisfaction. "I meant every word of it. That filthy man is finished at this school and at every other school in the system. He can go clean sewers, which is what he deserves. On the other hand, I deserve a medal, a bouquet of long-stemmed roses presented by a lispy, angelic child, and a year's sabbatical to Paris to brush up on my vocabulary."

"When did you notice the hole?"

"This morning, but I have no idea how long it's been there. It almost makes me ill. Not only could he watch us adjust panty hose and hike our skirts, he could probably hear every word said in the lounge when the door was ajar. Lord, I feel the need of a shower, or at least a rubdown with disinfectant."

I was in the midst of agreeing with her when the bell rang and students exploded into the halls. I retreated to the journalism room to meet my first-period class. Said group was silent and soberly watchful as I entered the room and sat down behind the desk. It took me a moment to recall that they were freshmen— and we all knew whom the freshmen had chosen as their candidate for Weiss's murderer.

After some deliberation, I decided to let things stand as they were. It did keep the class under control, in that they seemed to feel it necessary to watch me for signs of imminent attack upon their persons. I tossed over the roster book and leaned back to think about the murder, since I, armed with the wisdom of age and the inside track, knew the freshman class was mistaken.

I had reached no significant conclusions when the bell rang and the class galloped away. The second-period class came, milled around quietly, and left at the bell, as did I. The lounge was empty, which suited me well, and I was dozing on the mauve-and-green when the sound of water in the kitchenette roused me.

A Fury entered the main room, a porcelain cup and saucer in hand, and offered me a timid smile. Tessa Zuckerman had not been seen since her collapse during the distasteful events of the potluck, and Mrs. Platchett was difficult to confuse with anything except, perhaps, a bulldozer. Therefore, I deduced that it had to be Mae Bagby. And Caron swears my mental capacity is changing in inverse proportion to my age.

"How is Miss Zuckerman?" I asked. "Has she recovered?"

"She's still in the hospital, and the doctor wants to keep her a few more days. She hasn't been well for several years, you know, because of female problems, and her strength isn't what it ought to be." The Fury perched on the edge of a chair, her back rigidly erect, her knees glued together, and her ankles crossed at a proper angle. She looked dreadfully uncomfortable, especially to someone sprawled on a sofa. "We are taking up a collection to send her flowers," she continued in a thin waver, "although you certainly wouldn't be expected to donate anything since you hardly know her."

"But I would be delighted," I said. It was one of the perils of aligning oneself with any group, from secretarial pools to construction workers' unions. Someone's always being born, married, or buried—all of which require a financial contribution from co-workers. "Is there also a collection to send flowers for Mr. Weiss's funeral?"

Mae Bagby turned pale, and the teacup began to rattle as though we were in the early stages of an earthquake. "Bernice is taking care of that, I'm sure. Bernice is very efficient about that sort of thing. You might inquire in the office later in the day, or wait until there is a mimeographed note. There is one almost every day during sixth period. The collection for Tessa is a more personal gesture from those of us who frequent this lounge, our little group."

One of whom was apt to have poisoned Weiss. Before I could mention it, Miss Bagby stood up and drifted into the kitchenette to dispose of her cup and saucer. She then visited the ladies room (I hoped Pitts had retired from peeping), gave me another timid smile and a cozy wave, and left the lounge in a flurry of faint creaks from her crepe-soled shoes.

Once she was gone, I found myself wondering if she had really been there, or if I had hallucinated the presence of a shade, a ghost of teachers past. All schools were likely to have a few in the darkest corridors, moaning at the transitory fads and disintegrating moral standards. Rattling lockers at midnight. Reading faded files of students long since departed, in both senses of the word.

I was getting carried away with my Dickensian reverie when I was saved by the bell. Evelyn and Sherwood came in the lounge, followed by Mrs. Platchett and Mae Bagby, who was still insubstantial enough to warrant a second look. Once everyone opened Tupperware, took sandwiches from plastic envelopes, fetched drinks, and found seats around the table, I asked Evelyn if she had reported the custodian to Miss Dort.

"Yes, I did, but I don't know what's going to happen to him, and I really don't understand." She told the others what we had discovered during homeroom, which produced a considerable amount of outrage from all except Sherwood, who looked smugly amused.

"What did Bernice say?" Mrs. Platchett demanded.

Evelyn sighed. "She was horrified, naturally. Then she said things were too chaotic to deal with the problem immediately, and once we settled down she would inform the proper authorities. I presumed *she* was the proper authority. I put tape over the hole, but I won't feel comfortable in the ladies room until Pitts is gone—permanently."

"Nor shall I," said Mrs. Platchett. "I am surprised that Bernice did not react with more forcefulness. Surprised and disappointed, I must add. I could never determine why Mr. Weiss tolerated Pitts's slovenly work and disgusting presence, not to mention the possibility that he was corrupting some of our students. One must surmise Mr. Weiss had his reasons. Bernice should know better."

"What is Pitts rumored to be doing with students?" I asked.

Sherwood waved his pipe at me. "It's all speculation, of course, and the man has never been caught *in flagrante delicto,* but it is whispered in the hallways that Pitts operates a major retail operation from his lair. Not only is it said that he peddles ordinary cigarettes and alcohol, but also that he has such things available as funny cigarettes and contraceptives. Names of abortionists for students caught with their panties down."

"And this is tolerated?" I said, appalled by both the information and Sherwood's blasé tone of voice. "The custodian is allowed to sell illegal things to the students and send them to back-alley abortionists—and no one objects?" I stared at the teachers busy with their lunches. "Why hasn't someone reported him to the police? Don't you care?"

"I said those exact things," Evelyn said. "We've all repeated the gossip over and over again to Weiss. He always promised to investigate. When we tried to follow up, he would say that there was no proof, and that he couldn't fire Pitts or go to the police on the basis of idle gossip, especially from a bunch of students with big mouths and bigger imaginations."

Mrs. Platchett nodded. "He went so far as to imply that we also had oversized imaginations. It was monstrously insulting to those of us who have dedicated ourselves to the education of youth, and I was forced to say so on more than one occasion. I even showed Mr. Weiss proof that Pitts went through the refrigerator during class time, touching our food with his germ-ridden hands and helping himself to whatever caught his fancy."

I hadn't exactly warmed up to Mrs. Platchett in the past few days, but I felt a good deal more kindly toward her now. "What did Mr. Weiss do?"

"Nothing, Mrs. Malloy. He did nothing."

Miss Hart and her coach came in to the lounge, both aglow with young love and/or hunger. She greeted all of us with a warm smile, but Jerry continued into the kitchen and began to feed coins into the soda machine.

"I say, Finley," Sherwood called, "we're all dying to know what Weiss had on you. Be a good chap and share the secret with us. We swear we won't say a word to Mrs. Malloy's policeman."

"Can it, Timmons," growled a voice from the kitchenette.

Sherwood rolled his eyes in feigned surprise. "*Cave canem,* particularly those with sharp teeth and rabid temperaments."

"Leave him alone, please," Paula said earnestly. "It wasn't anything important, and Jerry doesn't want to talk about it. Mr. Weiss wasn't going to do anything; he was just—being difficult about a minor issue." She turned on the warm smile once again to convince us of her sincerity and unflagging faith in her coach. "Would anyone like some of my salad? I made the dressing myself."

Jerry stomped out of the kitchenette with a bottle of soda and a brown bag. "Don't you have a secret of your own, Timmons? Weiss's comment about the library sounded as if he knew something about you—something you might not want to get spread around the school. Did you kill him to keep him quiet?"

"Or did you get him first?" Sherwood sneared.

"Really!" Mrs. Platchett gasped.

"Jerry!" Paula Hart whispered.

"Sherwood!" Evelyn West muttered.

"Oh, my goodness," Mae Bagby sighed.

I, in contrast, did not make a sound. But I was scribbling notes on my mental clipboard faster than Miss Dort in her prime could have ever done. And praying I had every word down.

The remainder of the lunch period passed in silence. Each teacher tidied up and departed with noticeable haste. There were no companionable farewells. I made it through the rest of my classes without incident, although I cold-heartedly denied Bambi's request that she and the staff be allowed to return to the printer's to remind him the newspaper would not be forthcoming. The blue slips were too much to think about. My darling daughter kept her nose in her algebra book, pretending she was a motherless child. Thud and Cheryl Anne did not appear during their appointed hour; I marked them absent without a qualm.

During the last few minutes of the last class, a mimeographed page was delivered. It proved to be a missive from Miss Dort, containing information about the flower collection, a thinly-veiled threat not to miss the funeral, another about blue slips, and a final paragraph about the homecoming game and dance. Which was, I realized as a chill gripped me, slated for the immediate Friday. Miss Dort would not spend the week in search of a better-qualified substitute, since she would be occupied with the duties of assuming command, even if in a temporary capacity.

It was inescapable: I was going to chaperone the dance unless I solved the murder and resolved the journalism accounts in the next four days, in which case Miss Parchester could resume her duties and I could cower at my bookstore. It did not strike me as probable, considering the quantity of suspects, the wealth of opportunities, and the dearth of motives. I made a note to purchase shin guards and earplugs, not to mention a tranquilizer or two, and a stun gun, should the crowd go wild.

I was still brooding that evening when Peter came by. For reasons of his own, he was back to being Mr. Charm Himself. He stirred up a little warmth (he can, if he wishes, be quite adept), then politely asked if he might be presumptuous enough to request beer and sympathy.

I opened the beer, reserving judgment about the sympathy until I figured out what he was up to. "Any luck in the investigation?"

"I spent most of the day in Weiss's office, but it was a waste of time. Jorgeson says he feels more acned with each hour we spend in that damn place, and I'm beginning to feel the same way. I don't know how anyone can stand it."

"The teachers are a sincere lot. They've got to be dedicated to put up with the bureaucracy and low pay. There was an odd conversation today during lunch, by the way." I told him about Sherwood's crack and Jerry Finley's retort. "Both of them seem to have secrets that Weiss knew and was using to needle them. Did you find anything about either of them in the personnel files?"

"Nothing that I intend to repeat to a civilian who is not sticking her lovely nose into things that are off-limits."

He made a amatory lunge for the civilian, but she wasn't having any of it. "Then you did find something," I said excitely. "What was it—criminal records? Falsified credentials? Accusations from parents about incompetency? Was it something serious enough that one of the two would actually poison Weiss to stop him from exposing it?"

"There was nothing significant in anyone's file. Okay?" He tried a feint and a second lunge, but I slithered from under his arm and gave him a cool look.

"If you think I believe that, Peter, then you underestimate me. You will regret it, especially when I solve this case and prove Miss Parchester innocent of everything, from embezzlement to sloppy bookkeeping to murder. Your aversion to sharing information may slow me down, but it won't stop me."

"Would being locked up as a material witness stop you?"

"Not on your life." Which is precisely what it would cost him, along with beer, sympathy (should it be proffered at some future date), successful lunges, and incredibly witty conversation with a red-haired bookseller. He wouldn't dare.

"S"E"V"E"N"

The school was closed the next day for Weiss's funeral. Caron and I attended, as did a large crowd of faculty members and a fair number of students. The minister intoned the phrases, Cheryl Anne and her mother sniffled into sodden tissues, and Jorgeson (Peter's minion) watched impassively for hysterical, guilt-inspired confessions. We were at last dismissed, our ritual imperatives satisfied. Afterward, Caron announced she intended to spend the afternoon at Inez's house in the pursuit of algebraic mastery. She departed in a self-righteous glow that failed to impress me.

I decided to see if Miss Parchester had recovered from my last visit. I doubted I would be allowed to speak to her, but it seemed as good a plan as any on a lovely autumn day. I changed out of basic drab and drove out to Happy Meadows, determined to storm the bastion, or at least request an audience.

To my surprise, the guard let me in after a perfunctory search of car and purse. Person was not mentioned. I parked under a yellow oak and went inside, wondering if the inmates had taken over the hospital and declared a holiday from Anabuse and cucumber sandwiches. The sight of Matron shattered my fantasy.

"Well," she said with a frigid smile, "have we decided to bring our patient back so that we can try to recoup what ground we've lost?"

"We have no idea what you're talking about. I've come to speak to Miss Parchester." A sinking feeling crept over me as I studied Matron's less-than-cordial expression. "You haven't lost her, have you?"

"We do not lose patients."

"Do we misplace them?"

"It is possible that Miss Parchester has seen fit to leave Happy Meadows without being dismissed by her attending physician. It is most improper for her to do so, and she must return immediately so that the paperwork can be completed and her bill finalized. The insurance work alone takes hours to process."

"When did Miss Parchester leave, and how on earth did she get past the goon at the gate?"

Matron cracked a little around the edges. "We don't know exactly. We are certain she did not exit through the gate, since it is always locked at ten o'clock. Her room was empty this morning. She had arranged some pillows under her blanket to give the impression that she was sleeping peacefully, and I fear the night staff did not actually enter her room after midnight rounds. They have been reprimanded, and there will be notations made on their permanent records."

"But Miss Parchester managed to creep out of here at some point during the night and scale a ten-foot fence?" I said incredulously. "It's ten miles to town, and it was damn chilly last night. Did she have a coat? Have the grounds been searched? Did you call the police?"

My voice may have peaked on the final question, for the white-coated doctor came out of his office to investigate the uproar. When he saw me, he stopped and pointed his finger at me. "You are the woman who claimed to be an attorney! You put my patient in hysterics for several hours after your visit, and undermined hours of intensive therapy. I'm sure your visit was responsible for her subsequent actions. What have you done with her?"

"I haven't done anything with her, buddy. You people are supposed to take care of her, not allow her to stumble away on a cold, dark night. You'd better pray she didn't fall in a ditch somewhere and freeze to death! Then you'll have more attorneys around here than orderlies with butterfly nets and nurses straight out of *One Flew Over the Cuckoo's Nest*." I took a deep breath and ordered myself to stop frothing at the mouth. "Now, what have you done to find her and get her back?"

"Doctor has done everything possible," the Matron began ominously. I presumed she'd seen the aforementioned movie—and rooted for the head nurse. "He has followed policy."

Doctor's eyes avoided mine, and his fingers intertwined until they resembled a tangle of albino worms. "Thank you, Matron. I have indeed done everything to locate the patient. We have sent attendants out to search the estate, but we have nearly two hundred acres of meadows and woods. We fear the presence of the police may frighten the patient if she is hiding in the underbrush, so we have not yet called them."

I was torn between demanding they call the police and agreeing that they shouldn't, self-preservation being one of my primary instincts. My conscience finally won. "You'd better call the police immediately; your patient may be wandering down some back road in a daze. Ask for Lieutenant Rosen. He's been wanting to speak to Miss Parchester. . . ."

Doctor, Matron, and I exchanged uneasy looks. Doctor took a folded slip of paper from his pocket and handed it to me. "This was found on her pillow this morning during six o'clock rounds. Perhaps you can make some sense of it."

The spidery scrawl was hard to read, but I made out references to Bernstein, Woodward, and freedom of the press. I sank down on a ladderback chair and propped my face in my hands. Miss Emily Parchester, I bleakly realized, had taken up investigative reporting. Her reputation and her recipe for brandied peach compote were at stake. She was determined to expose a murderer and thus clear her name, along with the Judge's. But where was she now—and what was she doing?

I jerked myself up. "Before you call the police, I need to make one call. In private."

Doctor escorted me to his office. I dialed Inez's number, praying the girls would still be there. Inez's mother, a bewildered woman who has no inkling of her daughter's antics, assured me that they were in Inez's room, and soon I had Caron on the line.

I told her what Miss Parchester had done, then asked her to go to the escapee's neighborhood and watch for her to amble down the sidewalk in pink bedroom slippers. After warning her about the likely presence of a policeman on a similar assignment, I told her to call me at home if anything happened.

Caron was enchanted with the idea of playing detective. She suggested a disguise; I ruled it out and suggested she pose as an innocent teenager. She announced that she would be utterly terrified to go alone. I agreed that Inez was the perfect codetective for the stakeout. I refused to think up a code word, then hung up in the middle of a melodramatic sigh.

When I came out of the office, Doctor was hovering nearby, his fingers in a hopeless snarl. "I suppose we'd better call the police," he said, "even though the publicity will be most detrimental to our program. The newspapers will delight in hearing we've let a patient slip out of our care, particulary an elderly one in inadequate clothing, but I suppose it can be avoided no longer. I shall have the Matron place a call to this Lieutenant Rosen."

I shrugged a farewell and went out to my car. On the way home, I drove down Miss Parchester's street and then past the high school. Several little old ladies were out cruising, but none of them were slipper-shod. I pulled up in front of the house, planning to wait by the telephone in case Caron or Miss Parchester called, but I could not force myself out of the car. I knew who the first caller would be, if he didn't come by in person to harangue and harass me. Withholding evidence. Conspiracy to aid and abet an alleged felon. Bad attitude. Lack of trust. Tuts and sighs.

"Phooey," I muttered as I pulled away from the curb and drove back to the high school. Maybe Miss Parchester would attempt to find sanctuary with one of her old chums, who was apt to be a comrade. If I could get in the building, I could get addresses from the files and make unexpected visits. It was preferable to positioning myself for the inevitable, tedious, sanctimonious lecture. Some of which, I admitted to myself, just might be justified, if one ignored the humane element. I wouldn't, but others might.

There was a single car in the faculty lot. The main doors were locked. I took out my car keys and tapped on the glass until I saw a figure glide down the hall toward me. The sound had been adequate to rouse the dead; I hoped I hadn't. The figure proved to be Bernice Dort, clipboardless and less than delighted to let me into the building.

"Whatever are you doing here, Mrs. Malloy?" she asked once I had been admitted a few feet inside.

A bit of a poser. After a moment of thought, I said, "I came by to pick up the pages for the layout. I seem to have left them in the journalism room yesterday afternoon. So silly of me, but I'm a novice at this yearbook business."

She gave me a suspicious frown, but finally nodded and adjusted her glasses on her nose. "I presume it won't take long for you to fetch the pages and let yourself out this door. Make sure it locks behind you. I shall be in the third-floor computer room should you require further assistance. In the middle of tragedy, Mr. Eugenia continues to muddle his midterm data cards."

I waited until she had spun around and marched upstairs, her heels clicking like castenets in a Spanish café. "Thank you, Mr. Eugenia," I murmured as I hurried down the hall to the office.

The room directly behind the main office was crowded with black metal filing cabinets. As I expected, one was marked "Faculty/Staff." I was tempted to settle down with a stack of folders, but I was afraid Miss Dort might click into view at any moment.

I found the two marked "Platchett" and "Bagby," copied the home addresses on a scrap of paper, and eased the drawer closed with a tiny squeak.

My mission complete, I decided I'd better find a handful of layout pages (if I could identify them) in case I encountered Miss Dort on exit. The stairwell was gloomy, but not nearly as gloomy as the basement corridor. Some light filtered in through the opaque windows of the classroom doors, and an "exit" sign at the far end cast a red ribbon of light on the concrete floor. A boiler clanked somewhere in the bowels of the building.

I reminded myself that outside the sun was shining, birds were chirping, good citizens were going about their business. My fingers may have trembled as I turned the knob, but I did not intend to meet any psychotic killers or even any adolescent bogeymen. I switched on the light, snatched up a pile of old newspapers and a few pieces of graph paper, switched off the light, and started for the stairs and daylight.

When I heard music.

Country music, those wails of lost love and broken dreams in the best Nashville tradition. It came from the far end of the hall, in the proximity of the teachers lounge. Screams, groans, or howls would have sent me leaping up the stairs like a damned gazelle. Nasal self-indulgence did not.

Frowning, I crept down the hall and stopped in front of the lounge door. The music was indeed coming from the lounge, and below the door there was a stripe of light. The music faded, and a disc jockey reeled off an unfamiliar title and a tribute to some dead singer. A female vocalist began to complain about her womanizing lover.

It was not the stuff of which nightmares are born. As I opened the door, I considered the possibility that Miss Parchester had chosen the lounge as her port in the storm, and I prepared a bit of dialogue to convince her to return to the meadows.

There was a congealed, half-eaten pizza on the table. An overturned glass lay beside it. A puddle of glittery stickiness looked, and smelled, like whiskey. Another smell hit me, a very unpleasant one that was familiar. An image of Weiss vomiting during the lethal potluck flashed across my mind, unbidden and decidedly unwelcome.

"Miss Parchester?" I croaked. "Are you here?"

The female vocalist began to wail with increased pathos for her plight. I snapped off the transistor radio. "Miss Parchester? It's Claire Malloy, and I've come to help you."

Silence. The smell threatened to send me out to the corridor, but I gritted my teeth and moved toward the rest room doors. The men's room was empty. The ladies room was not. Pitts, the reptilian, slimy, disgusting, filthy, incompetent custodian, would never again be berated for failing to wipe down a chalkboard or mop a floor.

I went upstairs to the office and dialed the number of the police station. I asked for Peter, naturally. I told him what I'd found in the teachers lounge, then suggested he trot right over before I had hysterics. I hung up in the middle of the eruption and went to find Miss Dort in the great unknown called the third floor.

We were at the main door when the police armada screeched up, blue lights, sirens, ambulance, and all. Peter shot me a dirty look as they hurried past us, but he did not dally to congratulate me on my discovery and quick-witted action. Jorgeson settled for an appraising stare; he did not seem especially surprised to see me. One would almost think Peter had mentioned me on the way over.

Miss Dort and I followed them down to the lounge. She was white but composed, although her lips were tighter than a bunny's rear end. "This is dreadful," she said as we entered the room. "Pitts was despicable, but he did not deserve this any more than Herbert did. Someone is on a rampage and must be stopped. The students will be panicked by——" She broke off as Peter came out of the ladies room. "Mrs. Malloy seems to think Pitts was also poisoned with cyanide, Lieutenant Rosen. Is this true?"

"Mrs. Malloy has many thoughts; however, she seldom shares them with me," he answered. The smile aimed in my direction lacked warmth, as did his eyes. His voice might have halted a buffalo stampede.

"I called you immediately," I pointed out.

"Did you consider calling me from the Happy Meadows Home?"

There was that.

"Of course I did," I lied smoothly. "The doctor there said he would call you; it would have been redundant."

"It would not have been so four days ago. It would have been enlightening."

There was that, too.

"If you had asked me if Miss Parchester was at Happy Meadows, I would have told you." I decided to change the subject before it detonated. "Was it cyanide?"

The look he gave me promised future discussion, but Miss Dort's presence deterred him at the moment. "Probably so, but we'll send samples to the state lab. It looks as though it was introduced through food or drink."

We all stared at the table. "I would guess it was in the whiskey," I said. "I can't imagine poisoning pizza . . . unless someone sprinkled powder in the mozzarella, or slipped it under the pepperoni. But Pitts must have brought the pizza with him, which would make it all the more difficult. It would be much easier to dump poison in the whiskey bottle and leave it in the lounge. Pitts probably thought it was Christmas in November."

Peter was unimpressed by my well-constructed theory. "What an expert you've become in the modus operandi of murder, Ms. Malloy. How unfortunate the department can't afford to hire you, but thus far you've provided your services at every opportunity and at no charge, haven't you?"

Miss Dort interrupted his petty tirade. "This must be stopped, Lieutenant Rosen. The school will be in an uproar until this killer is apprehended, and the students will be unmanageable. As temporary principal, I have a duty to the school board and the community to operate this school efficiently and with a minimum of disruptions to the educational process. You can't believe how the press has hounded me—the calls—the interference from administrative paperwork to the ceiling—I don't know what I shall do."

Peter took her by the arm and escorted her to the lounge door. "I'll post an officer at the main door tomorrow to keep out the press, and I'm sure the administration people won't blame you for this. For now, show me the personnel file on the victim. I'll need his home address and next of kin, along with whatever there is about his past work record and personal data." He turned to glare at me. "Ms. Malloy, I will require a statement from you, but not at this time. Wait at your residence."

"Certainly." There was no reason to argue about the directive, not when I intended to ignore it. "I shall await your arrival with bated breath, Lieutenant Rosen. Do you need to write down my address?"

He sighed, shook his head, and left with Miss Dort. I guessed I had ten minutes or so before they returned, so I perched on the mauve-and-green and tried to look inconspicuous. In that my face was still greenish, it was moderately successful. The photographers snapped numerous rolls of film, and the fingerprint men dusted surfaces. The medical examiner came out of the ladies room, his face as green as my own despite his years of experience. Jorgeson directed traffic.

"Jorgeson," I said sweetly, "have you received the analysis from the lab concerning the cyanide that killed Herbert Weiss?"

"I guess it won't hurt to tell you it came from an organic source rather than a manufactured process. The Gutzeit test confirmed the presence of the compound in the peach compote, but we've asked for further tests to pinpoint the precise source." He scratched his chin. "Did you know peach pits contain cyanide, as do apple seeds, cherry pits, apricot pits, and a whole bunch of fruit like that? Gawd, I used to eat apple cores all the time. It seemed tidier. Gawd!"

"I suggest you throw them away in the future," I said without sympathy. Time was of the essence, in that Peter was apt to be displeased if he returned to find me grilling his minion. "Are we assuming the cyanide came from peach pits?"

"I don't think the lieutenant wants you to assume anything, Mrs. Malloy. He'd probably demote me if he found out I even talked to you. You'd better run along and wait for him at your house."

"I shall run along. Don't worry about demotion, Jorgeson; there's no reason why the lieutenant should ever know about our little chat, is there?" I gave him a beady look, then gathered up the newspapers and graph paper and went upstairs, wondering if Miss Parchester's recipe included such toxic ingredients as peach pits. Surely it would have been noticed over the years.

I took a few turns in the corridor to avoid the office. Once in my car, I checked the addresses and drove to Mrs. Platchett's house, a respectable little box in a respectable little neighborhood. She came to the door in a bathrobe, her head covered with bristly pink rollers. "Mrs. Malloy," she said through the screen, "how interesting of you to drop by unannounced. Is there something I can do for you?"

I considered a variety of lies, then settled for the truth about Pitts's untimely demise and Miss Parchester's escape from Happy Meadows. She was appalled, although it was difficult to decide which bit of information caused the greater grief. It proved to be the latter.

"Emily is wandering around Farberville with some wild notion that she will investigate Mr. Weiss's death?" Mrs. Platchett said, shaking her head. "Great harm is likely to happen to her. She is too trusting for her own good, and easily taken advantage of by anyone who claims an interest in the Constitution. You must locate her at once, Mrs. Malloy."

"I thought she might have come to you." I peered over her shoulder at the interior of the house. "Are you sure she's not hiding in a back room?"

"She is not here." Unlike some of us who shall remain nameless, Mrs. Platchett was not amused by the idea that she would aid and abet an alleged felon. "If you wait on the veranda, I will call Mae and see if she has heard from Emily, but it is almost inconceivable that she would make contact with either of us, and Tessa is still at the hospital. Emily knows we could not hide her from the authorities. It is against the law, and possibly unconstitutional."

I nodded. "Please don't bother to call Miss Bagby. Her apartment is on my way home, and I can stop by to speak to her in person." I hesitated for a minute. "Ah, do you happen to have any peaches, Mrs. Platchett? I know it sounds strange, but it may help Miss Parchester."

Unconvinced and visibly in doubt of my sanity, she disappeared into the house and returned with a lumpy brown bag. She handed it to me and watched through the screen door as I climbed in my car and drove away.

Mae Bagby invited me in for a cup of tea, although she did so in a listless fashion, murmuring that the funeral had drained her. I told her about Pitts. She closed her eyes, then took a swallow of tea and said, "This is truly dreadful, Mrs. Malloy. First poor Mr. Weiss, and now Pitts. Whatever are we to do?"

"The police will be unobtrusive tomorrow and finished with the crime scene by the next day. I suppose the students will appear to seek knowledge and the teachers to offer it to them."

"I don't know if I can bear to return to the school," she sighed. "It's not only the events of the last few days that motivate me to consider early retirement from my profession. The school has changed so much in the last forty years, and always for the worse. The students are so unconcerned about academics and morals, and they blithely break the law by consuming alcohol and drugs. Some of them actually engage in sexual activity to the point of promiscuity. It is all I can do to interest them in biology, in the discovery of the glories of nature. Perhaps I shall inquire about retirement."

I made a sympathetic noise, then asked if she had chanced upon the errant Miss Emily Parchester. Miss Bagby was as perturbed as Mrs. Platchett, but as firm in her avowal that she could not, under any circumstances, however justified, friendship or not, hide a fugitive. I gave her my telephone number in case the fugitive appeared, patted her shoulder, and drove home to conduct an experiment worthy of a Nobel Prize.

I was sitting on the sidewalk with the peach and a hammer when Peter pulled up to the curb. He almost smiled at what must have been a peculiar picture, then remembered his role as Nasty Cop. Slamming the car door hard enough to spring a sprocket, he stomped up the walk and glowered down at me. "I called earlier, but you were not here. I thought I told you to go home and wait for me."

I took a bite of peach. Yummy. "You did. What if I've been sitting out here since I arrived home?"

"I drove by several times."

"It takes me awhile to scurry home with my tail between my legs." I wondered where Mrs. Platchett bought her produce. Peach juice dribbled down my chin. I wiped it on my sleeve, finished the last bite of peach, and picked up the hammer. "I'll account for my whereabouts in a moment, but first I want to see how hard it is to get out the pit."

"And why would you want to ascertain that information?" he snapped, unmoved by my quest for knowledge.

"Peach pits contain cyanide; everyone knows that. Because the peach compote contained an organic cyanide compound, it does seem probable that the pits are implicated—if they're not impossible to extract."

"Not everyone knows the chemical structure of peach pits. When did you chance upon it? High school chemistry—or more recently?"

Lacking an acceptable answer, I ignored the remark and smashed the seed with a mighty blow. It bounced into a pile of dried leaves. "Damn, this is harder than it looks," I said as I crawled across the walk and started to dig through the leaves.

Peter leaned over and picked up the peach pit. "Let me try," he said in a grudging voice—since he hadn't thought up the brilliant experiment.

I handed him the hammer and sat back to watch him smash the seed. His expression was enigmatic, to say the least, but his single blow was forceful enough to shatter the outside covering and expose an almond-shaped pit. He studied it for a second, then handed it to me. "It isn't difficult. Anyone could do it."

"Not little old ladies with tremulous hands and poor eyesight," I said. "It takes the male touch to pulverize an innocent pit. We of the opposite persuasion lack the temperament. I really can't see delicate Miss Parchester on her hands and knees on the sidewalk, smashing peach seeds to collect the pits."

"Ah, Miss Parchester. Couldn't you have told me where she was—before she disappeared? You knew damn well that I wanted to question her, Claire. The fact that you knowingly failed to tell me her whereabouts borders on a felony."

As Mexico borders on France. "I felt responsible for her," I admitted in a wonderfully contrite voice. "I thought I could clear things up before you dragged her to the station to book her."

"But instead you lost her. Now she's playing Miss Woodward-Bernstein, and liable to dig herself into more trouble. If we'd had her tucked away in a cell, she couldn't have been a suspect in the custodian's murder. But of course she's trotting around town, no doubt with a purse full of compote and peach pits, and might have visited the high school during the funeral. I've issued a warrant. Good work, Ms. Malloy."

"Thank you, Lieutenant Rosen." I snatched up the hammer, put the pit in my pocket, and started for the house. "I'll give you a call when I determine who really killed Weiss and Pitts. In the meantime I have to wait for an important call."

"I have to take your statement. Now."

I faltered in midstomp. "No more sarcasm. I confuse it with the warm glow that comes from impacted wisdom teeth."

We went upstairs. He took my statement, then apologized and made amends. I accepted the apology, allowed amends, and generally forgave him for his boorish behavior. But I then shooed him away, worried that Caron might call while he was there. An apology was one thing, Miss Parchester another. And I *was* going to clear her name.

"E"I"G"H"T"

Caron's vigilance was not rewarded. She complained about it straight through dinner, then retreated to her room to sulk in solitude when I failed to offer adequate sympathy. I spent the night envisioning Miss Parchester supine in a pond or ditch, her slippers atwitch in her death throes. It did nothing to contribute to sleep, and I was not in a jolly mood the next morning as I arrived at what threatened to become my permanent classroom. I longed for the Book Depot, the jackhammer, my crowded office, the antiquated cash register with the sticky drawer, and the rows and rows of lovely books. It didn't do a damn bit of good.

Farberville High School had not closed its doors to commemorate the death of a custodian. During the morning announcements, Miss Dort assigned a few terse words to the tragic loss of an employee, warned the students not to speak with reporters, and went right on to the homecoming festivities—the very mention of which gave me goose bumps. I went right on to the lounge.

There were traces of fingerprint powder on the table and a lingering aroma that someone had attempted to overpower with pine-scented air freshener. I felt as if I'd been teleported to Maine. I contemplated a search for the other lounge, which to my knowledge was not yet a breeding ground for corpses, then reminded myself that I would learn nothing there. I waded through the pine cones and poured myself a cup of coffee.

Paula Hart came into the lounge. After a warm smile of greeting, she started for the ladies room, then stopped and shook her head ruefully. "I can't do it," she said with a small, deprecatory laugh. "I intended to be quite sensible about it, since the other faculty lounge is so far. But I can't make myself go in there—not after what happened to poor Pitts."

"You're the only person who's apt to be distressed by Pitts's death," I said. "Everyone else will celebrate—in a decorous manner, of course."

"He was a sad little man. He did so want to be a part of the staff, but he simply did not fit in with us. No education, a certain lack of—of physical fastidiousness, an inclination to grovel that encouraged certain people to ridicule him without mercy. All those rumors about him, based on student gossip, which can be fanciful. Heaven knows they come up with some wild ideas at times. The others were ready to lynch him, but I tried to give him the benefit of the doubt. I suppose I felt sorry for him."

It occurred to me that she and her coach had entered the lounge after the discussion of Pitts's peepery. I asked her if she knew about the spy hole in the ladies room.

"Evelyn told me. I wish I knew how long the hole had been there. I'd like to think he wasn't watching me adjust my panty hose every morning, but we'll never find out." She made a face. "It is awful, isn't it? Being spied on through a nasty hole in the wall. . . ."

"He was also privy to conversations when the door was open," I told her, making the same face but with a more mature set of wrinkles. "I guess he overheard quite a lot of personal conversations."

She fluttered a hand to her mouth. "Oh, I don't think he could hear anything, do you? Even with the door open, it's a thick wall and there's always noise in the halls."

"Let's test the hypothesis," I said, enamored of the idea of yet another Nobel-level experiment, this time in acoustics. "I'll go in his closet and put my ear to the wall. You take the tape off the hole, then go into the lounge and talk. We'll find out if he could have heard anything."

"What shall I say?"

"Anything. Your name and address. The alphabet."

She looked doubtful, but she stayed in the middle of the room. I went around the corner and through the storage room to the private sanctum. There were signs the police had examined the room, and I wondered if they'd found the alleged stash of illegal substances. I wryly noted a collection of empty whiskey bottles. Pitts would have done better to stick with his own brand.

I located the hole and put my ear to it, feeling rather sleazy even though I was conducting research for a good cause. I heard Paula chanting the alphabet as if she were inches away. Acoustical miracles, I supposed. Paula broke off in the middle of "L-M-N-O."

"Hi, Jerry," she said brightly.

"Why are you in the middle of the room reciting the alphabet?" he asked, not unreasonably.

I could almost hear the flutter of her hands. Our Miss Hart was not, to her credit, an accomplished liar, but it seemed she couldn't bring herself to expose me. Or maybe the truth was too silly for her true love to be saddled with.

"For a typing test," she gasped. "Third period. I'm going to time them on the alphabet."

"And you're not sure you remember it?" He chuckled at her, then cut off her flutters with what I presumed was a kiss. "Listen, my darling, I've got to find that blasted transcript before the police do. No, don't interrupt, please. If the police stumble onto it, they'll think I had a motive to murder Weiss. Honey, let me finish. I doubt it's in the regular file; Weiss wanted to dangle it over my head like a damned sword before he made it public. Maybe it's hidden in his—*what?*"

There was a long silence, punctuated by earnest whispers and a low growl. The door of the ladies room slammed shut, thus leaving the location of the mysterious transcript unspecified and my left eardrum aquiver in tympanic shock. I felt fairly sure Jerry wasn't going to offer further details, no matter how nicely I asked.

I was still listening to chimes in my head when I heard a noise through the hole. I waited a few minutes, then leaned against the wall once more, prepared to sacrifice scrupulosity and dignity in exchange for information. A toilet flushed, water ran in the sink, and the door was opened—and left ajar. Someone more considerate than the coach was in the lounge. Footsteps, the clink of the coffee pot against a mug, more footsteps. I decided the odds on a killer admitting all, particularly to a room devoid of an audience, were nil to none, and I was on the verge of abandoning my post when someone laughed.

"How's your student teacher faring in the face of all this mayhem?" Sherwood said. "Is she more *non compos mentis* than usual?"

"I suspect she'll flee back to the college to find another major." Evelyn sounded as if such flight held appeal. "The rest of us will end up with *delirium tremens,* complete with hallucinations and crazy ideas that this place isn't really a temporary stop on the way to the morgue. Policemen underfoot, newsmen in the parking lot, and Bernice Dort in command. Oh, Sherwood, I can't believe anyone would murder Herbert Weiss, or even pitiful Pitts. Maybe I am losing my mind."

"Surely you are not devastated by the loss of our *factotum,* our worthless dogsbody? We'll get a replacement, and we'll be better off for it, as will the building and the ignoble savages. By the way, I have arrived at a startling insight, Evelyn—one that warrants serious cogitation. It involves Pitts's vile habit of eavesdropping through that little hole. It must have been the precise size to accommodate his mind—which contradicted the tenet that *natura abhorret vacuum.*"

I did not take it personally.

"What do you mean, Sherwood?" said Evelyn. "And get to the

point without any incomprehensible asides, please. The first-period bell is going to ring any minute."

"It seems to me that certain information conveyed in confidence wormed its way upstairs to the domain of our resident Zeus. It has now been demonstrated that the walls have ears—perhaps they also have mouths."

"I understand your Latin better. What, Sherwood?"

"Among his other virtues, Pitts must have been a snitch. You heard Weiss's crack about the library, Evelyn, and only you and I knew about that matter. How else could he have learned of that absurd accusation, unless Pitts overheard our conversation and tattled to his boss?"

I willed him to explain. He didn't.

"That may be," Evelyn said, "but it's irrelevant now. Weiss and Pitts are both dead, so it doesn't matter what either of them heard. It's very convenient for you, isn't it?"

"*Mutatis mutandis,* a change for the better. May I presume my secret is safe with you, Evelyn?" There was a pause during which I prayed for a brief reiteration of said secret. There wasn't. "Ah, good, I knew I could trust you. We'd better retreat before the halls swell with the undeodorized."

A door closed. I rubbed my ear as I tried to make sense of the tidbits I'd heard. I did understand why Pitts eavesdropped; the conversations were entertaining and provocative, if not lucid. All I had to do was determine the meaning and what bearing, if any, these secrets had on two cases of murder. A transcript and an accusation about a library. Was either worthy of murder?

The bell jangled. I realized it was time for the first period and made my way through the outer room. I opened the door—and crashed into Sherwood Timmons.

"My goodness," he said, tugging at his goatee, "what have we here? Have I caught you *in flagrante delicto,* Claire?"

"You have caught me in the hall—and on my way to meet my first-period class. Now, if you'll excuse me, Sherwood, I must—"

"I fear I must insist you explain your presence in Mr. Pitts's closet. Were you seeking clues, or listening to your elders through a convenient hole in the wall?"

"Don't be absurd. I simply wanted to take a look around, to see if the police overlooked anything of importance."

"Overlooked—or overheard?" He moved forward until I could smell the wintergreen of his breath. "I had thought better of you, held you in the highest esteem, idolized your famed deductive prowess. Now I wonder if my Athena is but a mortal, as flawed as the rest of us."

"I am indeed flawed, but my vices do not include tardiness. It's first period, Sherwood, and I must meet my class."

"We shall meet again," he said, bowing slightly.

He stepped back and I hurried away, as pink as a small child caught in the vicinity of a forbidden cookie jar. A misdemeanor, but still embarrassing. I survived the first two classes by debating whether to tell Peter what I'd heard—or overheard, anyway. It was moot. On the one hand, he would be gratified that I cooperated, for once. On the other, he would not be gratified that I was still investigating. In mystery novels, the amateur sleuths are not hindered as they sniff around for clues and analyze casual remarks for Freudian slips. The police share all the evidence and are unflaggingly grateful for what assistance they receive.

I concluded that Peter needed to read more fiction, after which I might consider cooperating with him.

The second-period class wandered away, and I went to the lounge to ponder the puzzle. I was pondering away when Evelyn came in.

"What a nightmare," she said once we were settled cozily over coffee. "Especially for you, since you found the body. Why were you in the building yesterday afternoon, Claire? Did you really come back for the yearbook layouts?"

The speed with which gossip spread through the school was astounding, but I was beginning to get used to it. I told her about riffling the files for Mrs. Platchett's and Mae Bagby's addresses, and the reason for doing so. And the subsequent failure to find Miss Parchester at either residence. I did not tell her that I had also stained my jeans with peach juice, and allowed Peter to prove his manhood with a hammer.

"Poor Emily," she sighed. "She is so unpredictable, and I hope she doesn't do anything rash in the name of freedom of the press. It's her guiding force in life; she'll defend it to the death, murmuring about the Judge all the while."

"To the death?"

"No, that was hyperbole. But she is devoted to the cause, which resulted in a lot of rumbling about the *Falcon Crier*. There were some stories that were outrageous, filled with misinformation, adolescent ravings, and controversial stands on taboo subjects. I know Weiss bawled Emily out on several occasions, but she refused to censor anything her apprentice reporters wrote."

"Do you think this Miss Demeanor nonsense has anything to do with the murders? Most of it was drivel, but the business about the Xanadu Motel was different." I chewed on my lip, trying to recall a snippet of conversation that seemed as if it might have meant something. It remained steadfastly out of reach, like a mosquito bite in the middle of one's back.

Evelyn was staring at the wall. "It doesn't have anything to do with what's happened in the last week, Claire. I can't explain, but it really is irrelevant."

"Why can't you explain?"

"It was just a tacky little attempt on someone's part to stir up trouble," she said. "Once the newspaper was halted, so was the smear campaign. There's no point in worrying about it now."

I chewed off the rest of my lipstick, then said, "It was blackmail, wasn't it? You've got to tell me what it meant, Evelyn. It could be important, and I must know who was blackmailing whom—and why." When she shook her head and looked away, I took the obvious shot. "Do you and Sherwood visit the Xanadu on a regular basis?"

"I'm single, and so is he. We both live alone, so we would hardly pay for a sleazy motel room for an afternoon romp, would we? And even if we did, it wouldn't be much of a crime. A scandal, perhaps, but not a very big one in this day."

"Then who?" I demanded, forcing myself not to grab her by the shoulders and shake it out of her. I liked her, although her recalcitrance was straining the friendship. Caron evokes the same emotion in me.

"I can't tell you. You'll have to trust me when I say that it has no connection to Weiss's murder. It would make no sense whatsoever, and letting the gossip spread is unconscionable."

I let it go for the moment, although I wasn't prepared to accept her word. "Then let me ask you something else. What did you think about Weiss's comment in the teachers' meeting about Jerry's transcript? Is it possible that he falsified it, that he didn't really graduate and doesn't have a degree?"

"I don't see how," Evelyn said. "He has to have state certification to be employed as a coach and teacher, and the district office keeps the necessary forms on file. The state board of teacher certification grinds exceedingly slowly, but it does grind and cannot be avoided. I just thought Weiss was needling our golden boy, most likely out of petty jealousy."

"He did needle him well. I'd like to get a peek at the personnel files, though. There has to be something peculiar about Jerry's transcripts; he stormed out of the meeting and said some harsh things about Weiss afterward."

"Did he?" She studied me as if I had admitted poisoning the city water supply, then went into the ladies room and locked the door.

The bell rang (it was beginning to regulate my life) and the other faculty members appeared shortly for what proved to be a very restrained lunch period. Mrs. Platchett and Miss Bagby both gave me inquiring looks. I shrugged and shook my head to the unspoken questions. Ignoring me, Jerry sulked his way through a sandwich and left, despite Paula's unhappy sighs. Sherwood winked, but I managed to avoid an unseemly reaction; he did possess a key and I a healthy curiosity about the personnel files. Not to mention the journalism books, which I'd almost forgotten.

I retreated to the journalism room for fourth period. When Caron sauntered in, I tossed the roster to Bambi and beckoned for Caron to join me in the darkroom.

"Can you go to Miss Parchester's neighborhood after school?" I asked her. "I doubt she'll show up, but I don't want her to fall into the sticky arms of the law if she does."

"I wasted an entire afternoon there yesterday, Mother. It was Utterly Boring, and I see no point in putting myself through that ordeal again. Besides, Inez and I have to work on the Homecoming float."

"What Homecoming float? Is there to be a parade?"

"I was not referring to coke and ice cream," she sniffed. "The parade is Friday afternoon at three o'clock, and each class has to enter a float. The freshman entry is 'Broast the Bantams.' It's dumb, but no one could come up with anything remotely clever. We're working on it, stuffing crepe paper in chicken wire and that sort of thing, in Rhonda Maguire's garage."

"A float is not as important as Miss Parchester," I began in a sternly maternal voice. I realized that Caron was about to insist that it certainly was, if not a good deal more so. "All right, go work on the float. But if Miss Parchester is arrested for murder, you will not be writing the Miss Demeanor column next week. Or next year, or eons down the road when you're a senior. Keep that in mind while you're ankle-deep in crepe paper."

I left her to mull over her thwarted career and sat down at the desk to mull over my thwarted scheme. And my next move. Bambi McQueen approached, a sly look on her face. "If you'll write me a blue slip, I can take the absentee list to the office now, Mrs. Malloy. It's supposed to be turned in right after the beginning of class. Miss Dort doesn't like for it to be late."

"By all means," I said. I opened the desk drawer and took out a pad of blue slips. I noticed a key among the pencil stubs, a rusty thing with a tag marked "mailbox—office." "Does this open the Miss Demeanor box?" I asked with a flicker of interest.

Bambi said she thought it did, and I handed it to her with instructions to bring the contents of the box back with her. She waited until she had her trusty blue slip in pocket, then bounced away with a smug expression. Her expression was glum when she returned, however, and I was prepared for the announcement that the box was empty.

Once school was over, I walked slowly to the parking lot, not sure where to go, or what to do when I got there. Miss Parchester was not likely to appear at her apartment, and I had no theories about where else to search for her. A policeman of certain familiarity hailed me before I could reach a decision and beat a retreat.

"I have a message for Miss Parchester," said Peter. He leaned against my car, his arms folded and his smile deceptively bland. "Good news, actually."

"I'll be happy to pass it along when I see her," I said, miffed that he would think I was hiding her. Did he think I had her stashed in the trunk—or tied up in the attic?

"I brought in an accountant do a quick audit of the journalism books."

"Oh, did you? That was terribly clever of you."

"Thank you. The fact that you were involved in the matter gave it more significance than one would normally give it."

"Thank you. I didn't realize my presence was quite so ominous."

"Your presence is always ominous. Ominous, omnipresent, and according to some rumors, omnipotent."

"As much as I've enjoyed this repartée, I have more important things scheduled for the remainder of the afternoon," I said through clenched teeth. "What did the accountant find in the journalism books? If you're not going to tell, do it now."

"The accountant said that the books were basically in order. He said there had been crude attempts to make the account look short, but that the money was all there. He had a few other comments about Miss Parchester's system, which he found peculiar yet amazingly sound. I suspect she'll be relieved to find out that the embezzlement charges are going to be dismissed."

Leaving the minor matter of murder. "Who fiddled the accounts to make her look guilty?"

Peter shrugged. "I suppose I could hunt up a handwriting expert, but all he'd have to go on are a few smudgy numbers penciled in over the originals. Do you honestly think this has anything to do with the murders? A few dollars missing from a club account, easily located once the books are examined?"

"No, not really. It's damned odd, that's all . . . and it did result in Weiss's death. If Miss Parchester hadn't been accused and exiled, she wouldn't have left the compote in the lounge, thus providing someone with the vehicle to poison Weiss. I keep thinking it had to be planned; one doesn't stroll about a high school with a pocketful of peach pits."

Jorgeson appeared around the corner of the building and yelled at Peter.

"I'm needed," he said, charmingly reluctant to desert me. "Will you swear you don't have Miss Parchester tucked away somewhere?"

I dutifully swore (since I didn't), and went so far as to invite him to come by later in the evening. We parted amiably. I drove to the hospital to visit Tessa Zuckerman, the only Fury I hadn't questioned. I did not expect to find Miss Parchester hunched under a hospital bed, but I was running out of potential ports.

Miss Zuckerman resembled a limp, faded rag doll in the bed. Her arms were crowded with needles and tubes; her face was almost the color of the pillowcase that engulfed it. She appeared to be asleep, but as I started to tiptoe out of her room, her eyelids fluttered.

"Mrs. Malloy?"

"Hello, Miss Zuckerman. I came by to see how you were. Don't let me disturb you if you need to rest."

"No, it was so very kind of you to come, and I'm flattered by your concern. You must tell me the truth, Mrs. Malloy. Mae and Alexandria have taken it upon themselves to protect me from any outside news. Their decision is admirable but frustrating. They will tell me nothing about the dreadful—occurrence in the lounge. How is Mr. Weiss?"

I hedged for a moment, then told her. She closed her eyes for a long time, and I had decided she was asleep when she at last stirred. "Thank you for telling me," she said. "I wondered as much; he looked so ill and the bluish cast to his skin made me think of cyanosis. Have the police arrested anyone for the crime?"

"No, but they would like very much to speak to Emily Parchester about the brandied peach compote. They have not been able to find her, however. Has she been to visit you in the last few days?"

She turned her face away from me, and her voice took on a guarded tone. "I get so confused, Mrs. Malloy, that I cannot be sure whether my visitors are real or imagined. Let me think. . . . No, Emily has not been here that I can recall. I doubt she intends to come."

It was as convincing as Paula Hart's explanation of why she was standing in the lounge reciting the alphabet. Jerry might have believed his beloved, but I knew a lie when I heard one. And I'd just been offered a whopper.

"Please tell her I have good news—should she come by," I said. "I'll see you when you come back to school." Her eyes were closed again, but this time her breathing was deep enough to indicate that she had fallen asleep. I stopped at the nurse's station. "How is Miss Zuckerman doing?" I asked a shiny-faced young thing.

"As well as can be expected, but renal failure is very, very serious. Are you a member of the family?"

"In a way. Does her doctor have any idea how long she'll be in the hospital?"

The young thing gave me a long, solemn look. "The patient is not expected to recover," she whispered. "The endometrial cancer is no longer in remission. No other forms of treatment, including the less conventional ones, have had any significant effect, and she has refused further chemotherapy."

I forgave Tessa Zuckerman for her lie. I made a mental note to send flowers while they could be enjoyed, then thanked the nurse and walked out to my car. A woman nodded as she walked past me, a box of candy in her hand. A worried young man with a child hurried by, followed by an elderly couple and several teenagers. I gaped at their backs. Visitors. Emily Parchester had visited her dying friend, and would do so again.

The next set of visiting hours were from seven to nine P.M. I needed a couple of bodies for the stakeout, since I would have to entertain Peter. I drove to Rhonda Maguire's garage and steeled myself for both the incipient outrage and the sight of "Broast the Bantams." Neither would present a pretty picture. I was right on both counts.

After a hefty dose of cajolement coupled with money for hamburgers and milkshakes, Caron and Inez abandoned their classmates and left for the hospital. If Miss Parchester appeared, she would be tailed by two excited detectives with crepe paper in their hair.

When Peter came by, he was too tired to discuss the case. We drank wine and watched television like old married folks, and he was actually nodding when the telephone rang.

I grabbed it before the second ring. "Yes?" I hissed.

"Mrs. Malloy? This is Inez. Caron told me to call you and report what happened."

Peter's head was still lowered. I turned my back to him and hunched my shoulders around the receiver. "What happened, Inez? Why did Caron tell you to call? Why can't she come to the telephone herself?"

"She is in the emergency room. Even if she could call, I don't think she's in the mood to talk about it."

"What is she doing in the emergency room? What happened?"

"It's a long story, Mrs. Malloy, but Miss Parchester finally showed up at Miss Zuckerman's room. We were waiting in an empty room across the hall, ready to tail her to her hideout." She gulped several times. "Then, just as Miss Parchester started to go in Miss Zuckerman's room, a nurse spotted us and yelled at us to come out and explain what we thought we were doing."

"There must be more, Inez. Please get to the reason that my daughter is now in the emergency room and unable to speak to me."

"Miss Parchester jumped about ten feet when she saw us. Caron grabbed her to try to tell her that we wanted to help, but I think it must have scared her. Anyway, she sort of bopped Caron on the head with her umbrella and ran away down the hall."

"And Caron has a concussion from being assaulted by an old lady with an umbrella?"

"Not exactly," Inez said, sighing faintly. "Caron and I both started after Miss Parchester, but the nurse got in the way and we all ended up on the floor. Caron sprained her ankle. The hospital security people put her in a wheelchair and brought her down here to get it taped. I don't think they're going to let us go, Mrs. Malloy. My mother is going to kill me."

"No, she's not," I said. I could envision the fiasco from start to finish, from the lurkers in the dark room to the current extension of my daughter's lower lip.

"I have to go," Inez said in a very small voice. "They won't let me talk anymore. Will you bring bail, Mrs. Malloy? Caron and I have less than a dollar, and I think we're in worse trouble than that."

I assured her that I would be there within ten minutes and replaced the receiver. Peter was still asleep. There was no way to explain where I was going and why. There was also no reason to try, so I opted to let sleeping dogs lie. Better than I.

I left a note on his wineglass and tiptoed out the door.

"N"I"N"E"

I managed to extricate Caron and Inez from the clutches of hospital security, but it took an insurance card, a parental consent form to X-ray and subsequently wrap a twisted-but-not-sprained ankle, and an endless stream of avowals that neither girl would set foot in the hospital again unless they were preanesthetized in the parking lot. During all this fun, Caron limped out of a cubicle and shot me an icy look.

"This has been So Entertaining," she said. "It was all your idea, Mother. I told them that much, but they wouldn't listen to me. Anyway, I don't see how you can trespass in a public building. They Do Say this is a public building, don't they? That means the public can come in, doesn't it? I am public, aren't I?"

Nostrils aquiver, she beckoned for Inez to support her. The two hobbled out the door, leaving me to fill out insurance forms under the reproachful scrutiny of a nurse, who seemed to think I was some sort of modern day Fagin. Which I suppose I was.

There was a good deal of sniffing and puffing in the car, but no further rhetorical rampages or comments on culpability. Inez muttered a thanks for the ride and scurried into her house like a leaf caught in the wind. The inarticulate outrage continued all the way to Caron's bedroom door, where I was informed she could manage quite well without me. No thanks for the ride, either.

Peter was gone, saving me from the necessity of producing explanations (lame/mendacious) for the errand and for the noises that still drifted through the bedroom door. I made a cup of tea and retired to my bedroom to think about Miss Parchester. My theory that she would visit Miss Zuckerman had been right, but she had slipped away without divulging the location of her hideout. And she wouldn't return to the hospital. The debacle in the hallway would fuel her paranoia. I seemed to have perfected the ability to both find her and lose her. I considered what Peter would do if he ever found out about the scene in the hospital, when the fugitive had fled into the great unknown—again. In all probability, he would not be amused.

I went on to Pitts's murder, and wasted a good fifteen minutes wondering why he'd been poisoned. Sherwood suspected the custodian had carried tales to the principal, who then used the knowledge to apply pressure to various members of the faculty. Could Pitts have indulged in a spot of blackmail on his own? I glanced at the *Falcon Crier,* trying to imagine Pitts as the author of the nasty letters. Not Pitts, I concluded, although it would have been charmingly tidy; he hadn't been capable of penning insinuations and innuendos of such delicacy. Pitts had been, I thought glumly, more of a crayonist.

But his murder had to be linked to Herbert Weiss's death, which lacked any motive I could determine. Weiss hadn't been popular with the teachers I'd met, and probably wasn't any more popular with the other faculty members, but someone had taken an extreme view of things. Who? Pitts hadn't won any popularity contests, either. The rumors might be true, or they might well be the ravings of postpubescent imaginations. The same minds that evolved the concept of "Broast the Bantams" could surely assign nefarious motives to what might be innocent situations. I caught myself in a shudder.

The Homecoming festivities could no longer be ignored. After a gulp of tea to give me courage, I tapped on Caron's door. "May I come in, dear? I need to ask you something."

"Does it involve leaping off a cliff to help you with your investigation? Organ donation? Defenestration?"

Alert to the very real possibility of missiles being flung with lethal intent, I eased open the door. "Your ankle must be hurting. Can I bring you another pillow and some aspirins, or loosen the bandage? How about a nice cup of tea and some cookies?"

The patient was sprawled on her bed, the offending foot elevated on a pillow. Her glower had all the subtlety of a roman candle. "No thank you, Mother—you've done Quite Enough. I had to tell Rhonda I can't work on the float tomorrow afternoon, since I can barely walk. She demanded to know what happened. I had no idea what to say without thoroughly humiliating myself, so I made up some stupid story. I could tell she didn't believe me, and she'll tell everyone at school what a total klutz I am."

Better than the truth, which was likely to get back to certain cops alurk in the building. "Let's talk about the Homecoming schedule," I suggested, perching on the corner of her bed nearest the door. One never knows. "The parade is Friday afternoon?"

"Right after school at three-thirty, up Thurber Street and around the square. I was going to walk beside the float and do our class yell, but I doubt anyone will offer to push me in a wheelchair and I couldn't possibly keep up on crutches. The band would march right over me."

"You can see so much better from the sidewalk. Are you going to the game and dance? I need some advice about what to expect, and some support while I chaperone."

"Inez and I have to sell programs at the game to earn pep points. Maybe I'll sell more doing my Tiny Tim Cratchett imitation." She sucked in her cheeks and held out a cupped hand. "Please, sir, a penny for the crippled children's fund."

I almost laughed, but the sparks in her eyes kept me sober. "It will probably work, especially if you wear burlap. What about the dance? Are you and Inez going together—or do you have dates?"

The cupped hand went over her face, muffling the next words.

"No, I don't have a date, Mother. Some geek from my homeroom asked me, but the thought was nauseating. I told him I wasn't allowed to date until I was thirty. He's geeky enough to believe it. Inez and I haven't decided whether to go or not, but after Rhonda finishes telling everyone about klutzy Caron Malloy, I may not show my face in public again—ever."

"If you handle this carefully, you can win a lot of sympathy. You'll have all the boys waiting on you, bringing you punch and that sort of thing. It'll be fun."

"The geek will sit beside me all night, and I won't be able to get away from him," she sniffled. "I'll end up with pimples and herpes." She was already dialing for sympathy as I left her room.

The time had come for drastic measures if I was to avoid the Homecoming dance, save Miss Parchester's reputation, defend freedom of the press, discover the author of the Miss Demeanor blackmail letters, solve two murders—and keep Peter Rosen from locking me away for the rest of my life. I had forty-eight hours, tops. Or forty-eight years, if one used the actuarial tables.

I therefore yelled at Caron to get off the telephone, took several deep breaths, and called Sherwood Timmons.

After a round of diplomatic manuevers, I asked him if he was willing to let me in the high school that night.

"Ah, so you are still on the case of the fiddled books," he said, sounding delighted. "*Occasio facit furem*; the occasion makes the thief. Are we to wear rubber-soled shoes and use penlights to wend our way through the ledgers? Black turtlenecks and smudges on our faces? *Incognito et incognita?*"

"If you wish," I said meekly. Personally, I had on a wool jacket and my face was immaculate, but I decided to permit him his fantasies. The case of the fiddled books was no longer my primary motivation to search the office, since Peter had told me the money was still in the account. However, it seemed prudent to allow Sherwood to remain both incognizant and incognito, if he wished. I agreed to meet him in the darkest corner of the faculty parking lot. I then told Caron I had an errand and left her to continue her conversation with Inez about Rhonda—or Rhonda about the float—or the geek about hygienic distances—or something along those lines. She didn't even wave good-bye.

Sherwood loomed beside me as I climbed out of my car in the parking lot. "I must tell you how charmed I am by our little tryst, Claire. I do hope this will not be the only opportunity we have to get to know each other intimately. In fact, I've tucked a bottle of wine in my refrigerator in case we feel the urge for a spot of *vino veritas* once we complete our breaking-and-entering diversion."

I removed my elbow from his hand and gave him by best enigmatic smile. "We're merely entering, Sherwood, in that you possess a key. I realize it's unimaginative, but it's also less likely to get us arrested."

"Indeed. And we won't have to worry about the despicable Pitts appearing to fumigate, since someone has already exterminated him. *De mortuis nil nisis bonum*—but it is difficult not to interpret his demise as a gift from the gods."

"Then you believed all the rumors concerning drugs, alcohol, and back-alley abortionists? I was thinking about it earlier, but I wasn't around the school long enough to arrive at any valid conclusions about him."

"Only those on Olympus know for sure." He unlocked the door and held it open. "*Jacta alea est,* as Caesar was reputed to mutter; the die is cast."

The hall stretched like the interior of a monster, the lockers on either side glinting like rippled ribs. I hadn't cared for Sherwood's oblique reminder that we were alone, but I couldn't see him in the role of crazed poisoner. Praying my vision was accurate, I switched on my flashlight and led the way to the office and the file room beyond.

"Is this the most likely place to find ledgers?" Sherwood breathed on the back of my neck.

"Perhaps you should stay by the door in case someone's in the building," I said through the wintergreen haze. "Keep a lookout, listen for footsteps, that sort of thing."

I waited until he left, then found Jerry's folder and put it on top of the cabinet. After a quick glance through the doorway, I flipped it open and scanned it for dark, damning hints of an evil past or present. All I found was personal information of the innocuous sort, transcripts from Farber College and a midwestern university, and glowing recommendations from college coaches and professors. Jerry had maintained a high grade point average through graduate school, and had done nothing to disgrace himself that I could discover. Phi Beta Kappa and all that. No accusations of molestation or mismanagement of the team.

After a second glance through the doorway to confirm my sentry's position, I took out his file and looked at the contents. Nothing beyond the same sort of thing as in the coach's file. I closed the drawer and went into the main room. "I'm going to look through Weiss's desk," I whispered.

He nodded tersely. "I thought I saw movement at the end of the hall. Can't be sure. How much longer will you be?"

"Just a few minutes." I started for the inner sanctum, then stopped and went back to peer down the hall. "Did you really see someone down there? I don't especially want to be caught riffling Weiss's desk if there's a policeman in the building."

"Perhaps it's your policeman, dear sleuth. At least he wouldn't pull a gun on us and shoot us on the spot."

"Don't count on it," I murmured, deciding my lookout was too caught up in his assignment to be credible. I went into Weiss's office and sat down behind the desk. The drawers on either side were filled with forms, copies of memos, thick state regulation manuals, and other officious stuff. The middle drawer was crammed full of stubby pencils and confiscated goodies. A plywood paddle, worn shiny from use. Thumbtacks and ancient, lint-covered mints. A packet of letters held together with a rub-

ber band—and addressed to that paragon of propriety, Miss Demeanor.

I jammed the packet in my pocket. And without a flicker of
remorse, since they were already hot property, stolen from the
journalism mailbox. By the principal, presumably. Who'd been
murdered. Over a handful of letters?

My sentry coughed nervously. Ordering myself back to business, I dug through the drawer, but found nothing else of any
significance. I went out and told Sherwood I wanted to take a
quick look at Bernice Dort's desk.

He turned around, his face as garish as a Toulouse-Lautrec
portrait in the spray of my flashlight. "One wonders if you're the
least concerned about the journalism ledgers and poor Miss
Parchester," he said softly. "*Prima facie,* one might think you're
searching for something else, something to do with the faculty's
private business. Now why would one arrive at that conclusion,
my dear sleuth?"

I put my hand in my pocket. "I'm just checking things out,
Sherwood. This is the first time I've been able to—to look
around the office."

"For what?" He came toward me, his eyes inky shadows and
his voice disturbingly calm. "Were you looking for something
that might incriminate one of us? A letter, perchance, about me?
Did you overhear a conversation in the lounge while you were
innocently snooping in Pitts's sty?"

I edged around the counter, mentally cursing myself for the
wonderful scheme that had landed me here—with him. I have an
aversion to being menaced, particularly in a minty miasma. "I
don't know anything about that, Sherwood. I went in Pitts's
room out of curiosity, to see if there was any evidence that the
rumors were true. I didn't eavesdrop at the vile little hole." Not
much, anyway.

"*Suggestio falsi,* Ms. Malloy. I think you heard me discuss the
distressful situation with Evelyn. That's why you looked so guilty

when I caught you outside the room, and that's why you're suddenly so nervous, so worried that you shouldn't have come here with me, alone."

Bingo with a capital B. "Don't be absurd," I whispered, trying for an irritated edge to my voice. "I have no idea what you're talking about, and I don't want to know. If I thought you'd murdered Weiss or Pitts, I wouldn't have called you tonight."

"I would hardly murder Weiss over that idiotic accusation, even if I were perturbed that *vox audita perit litera scripta manet*—the voice perishes but the written word remains." He laughed, but it lacked a certain essence of mirth. "What's that you're clutching in your pocket?"

A diversion seemed timely, so I took out the packet and showed it to him. "I found this in Weiss's drawer, which explains why the journalism mailbox was empty. Why do you think he'd take the letters and stash them in his desk?"

"You'll have to figure that out on your own," he said, this time chuckling with some degree of sincerity. "Evelyn and I have wondered how long it would take the others—and particularly someone with your reputation—to deduce what's been happening."

"So you also know about the blackmail scheme?" I said. Enough retreating. I slammed down the packet and came around the counter, fists clenched, eyes narrowed. "Why won't Evelyn tell me the bare outline—if she's so damn sure it has nothing to do with the murders? For that matter, why won't you?"

"Because it's irrelevant, and Evelyn's determined not to encourage any gossip. She's gripped with some dreadful malaise called integrity; I tried to convince her otherwise, but she refused to tell me any of the juicy details, such as the identities of Aphrodite and her boyfriend. But she persisted, to my regret. Now, I do think we ought to depart before we get caught, don't you? I'd so hate to spend the night in the pokey."

I was about to persevere with the questions when a door

closed in the distance. Remembering my experiences a couple of days ago, with the music that led me to murder, I will admit I shivered—like a wet dog in a blizzard. "Did you hear that?"

My gallant sentry looked rather pale. "Someone in the building, obviously. A policeman?"

"Policemen don't prowl around in the dark. Earlier I wondered if Miss Parchester might have taken refuge in the building, maybe hiding in empty classrooms or closets until the building empties in the afternoon. I think we ought to take a look."

Ever so gallant, he gestured for me to precede him.

An hour later, we returned to the office. We'd been down every corridor, opened every door, peered into every nook (and there were a lot of them), and basically searched the entire building for the intruder. If Miss Parchester was determined to elude us, she was doing a fine job of it.

"Are you ready to leave?" Sherwood demanded, gallantry by now replaced with peevishness. "I have three sets of papers to grade, and we've wasted half the night. *Tempus fugit* when you're having fun."

I considered a lecture on the tedium of detection, but settled for a sigh. "Yes, let me get the Miss Demeanor letters and we'll go. I left them on the counter in the office."

The counter was bereft of packets. I checked my pockets and the floor. Sherwood swore he hadn't taken it, and even emptied his pockets to prove his innocence. After a further search and a great deal of grumbling, we left the building and went to our respective cars. *Vino veritas* was not mentioned.

I was still irritated when I arrived home, both irritated at myself for carelessness and at the unknown thief for tactlessness, among other things. I decided it would not be wise to ask Caron to stake out the high school the rest of the night. I confirmed that she was asleep, then picked up the last issue of the *Falcon Crier* to ferret out the identity of the nasty author if it took all night. *Tempus* might not *fugit*.

Dear Miss Demeanor,
Why does everybody make such a big deal about dates, anyway? Two girls can have a better time, and not have to put up with a lot of yucky kissing and grappling from some Nauseating geek.

Dear Reader,
Hang tight—someone will ask you out one of these days, and you'll discover the purpose of kissing and grappling, even with geeks.

After a deep breath and a moment of introspection as to my failure to provide adequate maternal guidance, I continued reading.

Dear Miss Demeanor,
How contagious is mono?

Dear Reader,
Contagious enough.

Dear Miss Demeanor,
If you were supposed to provide moral leadership to a bunch of people, and you had a choice between being divorced for adultery and bending one teensy little rule, which would you choose?

Dear Reader,
Miss Demeanor doesn't bend teensy little rules, because she has journalistic integrity. She doesn't stay awake at night worrying about being divorced for adultery, because (a) she's not married, and therefore (b) she can't commit adultery, even if she wants to. If driven to choose between such unpalatable options, she would probably climb in a closet and stay there. May I suggest the same for you?

I put down the newspaper and closed my eyes. It didn't take too long for the obvious to open my eyes, and eventually shove me to the telephone. I called Evelyn, apologized for the lateness of the hour, and asked if Herbert Weiss had been entertaining Bernice Dort in the Xanadu Motel every Thursday.

It took longer for her to respond, but at last she said, "I knew you'd figure it out, Claire. I had suspected as much since the first letter appeared in the Miss Demeanor column, but I saw no reason to speculate about it in the teachers lounge. They're both adults; they are entitled to behave however they desire—after school hours."

"But you're convinced of it now," I said. "You're not speculating any more. How can you be sure?"

"On the morning Weiss died, I was in the ladies room when they happened to come into the lounge. They discussed it rather loudly, I'm afraid. I would have preferred not to be there, but it was too late to show myself and pretend I didn't hear them. In any case, their affair couldn't have anything to do with his murder, so I chose not to mention it to the police or any of the faculty. Bernice wouldn't poison her lover, and there's no point in causing more grief to his family by exposing rather ordinary peccadillos."

"Well, someone else knew. If you weren't writing those blackmail letters—and I shall trust you weren't—then someone else was." I gnawed my lip until a fragment of conversation came back to me. "Cheryl Anne, Daddy's little princess, was the author. I happened to overhear her tell Thud that her scheme hadn't worked, that she would have to think of a new one."

"Weiss and Bernice didn't seem to know who wrote the letters, although I thought it was fairly obvious. I would guess that Cheryl Anne was hounding him at home to reinstate Thud, and using the column to keep him in a distraught frame of mind at school. The untimely cancellation of the newspaper put a stop to that. You don't think Cheryl Anne. . . ?"

"No," I said slowly, "I don't. I considered the possibility earlier, but the motive is feeble and the opportunity almost nil. After all, it's just a silly high school dance."

"You're one of the chaperones, aren't you?" Evelyn said. "Wait until you see how seriously they take these things before you dismiss it as a motive. Wallflowers have been known to transfer to other schools, and the intricacies of parking-lot misconduct dominate the conversations for weeks. But I think you're right about Cheryl Anne, Claire; surely she wouldn't poison her father over Thud's eligibility problems."

"Would Thud?"

"He'll end up in prison eventually, but it will be because of a barroom brawl, not a premeditated and well-planned crime. His mental limitations preclude that sort of thing. He'd be more apt to go after someone with a pool cue or monkeywrench, and in a mindless rage."

"That doesn't get us anywhere, then," I sighed. "It's tidier, but it doesn't get us any closer to discovering the identity of the poisoner. Cheryl Anne may have tried to blackmail her father, but she didn't poison the compote."

"Do the police still think Emily is the culprit? Have they been able to find her for interrogation, arrest, and execution?" Evelyn sounded as depressed as I felt.

I told her about the escape from Happy Meadows, the close encounter in the hospital, and the scene in the emergency room. Once she stopped laughing, she told me I ought to confess before Peter found out, interrogated, arrested, and executed a certain red-haired bookseller. She had a good point.

The next day my morning classes inched by without incident. The denizens of the lounge were almost mute during lunch, although Mrs. Platchett did report that Tessa Zuckerman was doing poorly. We all produced money for flowers and signed a gay little get-well card from "the gang at the office." She then gave me a questioning look, I shook my head, and we settled down to the soft whoosh of Tupperware.

Cheryl Anne did not appear during the Falconnaire period, presumably still in mourning over the demise of her paternal blackmail victim. Thud, presumably still ineligible, stayed hunched and unapproachable, although I wasn't sure with what I would have approached him. Or why.

Once I was free, I met Caron and Inez in the parking lot and drove them to Rhonda Maguire's garage, Caron having informed me she would At Least watch the work in progress. I went on to the police station, arranged a contrite expression, and asked to be admitted into the presence of Lieutenant Peter Rosen.

He closed his office door and put his hands on my shoulders to give me an unobstructed view of his eyes. The corners of his mouth twitched, but he gained control before he actually smiled. "To what do I owe the honor of your visit?"

It occurred to me that I really did like the man. It also occurred to me that I hadn't behaved well, and was apt to jeopardize the relationship if I continued on my blithe path. Getting a tad misty, I eased from under his hands and sat down on a battered chair. "I have come to confess all. You may then lock me up and swallow the key, but bear in mind that you will have to pick Caron up at five-thirty and fix dinner for her. She's incapacitated by a bad ankle, and I'm afraid her bark is as bad as anyone's bite."

He flashed his teeth at me as he sat down on the far side of his desk. "Before I order rabies shots, you'll have to tell me the extent of your crimes."

"The usual stuff," I said, squirming as if I were a teenaged truant facing Weiss's wrath and paddle. "Not mentioning little details to you, for instance. Prowling around the corridors in the dark to solve the murders and prove how clever I am. Evading the truth, although not as a rule."

"Are you going to elaborate?"

I elaborated for a solid thirty minutes. I told him how I'd been coerced into substituting, and why—which seemed to do odd things to the corners of his mouth. I recapped the conversations with Miss Parchester, the argument between Jerry and Paula after the teachers' meeting, the inexplicable comments I'd heard through Pitts's hole, the visits to the Furies, the hospital scene, the midnight prowl with Sherwood, and the enlightening discussion with Evelyn that led to the identity of the Miss Demeanor author. Then, making a face, I went so far as to admit how the letters had been stolen from under my nose. Not that they were still important, I mentioned in conclusion, unable to fathom the thoughts behind his expressionless face and somewhat uneasy because of it.

"You have been busy," he said. "Some of it I knew, and some I merely suspected, based on your track record. None of it surprises me, however, although for some naive reason hope springs—"

"Some of it you knew?"

He shrugged. "This morning hospital security reported an incident of minor importance. It did not require a brilliant flash of female intuition to guess the identity of two teenaged 007's in the room across the hall from Tessa Zuckerman, a witness in an investigation of particular interest to an unspecified party. The floor nurse related the details of the panicky visitor and the crazed attack that ended on the floor. One of the girls was rumored to be verbally precocious to the point the security men considered a tourniquet just below the chin. It was a good guess on your part, by the way."

"Thank you. What else did you already know before I came in here to grovel, apologize, and ultimately make a fool of myself?" I asked, resigned to the aforementioned trio.

"We asked the Xanadu manager for a description of his Thursday regulars, and he told us. No brilliance needed there, either. I discussed the affair with Miss Dort; I'm satisfied it was not a factor in Weiss's murder."

"Maybe she was jealous," I suggested. "Weiss was panting after Paula Hart, and we all know hell hath no fury. Miss Dort's efficient enough to crack a hundred peach pits in a precise row, grind the insides, put them in the compote, and shove a fork into her paramour's hand—all before the fourth period bell. There are likely to be notations on her clipboard."

"She said Weiss panted after women all the time, but that she was used to it and fairly confident after ten years that he lacked the balls to follow up on his lusting. She was scornful, not scorned."

I yielded for the moment, although I was not convinced. "You could have saved me a lot of trouble, you know. I had to learn all this the hard way."

"I'm not sure you ever learn anything, Claire." He shot me a discouraged look. "To continue, I also discussed the letters with Cheryl Anne, who was properly ashamed of her conduct and bravely offered to turn in her crown. Once she stopped sniveling at the idea, she pointed out that neither she nor Thud could enter the lounge without being noticed." He propped his feet on his desk, toppling a stack of folders, and crossed his arms. "That's pretty much what I've learned in the last few days. May I assume you've been equally open, despite your innate tendencies to the contrary?"

"You may assume so, Peter. I was trying to help Miss Parchester," I said, sighing. "I seemed to have muddled things more so than usual, and I'm sorry. If you're adamant, I will call Bernice Dort and tell her I won't be available to substitute tomorrow. No matter how deafening the jackhammer, I'll stay in the Book Depot and mind my own business. It needs minding, actually. I haven't been in for a week; the mice have probably invited all their friends in to nosh the paperbacks."

He rubbed his forehead, crossed his arms, rearranged the pile of folders, made noises under his breath, and generally allowed me time to suffer. I remained determinedly penitent. There were rumbles outside his office, cars coming and leaving, voices barking into telephones, lots of footsteps in the hall. All we needed were a few locker doors to be slammed, and we'd be in dear old Farberville High School between classes.

When I was about to exit with whatever dignity I could muster, he finally looked up and said, "You are convinced Emily Parchester is innocent. Despite your continual, maddening, eternally intrusive interference, I do value your opinion—if not your tactics. I suppose you might as well continue to substitute so that you can keep an eye on things in the lounge. You will, of course, report everything to me, without regard to your personal analysis of its value to the proper authorities."

"Of course," I murmured, somewhat disappointed I hadn't been ordered back to the bookstore for the duration. The thought had appealed. "May I be permitted to make amends to you?"

"Of course."

I gave him a bright smile. "Would you like to go dancing with me tomorrow night?" I suppose I might have mentioned the five hundred or so teenagers who would accompany us, but it must have slipped my mind.

"T"E"N

The events of the last week paled in the onslaught of the Home-coming madness. Most of the students wore some variation of red and gold in honor of the big day, and they chattered like starlings through the first two periods. The freshmen seemed to have either forgiven me for bumping off their principal or forgotten about it. No one paid any attention when I tried to quiet things down, so I settled for an aspirin and a long, solitary visit to the darkroom. Fourteen hours until the dance.

There were three bottles of aspirin beside the coffee pot in the lounge, standard equipment for such holidays. I gulped down another for luck, then slumped on the green-and-mauve, closed my eyes, and lulled myself with a pleasant reverie of books, book-racks, temperate bookbuyers, invoices, and quarterly tax esti-mates as yet uncomputed. The images evoked a quasi-religious rush of longing.

I kept my eyes closed as a few souls drifted in and out of the lounge, mission unknown. One was, I supposed, Evelyn's student teacher on her hourly breakdown; another was apt to be a Fury. I really didn't care. Now that Peter had asked for my help, I couldn't rally the energy to sniff out clues or grill suspects. *That* was too unsettling to think about, so I sank further into the plaid to doze.

"Burned out already?" Evelyn said in my ear. "Most of us survive a few years before we seek greener pastures elsewhere."

Yawning, I went into the lounge to get a cup of coffee. "I think it's psychosomatic," I called. "Anything to avoid chaperoning the dance tonight. The thought sends chills down my spine."

"You'll be in good company. Sherwood has the boys' rest room, Miss Bagby and I have the front door, and Jerry has the back door, to keep the smokers contained. Paula has the concession stand during the game, but I imagine she'll come with her beloved to ensure that he keeps his eyes on her and off the senior girls."

The coffee almost sloshed out of my cup. "Are you implying that Paula will attend this unspeakable function—even though she isn't required under penalty of death to do so?"

Evelyn laughed at my expression. "Paula's sweetness and light on the surface, but she has a stainless-steel interior. When she got fed up with Sherwood, she told him off with the acumen of a professional hit man, and he was so stricken he made nary a wisecrack in Latin for almost two weeks. It was truly amazing, not to mention refreshing. To everyone's regret, he finally recovered and is now much worse than before. I can count the Latinless sentences on one hand."

I stared at the formica table, trying to recall a bit of conversation that had occurred at the fatal potluck. "What did Weiss say to Sherwood about a manuscript that provoked a menacing Latin riposte?" I said, wrinkling my nose. "*Ars longa,* or something like that?"

"*Ars longa, vita brevis,*" Sherwood said from the doorway. "Art is long, life short. I didn't expect my delphic aside to be taken quite so literally by an unknown hand. Nor did I expect to continue to be your favorite suspect, Claire; I thought we'd resolved that last night, *in transitu.*"

"But have the sophomores abandoned you?" I said in a futile attempt to divert the direction in which we were aimed. It didn't work.

Evelyn raised an eyebrow at Sherwood. "Last night? I didn't

realize you two were getting all that cozy." She raised the other eyebrow at me. "You didn't mention anything when you called me to discuss the Miss Demeanor shenanigans."

Sherwood's eyebrows were up, so I raised mine, too, just to be companionable. "I asked Sherwood to unlock the building for me," I admitted. "I wanted to look at Jerry's personnel file to see if I could find whatever Weiss was holding over him. Sherwood was kind enough to comply, and we did discuss motives in passing."

"What did you find in Jerry's file?" Evelyn asked, thawing to early spring if not out-and-out summer.

I ignored Sherwood's glower. "I didn't find anything at all. It was all quite innocent—recommendations, teacher certification, good grades through graduate school, academic awards, that sort of thing. I was wrong when I hypothesized that he didn't have his degree. Degrees he has, and admirable ones."

Upon this seemingly innocuous revelation, Sherwood choked and sputtered through a mouthful of coffee and Evelyn turned an unbecoming shade of white. Both of them goggled at me as if I'd mentioned the coach's propensity for bestiality or the dismemberment of his first seven wives.

"What?" I said, unamused by their antics. "What's wrong with good transcripts and warm letters from old coaches?"

"Graduate school," croaked Evelyn.

"It's where you go after undergraduate school," I said. "I went to one myself, although I never got around to writing a dissertation. It's not a topic for 'The Twilight Zone' or 'That's Incredible.'"

"Jerry is a coach," Sherwood said, proving he too could croak. The pond was filling up; all we needed were lily pads.

"Jerry is indeed a coach, and probably a very good one," I said as tolerantly as I could. "He also has a doctorate in English literature, which is more than I can say after my three years of tuition, research papers, and white wine from a jug."

"A doctorate?" they croaked in unison. Lily pads couldn't be too far in the future, along with dragonflys and cattails.

"There's something you two aren't telling me. Why don't you calm down, sip some coffee, unstick your eyelids from your fore-heads—and tell me what you find so incredible?"

They looked at each other, shook their heads, looked at me, shook their heads, and looked at each other again. I was on the verge of an acerbic comment on the now-predictable pattern, followed by a repetition of my question in one-syllable words, when Evelyn found her voice.

"Jerry is a high school football coach. He's on the same salary scale as the rest of us, and it is determined by experience, contin-ued professional training—and educational level. No school would ever hire a coach with a master's degree, much less—" she gulped "—a doctorate, even if it were in physical education. He'd hardly warrant the top of the pay scale for two classes of general health, one drivers' ed, and study hall. They hardly hire any teachers with graduate degrees, since there are plenty with bachelor's floating around the market. So much cheaper that way."

Sherwood managed to find his voice, and it was laden with glee. "All Weiss had to do was call central admin and tell them about the degree, and our boy Jerry would find himself with his thumb out on the county line. *Empta dolore experientia docet;* painful experiences may teach, but not coaches with doctorates. Ooh, how delightful!"

"Sherwood," said Evelyn, "you do know you will not breathe one single word of this to anyone, don't you? If you so much as drop a hint in ancient Etruscan, I will call a press conference about your situation with that editor."

"The manuscript?" I prompted in a small voice, hoping they had forgotten my presence.

"*Et tu, Brute?* It was poppycock, and you know it," Sherwood growled at Evelyn. "Nothing was proven."

"It wasn't?" I said.

Sherwood grimaced so intently that his goatee trembled. "It sure as hell wasn't, Ms. Malloy. There was absolutely no basis for that slanderous allegation—everyone in my field uses the same reference texts and it's conceivable that a few phrases might sound somewhat similiar. Similiar—not plagiarized."

"An editor accused you of plagiarism, then returned your manuscript with a nasty letter?" I took a drink of coffee while I considered the implications. "Weiss found out, probably through Pitts's channel, and used it to make your life miserable and your career tenuous. You must have been furious."

Evelyn gave me a sad smile. "Sherwood told me about the letter the day after it arrived, and Weiss alluded to it for the first time that same afternoon. Sherwood's been frantic for weeks to learn how Weiss found out and what he intended to do, but it wasn't a motive for murder. The allegation was slanderous; it would have caused some degree of difficulty with other editors and certainly made it more of a battle to get published, but it wasn't life-and-death."

"No wonder you despised Pitts," I said to Sherwood.

His grimace eased. "I did. He was a despicable snitch, among his other qualities. He must have heard Jerry and Paula talking about the transcript and reported to Weiss, who simply sent for a copy. Holy Achilles, I wonder what Weiss had on the others. . . ."

"Something worthy of murder?" I said under my breath. The two must have heard me, for we all ended third period in a collective sigh.

At the end of the last period Caron informed me that I would have to drive her to the parade, since her ankle hurt and she wasn't about To Hobble Anywhere. As always, Inez was there to some degree. We parked behind the bank, made it to the square without too much hobbling, and found a flower box on which to sit.

Both sides of the street were beginning to crowd with students, parents, whiny children, and babies asleep in strollers. The sky was clear; the sunshine warm. I had about six hours until the dance.

Bernice Dort appeared behind us, sans clipboard. "How's your ankle?" she asked Caron. "I received a note that you were unable to participate in your physical education class, but one of the office monitors told me that you'd hurt yourself. I hope it's nothing too serious to prevent your participation in the freshman intramural volleyball tournament next week?"

Caron turned pink and said it ought to be better soon. Miss Dort nodded as if making a mental note to be transferred to a form, curled her lips at me, and started to march away.

I caught up with her at the curb. "This is my first parade," I said, despising myself for the ingratiating tone. "I understand the kids take the float competition very seriously."

"I am a judge, Mrs. Malloy, and I can assure you that *I* take the float competition very seriously. Class spirit brings the students together. It makes their formative years more meaningful, and encourages them to think fondly of their alma mater in years to come. I have not missed one of my class reunions in thirty years."

"Neither have I," I murmured as I crossed my fingers behind my back. Maybe I hadn't missed any of them; I'd never inquired. "You seem to be holding up well in the middle of all these tragic occurrences. The school continues to run well, and the students have already fallen back into their normal routines."

"Herbert Weiss was a great man as well as an inspirational leader of students and faculty. He will be sorely missed by all concerned." She leaned forward to peer around a pregnant woman. "It is three-thirty-seven now; the parade seems to be off schedule. Perhaps I ought to walk down the hill to find out what the problem is."

"Oh, they'll be along any minute," I said confidently. "I suppose you'll miss Herbert most on Thursdays."

She pulled off her glasses and watched them swing from the pink cord around her neck. After another glance around the pregnant woman, she pulled herself erect and looked me in the eyes. "I suppose I shall, Mrs. Malloy."

"You must have been panicked by the letters in the Dear Miss Demeanor column," I continued, "and willing to do almost anything to stop them. But framing Miss Parchester wasn't exactly the most humane route, was it? It caused all kinds of grief, and ultimately led to Mr. Weiss's murder."

"It was an unfortunate choice of actions."

"Your idea?"

"No, Herbert's. He was such an imaginative man. I do believe I hear the band in the distance; they're only eight and a half minutes late, which isn't too bad for this developmental stage. They do get caught up with themselves at times."

I heard the strains of an unfamiliar tune, but I wasn't about to be distracted by the promise of a parade. "So Herbert suggested you fiddle with the ledgers to make Miss Parchester look guilty, merely in order to halt publication of the *Falcon Crier*. The police have already determined that the money's been there all along."

"Neither of us condoned taking money from student accounts. That would be unthinkable, a violation of trust. Listen, they're playing a Sousa march."

"But it wasn't unthinkable to frame a little old lady who'd taught for forty years?" I said. Sousa be damned.

"Herbert had a truly creative mind," she said in a distracted voice as she tried to peer past the protruberent tummy. "It's surprising that he did not deduce the identity of the author of those letters. He could have disciplined his daughter at home, and saved both of us a great deal of worry, not to mention his time involved in devising and implementing the plan to stop the *Falcon Crier*. Luckily, my experience in bookkeeping proved to be a great value, although I was obliged to struggle with Emily's system before I could make revisions."

"What a shame to waste valuable time framing little old ladies."

"So we discovered," she murmured. "They'll probably begin the school fight song before they reach the square. It gives me tingles right down to my toes to hear the strains of 'Fight With All Thy Feathers, Falcons.' It's such a rousing tune that I just want to burst forth into song whenever I hear it." Her shoulders quivered with anticipation, and her lips lingered lovingly over the lyrics.

I wondered if she put equal enthusiasm and dedication into all her extracurricular activities. It was obvious that she and Herbert could have reached great levels of efficiency, if not ardor, in their lovemaking. Did she record climaxes on a monthly basis, with little checks and/or x's? I decided that she filled out all the "How-was-the-service?" cards and mailed them to corporate headquarters, even when postage was not guaranteed.

The crowd gasped at some unseen spectacle. Bernice stood on her tiptoes, straining to catch her first glimpse of the big event.

"Miss Dort," I said in a stern voice, "has it occurred to you that Emily Parchester is out there somewhere, frightened and alone, ashamed that someone might consider her guilty of a dastardly crime?" When I received a perfunctory nod, I upped my volume to compete with the growing noise of the crowd. "You did that to her, simply to cover up your affair. You've driven her into hiding, and I for one am terribly worried about her."

"If she knew she was innocent, then she shouldn't have poisoned poor Herbert."

"She didn't poison poor Herbert!"

"Who did?"

"Well, you might have," I said. "You might have slipped into the kitchenette and dumped powdered peach pits in the compote."

The pregnant woman turned to stare at us, then spun around and waddled away in an indignant huff. Bernice moved closer to the curb, but glanced back with a tight smile. "I had no reason to murder Herbert Weiss, Mrs. Malloy. I do not wander around educational institutions with powdered peach pits in my pocket, nor do I slip into kitchenettes to sabotage little jars of peach compote. I have personal standards."

"Prove it," I snapped.

"You prove it, Mrs. Malloy. I have floats to judge, and I do think I can see the tippy-top of the junior effort. Someone told me, in the strictest confidence, naturally, that its theme is 'Barbecue the Bantams.' Very clever, don't you agree?"

I glared at her back, which was all I was offered. When that paled, I returned to the flower box and sat down next to Caron. She and Inez made several unkind comments about the junior effort, and more about the Homecoming court creeping by in convertibles. The girls looked faintly blue in their low-cut gowns, but their smiles remained steadfast and their waves gracious. Cheryl Anne was in the last car, ever the modest reigning royalty of FHS despite the two kindergarten children on either side of her. The boy was wiping his nose on Cheryl Anne's dress; the girl openly bawling.

With a hint of satisfaction, Caron explained that they were crown bearers. It rather reeked of child abuse, but I let it go. The mayor went past in an antique car, followed by a junior-high band playing an arrangement never before heard by human ears. The sophomore float proved to be "Make Baked Beans of the Bantams," which Caron and Inez found, amidst giggles and snorts, Too Juvenile for words.

In the middle of this, I thought I saw pink bedroom slippers flash by in the crowd across the street. I poked Caron and muttered, "Look over there. Could that be Miss Parchester?"

"That is the drill team, Mother. Bambi McQueen's in the third row, and she can't even shake her pom-poms in the correct sequence. She's doing red-gold-red-gold, while everyone else does red-red-gold-gold. Her knees are too low, her hemline's crooked, and she has dumpy thighs. I don't know why they let her on the drill team."

"Over there by the post office door," I insisted, despite an urge to assess Bambi's thighs for dumpiness. "I can't see any faces, but I keep getting glimpses of fuzzy pink slippers."

"Some child dropped its cotton candy. Now the cheerleaders look a lot better than the drill team, don't you think?" She turned to Inez to discuss Inez's sister Julianne's talents in comparison to the mere distaff mortals dressed in crotch-length skirts and sweaters that would leave indentation in their flesh.

I stood up and tried to peer over heads at the other side of the street. Miss Parchester wasn't tall enough to tower over anyone out of elementary school; I was going to have to rely on the fuzzies on the sidewalk. There was a flash of plastic on a head, and perhaps the point of a furled umbrella. Very promising, I told myself as I began to push through the crowd and find a way to cross the street. All I had to do was grab the fugitive, drag her away for a quiet chat, and assure her that she was no longer suspected of embezzlement. Or murder—for the most part.

At this point, with my toe in the gutter, the full regalia of the Farberville High School Marching Falconnettes took over the pavement. Brass horns, tubas, clarinets, drums—the whole shlemiel right out of River City, and it started with a *P* and rhymed with *T* and basically translated into serious blockade problems.

I was hopping up and down, trying to see over a sea of plumed hats and tuba bells, when I felt a hand on my shoulder. It started with a *P* and stood for Peter, as in Rosen.

"Are you looking for a potty?" he asked politely. "There's one in the drugstore behind us, and I think it's free. If not, I'll be glad to loan you a dime."

"That's not funny."

"But you are, with this imitation of a human pogo stick." He gave me a look that forbode all sorts of problems. "What's going on, Claire? You're not the sort to be possessed by demons, nor are you one to make a spectacle of yourself—without cause. You're behaving manically, and you must have a reason."

I will admit that I should have told him about the pink fuzzies. I was the one who had concluded that confession was good for the soul, if not the ego, and that I would jeopardize the relationship if I continued to hide things from him. But I wanted to talk to Miss Parchester, and I wanted to do it alone. Okay, I wanted to do it first. She would be thoroughly spooked by a cop. I needed to calm her down, reassure her that the Judge's reputation was as safe as her own, and convince her she could come back to school—in time to chaperone the dance.

It would mean a great deal to her, this opportunity to show the students that she was, as always, above reproach. Having justified myself to myself, I gave Peter what I hoped was an enigmatic smile.

"I thought I saw an old classmate across the street, but the band cut me off at the pass. It's not important; I'll probably run into her some other time. Why don't you come sit with Caron, Inez, and me?"

The flower box proved adequate for four bottoms. The band finally passed on, in the literal sense, and was replaced by the senior float, "Bye-bye, Bantams." The girls looked rather nervous, sensing competition from the upper classmen, but they managed a few catty comments about the unevenness of the lettering on the banner.

Peter gave me a wry smile and put his hand over mine, just as if I weren't a treacherous, conniving, faithless quisling. He looked startled at my sigh, but I could only shake my head and look away as I tried to convince myself, as Caron would say, to Do The Right Thing.

As the moral dilemma raged, Jorgeson came over. "We lost her, Lieutenant. We spotted her in that jam of people across the street, and tried to sort of surround her without her noticing, but it didn't work so well. That dame can scamper like a frightened puppy, and the uniformed officer couldn't bring himself to tackle someone who resembles his grandmother. Said it was too cruel."

Peter glanced at me, then stood up and pulled Jorgeson a few steps away. "Does the uniformed officer with the unsullied conscience realize this woman is wanted in a murder investigation, that she may well have poisoned two people in the last eight days?" he said loudly enough to be heard over "Flaunt Thy Feathers, Falcons" or whatever. "Tell him to report to me in one hour. Now, alert all the patrol cars to watch for her on the sidewalk in at least a six-block radius."

Jorgeson saluted with one finger and hurried away to do as ordered, the back of his neck noticeably red against his navy jacket. Peter sat down next to me, harrumphed under his breath like an asthmatic whale, and stared fiercely at the rows of boy scouts straggling in front of us.

"Will you still take me dancing?" I asked.

A series of harrumphs ensued, punctuated with sighs and dark looks from under a lowered brow. "I have to coordinate a dragnet all over the damn town tonight. Beat the bushes. Search dumpsters. Find a suspect who has once again eluded us, although it seems she might have been apprehended had we been given a discreet tip."

"The dance doesn't start until ten-thirty."

"Perhaps you can persuade your old classmate to go with you."

"The sight of policemen was likely to frighten her, and she needed to be approached by a friendly, familiar face. I was going to convince her to turn herself in at the station."

"Class of what?"

"Nineteen aught three. We rode dinosaurs to school, wrote in cuneiform, and eagerly awaited the invention of the jitterbug."

"Well, tonight you'll have a wonderful chance to jitterbug till dawn. I will be occupied at headquarters those same hours, bawling out the uniformed officer and eagerly awaiting the apprehension of Miss Emily Parchester."

The conversation was clearly going nowhere, and I was clearly going to chaperone the Homecoming dance alone. I was saved from further remarks by the appearance of "Broast the Bantams," accompanied by hordes of goose-stepping freshmen yelling unintelligible things about the future of the freshmen, class of '90. They seemed to be predicting they would do "mighty finey."

"That doesn't rhyme," I pointed out to Caron once she and Inez had ceased their shrieks.

"Nothing ryhmes with 'ninety,'" she said. "We had to come up with something to yell at pep rallies and this sort of thing, but no one could produce a single acceptable rhyme."

"I'll have to agree with that. Who thought up 'mighty finey'?"

"I did, Mother."

Peter glowered from one side of me, Caron from the other. Miss Dort was undoubtedly displeased with me, as was a nameless pregnant woman, the denizens of the lounge, a paranoic Parchester, and the staff of Happy Meadows.

I told Caron and Inez to find a ride home, gave Peter a shrug, and exited to my bookstore, where there were no storms in the port. The jackhammer provide a pleasant drone that precluded thought. It was exactly what I needed.

"E·L·E·V·E·N"

The Book Depot grew dim as the day latened, but I did not turn on a light in the front room. The street crew had departed in a roar of dozers and dump trucks, and the ensuing tranquillity was too lovely to be disrupted. I waltzed about with a feather duster, savoring the solitude as I sneezed my way through a week's accumulation of dust. The teachers' lounge seemed very distant; naggish thoughts of the dance were firmly dismissed.

I was in my office at the back, nose-deep in a ledger that appeared to have been depleted by an embezzler, but in reality was depressingly self-depleted, when I heard someone knock on the door. Despite the "closed" sign, customers did occasionally insist on admittance. One would think *they* could read.

It was Evelyn, her cheeks flushed from the chill in the air and her eyes bright from, I supposed, the excitement of the parade. I let her in and invited her to the office for coffee.

"No thanks," she said, "we're going to have to hurry if we're going to be on time for the game. Because of the Homecoming activities, it begins half an hour earlier than usual, and the bleachers are apt to be packed."

"Is this some kind of cruel joke?"

She shook her head. I protested steadily as I turned off the office light and locked the door. I continued to protest as I was driven to my apartment to fetch a scarf, hat, and gloves; and I did not falter as I ate a hamburger, drank several gallons of coffee as a preventive measure against the cold night air, and actually paid money to a gate attendent to be admitted to Falcon Stadium, Home of the Fighting Falcons, No Alcoholic Beverages Permitted. At that point, my protests became not only redundant, but also irrelevant.

We joined Sherwood on the fifty-yard line. A red-and-gold plaid blanket awaited us, along with a thermos of coffee and a discreet flask of brandy. I had not attended a football game since high school, having managed to avoid them throughout college as a matter of principle. Scrunched between Evelyn and Sherwood, my feet already numbing, my nose beginning to drip, surrounded on four sides by screaming fans, I remembered why.

"Why did you do this to me?" I asked Evelyn. "I was having a perfectly nice time at the Book Depot. I planned to go home, read the newspaper over a Lean Cuisine and a drink, and prepare myself for the dance. My plans did not include freezing in the bleachers, spilling coffee in my lap, or watching a group of faceless hulks batter each other to pulp over an ovoid plaything."

Evelyn laughed. "But it's Homecoming, Claire. We must applaud the ladies of the court and cheer on the Falcons to victory. Where's your school spirit?"

"In my living room, curled on the couch."

"Try this," Sherwood murmured, handing me a liberally spiked cup of coffee. "It's my contribution to spirit. Enough of this and you'll be on your feet with the *optimates* screeching for a touchdown."

"I thought this was forbidden," I said. I sipped at it anyway; the worst they could do was haul me away to jail, which was probably a good deal warmer and quieter.

"*De minimis non curat lex;* the law does not concern itself with trifles, such as a dollop of brandy." He prepared cups for Evelyn and himself. "I heard an interesting tidbit from my fifth period *hoi polloi,* by the way. It seems that Immerson was reinstated at the fateful moment, and the Falcons now have a chance to broast, barbecue, and bake the Bantams."

"That's odd," Evelyn said. "He surely didn't produce a grade above a *D* on a pop quiz or turn in an assignment in his own handwriting. Word of that would have spread across the school more quickly than a social disease. Did Miss Dort actually relent and agree to let him play?"

"All I heard was that our Mr. Immerman was in the office most of third period," Sherwood said, "and Jerry was there during fourth period. His absence encouraged the drivers' ed class to engage in a brief but successful game of strip poker in the backseat of the Buick; an anonymous young lady was rumored to have lost *a capite ad calcem*——from head to heel." He waggled his eyebrows in a facetious leer, but I didn't doubt the story for a second. "But there is our principal *pro tempore* a mere dozen rows away; you might ask her why she changed the policy. Personally, I would rather consult Medusa about the name of her hairdresser."

I agreed with Sherwood, although I was curious. I finished my coffee and asked for directions to the concession stand. Once we had unwrapped the blanket, much as the Egyptians might have done to check on decomposition, I fought my way down the rows of metal benches and went to see if Jerry had confided the details to his beloved.

Paula Hart was in the back of the concrete shed, watching popcorn explode in a glass box. I inched my way through the crowd to a corner of the counter and beckoned to her. "I hear Immerman was reinstated," I said.

She gave me a puzzled look. "Yes, I believe he was. Can I get you a box of popcorn or something to drink, Claire? We have a limited selection of candy bars, but they're ancient and I wouldn't recommend them to anyone over eighteen."

"Did he convince Miss Dort to rescind the order, or did Jerry have a word with her?"

A frown that hinted of irritation flashed across her face, but she quickly converted it to a smile. "I have no idea. It's really too loud and crazy in here for conversation, and I do have to watch some of the less mathematically inclined when they make change. Perhaps you might ask Miss Dort."

"I'd love a box of popcorn," I said, determined not to be dismissed despite the jostling crowd and my disinclination to eat anything prepared by adolescents. When she returned, I began to dig through my purse. "Now that Miss Dort is acting principal, what do you think she'll do about Jerry's graduate-school transcript?"

Paula's hand tightened around the box until I could almost hear the popcorn groan. "I have no idea what you're talking about," she managed to say, her lipstick beginning to crack.

"I'd ask him, but I suspect he'll be occupied with this thing between the Falcons and the Bantams for the next two hours. Of course, it wasn't clear what Mr. Weiss intended to do. He sounded grim at the last teachers' meeting, however; you two must have been alarmed." The last bit wasn't exactly speculation, but it seemed tactful to pretend.

"The police haven't mentioned the graduate-school transcripts. How did you find out about them?"

"The police have the same problem I had initially," I said. "They saw them in the personnel file, but they didn't assume there was anything significant about the coach being exceptionally well educated. One has to understand the workings of the education bureaucracy to see why all teachers shouldn't be exceptionally well educated."

Her Barbie doll face crumpled. Ignoring the startled looks from the students beside her, she snatched up a napkin and blotted her eyes. "It was awful, just awful. Weiss made it clear he could have Jerry fired at any time. He also stopped me in the corridor late one afternoon after a club meeting and suggested that he—he and I engage in—in—a—oh, it was dreadful!"

"Did you tell Jerry that Weiss wanted sexual favors in exchange for job security?" I continued, unmoved by her display.

"Jerry called me that evening, and I just broke down." She sniffled bravely into the napkin. "He was furious, but I managed to calm him down and talk some sense into him. He wanted to go right over to Mr. Weiss's house, pound on the door, and make a terrible scene. It would have cost him his job for sure. With that on his record, he wouldn't have been able to coach anywhere."

Or buy a cottage and reproduce, I amended to myself. I was about to ask more questions when the bleachers above us erupted in a roar. The band took up the strains of the Falcons' fight song, competing with the opposing band's blare. Paula gave me an apologetic look and scurried away to blink bravely, if somewhat damply, at the popcorn machine. I left the crushed box of cold popcorn on the counter, and went back to join Sherwood and Evelyn on the fifty-yard line.

The band marched onto the field and arranged itself in some mysterious way that must have had some significance to those higher in the tiers. The cheerleaders bounced about like irregular pingpong balls, shaking their pompoms among other things and arousing the pep squad to frenzied squeals. The drill team formed two lines and shook their pompoms among other things. The scene reminded me of a primitive, sacrificial ceremony in which virgins would go to the grave intact. To the tune of "Fight Ye Falcons," no less. The crowd loved it.

The Homecoming court convertibles appeared on the track that encircled the football field. The girls perched on the backseats, their white, clenched fingers digging into the upholstery as they smiled at the crowd. They were escorted from their thrones by as-yet-unsullied football players to be presented to the crowd and to accept bouquets and admiration. Followed by the kindergarten attendants, Cheryl Anne clutched the arm of her darling Thud, who clumsily put a plastic tiara on her head and handed her a bouquet of roses. It brought back memories, distant and blessedly mellowed with time, of faces arranged in the yearbook, all grim and determined to succeed. I looked particularly stern under a bouffant hairstyle that always left Caron and Inez weak from sustained laughter.

The presentation of the court, sniveling babes and all, was touching. The next two-and-a-half hours of bodies flinging themselves against each other were not, except in the obvious sense. Grunts and thumps, the sound of helmet against helmet, the incessant screams of the pep squad, the boisterous verbosity of the fans—it verged on something worse than Dante had ever envisioned for the lowest circles of the *Inferno*.

The thermos ran dry. The flask went the same way. My feet forsook me and my hands turned blue. My nose ran a marathon. I was kicked from behind and elbowed from both sides. A coke dribbled down my neck during a particularly exciting play.

The majority of the plays were incomprehensible, although I did my best to follow both the ball and the seesaw score. The home team took the lead, then lost it via a fumble. Thud snatched the ball from a Bantam and scampered all the way to the goal line, sending the cheerleaders into paroxysms of glee. The Bantams doggedly scored once again. Everyone in the bleachers, with one exception, rose and fell with pistonish precision.

The final quarter arrived, along with a couple of Falcon fumbles and Bantam triumphs, causing the scoreboard to tilt dangerously to the enemy side. Just as I neared a frostbite-induced coma, the referees called it a night. The cheerleaders burst into tears on each other's shoulders, while the band played a version of the fight song that seemed more of a dirge. Cheryl Anne stalked down from the bleachers, paused to hiss at the forlorn Falcons, then led her cortege into the metaphorical sunset. Thud threw his helmet on the ground, having displayed enough foresight to remove his head from it first. The coaches shook hands and trudged across the field, their troops in straggly formation behind them.

"Shall we go?" I said, trying not to sound too heartened by the thought of a car heater and even a gymnasium.

Evelyn sighed. "It's such a shame to lose the Homecoming game. The kids really care about this sort of thing."

"Absolutely," I said. "Shall I carry the blanket? Where's the nearest exit?"

Sherwood glanced at me, but offered no editorial. We followed the stream out of the stadium. The students punched each other on the shoulder and verbally rehashed the final plays of the game; their liberal use of profanity was more than mildly disturbing to someone who would be obliged to restrain them in the immediate future.

I tugged at Evelyn's arm. "What precisely is my assignment at the dance?"

"You have floor duty. Emily always volunteered for it, swearing she enjoyed it, and no one ever argued with her for the privilege." Her voice dropped until it was almost inaudible. "You'll survive, probably."

"Floor duty?" I said.

Sherwood patted me on the shoulder. "You are the ultimate *in loco parentis,* dear sleuth. All you must do is keep the rabble from dancing too closely together—school policy is three inches and not a whit closer—and the ones sitting down to keep their paws off each other."

"And the band from singing obscenities," Evelyn added. "The lyrics can get pretty raunchy if you don't keep an eye on them."

"Don't let anyone drink anything that comes from a back pocket," said Sherwood. "No smoking, snuff, or chewing tobacco. No vodka in the punchbowl. No fistfights. Don't let the girls roll up their skirts or the boys unzip their jeans."

"That's all?" I laughed gaily. "And I'm going to do this all by myself, right? I won't have a squadron of marines to help me out, or even an automatic weapon. I'll just shake my finger at perpetrators, and they'll back off from whatever felonious activity they've chosen."

"Oh, you'll have help." Evelyn gave me a wry look. "I believe you're assigned with Mr. Chippendale and Mr. Eugenia."

"Wonderful," I sighed. And I had alienated Peter, whose presence might have saved me from what threatened to be slightly worse than root-canal surgery done by a drunken dentist—in a bouncing jeep. Just when I needed a whiff of nitrous oxide.

Evelyn drove us to the faculty lot. We went to the gym, which was dripping with red-and-gold crepe paper, and glumly surveyed the battlefield. I presumed it would be strewn with bodies by midnight; all I could hope was that mine would not be included in the count.

Speakers the size of refrigerators were arranged in front of a low platform cluttered with beglittered guitars and an intricate formation of drums. The acned boys in the band huddled on one side, their eyes darting as if they anticipated attack or arrest. They had long, stringy hair and feral expressions. A droopy banner taped on the wall above them proclaimed them to be "Pout," an ominously appropriate name. Evelyn and Sherwood wished me luck, then drifted away to their assigned posts elsewhere in the building, where they might not even be able to hear Pout's best efforts to deafen us.

Mr. Chippendale came through the door, metal chairs under his arms. "Ah, yes, Mrs. Malloy, are you prepared for the dance?"

"Certainly, Mr. Chippendale. I've made a new will, consulted a neurologist about potential auditory nerve damage, and booked a private room at Happy Meadows."

He gave me a startled look, then busied himself unfolding chairs along the wall. A grayish man with bifocals introduced himself as Erwin "Gene" Eugenia, Algebra and Trig, and took a stack of chairs to the opposite side of the vast room. Students drifted in to set up the refreshment table, all sober from the defeat at the hands (talons?) of the Starley City Bantams. I watched them carry in the punch bowl, reminding myself that I was assigned the formidable task of assuring their continued sobriety until the dance was done.

A short while later the gym began to swell with students. After a few false starts, Pout found its stride and broke into what was presumably their opening set. Mr. Chippendale took a post next to the stage, although I doubted he could isolate stray obscenities in the ululation that passed as lyrics. Mr. Eugenia stayed beside the punch bowl, leaving me to monitor the dancers for distance and the nondancers for discretion.

Once my ears grew accustomed to the volume, I realized I might survive. Some of the students from the journalism classes spoke to me, or at least moved their mouths in what I interpreted as amiable discourse. I smiled politely, though blankly. No one asked me to dance, which was for the best since I had had no training in that particular mode of stylized warfare.

During a lull, I spotted Caron and Inez near the door. For the first time since the onslaught of puberty, my daughter looked timid and vulnerable; Inez appeared to be in the early stages of a seizure. After a beady look at a leather-clad hoodlum with an earring and fast hands, I joined them. "I didn't see you two at the game."

Caron regained some of her usual superciliousness. "You went to the football game, Mother? Whatever for?"

"I was coerced," I admitted. "I sat with Mrs. West and Mr. Timmons in what I fear was the most vocal section of the bleachers. I suppose it was good practice for the decibel level in here."

"Caron and I sold programs at the south gate," Inez volunteered. "We turned in our money, then sat with Rhonda and some of the girls. Wasn't the game just dreadful?"

"I thought so," I said, suspecting our criteria were different. Pout roared into song once again; conversation was impossible. Caron grabbed Inez's shoulder, and they hobbled away to find seats amidst the wallflowers.

Despite the lack of a victory, the kids seemed to be enjoying themselves. I was beginning to feel somewhat confident when Cheryl Anne swept through the door and stopped to survey the scene, her mouth a tight red rosebud and her hands clenched at her sides. Thud hovered behind her, clearly uncomfortable in her wake.

The dancers nearest the door halted in mid-gyration and backed off the floor to make a path that would have led straight to the throne, had there been one. I was mildly surprised no one had thought to bring a red carpet.

Cheryl Anne snapped her fingers over her shoulder. "Don't just stand there, for God's sake. I want to dance."

Thud's eyes were almost invisible under his lowered brow, but he lumbered around her to his designated spot. "Come on, then—dance, damn it," he grunted. After a second of icy disdain, Cheryl Anne joined him and they disappeared into the mass of writhing bodies. I was not the only wallflower to let out my breath, Tupperwear-style.

At the end of the second set, the lead guitarist announced they were "gonna haf to break" for fifteen minutes so their "instruments could like cool off, you know." I slipped out the door to assess whether I had brain damage, and promptly bumped into my Baker Street Irregulars.

"I saw Miss Parchester!" Caron said, her fingers digging into my arm. "She's in the building."

"When did you see her, and where is she?"

"We saw her go around a corner when we went to hide in the rest room," Inez said.

"Hide in the rest room?" I said, momentarily distracted.

"The geek, Mother. He's here—and he keeps looking at me,"

Caron said. "Anyway, we tried to catch Miss Parchester, but we couldn't keep up with her. My ankle, you know."

"I know," I said. "Tell Mr. Chippendale that I've gone to the lounge for an aspirin, and that I'll be back after the break. Miss Parchester probably went to the basement to look for clues or some such thing. Perhaps I can persuade her to listen to me."

I headed for the basement, aware that I was spending an inordinate amount of time in the dark bowels of this building. My flashlight was still in my purse (I do profit from experience), and I switched it on as I scuttled down the stairs. The corridor was empty. The lounge was locked. The journalism room was dark and still and held no hidden presence that I could discern from the doorway.

As I paused under the exit light to think, I noticed one of the classroom doors was ajar. A taped card had Miss Zuckerman's name and a list of classes, which included such esoteric things as Steno II and A-V Machines: Advanced. Miss Parchester might have slipped in to pick up something for her friend, I decided as I eased through the door.

If she had, she was already gone. I shined the light on the far wall, which had inspirational messages taped in a tidy row. "Clean ribbons make clear copies." "Type right on your typewriter." The back wall exhorted the students to practice their swirls and curlicues. "Shorthand—your key to a good job." A travel poster that touted the charms of Juarez contributed the one splash of color in an otherwise drab decor. Miss Zuckerman must have felt quite naughty when she included it, I thought with a sigh. "Nimble fingers come from practice." My light continued around the room. "Join the Future Secretaries of America." "Speed and spelling equal salary."

I decided to search the room in case Miss Parchester had inadvertently dropped some vital clue, such as a motel key. I began with the rows of shrouded typewriters and worked my way to the desk drawers. I expected to find rosters and lesson plans. I did not expect to find a crude little cigarette in an envelope.

During the sixties, I had encountered such things, sometimes in an intimate fashion. That had been more than fifteen years ago, however, and I was not sure I could trust my aged nose to ascertain if this was truly a marijuana cigarette. It seemed absurd that Tessa Zuckerman would have one stashed in her desk; she was hardly my idea of a dope dealer.

I could have called the police station and told Peter about my discovery. He could have sent Jorgeson over to collect the evidence and deliver it to the lab to be tested. Then he could have arranged for Miss Zuckerman to be transferred to a cell next to Miss Parchester's, so that the two little old ladies could chat as they withered away in their prison garb. A murderer and a dope dealer, both with silver hair and porcelain skin. . . .

I took a book of matches from my purse and lit the thing. If it turned out to be some thug's innocent attempt to save a few cents on prefabricated cigarettes, then there would be no reason not to drop it in the trash can and go about my business. If it was illegally potent, I would have to tell Peter—at some point. I inhaled deeply and waited for the answer.

Oddly enough, I thought I could see Peter's face. I was sitting on the floor, my head against the desk, when the light came on overhead and footsteps echoed like a Poutian revival. Frowning, I squinted up at the face hovering above me. No body, mind you. It was very, very peculiar. I warned myself to watch out.

"Claire?" it actually said. It sounded like Peter's voice, which struck me as highly amusing, if not outright uproarious.

I clamped my hand over my giggle—my mouth—and said, "Where's the rest of you?"

The rest of him came around the desk and squatted in front of me. "What's wrong with you, Claire? Why are you sitting on the floor in a dark classroom?" His nose wrinkled (quite adorably, I thought), and he looked at the smoldering butt in my hand.

"Where did you get a joint, for Christ's sake—and why are you smoking it now? Here?"

"Don't have time later," I told him smugly. "I'm in charge of five hundred—count 'em—five hundred juvenile delinquents who want to dance all over each other. Want to show 'em how to jitterbug, Supercop?"

"You are stoned," he said in a stunned voice. "I presume there's an explanation for this, and that you're going to give it to me. Right?"

"I am not stoned. I am merely conducting an experiment, like the one I did with the pit peach. Peach pit. Remember when you saw me on the sidewalk with the hammer? It must have looked really funny." I started to laugh as I recalled his expression, then discovered I was helpless to stop—but I didn't mind one teeny-weeny bit. Finally I got hold of myself, or of something. It may have been Peter's shoe.

"Give me the joint." He held out his hand, and I obediently handed over the remains. He pulled me to my feet, which seemed to belong to someone else, and steadied me. "We are going to the lounge for a nice pot of coffee. I have a feeling you're not quite ready to return to the dance."

"I am too ready," I sniffed. "A little wobbly, perhaps, but more than capable of chaperonage. I may even dance, if anyone asks me. Maybe by myself. Anyway, the lounge is locked. We can't get in because we don't have a key. Not even Supercop can walk through doors that are locked. Will you dance with me?"

He mutely showed me a key, then propelled me down the hall and into the lounge. I was placed unceremoniously on the mauve monster, and informed that I was not to move while he made coffee. Which was dandy with me, since I wasn't sure I could move in any case. In any direction.

"If you want to arrest me, go ahead. I was chasing Miss Parchester," I informed the doorway of the kitchenette, "and I lost her again: That woman is as fast as a damn minnow, and as slippery as a damn sardine. We ought to stake out the public aquarium, Peter."

He came back into the room and handed me a cup of coffee. "I saw Caron in the gym, and she told me you were in hot pursuit of Miss Parchester."

"For the zillionth time," I agreed. "I thought you were on a stakeout, Sherlock. What are you doing at the school?"

"I came to check on you. You are, shall we say, at times unconventional in your investigative techniques."

"Unconventional?" That rang a bell somewhere, but all I could do was blink at him. Bravely, I hoped.

"As in overzealous, impetuous, and illegal," he said, holding the last of the joint in his fingertips.

I couldn't tell if his smile was sincere or sarcastic, but I did like the color of his eyes. When I said as much, he pointed at the coffee cup and turned just a tad pink. "This isn't my cup," I said, studying the intricate swirls of roses and pastel leaves. "This could warrant a firing squad—or worse, you know. After you finish locking up poor Miss Parchester and poor Miss Zuckerman, will you come to my funeral?"

"Miss Parchester is still at large, and Miss Zuckerman is tucked safely in her hospital bed. As for the funeral, I'll make a point of attending—it will be the one time I know exactly where you are and what you're doing."

I didn't much like that, but I decided to let it go. "Mrs. Platchett takes this cup thing pretty seriously. She was more upset at me for borrowing her cup than she was about the deviled eggs."

"Why was she upset about the deviled eggs?" he asked, not sounding especially concerned about my welfare.

"Well, she wasn't upset about the deviled eggs, because Pitts hadn't poked them. Did you know that broccoli doesn't take fingerprints?"

"Actually, it does, but we can discuss the technical aspects later. Why did she think Pitts might poke the deviled eggs?"

"He poked everything." I rubbed my forehead, which was beginning to ache. "I think I'd better have some more coffee."

"I think you may recover," he said with a smile. "Will you please tell me why I stumbled on to a stoned bookseller in the basement of the high school?"

I told him why. We agreed that I had erred in my decision to test the contents of the cigarette, and that I should have called him. I drank more coffee, my head propped on his shoulder, and told him about the problem of Jerry's transcript, Paula's reaction, and Thud Immerman's reinstatement. None of it amazed him, although he did seem interested.

"Paula's not as sweet as she acts," I said, snuggling into his chest. "She might have murdered Weiss to protect her future, or she might have persuaded Jerry to do the dirty deed in order to protect her virtue."

"He wasn't in the lounge, and neither was she."

"The murderer did have to enter the lounge between ten and ten-fifteen, when Evelyn came in to use the ladies room." I glanced at the closed door of said establishment. "If I'd known about the hole, I might have murdered Pitts myself."

"The hole was discovered the day after Weiss's funeral, so it could have been a motive in the second murder. We just can't find a decent motive for Weiss's murder, except vengeance."

"Meaning Miss Parchester?"

"I'm sorry, Claire. I don't enjoy the idea of chasing some elderly lady around Farberville to question her about her recipe for peach compote, but she did have a reason to be angry at Weiss. I do need to ask her a few questions, if only to permit her to prove her innocence."

"I know," I said, sighing. The fuzzy pink slippers must have been wearing thin, considering the miles they'd done in the last

six days. The hospital, the parade, the dance, probably the football game, and the school. The woman had been everywhere, but
was nowhere to be found—while the Judge rotated in his grave.
"What are you going to do about the marijuana in Miss Zuckerman's desk?"

"Ask her, although I would imagine she confiscated it from
one of her students."

"And failed to turn it in to the authorities? If she's like her
sister Furies, she's probably a stickler for regulations. Maybe she
found it the day of the potluck and did not have an opportunity
to deal with it."

He nodded. Before he could say anything, Caron limped into
the lounge. "Mr. Chippendale is frantic, Mother. He sent me to
search for you, because the band members took off their shirts
and he thinks they may take off more. He says they are virtually
Out of Control, although I don't know what he expects you to
do."

"Call in the cavalry," I said, smiling at Peter. "Surely you can
strike a chord of fear in their atonal souls."

We went to the gym. We didn't, however, jitterbug until
dawn. Actually, it was more like three in the morning.

"T"W"E"L"V"E"

I went the Book Depot the next morning and opened up for business, the ledgers having hinted at the desirability of earning a few dollars, if not an actual fistful or more. I sold books, straightened shelves, filed invoices, and griped long-distance about delayed orders. It was all fairly normal until Caron and Inez limped through the door, gasping and panting. As always, normalcy fled in the face of postpubescent theatrics. I could not.

"Did you hear about Cheryl Anne and Thud?" Caron demanded.

"No, I heard about a fire at a university press and something about an order shipped to Alaska by mistake, but nary a word about the queen and the jock."

"They Broke Up." Caron folded her arms and stared at me, willing me to blanche, grab the edge of the counter, and beg for further details. "They've been going steady for Two Whole Years," she added when preliminary fireworks failed to explode.

"A blessing for the future of the human race," I said. "I cringe at the thought of the offspring those two might have conceived."

Inez gulped. "It was terrible, Mrs. Malloy. They had a big scene in the parking lot after the dance, and Cheryl Anne told Thud to drop dead, preferably in the middle of the highway."

"In front of a truck," Caron added.

"He was furious." Inez.

"He called her dreadful names." Caron.

"Slut." Inez, with a shiver.

"Cheap little whore." Caron, without.

"She told him he was a miserable football player, that he ought to play against twelve-year-old girls." Inez.

"He said he'd played with little girls too long." Caron.

"He said he was ready for a real woman." Inez.

The Abbott and Costello routine was giving me a pain in the neck, physically as well as metaphorically. I held up my hand and said, "Wait a minute, please. I really am not interested in an instant replay of their witticisms, no matter how colorful they may have been. May I assume Cheryl Anne was upset because Thud failed to win the game single-handedly and ensure a Homecoming celebration fraught with significance and glistening memories?"

Caron and Inez nodded, enthralled by my perspicacity.

"And," I continued, "she was especially upset because she had worked so hard to see that he was eligible to play?" More nods. "By the way, how did Thud convince Miss Dort to reinstate him?"

"Nobody knows," Caron said, widening her eyes to convey the depth of her bewilderment. I wasn't sure if it came from the inexplicable behavior of her elders or the failure of the grapevine to ascertain the gory details.

"It's sheer mystery," Inez said. She attempted the same ploy, but she looked more like an inflated puffer fish. She needed practice. And perhaps contact lenses.

I shooed them out the door and sat down behind the counter. There were too many unanswered questions driting around the corridors of Farberville High School, too many petty schemes and undercurrents. Too many bits of conversation that might—or might not—have relevance. Way too much gossip.

I called Evelyn, my primary source of gossip. "Who has a key to the building?" I asked once we'd completed the necessary pleasantries.

"Very few," she told me. "Mr. Weiss decided several years ago that loose keys sank ships, or something to that effect. All of the teachers were required to turn in their keys."

"Sherwood has one."

"Sherwood lives next door to a locksmith. His copy is illicit, but it's saved both of us a lot of hassle when we've forgotten a stack of tests or one of the dreaded must-have-first-thing-in-the-morning forms."

"Have you heard of anyone else with a copy?"

"No," she said after some thought. "Weiss had one, naturally, as did Bernice. Perhaps school board members, although I don't know why. Head of maintenance, but no one on the level of Pitts."

"Miss Parchester or the Furies?" I said without much hope.

"Of course not. None of the teachers except an anomaly like Sherwood would want to have an illicit copy of the key. If something happened in the building after school hours, I certainly would like to be able to swear, under oath or polygraph, that I didn't have access."

"You're fond of the anomaly, aren't you?"

"I suppose I am." The confession sounded sad.

I told her that there'd been someone in the building the night Sherwood and I had indulged in a mild spot of prowling. She was fairly sure it couldn't have been a teacher—unless it was the one who'd let me in the building in the first place. I was fairly sure Sherwood hadn't stolen the letters from under my nose. I asked her if she'd heard anything further about the mysterious reinstatement of the jock, and she told me that she hadn't.

I bade her farewell, took a deep breath, and called Miss Bernice Dort. After eleven unanswered rings, I hung up in disgust.

When Peter wandered by later in the morning, I was still behind the counter, staring at the nonfiction shelves and grumbling under my breath. "Any progress?" I asked morosely.

"Miss Parchester continues to elude us, and she seems to be

our only decent suspect thus far. The lab reports are back, but they don't say much of anything we hadn't already suspected. Pitts ingested more than three hundred fifty milligrams of cyanide, which was dissolved in the whiskey."

"Was it also organic?"

"It was. A sample has been sent to the regional lab for a more precise analysis, but it'll take weeks to get the results. We're presuming Pitts was murdered with—well, with pits."

"Pitts poked the peach pits. . . ." I said, gnawing on my lip.

Peter grinned. "That's what you claimed last night, among other more whimsical things."

"There are too many damn p's in this. Pitts the peeper, peaches, Parchester, plagiarism, Paula, principals, pouters, poisonous pits, and parades! It's worse than the jackhammer."

"Not to mention policemen and prowling prevaricators."

"Stop the p's!" I gestured for him to accompany me to my office, where I offered (not poured) coffee and a dusty chair. "I am going to figure this damn thing out without any further alliteration. Let's begin with another source for the toxic substance."

"It's definitely organic," Peter said, leaning back with a tolerant expression. "Officers of the law do not dismiss coincidences; they leap on them. Toxic compote, made from . . . a certain fruit with a toxic interior."

"But Jorgeson told me that cyanide is found in the seeds of a variety of fruits. Apples, cherries, apricots, and so forth—why couldn't one of those be the source?"

"One of them could, I suppose, but we haven't come across any of them in the investigation."

I stared at him. "I may have, though."

He stared right back. "When? What?"

"It's just a wild guess—but there was a souvenir from Mexico."

"Lots of tourists go to Mexico, Claire; they all buy things to bring home and discard a few weeks later. Hundreds of thousands of tourists, I would estimate."

"And they go for a variety of reasons, both conventional and unconventional." I toyed with the theory for a few minutes, trying to find slots for all the disparate bits of information (not pieces of the puzzle, mind you). "Apricots and Mexico. The joint in the desk. Charles Dickens. It almost makes sense, Lieutenant Rosen, although it means we've been looking at this thing from the wrong side of the hole."

"Apricots, Mexico, Dickens, and dope? How many joints did you find in Miss Zuckerman's desk?"

"Just the one," I said distractedly. "It was evidence of a sort, although I don't think we'll need it for court. The murderer is going to get away with the crime. We couldn't see the apricots for the peaches."

"I'm not sure you've fully recovered from the effects of the marijuana," he said, looking at me as if I were atop the file cabinet with a rose clenched between my teeth. "We might run by the hospital and have you checked for lingering euphoria."

"My idea, exactly." I grabbed my jacket and hurried out of the office, followed by a bewildered cop (as opposed to a perplexed policeman). I directed him to drive me to the hospital, then clammed up and stared out the window.

As we neared the lot, I told him that I wanted to visit Miss Zuckerman before he arranged for a straitjacket and a handful of Thorazine. When he sputtered, I suggested we question her about the joint that was ingested in the name of scientific discovery. He agreed, albeit with minimal grace.

I stopped at the nurses' station to inquire about Miss Zuckerman's status. We were informed that she was critical, but allowed short visits by close friends and family members. She did look critical, more frail than she'd been a few days ago and even grayer. Her skin was translucent, her bruised arms sprouting needles and tubes that led to bags above her head.

She managed a smile. "Mrs. Malloy, how kind of you."

"I believe you know Lieutenant Rosen," I murmured. "We stopped by for only a minute, so please let us know when you're too tired for visitors."

"I intend to enjoy my visitors as long as I'm here," she said. "This morning Alexandria and Mae came by to tell me about the Homecoming game. So hard for the students to lose their big game, but they'll get over it. The resilience of youth in the face of disaster is remarkable, you know, as long as they can rely on the wisdom of their elders to protect them from true evil."

"Drug dealers, for instance?" I said softly.

"Wicked, wicked people."

"It must have been difficult to see Pitts every day when you knew what dreadful things he was doing to the students."

"He was *very* wicked."

"The marijuana cigarette was the last straw, wasn't it?" I prompted, ignoring Peter's sudden intake of breath behind me.

"I'd been observing him for several months, but this was the first time I actually saw him sell drugs. The student, when confronted, was properly contrite and vowed to never again purchase illegal substances, but I knew Pitts had to be removed from Farberville High School. Since Mr. Weiss seemed unwilling to take action, I felt obliged to act on my convictions."

"You happened to have cyanide with you—in your purse, I would guess—and you knew Pitts would eat anything that caught his fancy in the refrigerator in the teachers' lounge."

She gave me a beatific smile. "Very good, dear. I'm not sure that I intended to kill him; I hoped he would become very ill, and perhaps quit his job and go elsewhere. I crushed a dozen or so pills and mixed them in Emily's little jar of compote. I never dreamed Mr. Weiss would eat it first . . . but he wasn't a very nice man, either. He was supposed to set an example for the students, yet he was having an affair with Bernice Dort. I was listening at my post when Pitts sold the information to Cheryl Anne, who seemed to be pleased to learn her father was a philanderer. I was appalled, I must say."

I felt an elbow in my back. I ground my heel on a convenient foot, then bent over the hospital bed and said, "No one saw you enter or leave the lounge, Miss Zuckerman."

"No one ever noticed me. After all those years, I'm afraid I simply became part of the backdrop, a pathetic gray ghost who haunted the basement of the school. Once I made up my mind to teach Pitts a lesson, I assigned a lengthy paragraph to my Ad Sten class, slipped off to the lounge, and returned without my absence being noticed."

"Was there anyone in the lounge?"

"Mrs. West's student teacher was present, but she didn't notice me, either. Young people tend to find the elderly invisible; it helps them avoid facing their own mortality." She glanced away for a moment. "It hasn't been a very exciting life, but it has been rewarding. I did take a trip to a foreign country once; it was dirty, yet the cultural differences intrigued me. I would have liked to travel more."

"The clinic in Mexico?"

"Yes, but the doctors there said it was too late to control the malignancy. I followed the diet and took the vitamins, enzymes, and tablets, hoping for a miracle. It did not occur. Now, if you don't mind, I think I'd better rest." Her eyelids drifted down with a faint flutter. She began to snore in a quiet, ladylike way.

Peter moved forward, but I caught his arm and pulled him out of the room. "Would you explain?" he snapped as we started for the elevator. "Am I correct in assuming Tessa Zuckerman murdered Weiss?"

"She did, although she was actually after Pitts. It was her farewell gift to the school."

"She 'happened' to have cyanide in her purse?"

"Laetrile, made from apricot pits. You remember the controversy about it in all the newspapers several years ago, don't you? The proponents claimed it was the ultimate cure for cancer; the medical authorities claimed it was quackery to exploit those poor souls too terrified to pass up any possibility. Ultimately, those who chose to try it had to go to clinics in Mexico, where it was legal."

"And Miss Zuckerman went to such an establishment, and brought home a supply of Laetrile tablets, along with a travel poster," Peter said. "When she decided to rid the school of its dope dealer, she crushed a few tablets and popped them in the compote?"

I nodded. "She made the hole in the women's rest room so that she could spy on Pitts to determine if he was indeed the villain he was rumored to be. He was telling the truth the day he claimed he hadn't made the hole, although I imagine that once he discovered it, he did use it to eavesdrop and report to Weiss. He lacked the acumen to realize that it could be used two ways."

"So Miss Zuckerman observed a transaction and decided to poison him," Peter said. "It didn't work out as she intended, although she did not seem inordinately disturbed by the result."

"Married men with families should not have affairs," I said, shrugging. "It might prove dangerous—or fatal."

"I'll note that in the report," he said. He rewarded me with a glimpse of his teeth. It was unsettling.

We drove back to my apartment. As we reached the top of the stairs, Caron hobbled out the door, caught sight of Peter, and froze in a posture reminiscent of Pout's lead guitarist in a moment of spasmodic bliss.

"Oh," she breathed at us.

I tried to move around her, but she held her ground in the middle of the doorway. "You're supposed to go to the station," she said to Peter. "Right away, because of some emergency. They said to go right away."

"I'd better call in and see what's happening," he said.

"You don't have time to call. It's a terrible emergency, and they want you to hurry there without wasting any time on the telephone. Besides, Inez is talking to her sick grandmother in Nebraska."

He gave her a suspicious look, told me he'd call later, and left to face whatever dire trouble my Cassandra was so eager to predict. Once the front door closed below, said oracle stepped back and said, "Thank God we got rid of him, Mother. I wasn't prepared for him to be with you, and I couldn't think what to say."

"You made up that story? He'll learn the truth in about ten minutes, Caron, and he won't be amused." I went into the living room and stared at Inez, who was huddled in the corner with the telephone. "Why did Inez find a sudden compulsion to talk to her grandmother in Nebraska, for that matter? What on earth is—?"

"Miss Parchester," Inez whispered, pointing at the receiver. "Caron told me to keep her on the line until you got here, Mrs. Malloy. I think she's getting suspicious; you'd better take over now."

I grabbed the receiver. "Miss Parchester?"

"Mrs. Malloy, it's so lovely to have this opportunity to speak with you again after all this time. How are you?"

"I'm fine, Miss Parchester. Where are you?"

"I'm fine, thank you. I've seen you here and there, but it's been quite impossible to actually have a word in private. I seem to keep running into policemen wherever I go; it's so distressing."

"Where are you?" I repeated, determined to stay calm. "If you'll tell me where you are, I'll come right over and we can have many words in private. I have lots of things to tell you."

"I'd be delighted to have a little conference with you, since I realize you've worked hard on the investigation, but"—there was a long pause, during which I prayed she wasn't taking a discreet nip or two—"I do fear the presence of the police. They have been following me, and they may be following you, too. An undercover officer in a bizarre disguise literally attacked me at the hospital, but I was fortunate to elude him."

I was worried that Peter would storm up the stairs at any moment to discuss deception with my daughter. If I could only find Miss Parchester and allay her fears, then I knew I could persuade her to present herself at the police station. My track record wasn't very good, but I am an eternal optimist.

"Miss Parchester," I said with great earnestness, "I know who murdered Mr. Weiss. I know who fiddled with the journalism ledgers, and I know why. Don't you want me to come tell you about it?"

"I know all that, my dear," she giggled. "I'm a trained reporter, as you know, and I've been doing a little snooping. I feel incredibly akin to Miss Jane Marple. We're of a similar age."

As I gaped at the receiver, Caron tapped me on the shoulder. "Ask her if I can have an exclusive interview, Mother. We can put it on the front page of the *Falcon Crier,* with a byline, naturally, and maybe a photograph."

I made a face, took a breath, and searched my mind for the proper response to Miss Parchester's blithe assurance that she knew all that, my dear. My mind failed me. "You do?" I said.

"I've enjoyed our chat, Mrs. Malloy, but I'd better run along now," she said with the faintest hiccup. "I have an errand, and soon it will be teatime."

Before I could wiggle my jaw, the line went dead.

"You didn't even ask about the interview," Caron said, her lip inching forward in preparation for a scene. "Aren't you at all interested in my future in journalism?"

"I have a camera," Inez contributed sadly.

"You'd better worry about the immediate situation," I said as I headed for the liquor cabinet. "Once Peter returns, you may not have a future."

The girls discovered the necessity of retiring to the college library to work on reports for American history. I sank into the sofa and tried to find satisfaction in having identified Weiss's murderer, but it didn't leave me tingling with self-respect. Miss Zuckerman was too near death to be disturbed by the police; Peter would hide the report until she was gone, then file it away for posterity.

Miss Zuckerman had murdered Weiss, albeit in a haphazard manner. She had then been wheeled to the hospital, and had been incarcerated there ever since. Which led to an inescapable problem: Who poisoned Pitts? The memory of Miss Parchester's giggle began to haunt me. She seemed to be well informed of the identities of various players in the cast. Had she stumbled across the identity of the second murderer? Was she in danger?

She certainly couldn't defend herself with a fuzzy pink slipper. On the other hand, she had managed to avoid an entire police force for most of a week, so surely she could avoid a killer as well. If she wasn't one.

"She's innocent," I said, pounding the pillow. A lapse into alliteration, but justified. Where was she? I knew she wasn't at Mrs. Platchett's house, or at Miss Bagby's. She wasn't at home, the school, the police station, or the Book Depot (yes, I had looked). Peter had warned me that he had men at the hospital, but I decided she had enough of her wits left to avoid there. Happy Meadows would have turned her in like a shot, since "we" didn't want any problems with the police.

There was one place left, a fairly good possibility. I downed my scotch and hurried to my car, then hurried right back upstairs and grabbed the telephone book. The name was not listed. I hurried back downstairs, admittedly somewhat breathless by this time, and drove to Miss Bagby's duplex.

"I'm sorry to disrupt your weekend," I said when she appeared behind the screen, "but I need Tessa Zuckerman's address."

"She's still in the hospital, Mrs. Malloy."

"I was there earlier in the afternoon. I thought I might go by her house to water her plants and check on things," I said, not adding that the one thing I wanted to check on ran around town in bedroom slippers.

Miss Bagby had heard too many excuses about incomplete assignments and missing homework. "How remarkable of her to ask you rather than Alexandria or me," she said, her lips atwitch with doubt. "Did she give you a key?"

I considered telling her my dog ate it, but instead I said, "I walked right out of the hospital without it. She's doing poorly; I'd hate to disturb her about a minor detail like a house key, wouldn't you?"

After a moment of silence, Miss Bagby told me the address and the location of the house key, which was under the welcome mat. We're rather casual about that sort of thing in Farberville; it drives Peter Rosen et al crazy, but the burglars haven't caught on yet.

I drove to Miss Zuckerman's house and hid my car at the far end of the driveway. It was a tidy bungalow, similar to that of Mrs. Platchett—although I doubted a single leaf dared to fall on her yard. Here there were indications that no one had been home for several days. The shades were drawn, the door locked. The key was not under the welcome mat. Opting for simplicity, I rang the doorbell. Simplicity didn't work, so I sat down on the top step of the porch to consider my next move.

I was still sitting there, uninspired, when the pink fuzzies ambled up the sidewalk, with a few minor digressions to either side. Miss Parchester tried to pretend she hadn't noticed me, but I stood up, brushed off the seat of my pants, and trailed her into the house.

"It took me a long time to figure out where you were," I said. "I did accuse Mrs. Platchett and Miss Bagby of hiding you, but they were offended at the suggestion. I forgot to ask Tessa Zuckerman."

"She is a dear friend," Miss Parchester said. She took off her coat and plastic rain bonnet, propped her umbrella in a corner, and patted a few stray wisps of hair back into place. "She seemed slightly better today, although tired after her conversation with you and that nice policeman with whom you keep company."

"That nice policeman has been wanting a word with you for a week, as have I. In fact, that same policeman assigned several of his men to detain you, should you return to the hospital. Did you not encounter any of them?"

"I have been very cautious since I was attacked outside Tessa's room. Today I borrowed a bathrobe from a linen closet in order to pose as a patient; yesterday I wore a white coat and carried a clipboard. It presents a challenge, but the Judge trained me to utilize all my talents, and I have strived all my life to follow his wisdom." She hiccuped at me, then put her fingers on her lips and giggled. "It was most challenging to leave my country establishment without arousing unwanted attention."

"And how did you accomplish that?" I asked. As always, I supposed I ought to call Peter and share my discovery, but I was fascinated with her tale of exploits.

"In a laundry basket. It was unpleasant until I accustomed myself to the odor, and terribly uncomfortable. The laundry service is quite lax about leaving baskets in their vans; I must mention it to the matron so that she can speak to them."

"So you slipped out with the sheets in order to investigate," I prompted. "What have you been doing since then, besides avoiding an entire police department and attending school functions?"

"Would you like a cup of tea, Mrs. Malloy? I'm sure Tessa would not mind if we borrowed just a little and some water."

"No, no," I said hastily, "let's finish our chat before we indulge in—in tea. How did you learn that Miss Dort and Mr. Weiss were responsible for the errors in the journalism ledger?"

"The last letter to Miss Demeanor was, I fear, explicit. I turned quite pink at some of the language, but it was impossible to avoid the conclusion that the two were having some sort of relationship. The rest was obvious, wasn't it?"

After a fashion, and a week of reading old *Falcon Criers*. "Did you take the packet of letters from the school office?"

"Oh, my goodness, no. Although the letters should have been in the journalism mailbox, I happened to find them in Mr. Weiss's desk the afternoon of his funeral. I certainly did not take the letter in question with me as evidence; the Judge was very adamant about illegal search and seizure. However, I don't believe he ever gave an opinion from the bench about reading."

"You searched his desk, though."

"In the name of freedom of the press, my dear. The judge instilled in me a strong sense of priorities."

"How did you get into the building?"

"Mr. Pitts happened to be mopping the hallway and graciously let me inside. He even invited me to eat a meal with him, but I declined. Pizza is difficult to manage with dentures."

"You were in the school the afternoon Pitts died?" I said. "Did he mention anyone else in the building?"

"Pitts—died?" She turned white and put her hand on her chest. "I had no idea, no inkling of this. I feel quite stunned by the news. Mrs. Malloy, could you be so kind as to fetch me a glass of water?"

I went in the kitchen for water, then decided to hell with it and took the brandy bottle off the table. Once she was settled with a medicinal dose, her color improved to a pastel flush, if not a rosy glow. "You didn't know about Pitts?" I said.

"No, I am flabbergasted to hear of his death," she said. "I have not been able to watch the evening news, since I was worried someone might notice a light. Please tell me what happened to him."

"Let's discuss the murder of Herbert Weiss first. Were you aware that Miss Zuckerman spied on Pitts through the hole in the ladies room of the lounge, and overheard him selling certain information to Cheryl Anne?"

"She told me several days ago, but in the strictest confidence."

"Did she also mention that she laced your compote with Laetrile in order to poison him?"

Miss Parchester took a long drink of brandy, then looked up with a bleary smile. "Not in so many words, but I did wonder. I visited her classroom last night to see if her pills might be in a drawer, but I heard a policeman come down the stairs after me. I fled through the exit by the boiler."

"But you did know she had cancer, and had been to a Mexican clinic to try Laetrile—which is basically cyanide?"

"It seemed obvious."

The Judge had trained his daughter well, I told myself in an admiring voice. Or we had varying definitions of "obvious," with mine leaning toward "tentatively guessed after a week of agonized concentration."

"Tessa Zuckerman poisoned the peach compote and Herbert Weiss via a slight miscalculation, but she's been in the hospital since the day of the potluck. Who do you think murdered Pitts?" I asked her.

"I really couldn't say, Mrs. Malloy, I really couldn't say."

Damn. I'd been hoping it was obvious.

"T""H""I""R""T""E""E""N"

Miss Parchester announced that it was teatime, and went to the kitchen. I stayed in the living room with the brandy bottle, trying to work up enough enthusiasm to call Peter and inform him that I'd found his culprit. He wasn't apt to come roaring over with sirens and flashing lights, in that he knew she hadn't poisoned Herbert Weiss and her motive to murder Pitts was no stronger than anyone else's. Pitts hadn't been blackmailing Tessa Zuckerman, since she was unavailable for such things. He could have been blackmailing someone else, I thought tiredly, but it didn't seem likely. Blackmail requires secrecy; Pitts had been too eager to share his information.

Miss Zuckerman was the most promising candidate; she had admitted both motive and means, and the poison in the whiskey had also been an organic compound. She lacked opportunity, however. She was the only one who could not have left the whiskey for Pitts, I realized, sinking further into both the sofa and despair. Even Miss Parchester had visited the school, and had been invited for a cozy supper of pizza and whiskey. I wondered why her dear friend Tessa hadn't mentioned Pitts's death to her during one of their visits; Miss Parchester had been genuinely shocked when I told her.

I decided to ask her why, and went to the kitchen. The tea kettle was on the stove, but it wasn't whistling Dixie—or anything else. The cups and saucers were on the counter, along with a sugar bowl and two spoons. The back door was slightly open. Miss Parchester was thoroughly gone. It did not surprise me.

Once the tea things were put away and the African violets watered, I let myself out the front door and went to my car. I drove around the neighborhood for a few minutes, but I had little hope that I would spot her on the sidewalk, and I was proved right. Miss Zuckerman's house was located midway between the hospital and Farberville High School; I drove past both without success, then headed for home, aware that Miss Parchester would resurface in due time—probably disguised as a Maori, a nun, or a circus clown. Or all three, if she felt it necessary to operate as a tipsy, red-nosed, religious New Zealander.

As I unlocked my door, I heard the telephone ring. It was apt to be Peter, irate over Caron's lie and ready to bawl her out. Feeling as if I were trapped in a round of Russian roulette, I picked up the receiver. "I'm not available to come to the phone right now," I intoned. "At the sound of the ——"

"Claire, this is Evelyn. I've just heard the most astounding news, and I presumed you'd be interested." When I agreed, she continued, "Jerry and Paula have had a major falling out. She came over to sob on my sofa and repeat numerous times how utterly horrid he was. It seems the coach and Miss Dort have come to an understanding: He's going to become administrative vice-principal, a position more in line with his credentials."

"But he'll get a raise, won't he? That puts the cottage and babies in the immediate future, which ought to delight her."

"I pointed that out to her, but she sobbed harder and said I didn't understand. I didn't, for that matter, but I couldn't get anything more from her." There was a long pause in which I supposed we were both mulling over the inexplicable turn of events. I was wrong. "Sherwood had good news," she said, sounding oddly hesitant.

"His manuscript has been accepted?"

"Yes, by a university press. He is, quite understandably, elated.

After a stream of *Gloria in excelsis*es and other incomprehensible utterances, he said the classics department there had an opening for an assistant professor next semester and wanted him to come immediately for an interview."

"That *is* good news," I said. "You don't sound especially thrilled, though."

"I guess I'll miss his conversations, as obscure and oppressively pedantic as they were. It's difficult to envision the same with Mrs. Platchett or Mr. Chippendale."

We chatted for a few more minutes, then I hung up and made myself a cup of tea. Cheryl Anne and Thud had parted ways, as had Jerry and Paula. Miss Dort's long-standing relationship with Herbert Weiss was finished, too, although not by choice of either participant. Evelyn and Sherwood might miss the obvious and end up at far ends of the educational spectrum. I wondered if Claire Malloy might be facing the same fate, due to a well-intentioned attempt to tidy things up and present Peter Rosen with a solution.

It was late in the afternoon by now, and said cop had not returned to chastise my daughter and listen to my latest bit of treachery. I wasted a few minutes chastising myself for losing Miss Parchester—for the umpteenth time, then took a piece of notebook paper and a pencil and sat down at the kitchen table. Charts and timetables had never worked yet, but one did cherish hope.

I listed all the names and drew arrows hither and yon. The paper began to look like a highway map, but I persevered until I had sorted out the relationships. I circled Sherwood's name as the only possessor of an illicit key, and Miss Zuckerman's as the possessor of a notably lethal bottle of tablets. I then underlined her name as the possessor of the most brazen motive. But she had been in the hospital, I reminded myself as I decorated the circle around her name with flowering vines.

But she did have loyal friends. Who were likely to visit that evening at seven o'clock.

I was staring at the paper when Caron and Inez slunk into the room. "Peter hasn't called or come by," I told the mendacious duo. "He will, of course, so you'd best call in Perry Mason to conduct your defense."

Caron put her hands on her hips. "You're the one who bungled things, Mother. Inez and I kept Miss Parchester on the line; you were supposed to find her and deliver her to the police."

"I did find her," I admitted, "but she managed to slip out the back door. There may be a way for us to redeem ourselves, however. I think she'll visit Miss Zuckerman this evening at the hospital. If you two—"

"No way," Caron said. She picked up her notebook and her purse, shot me an indignant look, and hobbled toward the door. "Inez and I are not about to stake out the hospital. The situation was totally humiliating. Come on, Inez, we're going to Rhonda's house. At least we won't be Tackled and Thrown to the floor there."

"What about your career?" I said. "It's possible that we can sort things out so that Miss Parchester can return to her classroom Monday morning, and the *Falcon Crier* can resume publication. You'll have the opportunity to write the Miss Demeanor column."

"I have decided to drop the journalism class. My design for the freshman class float won first prize; everyone agrees I have a talent. Therefore, I have decided to apply myself to set design in the drama department."

Inez bobbled her head. "And Rhonda heard that Rosie is over the mono and coming back to school next week." They limped out the door, discussing the Untimely Recuperation and the Lack of Consideration shown by certain parties.

I sat for a long time, then went into the living room and called

Peter. I listened to a lot of unkind words about my darling daughter and admitted the purpose of the ruse. I then admitted I'd lost Miss Parchester, but that I had a good idea when next we might find her. He skeptically agreed to meet me at the hospital at seven o'clock.

That left an hour. I wandered around the apartment for a while, visions of arrows dancing through my mind. I called Miss Dort again, and listened to the phone ring in vain, then snatched up my jacket and exited, although not with Caron's style.

There was a car in the parking lot at the high school. I tapped my car keys on the glass door, and Miss Dort subsequently appeared. The first time I'd gone through the routine, Miss Dort had been irritated to see me. This time she smiled as she held open the door; the Cheshire cat couldn't have looked more pleased with itself.

"Did you forget the yearbook layouts," she asked as we walked to the office, "or did you just want to work in peace? I do enjoy the school when the students are elsewhere. At times I think we could be more efficient if they simply stayed away, but that wouldn't work, would it?" She giggled at her heretical proposal.

"No," I said, bewildered by her behavior. "I wanted to ask you why you allowed Immerman to play in the Homecoming game. I realize it's none of my business, but I hoped you might tell me."

"I simply felt it was best for the school, although the Falcons failed to win the game. Immerman's not as important as he thought he was."

"I guess Jerry was disappointed," I said, beginning to get a glimmer of an idea. A decidedly tacky idea. "After all, he made quite a bargain in order to get Immerman reinstated before the game."

Miss Dort patted her hair, if not her back. "An agreement was reached, but it had nothing to do with the issue of reinstatement.

Immerman was persuasive, and student morale is always upper-most in my mind."

"But you and the coach had quite a discussion."

"I called him in to inform him of my decision, but at that time I began to realize Coach Finley was much too valuable an asset to be left on a football field. Once we discussed the various direc-tions his career might take, he agreed most readily to take on the position of administrative vice-principal."

"That's not what Weiss intended for him, is it?"

"Herbert wanted to have him fired, but he was afraid lest he alienate Miss Hart. He was biding his time until he could find a way to dispose of Coach Finley. Someone disposed of him in the interim."

I saw no reason to enlighten her. "You weren't caught in the same dilemma, Miss Dort. Offending Miss Hart surely is not your worst fear. Being alone on Thursday afternoons might be, how-ever. Is that the bargain you made with Jerry—he stays on at Farberville High School, both as vice-principal and paramour?"

"I am getting older, Mrs. Malloy, and I have neither time nor inclination to join singles' clubs or prowl nightclubs. As acting principal of the school, I must maintain my standards."

"How persuasive was Immerman?"

"I fear it was a letter to Miss Demeanor that convinced me to let him play. Once I read it, I realized Cheryl Anne was the culprit, and quite vindictive enough to contact the school board with all sorts of misinformation about my little meetings with Herbert. She is incorrigible." Miss Dort gave me a tight smile. "To be succinct, Mrs. Malloy, she's a little bitch."

"That's how you discovered the identity of the poison-pen letter writer, isn't it? You took the packet of letters from the counter in the office. Sherwood and I searched the building for over an hour, but we couldn't find anyone."

"This is, as the students say, my turf. I suppose Herbert must have put the letters in his drawer and failed to mention it to me. It was most fortunate that you found them, Mrs. Malloy. They have since been destroyed."

"But Cheryl Anne and Immerman still know about the Xanadu. How can you be sure they won't use the information against you in the future?"

"Cheryl Anne is aware that I will report her blackmail scheme to the authorities should she try any more shenanigans. As for Immerman—we intend to discuss it on Tuesdays," she said. She settled her glasses on her nose, picked up her clipboard, and sailed out the office door.

A large percentage of my arrows had missed the target. Once I recovered from the shock and could move, I left the building and drove to the hospital, trying very hard not to dwell on the images that came to mind. Miss Dort would be caught eventually, and the school administration would not be impressed with her afternoon schedule. Thud was hardly a model of discretion, and Paula Hart was hardly the sort to give up gracefully. I was comforted with the knowledge that I would no longer be around the high school when the gossip started. Again. Rosie's journalistic integrity would be put to the test.

As I entered the hospital, I glanced around for undercover policemen and little old ladies in disguise but saw neither. Either I was wrong, or everyone was enjoying some degree of success. As I took the elevator upstairs, I prayed for the latter. Peter was waiting for me by the nurses' station.

"Miss Parchester can't possibly sneak in here," he said. "I've got men all around the building."

"She was here earlier this afternoon, apparently not too long after we were here. Did your men happen to notice her?" When he shook his head, I sweetly pointed out that she'd managed to avoid his men for a week, without having to miss any of her social obligations or school functions.

I was telling him about her escape from Happy Meadows when

Mrs. Platchett and Miss Bagby came out of the elevator. They acknowledged our presence with nods. We all trooped into Miss Zuckerman's room and positioned ourselves around the bed.

"How exciting to have so many visitors," she said. "It's almost a party, isn't it?"

"We're expecting one more," I said. "I think Miss Parchester will be here shortly."

The Furies exchanged looks. Mrs. Platchett at last cleared her throat and said, "Emily is a good and true friend, and she has been determined to spend as much time as possible with Tessa."

"Not that I have much time," Miss Zuckerman contributed. She looked at Peter. "I doubt you'll have an opportunity to arrest and detain me, Lieutenant, but I shall gladly sign a confession if that will assist you in your paperwork."

"For one murder—or for two?" I asked gently.

"Why, for two. I didn't intend to poison Mr. Weiss, but I seem to have done so anyway. I certainly intended to poison Mr. Pitts. I used exactly the same number of tablets."

"You couldn't have, Miss Zuckerman," I said. "You might have put the tablets in the whiskey, but you couldn't have taken it to the teachers' lounge and left it there."

She turned her head to one side. "But I did, Mrs. Malloy, and I insist on taking full responsibility."

At this point we heard a squeak outside the door. Peter and I stepped into a corner and watched as a green-clad orderly with a surgeon's cap and mask came into the room, pushing a wheelchair. It would have been more convincing if the orderly had not been wearing fuzzy pink slippers.

Mrs. Platchett and Miss Bagby tried to warn her, but Peter closed the door and positioned himself in front of it. "Miss Parchester, I'm Lieutenant Rosen of the Criminal Investigation Department. We've been looking for you."

"So I've noticed." She took off the cap and mask, then sat down in the wheelchair. "You really ought to speak to your men about their behavior, Lieutenant; it has bordered on police brutality. At times my civil liberties have been endangered by their youthful enthusiasm."

"We were discussing the identity of Pitts's murderer," I said as I came out of the corner. "Miss Zuckerman claims responsibility, but that's impossible."

"I did put Laetrile in the whiskey," Miss Zuckerman said in a firm voice that had stopped many a student in midstep. "I put one dozen tablets in the bottle. I would have put in a few more for good measure, but that was the last of them."

"Pitts was despicable," Mrs. Platchett said.

"He corrupted the students," Miss Bagby said.

"He had to be stopped," Miss Parchester added from the wheelchair. "Tessa's actions were warranted, even if they did violate his constitutional rights. The Judge was always harsh with criminals, especially those who were a threat to society."

Peter joined the circle around the bed. "But Miss Zuckerman did not buy the whiskey; someone else did and brought it to the hospital to be laced with poison. Someone then took it to the lounge where Pitts found and drank it. Either knowingly or unwittingly, one of you three ladies is an accomplice to murder."

The three looked back steadily, with nary a blink. One steely-eyed cop was no match for one hundred sixty collective years in the front of a classroom.

"One of you is guilty," he persisted, although with an increasing air of hopelessness. When he received no response, he looked at Miss Zuckerman. "Which one of your friends helped you murder Pitts?"

"If one of them is indeed an accomplice, she is guilty of no more than doing a small favor for a dying friend—and a major favor for the students of Faberville High School." She smiled, then closed her eyes and let her cheek fall against the pillow. We all tiptoed out of the room.

Miss Parchester announced that she needed to return the

wheelchair before it was missed. Miss Bagby opted to ride, and the three squeaked toward the elevator, leaving an unhappy policeman and a bemused amateur sleuth in the hallway outside Miss Zuckerman's room.

"Do you know which one did this 'small favor'?" he asked me.

"It doesn't really matter," I sighed. "Miss Zuckerman conceived and executed the plan; whoever delivered the bottle did so for her. You're not exactly loosing a homicidal maniac on the town."

He glanced at the closed door. "I suppose not, but what if they decide they don't like the new custodian? They can't be allowed to take matters into their own hands every time they encounter a potential source of corruption in the corridors of the school."

"Have a talk with them about retirement," I suggested. "I doubt you'll get an argument, and the three of them can take a nice bus tour of southern gardens in the spring. I'll check into watercolor classes." Of the three, I was fairly certain Miss Parchester needed the busiest schedule.

"I may check into Happy Meadows," he grumbled, but without heat. We walked out to his car and drove back to my apartment. I entertained him with an account of Miss Dort's intentions, and the likelihood of retaliation from Paula Hart. The teachers' lounge would continue to be a hotbed of gossip and intrigue, I concluded as we went upstairs.

"But you won't have to be there, or take it upon yourself to solve whatever mysteries arise," Peter murmured.

In that he was murmuring into my ear, I did not feel compelled to point out that I had solved the murders for him. In the midst of further murmurs, the telephone rang. It proved to be Sherwood Timmons, bubbling with the news about his manuscript. I let him bubble for a minute or two, then interrupted with congratulations.

"Thank you, dear sleuth," he said. "I shall cherish *ad infinitum* the memories of our minor escapade in crime."

"You had a key, even if it was an unauthorized copy," I reminded him. After all, Supercop was in my living room.

"I'll mail it to Miss Dort, accompanied by a note begging her forgiveness. She will make a terse note on her clipboard, but we will not have to listen to her crackly voice over the intercom or watch her lips purse with displeasure over——"

"We?" I inserted before he lost control of himself completely.

"Evelyn and I. I have proffered *vinculum matrimoniie,* and she has consented."

I congratulated him once more. After he said good-bye (*carpe diem,* actually, but I ignored it), I joined Peter on the sofa and told him about the impending *matrimoniie.* He gazed at me for a long time, looking terribly enigmatic. I opted for nonchalance.

"Claire," he at last said, "I can think of only one way to keep you out of trouble, and that's to——"

I stopped that nonsense. And with great charm, I might add.

The End

CAUSE AND EFFECT

BY

RALPH McINERNY

Published by special arrangement with Atheneum.

To Jim Carberry

ONE

Andrew Broom came out of the clinic into weak January sunlight, crossed the slushy parking lot to his car, opened the door, tossed in his topcoat, and then got in himself. Gripping the steering wheel with both hands, he stared vacantly ahead.

An hour before, his head had been aswarm with anxieties and hopes, plans and plots and projects in various stages of completion. Time had pressed on him as an amorphous commodity coming too swiftly but nonetheless in infinite supply. The future had been replete with possibility and indefinite in extent. He was forty-four years old.

It occurred to him now that he would never be forty-five.

His topcoat was a Burberry. His suit, soft gray, cost several hundred dollars more than that worn by the next most prosperous lawyer in Wyler, Indiana. His shoes, now bearing the marks of slush, were one of a half-dozen pairs from his bootmaker in Mexico.

What suit would they bury him in?

He twisted the ignition key and the Porsche murmured into life. This car was an affectation, bought for his wife; that had been the explanation, but Dorothy much preferred larger, more ostentatious vehicles. At the wheel of this sports car, Andrew had always felt twenty years younger, more. As young as Gerald. But not now. He drove out of the clinic parking lot, not so much as glancing at the low brick building where he had received the ultimate bad news.

He owned thirty-five percent of that building. The thought brought forth a tortured gasp—an attempt at laughter, a disguised cry of despair. Taking the precisely timed lights on Tarkington with precision, he found he could not stop the audit that had begun in his head, a ticking off of assets, a mental printout moving toward the bottom line.

He was a wealthy man. He had good reason to think that he was the richest man in Wyler, all of it earned money. Starting from nothing, he had worked hard, very hard, but he had also kept himself in good shape. He had stopped smoking so long ago it took an act of faith to believe that he had once consumed two and a half packs of Luckies a day. His drinking had dwindled to wine at the evening meal. He jogged every other morning and swam the days he did not jog. When he weighed himself that morning, he was exactly where he wanted to be: 172. He would have said that he was in excellent health for his age.

And so he had been. But no regimen is proof against leukemia.

He had had to wring the diagnosis from Dr. Lister, who had engaged in an orgy of circumlocution. You would have thought the doctor was flunking an exam when he admitted the results of the tests.

"We know so much more now than we did," Lister had said, unconvincingly. It was difficult to believe that this almost cringing figure was one of the excellent doctors Broom and his associates had lured to Wyler by building the clinic.

"It is fatal."

"With chemotherapy and radiation treatments..."

Lister had gone on and on, but Andrew tuned him out. His mother had spent her last days receiving chemotherapy. The very word filled Andrew with abhorrence. He had seen his mother lying empty-eyed and wasted on her bed, watching with animal wariness whenever a nurse entered the room, fearing the treatment more than the disease.

"Make them stop, Andrew," she had pleaded.

And finally Andrew did. His mother's final days had been almost serene.

He did not want to think at all of the way his father had died.

He was caught by a red light at the intersection of Tarkington and Byrd. The toot of a horn beside him drew his attention to a smiling face in the neighboring car. He did not recognize who it was, because the sun lay on the cloudy window in such a way as to create a mosaic of reflection and transparency. Nonetheless, Andrew answered with a broad smile and lifted his left hand. He might have been giving a farewell blessing.

That horn and greeting forced him back into the scheduled world that had been shattered by Lister's stammered news. Lister had insisted he come by, forcing Broom to reschedule appointments. Had he felt any apprehension on the way to the clinic? He had not. His thoughts had been full of strategy for appealing the conviction of Agnes Walz.

His watch read three minutes of eleven. When the light changed, he burned a little rubber getting the Porsche in motion. He would make that eleven o'clock meeting with his junior partner and nephew, Gerald.

TWO

First Cleary refused coffee, then he asked if Susannah had decaffeinated, finally he said okay, give me a cup, as if he were awarding a prize or finally giving in and admitting it was a screwed-up world. Nobody asked Agnes if she wanted a cup. She sat with her handcuffed hands in her lap, a wispy smile on her face, staring across the conference room at the wall of books that seemed enough to contain every rule invented by mortal man. Whenever Susannah came or went, Gerald caught a glimpse of the two deputies in the outer office.

"Where the hell is Andrew?" Cleary asked, addressing the question to the ceiling, along with a thin stream of smoke from his mentholated cigarette.

"Your coffee warm enough?"

"Can I smoke?" Agnes asked.

"Do you have any cigarettes?" Cleary answered. He winked at Gerald. Indicted, tried, and convicted, Agnes had lost all claim to Cleary's humanity.

"I'll get you some," Gerald said, happy to escape into the outer office.

Susannah looked at the clock, then raised her eyes. "Where did he go?"

"He didn't say. He just said, reschedule. But I couldn't get through to Sheriff Cleary in time."

"She wants a cigarette."

"Oh?" Susannah's hair was red. There was a spray of freckles on her cheeks. The eyes that now rounded in surprise were green.

"Agnes. Cleary is smoking and she wants one."

"Why doesn't he give her one?"

Gerald knew Susannah smoked. The problem was that she was a secret smoker. When her boss quit, she did too, at least she tried, and since he had shuffled off the habit with apparent ease, she could not admit that it was impossible for her. If Uncle Andrew ever detected the smell of smoke clinging to Susannah when she returned from a break, he said nothing. Gerald knew she had a package of Pall Malls in the bottom drawer of her desk, pushed far back. There didn't seem to be any way he could mention it.

"Go in and tell him that, will you, Susannah?"

She would do anything rather than admit she had cigarettes of her own to offer the convicted coconspirator in murder.

Meanwhile, Gerald took the elevator to the lobby, where he bought a package from the blind man at the candy counter.

"I didn't know you smoked," Louis said, aiming his snaggle-toothed smile and milky eyes in the direction of Gerald's voice.

"They're for a client."

"I was sorry to hear about Agnes." Louis's smile disappeared.

"Can't win them all, Louis."

"Win?" The blind man made tasting sounds with his mouth. "I was hoping they'd give the bitch the electric chair."

"Maybe next time," Gerald said cheerfully, heading back to the elevator.

Before he reached it, his uncle came sweeping in from the street.

"What happened to the meeting?"

"Everyone's upstairs. They've been there nearly an hour. Susannah couldn't get through to Cleary soon enough."

His uncle nodded, and that was all. Gerald found this a subdued reaction. Andrew Broom was impatient with anything less than perfection. Thank God, he made huge exceptions in Gerald's case.

"Those for you?" He was looking at the package of cigarettes in Gerald's hand.

"Agnes wanted a smoke and Cleary wouldn't give her one."

But when they came into the conference room, Agnes was holding a cigarette to her lips, using both manacled hands. A nonmentholated cigarette. Gerald would bet it was a Pall Mall. He slid the package across the table to Agnes. She arrested it with an elbow.

"Couldn't we remove those?" Andrew said, assuming the chair at the head of the table. "I guarantee your safety, Patrick."

Cleary puffed out his lower lip and shook his head. "Tell it to her husband."

Agnes turned her head to look at the sheriff. Gerald momentarily had no difficulty believing this woman and her lover had hired someone to kill her husband. The fact that the man had killed her lover rather than her husband had not been considered sufficient to acquit.

"Thank you for consenting to this meeting, Sheriff."

"You're late."

"And in my office."

"The heat's still out in the court house."

Andrew looked expressionlessly at the sheriff. "Now, if you'll leave the room, I wish to speak with my client."

"I'm not leaving her out of my sight."

"I want you out of hearing, not out of sight."

"How the hell am I supposed to manage that?"

"Don't light it," Andrew advised, when Cleary took a cigarette from the package in his shirt pocket, plucking it out with a clawed hand that put Gerald in mind of machines at the county fair. The claw stopped in midair.

"I do you a favor and you're telling me not to smoke?"

Having thus established his authority, Uncle Andrew allowed that the sheriff could smoke his cigarette in the outer office, from where he could also keep an eye on Agnes Walz. Agnes watched this exchange through a cloud of smoke she kept continuously before her face. It occurred to Gerald that the warning on the package would no longer seem particularly menacing to her.

Uncle Andrew watched Cleary out of the room, then reached for Agnes's cigarettes and shook one free. He put it in his mouth and found he had no match.

"Are you going to smoke that?" Gerald asked.

"Only if I get it lit."

Susannah brought him matches as if she were an accessory to a crime. She and Gerald watched Andrew inhale, then expel the smoke. If it pleased or displeased him he gave no sign.

"Now I would like to be alone with my client."

"He's smoking," Susannah said in wonder as they left the conference room.

"Maybe you ought to take it up again too."

"Don't tempt me," Susannah said.

THREE

Uncle Andrew's offices were located on the twelfth floor of the Hoosier Towers, the tallest building in Wyler, and Gerald had been given a room with a window facing west, providing him with an unimpeded view of a terrain flatter than that he had marveled at the first time he flew into O'Hare. A checkerboard moved out from the town, the gridded land Euclidean to a fault. The town spread out below him had a population of 60,000, give or take a soul or two. There was a Sears and a Western Auto, there was a shopping mall, there was an airport where twelve-seater Air Indiana Fairchilds brought terrified visitors from Chicago and Detroit and Indianapolis. The basketball team of the consolidated high school had been in the semifinals of the state tournament the previous year and was off to a good start this year.

Wyler, Indiana.

Hicksville.

It was not for this that Gerald had endured four years at Lehigh and another three of law school in Chicago. Spontaneous laughter would have sprung to his lips if anyone had suggested two years ago that he would end up on the lowest rung of a law firm in Wyler, Indiana. Gerald was prepared to believe that something had to fill in the geography of the country between major cities, but the less he knew of it the better. He had interviewed in Chicago and was a shoo-in at the First National Bank; he was on the short list for a position in one of the most prestigious law firms in the Loop. When Uncle Andrew called to say he would be in Chicago and would like to see his dear departed sister's only child, Gerald had been prepared to show a rube relative around the big city.

It had been a memorable reunion. Trying to find an image for it, Gerald vacillated between the return of the prodigal son, the conversion of Scrooge, and recognition of the peasant child as a prince of the realm.

"We drifted apart," his uncle had said in the Pump Room, where waiters swooshed past with flaming viands. He was referring to Cecilia, Gerald's mother, his older sister. It seemed an inadequate expression for the mutual repudiation his mother had told him about.

But Gerald had simply nodded and sipped the Barolo Uncle Andrew had ordered.

"She would have been sixty."

"Fifty-nine," Gerald corrected, and imagined his vindicated mother smiling on him from eternity. Even there she would not want to be thought a moment older than she was.

"It is a short-lived family. I refer to the women. Our grandfather lived forever."

Gerald nodded. The grandfather had been the cause of the falling out between his mother and Uncle Andrew. His mother had taken Gerald on pilgrimage to visit the senile old fellow, spotted as a leopard, drooling in the shade of oak trees. He did not know who Gerald's mother was. Most days he did not know who he himself was. Such longevity did not seem a triumph. Uncle Andrew had taken care of the old man's bills, but he had never visited him.

Gerald's mother and his great-grandfather were dead when he had the great reunion with Uncle Andrew. It was a reunion only in an exiguous sense. Uncle Andrew had seen Gerald just once before, as an infant of two months. Half a continent and a different conception of family ties had estranged the brother and sister.

"I wish she had accepted my invitation to visit."

"She thought you should visit us."

"Stubborn."

"That's what she said about you."

Uncle Andrew's laughter gave way to a thoughtful look. Gerald found it odd to think of his mother as Andrew's big sister.

"Tell me about your family."

"We managed," Gerald said. "My father didn't leave much."

"No." Andrew paid fleeting tribute to his late brother-in-law, the professor of classics in a prep school for spoiled boys.

"Not that I ever wanted for anything."

One eyebrow lifted and then the other. "No?"

"We were a very happy family."

Andrew nodded. "There is no substitute for that." He rolled the ruby Barolo in his glass and tried some on his tongue. "It is the great thing missing from my own life. From Dorothy's and mine."

No children. No heir. No family, save for Gerald. As Uncle Andrew was Gerald's sole link with any family past. Such thoughts moved his uncle more, but Gerald was not immune to their power. The sumptuous luxury of the Pump Room seemed an appropriate backdrop for deliciously melancholy thoughts on the tenuousness of life, the contingency of things, their evanescence.

"You have an unusual vocabulary," Uncle Andrew said, and it was half rebuke, half praise.

"I had an unusual father. He would have spoken of the *lacrimae rerum*."

"Ah."

"The tears of things."

"And now you are an orphan."

An orphan! Dear God, the power of words. Gerald had never thought of himself as an orphan. The word seemed to confer on him a pitiable status. The emotions it evoked, more than anything else, accounted for Gerald's susceptibility to his uncle's suggestion.

Wyler, Indiana.

It was the stuff of comedy. His uncle was actually suggesting that Gerald come with his law degree to Andrew's firm in the Hoosier Towers in Wyler, Indiana, there to labor both as junior partner and as heir apparent. That financial hardship need not follow on the choice of a modest scene for one's labors was a central theme in his uncle's pitch.

His local investments were various and lucrative.

The stock market was as accessible from Wyler as from Wall Street itself. Andrew Broom's portfolio was thick and varied and productive.

And there was the firm.

"General law, Gerald. There is nothing like it to keep the mind fresh and alert. In Chicago you will become a narrow specialist. You will know all there is to know about some corner of the law, and within a few years you will be bored by it. My practice is analogous to general medicine. I do corporate law, real estate law, copyright law. I do wills and estates. There is no facet of the law in which I have not practiced."

"Criminal law?"

"That too."

And his uncle had told him of his recent appointment by the court to defend Agnes Walz. There could be no doubt that Andrew Broom was giving the woman the full benefit of his legal knowledge. The enthusiasm with which he spoke of the case, as much as anything else, convinced Gerald that his uncle did indeed lead a fuller life, a fuller legal life, than the general run of Chicago lawyers.

"Do you golf?" Gerald asked.

A small smile dimpled the corners of his uncle's mouth. "I golf."

Andrew Broom, Gerald was to learn, had twice been state amateur champion. He was an all but scratch golfer and had played in some lesser pro/am tournaments.

"A good course?"

"Designed by Arnold Palmer."

"Just the one?"

On the tablecloth, Uncle Andrew drew a rough map of the area around Wyler, locating the golf courses for Gerald, ranking them as he did so.

There are those who will smile at the thought of a young man deciding so awesome a question on the basis of the golfing facilities available. Let these take comfort from thoughts of the blood ties, the assurance of inheriting, the opportunity to become versatile in the law. It would be too much to say that these did not weigh in Gerald's decision to move to Wyler, Indiana. But it would be false to deny that it was golf that proved to be the deciding issue.

He had come six months ago and he had played the course designed by Arnold Palmer until its contours might have been those of his beloved. But familiarity did not breed contempt. The best Gerald had scored thus far was a 79. He had yet to come within five strokes of his uncle. On net he'd tied him twice, thanks to his uncle's nonexistent handicap. He looked forward to the resumption of golf in the spring. Gerald had learned not to underestimate Wyler.

Thus far his legal activity had not been as various as doubtless it would become. The murder trial of Agnes Walz had demanded a good deal of ungrudged time from Uncle Andrew, and Gerald, fascinated, had followed the trial from the defense table. From time to time he had had to remind himself that this was not moot court, that the stakes were real, that his uncle's client was indeed on trial for conspiring with her lover to kill her husband. His uncle had been impressed with Gerald's mastery of the case. The truth was, he felt he had wandered into a fascinating soap and the facts adhered effortlessly to his mind.

In court, in consultation with her lawyers, Agnes Walz appeared sedated, so impervious did she seem to her plight. Her judgments of the principals in the case were pithy. Had she loved her coconspirator Jacob Fennel?

She worked her tongue about in her closed mouth. And then, "He pleased me."

"Did he love you?"

The thin lips stretched slightly. "He kept coming back."

"And what were your relations with your husband?"

She thought about it. "Husband and wife."

"Did you love him?"

She shook her head.

"Didn't you love him when you married him?"

"I guess so. He never bathed."

If she did not admit that she and Jacob Fennel had conspired to murder her husband, she never denied it either. Not that it mattered. The ace up the sleeve of the prosecution was a letter Jacob Fennel had left in his safe deposit box. In it, he recorded in detail the stages of the plot between him and Agnes to get rid of Wallace Walz. Fennel's movements were easily traced, and Uncle Andrew was to make much of them, conceding Fennel's guilt.

Twenty-five miles from Wyler, on the Indiana/Illinois border, was the town of Sorrento. On the Indiana side were blocks of frame houses, their paint corroded by the fumes of the cracking plants and refineries and chemical manufacturing plants that made Sorrento prosperous and uninhabitable. Prospect Avenue, the main street, traced the line dividing the two states. On the Illinois side were honkytonks, the last outpost of the Chicago mob.

The strippers in its clubs were zestful girls just beginning in the life, on the way up, and flabby veterans on their way down. Sorrento was down, so they had in fact arrived. In the dingy haunts of a dozen and a half garish clubs, these pathetic ecdysiasts did their stint upon tiny stages to taped music and then worked the meager crowds for watered drinks and a few minutes of ecstasy in the darker recesses of the clubs.

The customers were high school boys with prominent Adam's apples, laborers who had quarreled with their wives and were avenging themselves with a night on the town, and a fair representation of the slumming middle class, salesmen from suburbia reliving illicit moments of R&R in Asian cities of sin, professional men giving proof of the abiding truth of Stevenson's *Dr. Jekyll and Mr. Hyde.*

Besides the hookers and the customers, there were the hoods.

It was to Sorrento that Fennel had gone in search of someone to rid his beloved of the encumbrance of her husband. The prosecution had proved this to a fault, nor had Uncle Andrew's pro forma observations that they had never succeeded in turning up the paid assassin deflected the jury from the facts. The circumstantial evidence was overwhelming. And there had been the brooding presence of the surviving husband, Wallace Walz, staring at Agnes from a seat in the front row just behind the prosecutor's table. The man hired to kill him had killed his employer, Fennel, and if Walz savored the irony of this there was no evidence of it on his unforgiving face.

Gerald had gone to Sorrento, with his uncle and alone, to gather depositions. They were among the least informative documents ever to be typed out by a legal secretary as competent as Susannah. The hustlers in the clubs had difficulty remembering the day before, let alone months. In any case, given the pitiless turnover, no one hoofing it half-clothed on the diminutive stage of one of those clubs was likely to have been there more than a month.

This left the hoods, who made up the managerial class and the muscle. One of the former, Giulio Pompeio, had when first questioned indicated knowledge of Fennel's effort to recruit a gunman to murder Wallace Walz, treating it as an item in the public domain, but his deposition was as uninformative as the others. Uncle Andrew had been disappointed enough to send Gerald to see Pompeio again.

Pompeio reminded Gerald of the fat boy in every class he had ever been in. There was something vulnerable in his obesity. His little marble eyes rolled back and forth in the pouches around them as he conversed. The conversation was like a game Gerald was losing.

"I never said that," Pompeio answered, truly enough, when Gerald suggested that the manager of the Ecstasy had guilty knowledge of Fennel's search for a hired killer.

"Look," Gerald said, moving to the edge of his chair. He had always been able to handle the fat boy of the class. "Let's say I come to you because there is someone I want to get rid of."

"Yeah."

"I am looking for someone to do the job in such a way that I will not be blamed."

"Then it's dumb to tell me."

Gerald smiled. "Of course it is. But how else am I going to find someone to kill for me?"

"Who you want killed?"

"Let's say my wife."

"You're not sure?"

"Okay. My wife. I want my wife killed. How do I go about it?"

"Shoot her, drown her, I don't care."

Gerald was patient. "I want someone else to do it."

"For how much?"

"How much would be enough?"

"That depends."

"I want the best there is."

"Five thousand."

"You know someone who would kill my wife for five thousand dollars?"

"I probably know someone who would do it for free." Pompeio grinned. "I might do it myself."

"I am trying to have a serious conversation."

"Kill her yourself, kid. Keep it in the family. That's always best. A household accident, and nobody the wiser. You start talking around a place like this, well, that's dumb."

"Because the man I hired would tell the police?"

Pompeio slowly shook his head. "Naw. Because he would bleed you for the rest of your natural life."

"Blackmail," Uncle Andrew said, when Gerald reported this conversation. "Of course. I wonder if the man who killed Jacob Fennel was paid at all."

"Wouldn't he want the money in advance?"

"I doubt that Fennel would have been dumb enough to give it to him. Certainly not all of it."

More irony? The wrong man killed and the killer unpaid for his bloody labor.

Uncle Andrew nodded, smiling over Wyler like a benevolent deity.

FOUR

Left alone with his client Agnes Walz on the day he had received the fatal verdict from Dr. Lister, Andrew put the question to her.

"Did Jacob pay the man, Agnes?"

She had lit her third cigarette and now puffed away as if committing a species of suicide. She said nothing.

"You can keep that package, Agnes. I will bring you a carton in jail."

She nodded.

"Agnes, we're alone. I'm your lawyer, you're my client. You have been found guilty of conspiring to kill your husband. I don't see how the jury could have done otherwise. When the prosecution introduced Jake's letter, it was all over. All I could do was try to portray Jake as the kind of man who would try

25

to implicate you. Now, I am not asking you to tell me if you and Jacob tried to kill Wallace, not in so many words..."

"We did."

He did not show his elation at this confession. "And Jacob hired someone to do the job?"

"He did."

"Did you ever meet the man?"

"No. I left that up to Jake."

Andrew thought about it. It was a wonder the prosecutor had not produced at least one witness from that daisy chain of involvement. Andrew's attitude toward these events had changed, he recognized; no doubt that was inevitable in the circumstances. A man under sentence of death views the shenanigans of others in an altered light. Wasn't that the reason hermits had kept a skull in sight? *Memento mori.* One of the phrases he had picked up from Gerald, who in turn had picked it up from his father, the teacher. Why should Andrew Broom care if Agnes and her lover had tried to kill that dour bastard Wallace Walz? The fact that he never bathed had stuck in Andrew's mind. Surely that was extenuating enough? And if the killer had not been paid, as he had speculated with Gerald, why that was merely amusing.

"How much did you give him?"

"How much money is missing from the bank?"

"Your husband says ten thousand."

Agnes shrugged. Jacob Fennel had taken five thousand dollars from his bank account the day he was killed.

"That money Jake withdrew was meant for the killer, wasn't it?"

The little twinkle in her eye told him yes.

"Did he pay him?"

"Well, he didn't have the money on him when he was shot."

Suddenly Agnes was communicative. But he heard whatever she said with the ears of the prosecutor and thus framed the obvious objection.

"Was the ten thousand dollars missing from your safety deposit box the rest of the payment, Agnes?"

"He didn't earn it."

"Where is it?"

"I kept it."

"You kept it." All of this was new to him. It was as though he were having his first interview with Agnes. Thank God she had not told him this before the trial. Could he have defended her half so well if he had been unable at least to imagine that she was innocent? "Where is it?"

Her eyes darted to him. She shook her head. "I'd rather it was never found than that it go to him."

To her husband? "The money is his."

"Its ours."

"Even so."

She shook her head. "What would happen to that money, if it came to light?"

Well, it would be an exhibit if they got a retrial, a possibility looking less and less likely. Then it would go to Wallace.

"I'd give it to you first."

He decided not to tell her the spot they both would

be in if she told him where that money was.

She said, "You never called Wallace to testify."

"You were in enough trouble as it was."

"You should have talked to him."

The edge in her voice suggested how she must have talked to Wallace and how eventually she would have talked to Jake Fennel. Andrew admitted to himself that he believed Agnes had been the brains behind all this scheming. It was only fitting that she be the one to make the ultimate payment.

An inappropriate sentiment for a defense attorney.

"I want you to get another lawyer, Agnes."

She stopped smoking at this remark. "You gonna ditch me now?"

"Something has come up."

"What?"

"I mean with me. It's personal. I am going to have to withdraw."

She looked at him in silence. "I understand."

"No, you don't, Agnes." He hesitated. "I'm sick. I've just come from the doctor."

"Nobody likes to lose. I understand."

What an infuriating woman she was.

"I have been working on your appeal. I do not mean that I will simply abandon you. Agnes, what do you think should go into the appeal, to justify asking for a reversal?"

"Tell them I'm innocent."

Even after what she had told him, she managed to mimic a look of injured innocence.

"Of course."

Andrew walked to the window and looked out at

Wyler as if he were being subjected to one of the three temptations of Jesus. All this will I give thee ...But he had all that, in a manner of speaking, and soon it would slip through his fingers. No, it was his fingers that would slip away. The town would remain.

He closed his eyes and a pained expression altered his face. He was not used to such thoughts. A lawyer's life is caught up in the ultimate stakes, birth and death and all the crimes and misdemeanors in between, but he was totally unprepared for the knowledge that all his loans were being called in. In the muddle of his thoughts, it was difficult to feel concern for the fate of Agnes Walz. For a time it had worked, the idea that immersing himself in her case could obliterate what Lister had told him. But how long could he distract himself from the news that he was going to die?

"My associate, Gerald Rowan, will continue on the case, Agnes."

"That boy?"

"That boy graduated from one of the half-dozen best law schools in the country. He knows your case as well as I do. Of course, if you would prefer that the court assign..."

She was shaking her head. "No. I'll stick with the boy."

The boy. It was good that Gerald could not hear.

Agnes was taken away by Cleary and company, but before speaking to Gerald, Andrew closed the door of his office and made a phone call.

"Lister? Broom. About our talk earlier today?"

"Yes?" Why was it the doctor who seemed frightened and he who sounded matter-of-fact?

"That was a confidential conversation, was it not?"

"How do you mean?"

"Doctor and patient. Like lawyer and client. Privileged?"

"Oh yes, of course."

"Then I must ask you to proceed as if it had never occurred. I am going to seek a second opinion. Meanwhile, I do not want anyone to know what you told me."

"A second opinion." Lister's voice was that of an adolescent, seeking a register.

"Do you object?"

"Certainly not."

"How many people in the clinic know of that report?"

"None!" Lister yelped. "That report is confidential."

"It better be, Ted."

He slammed down the phone. He was acting absurdly. It was childish to blame his mortality on Lister. But he was filled with a passion to keep secret the awful news. A second opinion? He had no hope that it could alter things.

But another thought had begun to move amorphously across his mind as he spoke to Agnes.

FIVE

Billy's computer system was an electronic hybrid, a mating of a dozen different trademarks into an utterly unique configuration he had named, acronymically, GIGO, standing for "Garbage in, garbage out." Original? Hell no, but how many parents showed originality in naming their kids.

Billy had no kids, no parents, no family to speak of. The unspeakable exception was Rafe, his brother, who was doing hard time in Michigan City for armed robbery, assault with a deadly weapon, and DWI. Who but Rafe would have planned a job in minute detail and then tried to execute it while drunk?

The world of the computer enabled Billy to escape the world inhabited by Rafe. It was as though he floated right through the amber screen of his monitor and got lost among the circuitry. He spent up to ten hours a day fiddling with it, his modem enabling him to tap into banks and state bureaus and the main frame at Purdue.

And to write.

On the one occasion he himself had done time, left in the lurch by Rafe, Billy had taken a writing course by mail. Fiction. He had begun writing his own life, but the far-off instructor assumed it was a novel so that is what it became. Billy found his own life a more attractive subject if he could mold it to his dreams and desires. It now occupied 900 megabytes on his hard disk and was backed up on four diskettes.

He called it "My Story," the title a fairly good indication of its contents. There is a dank corner of purgatory awaiting the correspondence teacher who encouraged Billy's writing. His syntax and spelling were terrible. As for the story, in it Willie (aka Billy) was a wimpy naif who was forever getting the shaft from his brother and assorted alleged friends. Popping away at the keyboard of his computer, Billy really believed this portrait of himself.

It was a lot more comfortable to think that Rafe was the bad apple.

When he wasn't sitting in his corduroy bathrobe in front of GIGO in the upstairs bedroom of the house in which he and Rafe had been raised by an aunt and uncle, Billy looked after things down at the Ecstasy in Sorrento.

The hours were right, ten p.m. to four a.m.

And whoever it was that finally paid his wages would not be curious about his background.

Altar boys did not apply for jobs keeping order in clubs like the Ecstasy. They were more likely to be among the citizens Billy had to subdue when the drink and animal spirits put out the light of reason in them.

Billy talked that way. It broke up Giulio and the girls, and he could understand how it sounded to them, but how could he hope to become a writer if he did not expand his vocabulary? Even John Steinbeck, Billy's hero, used words Billy had never heard of but which he dutifully looked up and then, faithful to the practice recommended to him by his correspondence instructor, used at least six times the same day.

"A fastidious employer would not have us," he said to Janette.

And later, "Aren't you being overly fastidious, Giulio?"

The one that brought down the house was "Goddam it, Bennie, bring a rag and make this bar more fastidious."

That was the day he got to know the lawyers from Wyler. And also got a much needed lesson in always keeping his mouth buttoned.

His assumption had been that they had just come in off the Interstate to see what there was to see in sin city, a completely adventitious coming.

"Adventitious," the younger man, Gerald, repeated, crinkling his nose.

"It means like it might not have happened."

"I know. As improbable as finding someone like

you here." When he gestured, a starched cuff emerged from the sleeve of his suit jacket and a gold link glinted.

"We're here on purpose," the older lawyer said. "I am defense counsel in a murder case in Wyler, Indiana, about thirty miles southeast of here."

They were sitting at a table near the front door, Billy's back to the stage, where one of the girls was grinding through her routine to soft rock. It was something the way the lawyers kept their eyes on the dancer yet managed to go on talking to him. Long before they mentioned the name, Billy was on the alert.

Agnes Walz.

"I read about it." Why the hell did he have to say even that?

"Have you talked to the prosecution already?"

Billy pushed back from the table. "You better talk to Giulio."

They talked to Giulio, that night, other times, if the information Billy got was correct. The prosecution insisted on talking with Billy.

He dummied up. Did they expect to straighten out the world by asking people a few questions?

"A place like this," he tried to explain, "it has no regulars. Understand? People come here once and usually that's it. Or months go by and they come again, and by then it's like a new place."

"Different girls?" The young male attorney from the prosecutor's office had trouble keeping his eyes from the dancer too. The woman with him, under thirty, wearing a charcoal gray suit and a pink silk blouse, her hair all done up nice, stared straight at Billy, but unless her peripheral vision was shot to hell she had to know what Bridget was doing up there on the stage. Bridget was the kind who made little shouts and moans of pretended abandon as she discarded her bra and then grabbed the edge of the curtain and began engaging in adult relations with it. Billy enjoyed watching the young lady lawyer's discomfiture.

"Discomfiture?" The male prosecutor tore his eyes from Bridget.

"Unease," Billy said helpfully. "Most people feel it the first time they come here."

"You get used to it though?" the girl asked. She acted like if they could make this a sort of scientific subject—how long does it take before the sight of a naked woman squirming on a stage does nothing for you?—it would be tamed and tolerable.

What they were all after was someone who could identify the man who had come looking for someone to commit murder for him.

Billy was surprised when his boss turned cooperative.

Giulio shrugged and his eyes rolled from one corner to the other. "Know why? The sonofabitch is dead. He wanted someone shot and he ended up shot himself. How about that?"

"Poetic justice."

Giulio squinted and looked away. In conversation with Billy, he found it best to let every other remark go unanswered.

"I'm not remembering well enough to do them any

good on the stand. They going to prosecute the guy's woman. Anyway, they located a dancer who was here at the time and she said sure he had asked her about it."

Billy remembered the guy. He wore a dark blue mesh cap with International Harvester on it. When he relaxed there was a pattern of white streaks where the sun hadn't got at him because he was squinting. His hands looked like weapons. He said his name was Casper something or other, but he was Jacob Fennel. The story made the Chicago and Gary papers, so Billy had a chance to study the photograph. Imagine coming into a place like the Ecstasy and talking to strangers about wanting to hire a killer.

He had talked to Billy too.

And Billy sure as hell was not going to talk to anyone about it, not the defense lawyers, not the prosecutor.

He was staying *hors de combat*.

He was into foreign phrases now.

This one sounded like a pugnacious prostitute.

Pugnacious had been last Wednesday.

Prostitute was every night of the week at the Ecstasy.

SIX

Gerald Rowan had been attracted to the law when watching reruns of Perry Mason on television. Like most law students, he initially imagined he was destined for criminal law. But criminal law, despite the glamour and no matter which side of the table one sat on, was not where the big bucks were.

Wanting the big bucks came quickly in law school.

He had not succumbed to the blandishments of Uncle Andrew and come to Wyler in order to practice criminal law. Nonetheless, a good deal of his attention and energy had been claimed by the Agnes Walz case, if only because Uncle Andrew was so involved in it. He could not say that he regretted it.

He liked the fact that his uncle took so seriously a court appointment as defense attorney. He had nothing to gain from the case. But he did have something to lose. The case. Uncle Andrew did not like to lose. He was not accustomed to losing and clearly had no intention of acquiring the habit.

But he had lost.

The jury had found Agnes Walz guilty as charged, coconspirator with the late Jacob Fennel in an attempt to murder her husband, Wallace. It would have required a miracle for any other verdict to be returned after the document Jake had left in his safe deposit box came to light. There it all was, the plot he and Agnes had engaged in to get rid of her husband. Uncle Andrew had taken it well and had immediately turned his attention to the appeal. Gerald had been impressed.

Until now. After being alone with Agnes in the conference room for fifty minutes, his uncle had gone to his office and closed the door. They were to lunch together at the Athletic Club at twelve fifteen. Five minutes was more than enough time to walk to the club and no one was going to turn Andrew Broom away because he was late, but Gerald was hungry and at twelve ten he buzzed his uncle to remind him of their date.

"Gerald, would you mind going without me?"

"You forgot."

"I'm afraid so. Do you mind?"

As a matter of fact he did not. It gave him an excuse to change his venue from the all-male dining room of the Athletic Club to the country club, where there was a better than even chance he might see Julie.

Julie had honey blond hair and was five feet seven

in bare feet, requiring her to direct her clear blue eyes slightly upward at an angle to meet Gerald's. The plush fold of her lower lip, the classic contours of her nose, her body, which had been toned but not toughened by swimming and tennis and golf—making an inventory of Julie's assets had become one of Gerald's favorite indoor sports. Even if every other aspect of the move to Wyler had proved a disappointment, the presence in this town of the adorable Julie McGough would have overshadowed it.

Frank McGough, her father, hated Andrew Broom and thus, by illogical transitivity, Gerald as well. Matters had not been helped when Gerald, the new boy on the block, had bested Stan, the scion of the McGough family, in the country club golf tournament in August. But enmity had obtained between Frank McGough and Andrew Broom since they had returned to their native town from law school in the very same year and commenced the competition that had enriched them both, redounded to the benefit of Wyler, and made them implacable foes.

Uncle Andrew professed to be impervious to the charms of Julie.

"She reminds me of her mother."

"Her mother is beautiful, too."

"I was referring to her disposition."

"She is an angel."

"There are fallen angels."

The thought of taking a fall or two with Julie was enough to blur Gerald's vision. And his thinking. He had underestimated the intensity of the dislike Uncle Andrew felt for all things McGoughish.

"There are dozens of other girls, Gerald."

"She is the most beautiful, the most attractive, the most..."

"Anyone but Julie McGough, Gerald."

Julie, of course, was receiving the same stern advice about Gerald from her father. How could two young people, thus forbidden one another, possibly resist the attraction?

By September they were playing the back nine in the failing light of evening, timing their progress so that they would have reached Number 16 when further play was out of the question. Number 16 is a par three, the green an almost-island in a small pond. A wedge and luck were sufficient to loft the ball onto the putting surface. Players then had the choice of a land route that would bring them circuitously to the green or they could take the flat-bottomed boat docked just below the tee and row to the green. No matter the dying of the light, Gerald always hit a ball before they clambered into the boat and pushed off into a setting so romantic he found it physically painful not to burst into song. His off-key humming was not repellent to Julie.

The first time he kissed her was in that boat, afloat among the lily pads, the twilight harrumphing of frogs as accompaniment. That there was no way to get comfortable in the boat, that pressing his lips to Julie's entailed jamming his knee painfully against the ribbed bottom of the boat, that the whine of mosquitoes crescendoed as they drifted close to shore— none of this could detract from the magic of the moment.

"Are you going to putt out?" Julie would ask.

He nuzzled into her golden hair. "I'd love to."

Her laughter was as golden as her hair, and he imagined old duffers on the porch of the clubhouse hearing her and feeling the pain of loss.

"Marry me."

"Don't joke."

"I never joke about marriage."

"We can't."

"Why?"

"You know why."

"I will not sleep with you unless you are my wife."

This excited her and she pressed her lips to his, tightened her embrace, increased the pain in his knee. It was wonderful. The boat bumped against the shore, and they tried to get more comfortable. Without success. The rowboat was as effective as a chastity belt.

For a time such furtive rendezvous had their attraction; it was exciting to have such a tremendous secret with Julie. But eventually Gerald felt the need to declare his passion to the world. The country club equivalent to this was to invite Julie to the autumn equinox dance. Her lovely face became a mask of sadness.

"Patrick Hennessy has already asked me."

"Poor fellow."

"Gerald, I accepted. The dance is public."

Meaning they could not attend together.

"Julie, we can't go on like this. I love you."

She put her finger on his lips. It was like a blessing. "I cannot oppose my father."

"Then we must present him with a fait accompli."

She frowned incomprehension.

"Elope," he explained.

"Gerald, I couldn't. My parents have been planning my wedding since I was a child."

A child. He took her hand. "If you were pregnant..."

She squeezed his hand, a signal for him to go on. She would not be the first bride to have anticipated the joys of marriage. In this day and age...

But she shook her head, stopping that line of reasoning. Julie was her father's daughter. That the multitudes might be doing such-and-such could never be an argument for her doing something. Gerald returned to basics.

"I love you. I need you. I want to hold you in my arms, in a bed..."

Her breathing became a roar in his ear.

The dance was on a Saturday. The plan was that on Friday night he should share her bed in the McGough home. Stan and her parents were going to Chicago for a White Sox game. (Uncle Andrew, needless to say, was a Cubs fan.) The coast would be clear. It would be their honeymoon. In their hearts they would get into bed together as man and wife, regardless of the legality of their union.

Thus on Wednesday the anticipatory pleasure of seeing Julie, just seeing her, catching a glimpse of her across the room and knowing that in two nights' time she would be his, brought Gerald palpitating into the parking lot of the country club.

And catch a glimpse of Julie was all he could do. She was surrounded by femininity—the monthly luncheon of the Association of University Women, of which she was recording secretary—and so busy that she seemed oblivious to Gerald's presence in the dining room. He took a table by the window, ordered a luncheon steak and a salad, beer with the meal, coffee later, and settled down to enjoy his beloved from afar.

Julie was not at the club today, and while he ate lunch, Gerald was assailed by thoughts of his uncle. Something was wrong. First, the postponement of the long-anticipated meeting with Agnes Walz in the conference room of his law office. Uncle Andrew had made it a matter of honor to consult with his client there, to underscore the fact that she was not a dangerous murderess. As her counsel, he could not of course accept the trial verdict as final. And he had badgered Cleary into bringing her to the Hoosier Towers.

There had been the planned newspaper coverage, but Andrew Broom was absent from the photographs. The plan was for him to welcome Agnes with an exonerating hug at the door of his office. Gerald had stood in for his uncle, substituting a warm handshake for the embrace. Maybe Mr. Walz never bathed, but Agnes was no beauty either. That she had excited the passion of Jacob Fennel was no test of her seductivity. After losing Agnes to Wallace when they were in high school together, Jake had never married.

The rivalry between the two men had continued, transferred to an agricultural plane. Their holdings grew in every direction. Even in lean years they both prospered. The one thing Wallace could not produce was an heir, and this failure hung like a black cloud over his home farm, the fertility of whose acreage was legendary, the productivity of his pullulating poultry, cattle, and swine cause for comment as far away as Purdue. It was a totally new world to Gerald.

"I'm becoming interested in animal husbandry," he told Julie during the pre-trial preparation for the defense of Agnes.

"You're awful!" But she tugged him close, grinding her lips against his.

Gerald's foreboding about his uncle increased when he returned to the office and was told that he was to assume chief responsibility for the appeal of Agnes Walz's conviction.

"How do you mean?"

"You are her lawyer now. Unless of course you want to refuse."

Despite the fact that he himself was apparently defecting from the cause, Uncle Andrew made the thought of Gerald's not taking on the task a treasonable one.

"I've always thought you were spending more time on the case than it deserved."

"Defending a person accused of a capital crime is not my idea of wasting time."

"You know what I mean," Gerald protested weakly.

"I wish I did."

Gerald retreated to his own office to brood over developments, and it was only later that he realized his uncle had given no reason why he was passing the Agnes Walz matter on to Gerald. He buzzed Susannah and asked her to come into his office.

"I am taking over the Agnes Walz appeal."

"I know."

"Do you know why?"

In Susannah's wide eyes there was wonderment and fear. Gerald had never seen this extremely competent woman look even momentarily confused. He opened the box of cigarettes he kept on his desk for clients. Susannah took one and he lit it for her.

"To hell with it," she said and inhaled deeply, letting the smoke flutter forth as if she were giving up the ghost.

"Where did he go this morning?"

"Did you ask him?"

"He put me on the defensive."

She smiled. "I know."

"Where did he go?"

"He got a call from Dr. Lister at the clinic."

Gerald remembered that his uncle had had a physical a week ago. No doubt the test results had been ready. Susannah agreed.

"Do you think anything is wrong?"

"He looks healthy to me."

"He is healthy," Gerald insisted. He knew his uncle's stamina on the golf course and on the tennis court. If there had been any slowing down, it had gone unnoticed by Gerald.

But Uncle Andrew had turned over the Agnes Walz appeal.

He had forgotten their luncheon date.

He had postponed, or tried to, a dramatic encounter with his client in the Hoosier Towers. Something was definitely awry.

"There's nothing to worry about," he assured Susannah.

"I know."

She stubbed out her cigarette and stood.

"He'll bury us both," Gerald said as she went to the door.

She opened it and gave him a radiant smile before leaving.

What an actress.

Gerald felt a need to talk to someone, but who was there? He had already talked to Susannah and they had entered a mutual and tacit pact to lie to one another. Aunt Dorothy?

If anyone would know whether Uncle Andrew was in poor health it was his wife, Dorothy.

SEVEN

Andrew liked to say that Wyler was the world writ small, and Dorothy agreed.

"Very small."

"If we lived in Chicago, you think it would be on the North Side, near Water Tower Place, something like that? Maybe now. But where we would have started would have been Evanston, Winnetka, Skokie even, one of those, and if they aren't small towns I don't know what is. Chicago is just a lot of small towns strung together. Same thing with L.A. and New York. You know anyone who lives in New York? Look where your classmates live. Scarsdale, White Plains, Chappaqua. Wyler is a big city compared to Chappaqua."

"I'm surprised we don't have a big league team. The Wyler White Sox?"

A conversation with Andrew was largely a matter of listening; Dorothy had stopped fighting that years ago. She kept one eye on the TV or on her book, and every once in a while, when he took a breath, she slid in a remark of her own.

He had a theory about everything. Other people thought this or that, had an opinion, but Andrew Broom had a theory. Thus he never admitted being surprised at anything. Whatever happened fit right into the old theory, as if he had predicted it.

Her miscarriages? He traced them, at least to his own satisfaction, to the dieting and exercise that had gone into her thwarted dancing career. She couldn't believe it.

"How many ballerinas have babies?" he asked.

"It's not because they can't have them."

He smiled. At the time, she thought, well, anything that reconciles him to the fact that there isn't going to be any Andrew Broom, Jr., is all right with me. She had cried herself to sleep more than once regretting the darling daughter she would never have. It is not easy to accept the fact that you cannot reproduce yourself. All the babies in the world unwanted, unplanned, women turning them out at the drop of a hat, girls too, and she couldn't do it.

In her heart of hearts she blamed Andrew and supposed he blamed her in turn. A companionate marriage, mere sex partners? Think of it as shacking up? But it is hard to sustain interest in a man who is only a bed partner. Just as she sensed he had lost interest in her.

He had always been a handsome, manly man and in his mid-forties he still was, but looking at him now all she saw was a man who had failed to have children. She herself was beautiful. She had known she was beautiful from the time she had known anything, and she had grown more beautiful with age. Catherine Deneuve, that's what people said, and Dorothy could see the resemblance.

People did not understand that beauty is boring. Too much is expected of a beautiful woman. She must be poised and intelligent, graceful and good. Once Dorothy had seen Sophia Loren angry as a fishwife in an Italian-made movie. No American actress would have taken the part. But the anger had turned a beautiful woman into a person.

Andrew had deflected his paternal instinct into his work and become a town father. The actual phrase was often used. Well, he had produced the new Wyler without the aid of a wife, no matter what he and others said at banquets and awards. She had no interest in his work, in this town, in him. Andrew bored her and she bored herself.

Five years ago, he had gotten caught up in genealogy, searching the past for relatives he did not have. He had known all along of his sister, knew she had a son, but it would have been too simple just to look them up. Andrew, being Andrew, had wanted to create a family; his sister and Gerald were already there needing only to be recognized.

Genealogy having turned up no alternative, Andrew finally got in touch with Gerald and now it was a whole new world. It was the best thing he had done since building the clinic and attracting its staff to Wyler.

Dorothy lived in dread of one thing, cancer of the breast. She was certain she would commit suicide rather than subject herself to a mastectomy. Her breasts were perfectly proportioned to her body; they were far from being her most attractive asset, but she could not imagine life as a maimed woman, hiding her deformity with padded bras. Whenever she palpated her breasts, eyes closed, holding her breath, dreading the discovery of a telltale lump, Dorothy murmured half-forgotten prayers of childhood. She did not think it a bit comical that a woman of forty-one should be sitting at her vanity, her slip dropped to her waist, feeling her breasts and whispering, "Now I lay me down to sleep, I pray the Lord my soul to keep." She did not know if she believed in God, but she believed in the trusting child she had been when any pain could be taken away.

Like an idiot she connected her fear of breast cancer to dancing. As a dancer she had wanted to be flat-chested and had bound down her breasts. She would never have told Andrew this. She refused to be proof of one of his silly theories. But thank God he had built the clinic and brought first-class medical people to Wyler.

Ted Lister came with the clinic.

There had been a Peg Lister in her class at Vassar and though she proved to be no relation of his, it had gotten them off on a good footing and Dorothy still

half believed that they had somehow known one another or been connected in a mystic fashion before he
came to Wyler.

It was Ted who allayed her fears about breast
cancer.

More important, he had lifted the weight of child-
lessness from her. He ran tests. He was certain.

"You could have had children." He toyed with his
stethoscope and then looked directly at her. "You
still could."

"But I had three miscarriages."

He nodded. "You would have to be careful during
the first two months. Isn't that when you lost the
other babies?"

It was.

"Tell your husband. There's no reason you couldn't
have a baby now."

"How old do you think I am?"

"I know how old you are." He indicated her folder.

Get pregnant at forty-one? He must be out of his
mind. Then why was she grinning from ear to ear?
She wanted to hug him, it was such a relief to know
that she could have had children. There was nothing
wrong with her.

She did not tell Andrew. Would he even care? But
the reassurance she had received from Ted Lister restored a lost balance between her and her husband.
She cherished the knowledge she now had as if it
were a weapon to be used against him. The fear of
breast cancer was harder to get rid of. To convince
her, Ted agreed to see her often. In case anything

started she wanted it discovered immediately.

"I would never do a mastectomy in any case," he said.

"Why not?"

"I don't believe in them."

"But if I got cancer..."

"It could be treated in a far less drastic way."

On another occasion, he asked what her husband's reaction had been.

"To what?"

He seemed embarrassed. "When you told him you could have children."

"I didn't tell him."

No need to say more. He got the picture. Knowing Andrew as he did, Ted must have seen that there was no longer a romantic relationship between them.

Ted Lister became a symbol of restored self-confidence. Not that things happened without Dorothy's realizing what was going on. She knew when she began to look forward to her monthly checkup as if it were a date as much as an appointment. She saw Ted at other times too; he had joined the country club, and she took up tennis. She had never wanted to compete with Andrew, but it was different with Ted. She saw him socially, yes, but the first time he made love to her was in his clinic office. After hours. On the examining table, as if it had sentimental associations for them.

She had never felt like this toward Andrew.

Her marriage to Andrew had been as much an arranged match as is possible in this day and age. They were the perfect couple, a wedding cake couple, beautiful alone, beautifully matched. So far as Dorothy knew, what she felt for Andrew was what women felt when they loved a man. There had been no standard to measure her feelings against, and now she realized she had never loved anyone before Ted.

Ted was divorced. His wife had refused to make the move to Wyler. Leave Boston for Indiana?

"I can understand that," Dorothy had said.

"Do you know what an opportunity moving here was for me?"

"I know what it means to me."

That was the dark side of her love for Ted. There was no point in thinking that he would take her away someplace else where they would live happily ever after. The clinic in Wyler was the best thing that could have happened to him professionally; he had sacrificed his marriage for it, and anything they were going to have they would have to have in Wyler.

The fact that Ted was in effect Andrew's employee made things more complicated still. Dorothy thought that, if she and Ted could marry, even Wyler would be tolerable.

More and more Andrew loomed as a roadblock to her happiness.

"He will kill himself with work," she said. How often had she said that, scarcely knowing what she meant. Ted shook his head.

"Not Andrew. He's in perfect health, as strong as an ox."

EIGHT

Gerald had no idea how he was to make a case for Agnes Walz when she was so obviously guilty as charged and as determined by a jury of her peers. Uncle Andrew, increasingly preoccupied but unable to let go of the case completely, listened to Gerald and held up his hand.

"You have to provide an alternative object of suspicion."

"He's dead."

A grudging smile. Andrew needed a session under a sunlamp. How long had it been since he had played a round of golf or some tennis? What he should do was go south, follow the sun.

"You think Agnes is dead?"

"So saith the jury."

"Maybe. I don't know. Think about it. If she and

Jake conspired to have her husband killed and if Jake was killed instead of Wallace, what does that suggest to you?"

"I'm listening."

"Somewhere there is an unpaid assassin. Produce him and you will muddy the waters enough to give Agnes a shot at a new trial."

Once it was pointed out, it was painfully obvious, but Gerald had no illusion he would have thought of it himself. How could he think Agnes guilty and at the same time regard the hired assassin as a figment of the imagination? The early hope of Agnes's defense was that they would be able to show Wallace had killed her lover. Even when he came up with an air-tight alibi, Gerald had continued to think the husband had done it.

An unpaid assassin? He remembered the search of the Walz bank account and the failure to turn up any large withdrawals. But if he expected Uncle Andrew to applaud this memory he was mistaken.

"From the checking account. But she cashed in a ten-thousand-dollar CD."

"Where is it now?"

"It wasn't buried with Jake."

"How long have you known that the killer wasn't paid?"

Uncle Andrew looked at his watch. "Less than forty-eight hours."

Had Agnes told him the day before, during their talk in the conference room?

The possibility had a fascinating quality to it, providing endless delight as he turned it over in his mind. Gerald was certain that sooner or later he would see how it could be put to good use.

The first thing was to feed it to the newspapers. This meant Healy, the editor of the Wyler *Star*, the local paper that, after years of appearing in the evening, had been transformed into a morning paper so as not to have to compete with television. Healy had never succeeded in getting his internal clock to make the transition and, in the early afternoon, when he should have been in bed, his body was still aiming toward the afternoon deadline. So he sat in the Roundball Lounge sipping whiskey sours and holding court. Gerald telephoned in the hope that he could speak to the editor in his office, but was told to make it the Roundball.

"If I don't get a little bit drunk I get no sleep at all."

So he fed it to Healy in his booth at the Roundball. The paper coasters were shaped like basketballs. Gerald shuffled three of these around on the table between Healy and himself.

"Say Agnes is guilty."

"I do," Healy said. "Now that's okay. No more alleged, accused, and the rest. She has been found guilty."

"Of conspiring with a murdered man to murder her husband."

"So the wrong man got shot."

"The killer gets his money, he shoots the victim."

"If he does it right. This time he didn't."

"He shot his employer."

"One of them."

"So who paid him?"

Healy's drink looked like a fruit bowl. He stopped nibbling on an orange slice and studied Gerald successively through each of the sections of his trifocals. Hair sprouted from his ears, but for all that he was something of a flashy dresser. Glen plaid suit, blue shirt, solid tie, navy blue.

"What are you telling me?"

"Maybe the hired killer never got paid."

"Sonofabitch." Healy finished his drink and licked at the sugar on his lips. "Broom could have made something of that at the trial, why didn't he?"

"He didn't know for sure. Besides, it would have meant adopting the prosecution case."

"And the prosecution had no interest in making that point. Well, well."

Healy's third whiskey sour was being delivered when Gerald left. The story would be on the wire within the hour. So what if it did not appear in the *Star* until tomorrow morning?

NINE

The kitchen was the heart of the house, which is the way Agnes had wanted it, but so had Wallace. That's the way it should be on the farm. He had been raised just south of Wyler on a piss-poor eighty-five acres his folks had rented and made profitable and then had to move out of for one of the sons of the owner. As a kid of thirteen, Wallace had considered that robbery.

He himself had paid the same favor to more than one tenant—not replacing him with a son, but letting the poor bastard improve the property and then booting him out on his ass. The lesson he learned as a kid was not the Golden Rule but to get his and hang on to it.

There was an island stove in the kitchen and a

boomerang-shaped breakfast bar, and at the far side, in an alcove that was all windows and fluffy curtains, the table where they ate meals other than breakfast.

Agnes had not been one for using the dining room. He could count the times they had eaten in it, but it was there, just in case. That's what making it meant —you always had more than you needed, just in case.

Wallace, a tall, lean man wearing fresh Levi's and a Pendleton shirt, took his mug around to the stove and got a refill of coffee. He tried it there, the thick lip of the mug pressed to his mustache, squinting toward the picture window that looked out on an unimpeded view of the southern expanse of the Walz main farm.

"That's a great view," young Rowan said.

Wallace nodded. "Sure you don't want more coffee?"

"One's my limit."

Wallace could not imagine drinking one cup of coffee and calling it quits. Or one beer. One anything. He was a man of gargantuan appetites.

It had helped his view of the world as a place friendly to people like himself that he had found Agnes. When he first met her she looked like a boy with tits, but Wallace had seen the depths of her gray eyes. This kid had known life, that was their message. She was of the farm, had been in on the birthing, the butchering, the breeding of cattle, and knew life raw and red and pulsating. He had known that before they had talked much. She was his spiritual twin.

The other half of my soul. Where had he read that? Some poet's fanciful description of what the perfect marriage is, finding the lost other half of your soul. Wallace had left the magazine around, hoping Agnes might read it. He would never have said such a thing out loud to her.

That was not what their life together had been. It had been lived in this kitchen, at the desk in the front hall where he did the accounts, and upstairs in their bedroom where, under a mountain of comforters in winter and bare-ass naked on a sheet in summer, they had nightly screwed till their ears rang.

Young Rowan wanted to know if he bore his wife a grudge. Wallace smiled.

"I try to remember the good times."

"Writing the appeal isn't easy. I can tell you that I was no more surprised than you were when the jury brought in its verdict."

Wallace came back to his stool. "Why is Broom unloading it on you?"

"He isn't unloading anything." It was the first genuine emotion the young man had shown. If he thought he was getting close to Wallace with his phony sympathy for the wronged husband, forget it. Broom had tried to pin Jake's death on him.

"How do you describe it?"

"I have taken over the case. I have been in on it almost from the beginning. Unloading might apply if he had just turned it back to the judge."

"What do you stand to make from it?"

"I don't know."

"You don't know. You go to the Santa Claus Law School?"

"There is a set fee for court-appointed attorneys. Your wife has a court-appointed attorney because you refused to pay for one, and in the circumstances that is perfectly understandable."

"Thank you."

"Why did she want you dead?"

It came at Wallace like an overhead serve, meant to be an ace.

"I guess she was tired of me."

"And in love with Jacob Fennel. Tell me, did you know Jacob Fennel?"

"We were all kids together, Jake and Agnes and me."

"From what I've learned of Fennel, I find it difficult to believe any woman would actually kill for him."

He laughed, he couldn't help it. "Well, Agnes is no bathing beauty anymore either." Good in bed, but a little lazy about personal hygiene. She had never forgiven Wallace for hinting about more frequent bathing.

"Next to him she is."

"Son, if you expect me to explain the ways of women to you, you've come to the wrong door. You don't try to understand women, you enjoy them."

"What would your reaction be if the appeal were successful, if there were a new trial and Agnes were acquitted?"

"That's your plan?"

"The chances of bringing it off are minimal. But I am going to try. She deserves that and I mean to see she gets it—an honest effort."

"Good."

"Where's the money?"

Wallace twisted on his stool and stared into Rowan's eyes. "That's twice, son. I don't like lawyer tricks. What kind of question you asking?"

"Your wife and Jake Fennel hired someone to kill you."

He nodded.

"If you hired such a person, when would you pay him?"

He thought about it. A good question. "Some before, the rest later."

"Okay. So the killer didn't get paid in full."

"How do you know that?"

"Agnes. Jake paid him some, but the money Agnes took out of the bank was never paid."

"Better ask Agnes then."

"We have."

"What did she say?"

"The trouble is, if she has it, it is not in her purse. Plus the fact that she isn't likely to have much use for money where she's going."

"You figure that money will be your fee?"

Rowan looked away and his jaw worked as he got control of himself. "No. The money belongs to you and you are not our client." He picked up his cup and turned it slowly in his hand, studying its contents. "Has it ever crossed your mind that the killer might still try to earn his fee?"

"You mean try to kill me?"

"Admittedly a dumb idea. But we are not dealing with a genius, a man who will kill for money."

"Most people would."

Rowan looked shocked. "Mr. Walz, one of the reasons I came here was to inform you of something we are going to do. In an effort to smoke out the assassin, we are going to float a rumor that the ten thousand dollars was paid him. If he wasn't paid, that is going to get his attention. What he will do then is anybody's guess."

"Sounds dangerous."

"That's why I'm telling you."

Wallace did not like it. He liked it less when Rowan said they were floating several different stories: that the killer had been paid, that his money had been stashed somewhere for him, and that he had not been paid. Rowan was right in saying that nobody had given much thought to that payment, which, when you thought about it, was an essential ingredient in the plot.

"How's Agnes doing?" he asked, when Rowan was on his way.

"Any message?"

He thought for a moment, pulling at the corners of his mouth so he would not smile. Finally he shook his head.

"No. She'll know what I'm thinking without my telling her."

He watched Rowan on the way to his car, shifting his briefcase from one hand to the other to fish the keys from his pocket. Under thirty for sure. Poor

Agnes, to have her thin thread of hope in the hands of a kid like that. But Wallace envied Rowan his youth.

He himself had been living like a monk, except for several excursions to Chicago and a flight to Las Vegas. For years there had been no interruption in the marital routine he and Agnes had established, but with her arrest that had been arrested too.

Agnes would not expect him to get along without loving. It was not in his nature.

Restless, he wondered about driving to Chicago, but thoughts of rush-hour traffic were not welcome.

Maybe Sorrento. That was close and had all the action a man could want.

He nodded, as if winning an argument with himself.

Sorrento it would be.

TEN

Everybody thought it was funny as hell. Rafe called from Michigan City to ask what Billy knew of it and said that he and his colleagues wondered what was happening to the world in their absence. Billy said he would keep Rafe posted.

Posted. He batted out a newsy letter once a week on GIGO for Rafe and anyone else he wanted to pass it on to in Michigan City. Damned if he knew why Rafe cared what was going on outside. Short of a miracle, the only way he would get out of there was in a box.

Giulio laughed so hard he couldn't get his goddam cigar lit. His fat face gleamed with sweat and excitement at finding someone stupider than he was.

"Think of it, Billy. This dumb shit agrees to kill the

husband, makes a mistake and kills the boyfriend instead, and for all this he gets nothing."

"That what you heard? He got nothing?"

"What I heard? I only know what I get from the news. I *know* a guy as dumb as that, I might shoot him myself."

Billy grinned and shook his head. It was the hot topic on the strip. Even the girls were talking about it, though mainly they wondered what the woman, Agnes Walz, was doing.

Giulio said, "What gets me, people will think that dumb shit is from here. 'Cause the guy that got nicked was asking around here for someone to shoot the husband. They're going to think he found someone here, someone dumb enough to shoot the wrong guy and then not even get paid for it."

"That's right."

"We ought to be able to protect ourselves against that kind of publicity."

"I think it's helping us."

"How so?"

"Business is up."

"Tourists," Giulio said with disgust.

"Tourists, sure, but not only. Besides, some guy comes by here, just looking, comes with friends of his, he's going to come back alone, once he gets a look at what we got going."

"You think that, huh?"

"Look at your receipts. I'm guessing. You ought to know. Either it's true or it's not."

It was true. Billy needed no set of books to know that, besides the large number of gawkers driving along the strip, checking out sin city, tourists, there were also more customers. The Ecstasy was hopping and the girls were complaining, wanting more help on the floor.

One of Billy's jobs was to make sure no funny business went on in the dark booths in the back to which the girls took their johns. There was always the chance some weirdo would decide to use a razor on a girl's breasts or just start beating the hell out of her. Billy threw them indiscriminately out the back door into the night. The Ecstasy was not likely to prosecute or call in the cops. If they could count on the cops for that sort of thing, Billy would be out of a job. But mainly there were arguments over money.

Not what the guy paid but what he realized was missing from his pocket after the private show was over. There had been a policy about that, about girls picking the pocket of the john to whom they were attending and who was momentarily feeling no pain, but Giulio did not enforce it. That was money that might have gone into the till, Billy thought, but Giulio disagreed.

"Naw. Once they been in the back they're going to leave. They might go on to another club once they revive, but we've seen the last of them. Let the girls take their bonus."

Billy did not like it, but the whole strip was a con game. Watered drinks, cheap whiskey in expensive bottles, the prices sky high; the girls on stage were the closest there was to the real thing. What you saw was what you saw. Everything else was con. Tease. If the girls could have gotten the money without doing anything for the poor sonsofbitches they lured into the back, most of them would have done it. Just take the money and run.

Giulio's only restriction was on lifting money from johns seated at the bar. Once they agreed to go into the back, they were fair game. But at the bar, leave them alone. Hustle drinks, sure, tell them about the unheard-of pleasure to be had in the back of the room, okay. But keep hands off, at least off their wallets.

It was while everyone was still getting a charge out of the hired killer who didn't get paid that the farmer came in.

Billy was toward the back, leaning against a pillar, talking with Carole. Carole was about five four and agile as a monkey on the stage, but if you noticed her eyes you could see she was a million miles away. It was a job, she wasn't ashamed of it, but unlike the other girls she thought beyond it. She wanted to get into management.

"Start a house," he suggested.

"C'mon."

"Why not?"

"With housewives doing it right and left, what's in a house?"

"Look at this place."

"This place." She wrinkled her nose.

"Don't knock it."

"What am I saying? I want to move up in the organization."

"Talk to Giulio."

"Giulio! I want to talk Braille I'll talk to Giulio. The fastest hands in town."

"Give a little, get a little."

She moved against him, her head about as high as his elbow. "What do you have in mind?"

"I'll show you my computer."

"I'll show you mine."

That was when the farmer came in. Billy was so surprised that he put his arm around the snuggling Carole and hugged her to him. Too hard.

"Billy, you're hurting me."

He let her go. He apologized. He laid a massive hand on her red curls. But he kept his eyes on the farmer.

Blue flannel shirt under a corduroy jacket with leather patches on the elbows, and Levi's. Cowboy boots. What else? Like most people who weren't regulars, he stood there for half a minute, seeing nothing, and this gave the girls a chance to look him over. Charlene was the first one to make a move. She got hold of his hand and tugged him toward the bar. He smiled down at her, but he couldn't possibly see her clearly yet. Which was to Charlene's advantage.

Carole said, "Think he's got the rent money on him?"

"He'll ask about using credit cards."

And the answer would be no. Elsewhere, the organization was heavily into plastic, but here on the strip it was cash or so long Charlie. The only traffic in credit cards here was through the girls, who sold those they stole.

"We were talking," Carole reminded him.

"Later."

"It's a date."

She had a sassy ass as well, and she made it move as she walked away, looking back at him with lidded eyes. As a rule, Billy kept things on a business level in the club. He had seen too many guys go down the tubes because they had started treating the girls as a fringe benefit. But Carole was different. For Carole, he made an exception.

He studied the farmer from four angles, moving around the room, but he had been sure from the start. What the hell was he doing here?

Giulio said, "Maybe he's come looking for the stupid bastard who agreed to kill him."

"And do what?"

"Return the favor."

"That doesn't make any sense. Nothing happened to him. He should be happy. He's rid of both his wife and her boyfriend and he didn't pay a nickel."

"Nobody paid a nickel, Billy. That's what's so goddam funny."

Within half an hour, the farmer went into the back with Charlene. They were gone so long, Billy checked the booth. It was empty. He asked Carole if she had seen Charlene.

"She's in the back."

"I just checked."

"I told you to keep the back door locked."

"Wait'll he sees Charlene in the light."

"Funny. I just hope she's safe."

Billy didn't like it. Girls on duty were on duty and there was no slipping out the back door with a guy, not if they wanted to go on working there. An arrangement after hours, that was nobody's business, but when you worked a club you worked indoors and until your shift was done.

"You want I should fire her?" Giulio asked. He was reading a dirty magazine. He ran a strip joint, he had live meat all around him, and he sat there in his office looking at dirty pictures.

"I'm not telling you your job."

"It seems to me you are. And not for the first time."

"Forget it then. I never noticed she was missing."

Charlene came back two hours later, grinning like the cat that ate it and two hundred bucks to the good. Well, until Giulio heard and took his cut. Down the middle, fifty-fifty, same as in the back booths.

"Plus I'm docking you two hours. Now get on the stage and shake it, you missed a turn."

Charlene suddenly smiled. "Honey, I didn't miss anything."

Billy talked to Charlene about it. The farmer had taken her to a motel, a hot-sheet place on the Indiana side. Much talking?

"Talking was not what he had in mind."

He asked Carole to find out if there was anything else, and later, at the house, before he showed her the computer, he made her a drink and they talked about it.

"They just did it, Billy. Like three times. The guy must have been for a stay on the moon he needed it so bad."

"I wonder who he was."

"Why?"

"He didn't remind you of anybody?"

"You know the guy, Billy?"

He got out the newspaper, what the hell, and let her see for herself. Carole moved her lips as she read, but she recognized right away who the guy was.

"Jesus H. Christ," she said.

"Don't swear."

She looked at him. She wore a sweater and slacks, not much makeup. Who would know how she made a living? "Sorry."

"I was raised here in this house. My brother Rafe and me."

She accepted that.

"Wanna see my computer?"

She took his arm and rubbed her head against his chest.

"I thought you'd never ask."

ELEVEN

It was a telephone call that put Andrew Broom back into the Agnes Walz appeal.

Three days after he got the news from Lister, he had gone to Chicago, checked into the Palmer House, called room service, and proceeded to get drunk as he had not been drunk since before he married Dorothy.

Dorothy.

The big question was, should he tell Dorothy? But big as it was, it was not the first question. Quite understandably, Andrew's first thoughts were of himself.

From being stunned, he became angry at the thought that he must die. On the flight to Chicago, in the cab from Midway to the hotel, in the goddam lobby of the Palmer House, there were people, people, people, all of them alive, going about their day. He wanted to lose himself in the anonymous crowd, join those riding up and down the escalators, hide from the grim finger that had pointed out Andrew Broom and no one else.

Three days before, if he had been asked his thoughts on death, he would have replied matter-of-factly that death is a fact of life. When his time came he would face it calmly, bravely, without complaints. But that was when he would have assumed he was talking of some date in the remote future, a scarcely believable rendezvous that he like all others must eventually keep.

But now? Goddam it, it wasn't fair. Why me? Let it be somebody else. If you let me live...

He was speaking to someone, but who? God? Halfway through the first bottle of J & B he got religion. He knelt beside his bed and, tears streaming down his face, bargained with the deity. Give me ten more years and I will build hospitals, feed the hungry, do a dozen things. God, give me a year, just one year more.

No one answered. He finished the bottle in the chair by the television, looking at the gray unlit screen. What would be the difference ten years down the road or even one? I'll be ten years older, a year older. That seemed difference enough.

He slept for several hours and woke to a dark room and for a moment did not remember where he was, did not know where to reach to turn on the lights. Panic. Had he already died? Was he in his grave, underground, come awake in his coffin, victim of a horrible mistake?

He lifted one hand slowly, palm turned up, dreading that his still-living flesh would press against a satin interior.

And remembered he was in a room in the Palmer House. His head was like a balloon. He found the lamp beside the bed and when he turned it on it hurt his eyes. He was still fully dressed, still wearing his tie, for God's sake, carefully knotted, pulled up tight under the buttoned collar.

He undressed on his way to the bathroom, scattering clothes, and stood in a tepid shower, letting it sting his face and body. Easing the knob to the right, toward C, he stood there as long as he could and then jerked the knob to the left and waited for the frigid water to warm. It turned hot so quickly he had to jump out of the tub to avoid being scalded. He wrapped his arm in a towel before reaching in to adjust the temperature again. His head felt better. And he was thirsty.

He took a drink, Scotch on the rocks, back to the steam-filled bathroom, and it seemed almost medicinal, sweat running down his face, cold liquid flowing down his gullet.

The shower had all but driven from his mind the realization that he was dying, but he could feel the bad news crouched somewhere in the room, waiting to pounce. So why stay in? This was Chicago, it was the shank of the evening. We who are about to die salute you.

He sat on the edge of the bed with the phone book on his knees and looked up escort services in the yellow pages, stabbing his finger at random. Within minutes he was getting dressed, June was on her way. First a good dinner, then a few clubs, after which, who knew, he might bring her back to the room and he might not. There was something morbid in the thought of crawling into the sack with a strange woman while the knowledge he was dying rode his back.

"Honey, there's something I should tell you."

"Yeees."

"I'm dying."

One possible response would be a scream, a cry of alarm and disgust, a hasty withdrawal.

Or, maybe she'd have a sense of humor. "I wondered what you were doing."

Or, "Spare yourself. You should have seen the guy I was with last night."

The only reaction he could not imagine was sympathy. Pity, horror, repugnance. But not sympathy. Turn it around. Think of himself, in his health, in bed with a girl who tells him she's dying.

But he had not gone to bed with strange women when he was healthy. He had been incredibly faithful to Dorothy. In fact, he and Dorothy had not been doing all that much lately. That sort of thing had stopped, or all but stopped, when?

He knew when. Dorothy got pregnant, then lost the baby. Once, twice, a third time. Struck out in the one department that really mattered. He had not known how much it mattered until the realization got through to him. He would never be a father. He would never have children.

With Dorothy.

So why not divorce her, find someone else and have another try? A man never got too old for that and he was only in his mid-thirties when they had finally faced the facts. But divorcing Dorothy would have been like ceasing to be himself. His relation to her was that profound, beyond the reach of assent or dissent. It entered into what he was. Leaving Dorothy would be like killing himself.

Suicide.

June called from the lobby, her voice lilting, carrying a little tune like door chimes. He told her to come up.

She could have been a schoolteacher. A nurse. A secretary. She would be anything he wanted her to be, it turned out, and what she assumed he wanted was a sedate companion, so that is what she somewhat disappointedly became.

They had dinner in one of the hotel restaurants. They went on to a nightclub, also in the hotel. During dinner it was like being at the country club, June the wife of a new member. Her hair was very dark and abundant, her skin porcelain, her lips made up with a precision they scarcely lost as she ate. They spoke of the Bulls, of the news of the day, of the current squabbling between the mayor and the city council. In the lounge, where the lights were low, she said she would have Scotch too.

"Are we going to go to bed?" she asked.

"Is that part of the deal?"

"If you wish."

He looked at her and she smiled, receptive. It seemed unbelievable that he was doing this.

He said, "I wish."

"Then let's not waste time sitting here."

He had never been the passive partner before and it was a revealing experience. Looking up at her serene smile and at the well-shaped breasts she lowered teasingly toward him, he wondered if this was the answer. Oblivion through sex. Could he screw himself to death?

Whatever he wanted, that was the deal. He decided he wanted to be surprised, and June surprised him. Twice, almost three times, but after all he was over forty. They had a drink then, and he resisted the impulse to ask her about herself, how she had gotten into this line of work.

"Anything else?" With a smile. She was at his disposal.

He shook his head.

"I'll sleep with you, if you want."

"No. I don't think so."

"You shouldn't keep drinking, you know. Get some sleep. What about tomorrow?"

"I'm dying."

She looked at him. "We all are."

"My doctor gave me the bad news a few days ago."

She thought about it. "I guess this is as good a response as any."

"It doesn't disgust you?"

"No."

He asked her to stay. He held her tightly in his

arms and fell asleep like that, consoled by a stranger. She was in the bathroom when he awoke. They parted on a businesslike note. She took down information from one of his credit cards. He asked how much it would be and she told him.

"Double it."

"Thank you."

In the cab back to Midway, he realized that he had no hangover, felt no ill effects from the drinking or the bout with June. Could that be an effect of his illness? It made no sense.

The damnable thing was that he had never felt better in his life.

He loved the look of the Midwest from the air, the gridded polychrome squares, fields, roads, a stand of trees, and the buildings. It was the most fertile land in the world, stretching for hundreds of miles in four directions. Dying was a way of returning to the earth.

The hum of the Fairchild's motors in his ears— there were only four other passengers—and the smallness of the plane really gave the sensation of flying; he had felt a flutter of fear on takeoff when, as the plane banked up and away, there was a shudder of resistance and he could imagine a stall and then a vertiginous downward spinning into darkness.

He almost wanted it to happen, much as it frightened him. But it wasn't fair to the other passengers, wanting to take them with him.

His father had committed suicide.

There. He had finally let the thought form in his mind. That was what he had been avoiding since leaving Lister's office. It was what he had fled by taking this trip to Chicago, what he had tried to lose in the warm otherness of June. At 12,000 feet, approaching Wyler, he almost welcomed the memory.

His father had committed suicide.

He had been found slumped behind the wheel of his car in the garage. The motor had run until it was out of gas and neither Andrew nor his mother had heard a thing. Painless was the way everyone described his father's death, but that did not take into account what it had done to his mother and to him.

They had been left with the pain. His father had drifted off to wherever the dead go.

He could have been more considerate. There were ways he could have done it that would have hidden what he did. You could kill yourself without hurting others the way a suicide hurt. It was possible.

Back in the office, Susannah said, yes, she had called Mrs. Broom and told her of the unexpected flight to Chicago.

"How did it go?" she asked, a routine question. Or was it? Susannah, at thirty-five, was a very attractive woman, devoted, single, more valuable than a partner. He had the odd certainty that she knew what he had been up to in Chicago.

"Everything came out all right."

"Good. There have been some calls."

"Anything urgent?"

"More strange than urgent."

He studied the slip she gave him. No name, just a number. The caller had not given a name.

"It has something to do with Agnes Walz. Should I give it to Mr. Rowan?"

"No. No, I'll return it."

There was something about the number, he didn't know what. He wanted to figure that out before he called it. He thought about it by trying not to think about it and then he had it. As he left the office, he told Susannah that, if the man called again, she should tell him to be patient. She should not pass the call on to Mr. Rowan.

Susannah never questioned his orders. In her way, she was like June.

York looked dubious when Andrew made his request, but he could not refuse it. Andrew waited patiently while the prosecutor made a pretense of doing him a favor. If York belonged to Andrew Broom's party, the lawyer would have made sure he never got the nomination for reelection. York had a gray crew cut, a scar on his head, eyes that seemed an afterthought in his puttylike face. But he was a good prosecutor. Andrew gave him that.

"This is for the appeal?"

"That's right."

"You'll be turned down."

"I know."

"But duty calls, huh?"

"You would do the same thing, York."

A nod of the close-cropped head. And then the phone call. Mr. Broom is coming to inspect the exhibits from the Agnes Walz trial.

The bag holding the effects found on Jacob Fennel

was not heavy. It was the billfold Andrew was interested in and the slip of paper that contained columns of numbers.

5000

267.12

2322960

606726

Curious. Those numbers had never figured in the trial. No one quite knew what they represented. The first entry would be the down payment Agnes had told him about. They had identified the last number. Fennel's Marine Corps ID.

And now Andrew knew what 2322960 was.

It was a telephone number.

It was the number Susannah had handed him when he returned to his office after his trip to Chicago.

He checked the stuff back in and walked down Tarkington in the afternoon sunlight. Should he just call the number or should he run a check on it and find out who his caller was?

What he found out by dialing was that the number did not exist locally.

So where was it?

And then a hunch. Coming from the same place the memory of those numbers in Fennel's billfold had come from. He looked up the area code for the northwest corner of the state, dialed that, and then the number on the slip.

He listened to the phone ring and ring.

"Yeah?" A man's voice.

"Who is this?"

After a pause, the voice spoke again, as if just answering the phone.

"Ecstasy Club."

TWELVE

Was it Ted's weakness that attracted her? Dorothy wondered. God knows it couldn't be his strength. Telling him about Andrew's unscheduled trip to Chicago had been a mistake, but her only thought had been that they could spend the night together.

At his place. She loved his apartment as she could not love her own house. Everything in the house she had chosen. It had no power to surprise.

But the excitement with which she had come to him evaporated before the panic he showed when she told him Andrew had gone to Chicago.

"Oh, my God. Where in Chicago?"

"Where? What difference does it make?"

· "He's gone for another opinion! He said he would and that is what he's doing."

Dorothy had assured Ted that Andrew had said

that only to ensure the secrecy of the test results. But he had only half believed her then, and now he was wild-eyed with worry.

"Ted, what is the worst that can happen?"

"The worst? Only one thing can happen. He will be told he is in perfect health."

"That's right."

"After I told him he's dying! Dying of leukemia. He'll fire me. He'll kill me. He'll sue the pants off me."

She shook her head. "No. Think about it. He will be so relieved he will want to kiss you."

He just stared at her, trembling. She took him in her arms and he blubbered like a boy. He was almost five years younger than she and so what if there was a maternal element in what she felt for him? She rocked him in her arms and listened to him sob that he had thrown away the best position he would ever have. The clinic was a godsend. Not just the salary, although his salary *had* doubled when he made the move, and the divorce had been a standoff with both of them claiming desertion. He went on, as if he had been rehearsing this tale of woe ever since Andrew had telephoned to tell him he would seek a second opinion.

That had surprised Dorothy too, if the truth be known. The plan had been simple, simple enough to work. Ironically, the case Andrew was on, his defense of Agnes Walz, had suggested the idea to her. Dorothy had attended the early sessions of the trial, wanting to look at this rawboned, unattractive woman who had conspired with her lover to murder her husband. She said the usual things when she talked about the case—and everyone talked about it —but in her heart Dorothy admired Agnes.

She had just let the idea come out when she talked about the trial with Ted.

"She was dumb," Ted said.

"How so?"

"Bringing in someone else."

"You think she should have killed the husband her-self?"

"At least she would have known which one he was. No, she should have had her boyfriend do it."

"Would you kill Andrew so we could be together always?"

A parlor game question, speculation, fantasy, what if...She made Ted think of ways he could get rid of Andrew. It excited her, this game, and she wondered how Agnes Walz and Jacob Fennel had reached the point of really meaning it.

"You never think of obvious ways, Ted."

"What do you mean?"

"Obvious to you, I mean. Ways only a doctor could do it. Kill someone."

This shocked him, to his credit, she supposed, and she realized that she was a very long way from turn-ing the game into a serious discussion. Until she saw she was going about it the wrong way. The way to a man's mind is through his loins.

It was in bed that she brought her lover around and persuaded him to be a killer.

And she had hit upon the perfect plan.

Frighten Andrew to death.

Bring him to the point where he would kill himself.

"His father committed suicide."

"Oh? He never told me that."

"He told you his father was dead, didn't he?"

"Yes. But I believe he said he wasn't sure when I asked the cause."

"He committed suicide." She leaned toward Ted and put her finger in the exact center of his lips. The cleft in his chin, the furrow in his upper lip, the quotation marks just above the division of his eyebrows —what a symmetrical face he had. "He killed himself because he thought he was dying."

Ted had had a patient in the East who committed suicide when he told her she had cancer. He had blamed himself for it at first, but had come to see that he had no right to withhold such information for fear of how it might affect a patient.

"If Andrew were told he was dying he would do what his father did."

"You can't know that."

"It is one of the things I do know. Andrew and I know one another, Ted, far below the level of words. He knows what I would do, I know what he would do."

"Then he must know about us."

"No." She could not tell him that this would not be important enough to Andrew.

"You still love him." He said it like an accusation. She knew there was no point in replying directly.

The way to a man's mind is through his loins.

It was Ted's libido that decided him to do what he

would never have done without the erotic pressure Dorothy put on him. She had to remind him that as a doctor he was an authority figure.

"If you told him his penis was abnormal, he would believe you."

He laughed.

"Ted, if you told me I had breast cancer, do you think I would doubt you?"

Evoking that old fear convinced her what Andrew's reaction would be. It enabled her to get Ted to agree.

Andrew went for his regular examination and all sorts of lab tests were involved.

Andrew being Andrew then forgot all about it. He had no doubts about his health.

She had had to convince Ted to call him, tell him to come to the clinic. The fact that he had not himself telephoned for the results of the tests suggested all kinds of terrifying possibilities to Ted.

"He may have an informant in the lab."

"Nonsense."

"If he asked one of the nurses to check on it, she would. Who wouldn't do what he asked?"

"He hasn't done it, Ted. He never does. He isn't worried. You are going to have to call him."

Dorothy sat in her car in the slushy parking lot while Andrew was inside with Ted. She was already there when he spun into the lot, hopped out of his car, and strode toward the clinic, his open Burberry flapping in the wind. Portrait of a man in excellent health.

He looked completely different when he came out,

and despite herself Dorothy's heart went out to him.
If he had really had leukemia, she would have shown
him tenderness, cared for him, relived the way it had
been between them once. He threw his coat into the
car, got behind the wheel, and then just sat there.
What terrible thoughts must be churning through his
mind.

If she had ever doubted what such news would do
to him, she no longer did. He would not wait to
waste away and die a painful death.

Dorothy's concern turned to Ted, cowering inside
the clinic. Was he at a window, watching Andrew
sitting in his car? Dorothy was immobilized until
Andrew left. Then she could go inside to Ted. He
would need her now.

Suddenly a doubt crossed her mind. What if Ted's
nerve had failed him at the end and he had not gone
through with it? But why then would Andrew be so
despondent? Because Ted had blurted out the whole
truth and Andrew was sitting stunned behind the
wheel of his parked car trying to take in the knowledge that his wife had conspired with his doctor to
give him a false diagnosis of a fatal illness.

Andrew would be in a mood to kill if he had been
told that, and she would be his victim.

His almost willing victim.

She could not live in the same world with Andrew
if he found out what she and Ted had conspired to do
to him.

Andrew finally drove away and she ran inside. A
trembling Ted came to her in the examining room
where they had first made love. He was so drained

by what he had done that he could not have repeated the feat.

He was still half panicked when she left, but the worst was over.

The rest was up to Andrew.

"Yes, he got back half an hour ago, Mrs. Broom." Susannah had never played coy with the boss's wife. Dorothy wondered what Susannah really thought of her. She wondered what Susannah really thought of Andrew. The cliché was that the loyal secretary was half in love with the boss. Susannah did sound happy Andrew was back.

"Put me through to him, please."

"Oh, he went out again."

"Where?"

"He didn't say. He did say he would be back soon."

"Would you have him call me? I'm at home."

She sat staring at the phone while the minutes ticked by. Some of Ted's nervousness had taken possession of her. Panic is contagious. She gave a start when the phone rang.

"Mrs. Broom? Your husband."

"Thank you, Susannah. Andrew? Where on earth have you been?"

"Dorothy, something very interesting has just come up." There was a lilt in his voice. She closed her eyes. He did not sound like a man who thought he was going to die.

"Can you tell me?"

"About Agnes Walz. I can't go into it now, but for the first time since the trial I think we have a chance with the appeal."

"Is that why you went to Chicago?"

There was a moment of silence. "Yes, that's right."

"Oh, darling, I'm so happy for you."

Her relieved elation seemed to remind him of something. He thanked her in a preoccupied way, and Dorothy knew that he was once more thinking of himself, not Agnes Walz.

She hung up and immediately dialed the clinic.

THIRTEEN

Gerald had felt the way Wallace Walz had, that Uncle Andrew was more or less dumping the Agnes appeal on him. Tired of losing, wanting to get back to something he knew he could win? Hard to say. But Gerald had accepted the assignment along with the hint about the unpaid assassin and gone to work.

Now Uncle Andrew was moving back in.

"I've got a new lead, Gerald. I think I'd better pursue it."

Winter sun came through the vertical slats in the blind on the window behind Uncle Andrew, creating a surrealistic effect. It would have been more effective if Uncle Andrew had not explained to him how carefully chosen the blind had been for its impact on visitors. ("Particularly if someone is under indictment, laying those stripes on him puts him in a docile mood. Clients ought to know what awaits them without our help.")

"You're not showing much confidence in me."

The flesh on Uncle Andrew's face was taut. There were slight circles beneath his eyes but he still looked much better than he had two days ago.

"Gerald, this is more complicated than I thought. And dangerous."

"How was your trip to Chicago?"

One of Uncle Andrew's own tricks. A quick jab from an unexpected quarter. He frowned at Gerald.

"Fine. I needed the rest."

"I thought it was business."

"Mainly monkey business."

"Sure. As soon as you come back you want to bump me from work on the appeal."

Uncle Andrew nodded as he thought about that. "A reasonable inference. False, but valid. This has nothing to do with my trip to Chicago."

"Which was just for relaxation."

A small smile played at the corners of Uncle Andrew's mouth. "Next time I'll take you along." A cloud passed over his face, erasing the smile. "Next time," he repeated.

"What happened to change your mind?" Gerald asked, momentarily put off by his uncle's mournful tone.

Uncle Andrew put up a hand. "Okay, you're right, Gerald. I should tell you in any case." The cloud darkened, then lifted. "I got a phone call while I was gone. The caller left a number. It had a familiar look, I didn't know why, and then it clicked. Do you remember the list of numbers on the slip of paper found in Jacob Fennel's wallet?"

Gerald had not actually seen the effects of the late Jacob Fennel. Nor had they figured in the trial. He shook his head.

"A bit of advice then. Always inspect everything made available to you in the course of preparing a case, particularly a criminal case. If there is stuff the prosecution does not introduce, it may be for a very good reason."

"And they had a reason for not bringing up that slip of paper?"

"I doubt it, Gerald. The numbers made no sense in the aggregate. But one of those entries matches the telephone number our caller left."

"No shit."

"Yes." Uncle Andrew considered profanity an indication of an empty head, a minimal vocabulary, weakness of imagination, and other vices. "No shit, indeed."

"You called the number."

"Yes."

"And?"

"It is the number of the Ecstasy Club in Sorrento."

"Wow." He should have saved his No shit for this. He got to his feet and looked down at his uncle. "Who answered?"

"I don't know. Possibly the manager. What was his name . . ."

"Pompeio. Giulio Pompeio."

Uncle Andrew smiled approval and Gerald saw that it had been a test.

"When he identified the place, I hung up."

"I'm going over there."

"To do what?"

"For starters, I'll find out who called here."

"Why don't we wait for him to call back? There is no point in rushing to Sorrento and scaring the bejesus out of someone who might conceivably be of help in the appeal. No. Patience is required. A precipitous move now and all might be lost."

"*Festina lente?*" His father would actually slow his pacing back and forth in front of his class when he repeated the adage. ("Make haste slowly, gentlemen. Oh yes. Do not rush heedless into the breech.")

"Exactly," Uncle Andrew said.

"The call is in response to the wire report in the papers. The big joke on the assassin."

"Infuriating the man and prompting him to call the defender of his employer?"

Gerald sat down. "He wants his money."

"I'm sure he does. God knows he earned it. A life is a life, so far as the risk goes."

"Maybe he thinks he should fulfill the original agreement?"

"Maybe we should wait to see if we get another call."

"Just sit and wait?"

"*Festina lente.*"

Gerald did not like it. He liked it even less when Uncle Andrew settled back, buzzed Susannah to ask

that she bring them coffee, and drifted into a philo-
sophical conversation. It began with the reminder
that they might be putting Wallace Walz's life in
danger and then shot into the stratosphere.

"What would you do if you knew you had a precise
amount of time to live, Gerald?"

"I do."

"I mean if you knew exactly what that amount
was. Say, one year. Or a month. A day. What would
you do?"

"Sweat."

"Yes. And pray perhaps?"

"Perhaps."

"Did you ever hear the answer a saint gave to my
question? He said if the news came to him that he
had five minutes to live while he was playing billiards he would go on playing billiards."

"I never thought of saints playing billiards."

"What do you think they do in heaven? Seriously,
Gerald, the point is a good one. He meant he would
die with his boots on. That's what is expected of us.
Just doing well what we're doing."

Uncle Andrew was not in the habit of preaching,
nor was this kind of speculation his cup of tea. The
thought grew upon Gerald that there was more than
the phone call behind his uncle's renewed interest in
the Agnes Walz case.

They had two cups of coffee together; Gerald
agreed that they should wait upon events. He
stopped at Susannah's desk on the way to his office.

"Where did Andrew stay in Chicago yesterday?"

Her brows lifted before she raised her eyes to him.

"He didn't say." She added, significantly, "And I didn't ask."

"Where does he usually stay?"

"In Chicago? The Palmer House."

Back at his desk, he telephoned the Palmer House and asked to be put through to Mr. Andrew Broom. A bit of half-audible fussing and then, "There is no Mr. Broom registered in the hotel."

"Oh, but there is. He checked in yesterday."

"One moment."

Gerald turned in his chair and looked a thousand miles into the distance. More. Ninety-three million miles. He shaded his eyes from the sun. Why was he making this call? Why was he checking up on his uncle?

"Mr. Broom checked out of the hotel this morning."

"Thank you very much."

Nothing. Nothing to equal a man's answering and saying Ecstasy Club, so why did he feel he was on a spoor he must pursue? He consulted the prairie stretching away from Wyler but it told him nothing. Standing, he looked down at the town, his uncle's town. The bank, the steeple of the Presbyterian church, the clinic...

The clinic. Things had turned odd four days ago when his uncle had wanted to postpone the meeting with Agnes that he had arranged to have in his office, despite the opposition of York and Cleary and the Wyler *Star*. An editorial in the latter argued from feminist premises to the conclusion that Agnes must now be treated exactly like every other tried and condemned criminal. Uncle Andrew had overcome all that and then been late for the meeting. Because of an unscheduled visit to the clinic.

Gerald went out, sat in the chair next to Susannah's desk, and offered her a cigarette, which she refused. He lit one himself and sighed forth smoke. Susannah went on typing.

"Say hello for me," Gerald said.

"What?" Her hands hung over the keys, the machine momentarily silenced.

"Who's a good doctor?"

She turned off the machine. "Something wrong?"

"I don't think so. But I haven't had a good physical for over a year. Maybe I should."

"Go to the clinic."

"Just drop by?"

"I'll make an appointment for you, if you'd like."

"Good. Set it up with my uncle's doctor."

"Dr. Lister? Good. I would have anyway. He's supposed to be the best."

"What's his specialty?"

Susannah thought. "Internal medicine? He is also the chief medical officer there."

"That makes it sound like a big operation."

"The Wyler Medical Clinic is one of the best things your uncle has done for this town. And he has done a lot."

"I know. Make the appointment for as soon as you can, will you? It's too bad they couldn't take me today, there's so little going on here this afternoon."

"I'll ask. As a favor to you know who."

He leaned over and tried to kiss her, but Susannah lifted one shoulder and ducked her head toward the other.

"Never kiss the help," she murmured.

"Kiss you? I was going to blow in your ear."

"Go to your office."

"Yes, Mom."

While he waited to hear from Susannah, he called Julie McGough and told her he was going to have a physical at the clinic.

"I want to come to you pure and whole."

"Come the day I do volunteer work. Maybe I can get a peek at you in your skivvies."

"Your day is Tuesday, right?"

"Today is Tuesday. I help out on Mondays."

"I don't know if I can wait. The pain, the pain."

"Is something wrong?"

"Acute frustration."

"I know what you mean." Her voice lowered and seemed to seep into his ear.

"I'm being buzzed."

"I never heard it called that before."

"Later."

He punched the button and Susannah said that if he could be at the clinic in fifteen minutes they would be happy to give him a physical.

"Most of it is done by nurses, you know."

"I'm counting on that."

Susannah hung up. Not gently.

FOURTEEN

Although he was not working, Billy was in the office when the phone rang and Giulio answered. He looked at the receiver, said, "Ecstasy Club," then dropped the phone into its cradle from a height of maybe a foot.

"Sonofabitch hung up."

"Wrong number."

"Yeah."

Maybe it was dumb leaving the number of the club, but it was smart too. Billy couldn't just come right out and let the lawyer know who was calling. Besides, he didn't know what the hell the phone call was supposed to do. All he knew was that he was sick and tired of people laughing about the dummy who shot the wrong guy.

And then the farmer shows up. Why would he pick

the Ecstasy of all the clubs on the strip? Why would he decide to come to Sorrento in the first place?

Things happen and the way to live was to let them happen, don't get in the way, move with it. Rafe had always had these well-thought-out plans that eventually got screwed up. Billy had always done much better when he acted on the spur of the moment, prodded by something that just happened.

He did not know the meaning of what had been going on these past months and weeks and days. Sitting at GIGO, pondering the meaning of events, letting it all hang out there on the amber screen and storing it away on the hard disk, backing it up on floppies, he just let his mind trail along after the cursor, watching the letters show up on the screen, forming words, forming sentences, expressing thoughts he did not know he had before he expressed them, waiting for the answer to emerge.

The shotgun was in the basement, propped in a corner of the coal cellar, what used to be the coal cellar but was not just a boarded-off dusty pen, not the best place to keep the gun, but what the hell, it was nothing special. He had bought it at a discount house in Gary, the only white in the place, and no questions asked, man, just give me a name, any name. Billy wrote down the name of the principal of the grade school he had gone to, Timothy Grady, figuring the man was dead or senile by now anyway.

The gun had a hell of a kick and Billy remembered how they had strapped on the M1 at the firing range, belting it in close to the body, so that you felt it was a part of you. Your rifle. This is my rifle, this is my gun...

The jingle came back to him while he was at the keyboard, so he fed it into "My Life," where it belonged of course, along with all his memories of Marine Corps Base San Diego, lying right beside the main runway of the San Diego airport, civilians lifting off every minute it seemed, going everywhere, anywhere else, while you were as bad as in jail for eight weeks, jogging around that goddam parade field that was at least a mile long. In summer, with the sun on it, it was a sea of mirages as you looked back toward the buildings, the theater where you watched movies and listened to the preacher, and he wondered what in hell had prompted him to sign those papers.

Rafe. Rafe had told him a stint in the Corps would open a dozen doors in the future. Well, it had opened the gate at Michigan City to him once, and that was all there was going to be of that. In the Corps he had been in the shore patrol, on the right side of the wire, and that, along with his graduate course at Michigan City, had landed him the job at the Ecstasy.

Something else would turn up, this was only a phase of his life. He did not want to get into management, like Carole did, unless it just happened; he wouldn't say no but he wasn't chasing after it either. Not chasing after anything. He thought of himself as a kite, a balloon, ready to catch the best breeze blowing.

The breeze had blown in the country boy called

Jacob Fennel. He was calling himself Joe Harper at the time, but Carole checked out his billfold and Billy confronted him with his real name.

Fennel had been nervous before. Now he was frightened. There was a space between his front teeth and when he smiled Billy thought his face would crack.

"What I said? Don't think I was serious." He lifted his beer in explanation.

"I never thought you was."

"I wasn't."

"Coming in here and asking this one and that one where you could find somebody to kill a friend of yours. Nobody's that dumb, Jake."

He nodded eagerly. He got off the stool but could not leave his beer undrunk. Billy blocked his way.

"I have the man you want."

It was the way the man's face twitched then, flickering back and forth between a smile and a serious expression, that put Timothy Grady in Billy's mind again, after all those years. Grady had had trouble knowing what expression to wear when he confronted the school assembly.

Fennel was hooked. Billy took him to a booth and they talked around the subject for an hour. It took that long to make it clear that they were doing business, the two of them.

"The woman in on it?"

Fennel nodded. "I wouldn't do it if she weren't."

"She'd know it was you?"

"That's right."

"Won't everybody else?"

"Maybe. But they won't be able to prove any-thing."

"Why do you want this man dead?"

"I want his wife. I want everything he's got."

It was the first time Fennel had shown any fire. He wanted Wallace Walz dead, there was no doubt about that. He wanted it real bad.

"You can't afford it, Jake."

"Maybe not."

"A thing like that, it's not like hiring someone to do something around the farm."

"No, it isn't."

"It costs."

"How much?"

"A million dollars."

Fennel giggled. "In cash?"

"How much you prepared to pay?"

"What would you suggest?"

"I told you, a million dollars."

"I think a thousand dollars is a lot of money."

"I think your head is full of shit."

Billy was sure that Fennel enjoyed it as much as he did, the haggling. They were going to make a deal and they knew it. Carole said it was like a john, when you started talking money, you had him by the balls. When they settled on the price, Billy wondered if he shouldn't have held out for more.

"Five is a lot of money down," Carole said. There was a lot more respect in the way she talked to him now.

"You think I ought to do it?"

"I thought you already agreed."

They were sipping orange juice and vodka, half and halfs, in Billy's bed, and it was as easy to talk to her as to his computer. That impressed her too, the equipment on the trestle table along one wall of the room. He had promised to show her how to use it.

"Word processing," he said. "It's more or less like typing. Knowing the computer I can do anything."

"It does everything but screw."

"Some things I want to do myself."

She spilled a bit of her drink on his chest, reaching across him to put it on the table, and then she licked it up. Billy's vision blurred. He had a partner in Carole, something he said he would never do, but right then it seemed the perfect arrangement.

Later, in the semidark created by the tent she had made of the covers, she said, "How you going to do it?"

"I'm thinking."

"I don't want to know. I wish you luck, but I don't want to know the details. That's best."

Of course it was. But he was disappointed. Still he had GIGO to talk to and he worked it out on the amber screen, after a few more talks with Fennel.

They met in Gary, in a bar half a mile from where he bought the shotgun, and Fennel brought sketches and diagrams and too goddam many instructions.

"I don't like all these plans," Billy complained.

"It's got to be planned."

"Plans go wrong."

"There's no other way."

"Sure there is. You finger the sonofabitch and I take him out."

Jake brought a picture of Walz. It was funny how much the man looked like Fennel. The snapshot had been taken in winter, but he and the woman wore no coats as they stood just outside the door of a house, snow piled to the windowsills, the sun picking up their faces but leaving their bodies in shadow.

"That the woman?"

Fennel nodded. "That's Agnes."

Billy looked hard at Walz. He said, "Why don't you just leave it all up to me? One day you'll find out like everybody else that he's been shot."

Fennel shook his head. "We considered that. Agnes and I. It won't do. It's important where the two of us are when it happens."

Billy thought of going ahead as he wanted to anyway. After it was done, Fennel and the woman would see that was the way to do it. But Fennel was crazy about planning.

The poor sonofabitch. Finally Billy made him accept his way. Give me a call, finger the guy, and whammo.

It hadn't been easy, afterward, listening to everyone joke about it. Carole shook her head. "Billy, that's the best thing you've got going. Let them laugh. We know better."

She was right. He had his five, as much as such a job was usually worth, so what did he care if people laughed about the dummy who hadn't got paid, who killed the wrong guy?

Leave it to Fennel to cover himself with that goddam letter in his safe deposit box. A guy who planned everything had to take out that kind of insurance, a notarized statement detailing the conspiracy he had entered into with Agnes Walz to have her husband killed. Billy was on his way to O'Hare without so much as a kit bag after he first heard of that letter. From Miami he telephoned Carole.

"Come on home, honey. It names no names."

"They'll look into everything he did, everyone he talked to."

"Billy, it wasn't you he was protecting his ass from. You don't figure in it at all."

She was right. He came home. She met him at the plane and they spent a night at the O'Hare Hilton. Most of the time it was enough that Carole knew. They could talk about it. He could work it out at the computer.

"It'll die down," Carole said. "It already has."

And then the farmer showed up at the club and now the papers were full of gobbledygook about the unpaid gunman.

"Ignore it," Carole said. "It's some kind of trick."

But she had no good explanation for why Walz showed up at the Ecstasy other than the explanation Charlene had. He had needed a woman. Billy hadn't liked it.

Just as precaution, he decided to get rid of the shotgun. He went down to the basement and groped around in the coal cellar. Puzzled, he went upstairs for a flashlight. He pointed it into every corner of the coal cellar, then went on to search the rest of the basement.

It wasn't there.

The shotgun was gone.

He telephoned the club from O'Hare and, pinching his nose, asked for Carole.

"You the guy called earlier?"

"Yeah."

"You want to talk to Carole?"

He could imagine the expression on Giulio's face, big shot, making up for being hung up on before. He waited and Giulio said it again.

"You want to talk to Carole?"

"Please."

"That's the magic word."

When she came on he asked if Giulio was there still.

"That's right."

"Carole, I'm at the airport. I've got to get out of town."

"Tell me about it," she said brightly, but he could hear the edge in her voice.

"My shotgun is missing."

"I know."

"What!"

"I know."

"Who the hell took it?" Visions of Rafe's friends assailed him.

"Yes, I did."

"You did!"

"That's right."

"Then where the hell is it? I want to get rid of it, where it will never be found."

"Where did you have in mind?"

"The Calumet River."

"Yes, it is."

"What are you saying?"

"I put it there myself, honey, so why don't you be a good boy and relax."

Relax wasn't the word for it. "I think I love you."

"Talk, talk, talk."

"I'll be there in half an hour."

FIFTEEN

The first effect had been like seeing the skull beneath
the skin, life as a mockery, the flimsiest of disguises
for death. Breathing was an inhaling of dust and
ashes.

Fear, anger, then disgust.

But now he felt differently. The fact that he was
dying seemed simply a lens through which to look at
the world and, if it had a different look, a very different look, it had not lost its capacity to charm.

June, for one, and the simple elemental lust he had
known with her. He would not have wanted to make
a career of that sort of thing, he did not relish the
realization that he had been unfaithful to Dorothy,
but he could not really regret that session in his
room at the Palmer House either.

That almost impersonal reminder of the warmth

and need of humans for one another had been salutary.

And then the feeling he had, flying into Wyler, looking down at the land, the source of sustenance, the source of life, the start and finish of it all. The earth was his destiny, at least the destiny of his bodily self, and he found himself submitting to the implacable necessity that to the earth his body must return. What was the Lenten reminder? *Remember, man, that thou art dust and into dust thou shalt return.*

From June to the midwestern terrain, from earth mother to mother earth.

There was a religious aspect to the realization. Four days after getting the grim news from Dr. Lister, Andrew Broom felt reconciled to his fate.

Not that he was disposed to be completely docile and passive. If death was coming for him, he was willing to go halfway and meet his fate.

My father committed suicide.

When he had been able to admit that thought, he was through the worst of it. He was, in the phrase, a self-made man, wresting from the world the success he had known, surmounting humble origins as the American myth decreed. His life had been more or less deliberately fashioned according to his own effort and plan. The same would be true of his death.

But unlike his father he would not make a mess of it. He would not leave a burden for others to bear. The best suicide is that which cannot be detected. But the death by natural causes, if leukemia counted as natural, that could be his, he did not want. What then?

Death by violence.

For months his head had been ahum with the details of the Agnes Walz trial, and it was not surprising that he began to meditate on the elements of that event. Agnes and her lover had conspired to murder Wallace Walz. They would diminish the risk, as they thought, by employing a third party. A hireling. A stranger. And, when the deed was done, they would be visibly busy elsewhere.

In the event, the plan had disintegrated. Jake Fennel, not Wallace Walz, was blasted into the next world. And, an odd tribute to the love he had borne Agnes, Jake had carefully set down the plot on paper, had the paper notarized, and put it in a sealed envelope in his safety deposit box. Insurance? It had proved the downfall of his supposed beloved. Together with the ten thousand dollars Agnes had withdrawn from the bank three days before the shooting, it had made a guilty verdict a foregone conclusion.

It was easy to imagine what had gone wrong with the plan. That had been the topic of conversation, it seemed, since Jake's damning testament came to light. Andrew Broom saw those events now in a different light.

To die by his own hand, but at one remove. Not to pull the trigger himself, but to arm his assassin. He wanted only one part of the plot concocted by Agnes and Jake. And it seemed possible that he could tap into the identical cast to find the player he sought.

The only thing that gave him pause was the apparent stupidity of the actors. To contract to kill one man and then by accident kill the man who had hired you? It seemed incredible. Throughout the trial, Andrew had been worried by that thought, a chipped tooth infallibly found by the probing tongue. The degree of stupidity involved was hard to credit. And Agnes was no help.

Not even now, after the conviction, when at last they spoke frankly to one another, was she any help on the crucial point.

"Did you ever talk with the assassin?"

"That's a grand word for a paid killer."

"Call him what you like. Did you meet him?"

"Jake took care of everything."

He listened for a trace of bitterness, for sarcasm, for some indication that the way things had turned out had turned her against her lover, but her voice was that of a robot, flat and even and unrevealing.

"He sure picked a lemon."

She looked sharply at him, then smiled. "I thought you meant me."

"You picked the lemon, Agnes."

"Wallace is a good man, according to his lights."

"I didn't mean Wallace."

But he could not draw her into criticism of the man whose stupidity had meant his own death and very likely hers as well.

"I wrote him a letter." She turned over a sealed blue envelope.

"Who?"

"The assassin."

He looked at her. How vacant her eyes seemed. He picked up the envelope. "There's no address."

"I know."

"Pretty stationery."

"It was a gift from Jake." Her expression did not soften. "I want you to deliver that."

He put it in his pocket. If he could ever accomodate her wish, he might be able to accommodate one of his own.

Telling Gerald of the match between the number left with Susannah and the number on the slip of paper in Jake Fennel's wallet had been done on the spur of the moment. He had wanted to impress Gerald with his memory; no point in denying that vanity had been at the bottom of it. But there had been cunning as well.

Half-consciously he was recruiting his nephew into a plan that was still amorphous in his own mind. Andrew had no doubt it was the assassin who had telephoned. He had to find that man. At the same time, he wanted Gerald to know of the call from the Ecstasy Club.

A call from the club alone would have meant nothing. The prosecution, he himself with Gerald, had been there gathering depositions before the trial. The significant fact was that the telephone number matched the one in Jake Fennel's billfold. It corroborated the claim in his testament that it was to Sorrento he had gone to seek a hired assassin.

Jake had been remembered in the Ecstasy. As a fool on a fool's errand. Who would enter into a compact with someone stupid enough to advertise that he was looking for someone to commit a murder?

It seemed common sense that no one would have fallen in with his plan. But someone had. The same someone who had bitten at the speculation that he had not received his payoff.

That night, Andrew took Dorothy to the country club for dinner. They dined with friends, they danced, Andrew even exchanged some civil remarks with McGough. For a moment resentment boiled up in him that he must die while his old rival remained behind on the field of battle.

He got over it. McGough's hour would come. No one could escape it.

When he swung up the drive to the house, he said to Dorothy, "Sweetheart, I'm going to drop you off and go back to the office."

"At this hour!"

"Suddenly I think an appeal of Agnes's conviction may be successful. I want to keep at it."

"You must take care of yourself, Andrew. You work too hard."

Such tenderness was not customary. It had a powerful effect on him, as if she could know the truth and was speaking out of that knowledge. But that was nonsense. Lister would not have dared.

"How *are* you feeling, darling?"

"Never better."

"You look tired."

"There's a reason for that."

"Oh?"

"I'm tired."

He leaned toward her and she chastely kissed his cheek. A tactile memory of June teased his mind and he smiled.

"Don't be late."

"If it gets too late, I'll sleep on the couch in my office."

"Oh, Andrew."

She stood under the porte cochere, hand raised, concerned wife bidding adieu to husband off to do battle. Andrew waved and began the drive to Sorrento.

SIXTEEN

Dorothy watched the car swing down the drive and into the street. She remained in the doorway even after the red taillights went out of sight as Andrew turned the corner. And waited.

Ted Lister had been haunting her evening. At the club, he had peeked out of the bar when they came in; he took a table in the dining room as soon as they were settled, and Dorothy changed seats with Peg Bilans so she wouldn't have her appetite ruined by the plaintive, desperate gaze of her weak-kneed lover. When they danced, Ted prowled the edge of the dance floor. If he had tried to break in, Dorothy would have politely refused. No scene, just for the love of God go. We'll talk when we can talk, but this is not the time nor the place.

Two minutes after Andrew had gone out the drive,

Ted roared up, his Mercedes coupe coming to a stop in the very spot were she had moments before gotten out of Andrew's Porsche.

She held the door open and a trembling Ted came into her waiting arms. She embraced him in self-defense as much as anything, and had to pull him back out of the doorway. Discretion had obviously lost its meaning for Ted, but Dorothy was still aware that the wrong pair of eyes might see her welcoming him with open arms just after she had seen her husband off into the night.

"Dorothy, we are in deep, deep trouble."

"Come into the den and tell me about it."

Her calm tone infuriated him. Holding her wrists tightly he stepped back and stared at her. "You're not worried?"

"I don't know if there is reason to worry."

He spoke with exaggerated control, a word at a time, as if he were trying to keep his message within a certain limit. "Your nephew Gerald came to the clinic this afternoon."

"He is Andrew's nephew."

Ted pressed his eyes shut in protection against this irrelevancy.

"Before he talked to me, he talked to two of the staff. Thelma Nailer, a medical technician, and Bobbie Burke, a nurse. He was asking them questions about the physical Andrew took last week."

"And what did they tell him?"

"Nothing! Thelma reported it to me almost immediately and Bobbie was quite open about it when I talked to her. Neither one of them gave out any confidential information nor did they hint at the outcome of the tests. Bobbie wouldn't know and Thelma is too experienced to be sweet-talked into talking."

"Sweet-talked? Gerald?"

"The word is Thelma's," Ted said defensively. "Can we please stick to the point?"

She had managed to lead him toward the den where she closed the door behind them, settled Ted into a corner of the leather couch, and pulled a hassock up for herself.

"And then he came to you?"

"Then he came to me." Ted's eyes darted toward the cabinet that served as a bar. Dorothy got to her feet, opened the cabinet, and dropped ice cubes clattering into a low glass.

"Bourbon?"

"Please." Ted had acquired a taste for bourbon since moving to the Midwest.

He waited for the drink with an eagerness that was not lost on Dorothy. Another indication of weakness. What did she see in this poor excuse for a man? Why would any woman jeopardize a life with Andrew for a liaison with Ted, let alone enter into a criminal plot with him?

The answer is lost in the obscurer reaches of the heart and loins. The mind master—or mistress—of the flesh? This is so rare as to be the exception. Her love for Ted made sense just because it made no sense. It was a way of revolting against her husband, her life, herself. To what purpose? Why does a terrorist drive a truck loaded with explosives into the camp of the enemy? It was the appeal of negation, of nothingness.

Gerald—Andrew's nephew, she insisted on that; she had no wish to be anyone's Aunt Dorothy—Gerald would indulge such thoughts when they engaged in bantering conversation. Like Andrew, she gave him credit for having been raised in an academic environment, as if he had inherited with his genes the knowledge his father and his father's colleagues had acquired over long years of effort. But such matters could be discussed only in a lighthearted way, as a forgivable recess from acceptable topics of discourse.

Ted was no more inclined to acknowledge that she had a mind than Andrew was.

"How did he bring the subject up with you?"

"He said he had been worried about his uncle lately. Not only the prolonged strain of the Agnes Walz trial, other things. For personal and professional reasons, he was concerned."

"Asking no direct questions?"

"A transcript of our conversation would make it seem perfectly harmless. Nothing threatening at all. Even a recording of it would reveal nothing."

"But you know otherwise."

Bourbon ran down his chin when he pulled the glass angrily from his mouth. "He suspects something, Dorothy. He knows something. It was there in his eyes and manner. Andrew must have said something to him."

"That I very much doubt."

"Then why did he come to me?"

"He gave you perfectly plausible reasons. Andrew

has all but turned the Agnes Walz case over to Gerald. He went off to Chicago yesterday in a very secretive way."

"To have another physical!"

"Do you know that?"

"I would have to be a fool to think otherwise. He said he was going to do it. Who wouldn't want another opinion after getting the kind of results I gave him?"

Dorothy poured a little bourbon for herself when she freshened Ted's drink. He was gulping it down and she was inclined to encourage it. He might make more sense drunk than he did sober. She took her seat again on the hassock and laid one hand on his knee.

She tried not to sound too calm, she did not want to enrage him, but she talked and talked, dominating the conversation, giving him time to work on the very strong drink she had made for him. She spoke as much to herself as to Ted, putting together his account of Gerald's visit, Andrew's behavior since the fateful visit to the clinic, and what she knew of her husband after all their years of marriage. There was no cause for concern. That was her message. That was her belief.

The difficult part was to get Ted to accept it, lest he screw up everything now in a fit of panic.

He could not give her any basis for the panic he had felt when talking to Gerald. He had simply projected his own fears and conjured up suspicions that were not there. Gerald's ostensible reasons for going to the clinic were more than good enough.

"He also wanted a physical. Did I say that? In a way, that was his real excuse for coming. That is how he started the conversations with Thelma and Bobbie. What did it entail, how long did it take, when would he know the results? Thelma assumed he had picked up a venereal disease and was worried about it."

"She did!"

"Nobody just comes out and says it."

"She really thought that of Gerald?"

"No one is above suspicion."

"Ted, you're not serious."

But Ted did not reply. She thought he was going to cry. His lower lip trembled, glistening with bourbon, and a muscle in his cheek twitched. He pressed the glass tightly against his lips, gaining control.

"People with a fatal illness will go to any lengths to find a cure, hopeless as it is. There are clinics in Mexico where charlatans make millions dispensing useless nostrums to people dying of cancer. They want to believe in the cure. They cannot accept the fact that they are dying. Oh God, why did I get into this?"

She knew about cancer patients. She also knew that Andrew would not be numbered among such cringing fools. Already she detected in him a defiant acceptance of the inevitable. That was why she was sure he would not fight his fate by seeking even a second opinion. It would never occur to him that Ted could make a mistake about something like that, let alone that he would deliberately mislead him.

She understood Andrew because in this they were alike.

The danger that Ted feared she relished. Of course there was the chance that they might be discovered, with results almost impossible to predict. What would Andrew do to them—to Ted, but particularly to her—if he found out that they had conspired to tell him he was a dying man when his health was as good as it had ever been? The fact that that chance existed excited rather than panicked Dorothy. It frightened her, yes. She did not want to think what an infuriated Andrew would do. But either things would turn out as she had planned or they would not. Andrew, told he was dying, would take his own life, and then hers would open up as it had not in years. Or, Andrew would find out and...

What would Ted say if he knew that she was almost as excited by the prospect of failure as she was by the thought of success?

"Where did he go?" It had belatedly occurred to Ted that Andrew had conveniently gone off and given him this opportunity to weep on her shoulder.

"Don't worry. Have another."

He handed her his glass, as if accepting needed medicine. "He's not coming back?"

"He said he was going to his office."

"You don't believe him?"

"The main thing is, he's gone. Wanna mess around?"

"Now?"

"When did you have in mind?"

"Dorothy, ever since your nephew...Gerald... came to the clinic, I have been a nervous wreck. I would be no good to you."

"Maybe I can be of help."

But fear had rendered Ted impotent. He acted as if the memory of their lovemaking now made him physically sick. He had never bargained for this. The loss of his job. A lawsuit that would discredit him forever, to say nothing of the possibility of jail. Dorothy danced her fingers over his knee. But for once he was not susceptible to her seductive wiles. She accepted it. What a fatalist she had become. *Que sera, sera.*

SEVENTEEN

Gerald followed Uncle Andrew from the country club, watched him drop Dorothy off and, parked on the opposite side of the road, had to duck down when Andrew drove out again. He looked up just as the taillights disappeared around thee corner. What the hell?

He wasn't sure why he hadn't taken Andrew aside at the club, except that he didn't know quite how to put his suspicion. That difficulty explained why he was still parked across the road from his uncle's house when the Mercedes whipped up the drive and Dr. Lister jumped out and ran into Aunt Dorothy's arms!

What in the hell was going on?

There was no mistaking the nature of that welcoming embrace. This was not the chaste hug and pro forma kiss that had become customary among friends, trivializing personal relationships. This was a lover being taken into the arms of his beloved. Aunt Dorothy? Gerald was astounded.

Like most men in their twenties he assumed tacitly that couples over forty had long since hung up their loving cups. Andrew, unlike most men, did not lace his conversation with raunchy remarks, had no repertoire of semi-funny dirty jokes, seemed as proper as a clergyman. As for Dorothy, well, she certainly was attractive for her age, and she was flirty in the way of middle-aged women, as well as being a matchmaker. That as much as anything seemed to indicate she was personally over the hill. She had encouraged Gerald with Julie.

"The famous feud? Forget it. It was silly to begin with, but to wish it onto the next generation is absurd. Julie is a lovely girl."

Gerald agreed. Doubtless this budding love affair reminded his aunt of her youth, of that great long ago when she and Andrew had been young and romance had been a part of their lives.

It took some adjustment to accept this undeniable display of affection on Dorothy's part, but to Dr. Lister? Gerald had had trouble taking Lister seriously when he finally got into the man's office.

"I wondered if I'd meet at least one honest-to-God doctor while I took this physical."

Lister frowned. A man without a sense of humor. "I assure you that our system is both efficient and reliable."

"So my uncle tells me."

"I'm glad to hear that." Lister's voice sounded like a yelp.

"He just had a physical himself."

"I know that."

"Of course. When do I get the bad news?"

"What do you mean?" Lister was the most skittish doctor Gerald had ever seen.

"All these tests I've taken. When do I get the results?"

"You will be notified."

"That's right. My uncle Andrew was called over here the other day. Fouled up our schedule. We had a meeting set with Agnes Walz. Have you been following that case?"

"I think everyone has been."

"I'm worried about Andrew."

"Why?"

"I'm not sure. Ever since he got the results of his tests..."

"Did he discuss them with you?"

"No."

Lister nodded vigorously. "You said you're worried."

"He seems tired and distracted."

Lister ran an index finger down the bony extent of his nose. He was waiting to see what else Gerald might say.

"You work with someone you notice those things."

"Well, let us take care of you." Lister strapped the blood pressure equipment around Gerald's arm and began to pump it up.

"He's in good health, isn't he?"

"You seem to be, Mr. Rowan," Lister said, studying the dropping pressure line as he eased up the black rubber ball.

It was there in Lister's office that Gerald developed the theory that the doctor had discovered something bad as a result of Uncle Andrew's physical, and had been too cowardly to break the news to the man who was, after all, his employer. He could believe that Lister would do such a thing out of weakness, and then be too frightened to correct the mistake once he had made it.

He thought of Andrew, ill, maybe very ill, yet walking around with the false assurance that his physical had turned up nothing.

"You'll tell me if something bad shows up in my tests, won't you?"

Lister was impatient. "Mr. Rowan, is there something in particular you would like us to be on the lookout for?"

"Like VD?"

"Like VD. Do you think you may have contracted it?"

"Doctor, I don't even use public toilets."

The more he thought of it, at home in his apartment, taking a shower to wash off the feel of dozens of strangers palpating and probing and sampling his body, the more Gerald was inclined to think that Dr. Lister had withheld bad news from Uncle Andrew.

And he engaged in imaginary conversations with Uncle Andrew:

ANDREW: What basis do you have for saying that, Gerald?

GERALD: It's hard to say. Talking with him, I got the feeling...

ANDREW: The feeling?

GERALD: He's such a creepy bastard. Sorry. But he's furtive, sneaky.

ANDREW: Why do you say Dr. Lister falsified the results of my physical?

GERALD: I'm trying to explain.

ANDREW: You're not succeeding.

He couldn't find a way to put it that didn't sound ridiculous. The thing to do was to ask outright what Lister had told Uncle Andrew. If Andrew said he'd been given a clean bill of health, Gerald could then proceed in a roundabout way, asking his uncle if he thought a doctor would ever deceive a patient about such results. A doctor like Lister. The doctor examines his boss, his employer, his benefactor (one of the above) and discovers something he doesn't want to tell the man. He will be held responsible if something has developed while the man has been under his care, so...

Sitting in his parked car outside Uncle Andrew's after seeing Aunt Dorothy welcome Lister, Gerald felt he had the explanation. Dorothy was having an affair with Lister. By repressing the news of Andrew's illness, deflecting him from seeking the care that might save him, the aging lovers could remove Andrew from the scene and live happily ever after.

Gerald hit the steering wheel with the heel of his hand, once, twice, in anger. The third time, he hit the horn and startled himself when the noise of it split the night air. He reached for the ignition key and twisted the motor into life. But he did not just take off down the road as was his immediate impulse.

He turned into the driveway and had a little difficulty getting traction because the surface was icy and he did not have much momentum, but by easing up on the gas and letting the idle speed take the car up the slight incline, he came to a stop behind the Mercedes. At the front door, he stamped snow from his shoes and pressed the bell.

Puffs of frigid breath, an undeniable chill in the air. The temperature must have dropped fifteen degrees since sundown. He rang the bell again.

"Gerald!" Dorothy cried when she opened the door. "What a surprise."

Did he imagine relief in her voice? But Uncle Andrew would not have rung the bell if he returned.

"Is Andrew in?"

"He's at the office."

"The office. I never thought of that."

"Is something wrong?"

"I'm not sure. Whose Mercedes?"

"Dr. Lister is here. Gerald, come in out of the cold while you make up your mind what to do."

"I thought I saw the two of you at the club to-night."

"Were you there?"

"I ate in the grill."

"Why don't you phone the office if you want to talk to Andrew?"

"Good idea. I'll use the phone in the den."

He had noticed the light, had wondered where Lister was hiding. When Gerald entered the den, Lister held a magazine open before him and looked over it in feigned casualness. Gerald was sure the doctor would not have noticed if the magazine were upside down.

"Dr. Lister."

"Hello, Gerald."

"Aunt Dorothy said that was your Mercedes out front. Some car."

"I like it."

Gerald picked up the phone and dialed the office. Dr. Lister watched as he did so, and Gerald realized that Dorothy was in the doorway doing the same. Suddenly he was certain the phone would not be answered.

It wasn't. But, pressing the receiver to his ear lest the sound of the ringing be audible, he carried on one more imaginary conversation with Uncle Andrew.

"I'm at the house, stopped by on my way from the club." Pause. "I know. I saw you there. Should I come down there? I want to talk." Pause. "No, it'll keep. It's not that important." Pause. "Sure, sure. I understand. Okay. Until tomorrow." He put the phone down quickly, snuffing a final ring.

"I'm glad I called."

Dorothy said, "He doesn't want to see you?"

Gerald looked at Lister, whose eyes slipped away, then returned, trying to hold as Gerald said, "He isn't feeling well. He's coming home, but he doesn't want to talk."

That should put the kibosh on anything the two of them had planned. Inside Uncle Andrew's house, seeing that goddam Lister ensconced in the den, Gerald felt another surge of anger. The sonofabitch. He was so angry, he left the den and made a beeline for the door.

"Don't just run off, Gerald," Dorothy coaxed. "Stay and have something to drink."

He shook his head, pulled open the door, and standing in the arctic blast, turned to say good night to his aunt.

"Sure you won't stay?"

"I don't want to be here when Uncle Andrew gets home."

EIGHTEEN

The lawyer Broom stopped at the office to let Giulio
know he was there and then came into the club and
stood for a moment peering into the gaudy darkness.
He turned and watched Sadie on the stage, smiling
to cover whatever unease or embarrassment the
sight of a naked woman doing what Sadie was doing
in public might give him, and then he left.

Billy asked Carole to go after him and ask him
what in particular had brought him to Sorrento.

"If he says a phone call, tell him to wait."

She was back in a minute. "He's waiting." She put
a hand on his arm. "Be careful."

Men in every walk of life had been seen on the Sorrento strip from time to time, but the lawyer looked
as out of place there as anyone ever had. Billy almost felt sorry for him.

"Where are you parked?"

He looked at Billy and Billy met his eyes. "Your name is Billy, as I remember. Are you the one who called my office?"

"That's right."

He had parked the Porsche right there on the street, a pearl among swine.

"You're lucky it's still here."

"I don't feel lucky. Where are we going?"

"Just drive. We can talk in the car. It's safe." He lit a cigarette, after the lawyer refused one. "For both of us."

"Do you think I'm taping this?"

Billy looked around. "I wouldn't be surprised. Are you?"

He touched something on the dashboard and a cassette slid into view. He showed it to Billy, then put it in his pocket. "Not anymore."

It seemed important not to be impressed. Billy gave the man directions, and that made him feel in control of the situation again. He decided they would stay in Illinois.

"My client owes someone ten thousand dollars and is anxious to pay."

"Who's your client?"

"I think you know. We have talked before, Billy."

He nodded. "I remember."

"You told me nothing."

"Just what I told the other side. The police."

"Agnes wants to talk to you."

"Where?"

"She is still in the county jail in Wyler, Indiana."

"I'm not going to no jail."

"Why not?"

"I don't like jails."

"Neither does Agnes. But it's the only way you will get the ten thousand."

Billy looked at the dash, wondering if this was being recorded despite the way the man had taken that tape out and put it in his pocket. Whatever he said now, he was admitting something, accepting that he was the man Agnes owed the ten thousand.

"How can she get at it?"

"She said you would already know."

"Tell her to send the message by you." He rolled down the window and tossed out his cigarette. They were close to the refineries now and the stench was strong. The lawyer did not wait for directions, but took a turn to get away from the smell. Billy didn't care. They weren't going anywhere in particular.

"She anticipated your request. The answer is no."

The original deal was the ten thousand would be put somewhere he could get at it and they would let him know afterward where to get it. The unstated guarantee was that he would do for them what they wanted done to her old man. The way things had turned out, Billy wasn't surprised he had received no message. Nor could he say she was reneging.

Broom said, "I might be able to have her brought to my office. You could talk with her there."

"Anyone seeing me talking to her is going to put two and two together."

The lawyer, to Billy's surprise, agreed. "I explained that to her. She seems to think you wouldn't care."

"Just because she's got no more worries doesn't mean I'm crazy."

The conversation changed abruptly. "Good. You're not a damned fool and I'm glad. You would have to be very stupid indeed to agree to any version of what Agnes wants."

"I'm not stupid," Billy said.

"I believe you. I think what she wanted was a chance to talk to you."

Billy bet she did. She would want to know what the hell had made things go so wrong. He did not know if she would believe him when he told her. He could tell the lawyer he wasn't stupid, but he had been stupid then. He should have known that the man on the phone was not Jake Fennel. Agnes would figure what Billy did, that her old man had found out what she was up to and used the plan against her.

"So where does that leave me?" Billy asked.

"Where can we talk?"

"We're talking now."

"I want to look at you when we talk. I have a proposal to make."

Billy directed him to the house, why not? Where he lived was no secret and it was no secret that the lawyer had been to the club. This could be just one more pointless conversation meant to help the man's client. The man did not show much interest in the house, left his coat on, but took the beer Billy offered and didn't mind drinking it out of the can.

"You said you have a proposal?"

"How would you like to make another ten thousand dollars?"

"Another?"

"Twenty in all."

"How?"

"The same way."

"The deal before was fifteen."

"This will get you the ten you have coming and another ten."

"You don't sound like a lawyer, offering a deal like that."

"I have a fool for a client."

"Who gets taken care of this time?"

He tipped his beer up, turning his head so he could keep one eye on Billy while he drank. He put the can down carefully, as if the table in front of the old sofa could be hurt.

"Me."

"Funny."

"I'm serious."

"You want someone to take you out?"

"That's right."

The man wasn't laughing. And he seemed serious so far as Billy could tell.

"Why?"

"What difference does that make to you?"

"I mean, why someone else? Why not do it yourself?"

"I would be, only at one remove."

Billy crushed his beer can. He always crushed his beer cans. "You don't want to know when, is that it?"

The lawyer nodded.

"I don't know."

"It's a package. As I said. You take this or you don't see the ten Agnes owes you."

"How will I get the money?'

"Does that mean we have a deal?"

"Only when I get the money."

"That's fair enough." He reached into his pocket and pulled out an envelope. He tossed it on the table, next to his beer can, and rose. "That's from Agnes."

Billy went with him to the door. The Porsche was still at the curb. You never knew in this neighborhood. "Don't call me at the club."

"How will we get in touch?"

"I'll call your office."

"Tell me. Why did you call before?"

"To get something started. And it worked."

Broom half pulled his hand from the pocket of his coat, then jammed it in again. It would have been weird, shaking hands after a conversation like that. Billy watched the man get into his car and drive off up the street. He shook his head and went inside.

The world was getting crazier all the time. But it could be as crazy as it liked so long as he got what was coming to him. And more besides. Another thing, he told himself, I won't even tell Carole.

The thought stopped him. He had picked up the envelope the lawyer had left on the table and stood tapping it against his hand, wondering why he had thought that about Carole.

It wasn't that he didn't trust her. He didn't trust anybody.

One thing was for sure. If he got out of this with the kind of money they had been talking about, Sorrento would have seen the end of Billy Sciacca.

The envelope was pale blue and smelled of perfume. It was sealed and didn't look like it had been tampered with. It was pretty obvious it didn't contain any ten thousand dollars. Broom would never have delivered it if it did.

Billy slit it open, unfolded the pale blue sheet inside, and read.

"Make money the old-fashioned way. Earn it!"

It took Billy a minute, but when he got it, he laughed. The old girl hadn't lost it all, sitting in jail.

Besides, it seemed fair enough when he thought about it. And he felt a lot better thinking about things now that the lawyer Broom had been here. Agnes wanted what she was paying for, what she hadn't gotten yet but was sitting in jail as if she had.

Okay.

A deal was a deal, no matter how screwed up it had been to this point.

NINETEEN

Two phone calls.

The first from Agnes, for God's sake. It was like a call from beyond the grave. Wallace had written her off since the arrest, to say nothing of the trial, and then to hear her voice on the phone. In the kitchen. He had answered it there and was standing in Agnes's kitchen to hear her say it.

"Your turn."

That was all. No conversation, no how are you, go to hell, or anything like that. Just two words.

Wallace got hold of the prosecutor's office and they said, yes, she could use the phone, with restrictions, of course, but she had not lost all her rights as the result of the trial. Did he have a complaint?

He said he had been surprised, that was all, and no, he didn't want to be put through to Agnes now.

The second call was worse.

He recognized the voice, for one thing. How could he ever forget it? The voice of the executioner. Wallace had, in the smartest move he had ever made in his life, used the plan Agnes and Jake had cooked up against him.

At the time, he wasn't sure it would work. He had been putting two and two together for months, ever since the big truce between Jake and himself, after all those years, the truce engineered by Agnes. If anyone had told him that Agnes would get into something with Jake, Wallace would have laughed. Jake had been a pipsqueak in school and he had not improved, not that Wallace could see. And Agnes was being taken care of in the love department. If she had been hanging by her thumbs, it might have made some sense, but their routine had not changed. As good as every night. And not just run-of-the-mill rolls in the hay. After it all happened, when he thought of himself and Agnes upstairs in their bed, Wallace wanted to cry out in agony, he missed her so, it hurt so much that after years and years of being that close she should have betrayed him with Jake Fennel!

What is it about women, this secret desire to destroy, themselves first of all? The attraction of the weird and the weak, maybe that was a flaw that came from strength, from compassion and tenderness. Dancing girls flocking around that dwarf French painter who did the posters, and the handicapped exerting a strong, perverse pull. Same thing, white women and blacks, so far as Wallace could see.

It helped him to understand what Agnes had done, helped some, but finally did not stop him from crying out loud when he was alone in the deserted house.

Following them around in the rented car, like in some goddam movie, the betrayed husband tracking his wife and the sonofabitch she was sleeping with. At motels all over the countryside, Wallace could have provided a list, even at the bastard's own house. And still, every night, ready for him. God, what a woman. Disgust and wonderment mixed in his mind as he thought of it.

She never kept away from their bed during all that time. He could wipe away the agony of the afternoon, the following, the imagining, just like that when he held her in his arms. Must have been the same with her. It didn't matter. He meant to kill Jake Fennel and in such a way that everything would be back the way it was, except Jake would be playing a harp—or more likely using a pitchfork. He sure as hell did not intend to spend the rest of his life in jail just for the satisfaction of taking care of Jake once and for all.

The way he tracked them, he went to Jake's first and then witnessed the rendezvous, Jake pulling into a motel where the red Olds was already parked. Jake went to arrange for the unit and then through the door leaving him to stew and imagine and hate until they came out again. He learned patience. He learned how to plan for the kind of resolution that would leave him untouched. He would kill the sonofabitch and never be suspected.

And then he learned that they were planning to kill him.

One day Jake set out, picked up the Interstate and headed north, and Wallace was about to turn back, figuring this had nothing to do with Agnes, but something made him stay with it, and when Jake pulled off at Sorrento and made for the strip, Wallace wondered if he had ever really known his old rival. Jake was as bad as Agnes. He couldn't get enough. Banging her almost daily and now off to the honky-tonk to get some strange.

That was how he learned that Jake had been inquiring about a hired assassin. Jesus. The girl who told him laughed and said the guy must be buggy thinking someone would say, Why sure, I kill people, who'd you have in mind? The girl Carole took the fifty he offered her and promised to keep him posted. There was a hundred more for her if she passed on important information.

She did.

Billy Sciacca. The muscle of the Ecstasy Club. Just talk? Carole said no. He peeled off three hundred-dollar bills and told her to keep on the alert. Two days later she said the deal had been made.

"When will he do it?" Something happened to the skin on the back of his neck, there was a ripple down his back that ended with a tightening of his sphincter. He was referring to his own death.

"Soon. That's all I know."

"Keep your eye on him."

Carole called when Agnes was home and he took the message while he looked across the kitchen at her laying strips of bacon in the frying pan.

"He is waiting for a call," Carole said, her voice tense. She was running her own risk, taking his money to make these calls.

Carole had already given him the number where he could reach the guy, call about noon, that was the best time.

"Who was that?" Agnes asked.

"Quirk at the bank. I've got to go to town."

He should have come up with a better excuse. Mentioning the bank got Agnes nervous. No wonder, after she had cashed in a CD for ten thousand without telling him about it. And she was right to be nervous about Quirk; it was something the banker said that, along with everything else that was going on, had made Wallace look in the safe deposit box and discover a CD was missing.

"Are you going to use the Olds?"

Wallace said, "I can use the pickup."

"No, use the Olds. I have to do anything, I can take the pickup."

That had made it much easier. When he called the man at noon he told him today was the day, sounding so much like Jake when he said it that he could have fooled anyone. He gave Billy the number of a pay phone at the bottom of the exit ramp off the Interstate.

"Wait there. I'll spot him and let you know."

Something would go wrong. He kept telling himself that. Today they would not get together and Billy would be pissed and they would find out he knew and what then?

But it did work. When Wallace followed Jake to the motel they had been using a lot, the Lullaby, on old Highway 12, the pickup was there. Jake pulled in and in fifteen seconds the lovers were behind the locked door of Unit 7.

A mile up the road, Wallace made the phone call. The unit number. The license tag of the pickup. What the guy was wearing. Do it.

He did it. Wallace saw him do it, picking it up with binoculars, a ringside seat. The weird thing was, he had not seen Billy show up, the guy moved like a ghost, and when the door of the unit opened and, same as always, Jake with his head tucked down into his chest started for his car, Wallace swore, certain nothing was going to happen. He was wrong. The first blast threw Jake back and he might have tumbled into the motel unit again but his shoulder hit the door frame, spinning him into perfect position. The poor bastard was looking right at it when the second blast all but took his head off.

It was the damnedest feeling. Wallace wanted to cheer he felt so good, but at the same time he could almost feel what Jake had felt when the charges hit him. After all, Jake was taking his place.

The big guy, Billy, calm as could be, broke the shotgun and reloaded before getting back into his car and driving away. Wallace waited until Agnes appeared, naked terror on her face, her mouth open. She was screaming, but he couldn't hear her.

People came piling out of the other units and a deputy who had been having coffee in the motel office came on the run, uniformed and everything. Nobody seemed to have seen Billy drive away.

That is what they meant to do to me. He kept saying that, over and over, as he drove home. That is what they meant to do to me.

Agnes never came home again. He had never talked to her since. They wanted to question her about what had happened, of course, she could not have gotten out of that.

The swiftness of the arrest had surprised Wallace. Sometime during the day he had decided that Agnes must go too. That would be more difficult, but not impossible. She would commit suicide, at least that is how it would look. Remorseful housewife kills self when plan backfires.

The arrest seemed to make it impossible. Not that he gave up. He filled one of Agnes's bottles of artificial sweetener half full of strychnine, figuring that when she asked for her things to be brought to her, the sheriff would deliver it. But she asked for nothing, and Wallace sure as hell couldn't volunteer. It would have been risky enough if the sheriff just included it among Agnes's things. He put the bottle of sweetener in the cupboard, with the bottles of Agnes's pills.

And now today, after Agnes had phoned, a second call and that unforgettable voice.

"Wallace?"

"Yes."

"Your turn."

The phone clicked. Returning the receiver to its cradle, Wallace suddenly felt in the bull's-eye of a target.

The house, built on a rise with lots of windows so he could look out in any direction and see his property stretch away toward the horizon, now made him vulnerable. He knew how crafty Billy was, how invisibly he had arrived when he took out Jake. Wallace, who was looking for him, had not even seen him come.

He had to get out of the kitchen right away, it was like being in a greenhouse, but first he went on hands and knees to the windows looking out at the barn and the shed in which they kept the cars. The red Olds and the pickup and the snowmobile Agnes had wanted but which neither of them had used much. Nothing.

Not yet. The man had just phoned. Think. He had time. The man would have to come for him here, on his home ground, that was an advantage.

He knelt by the window, watching snow flutter down, silvery in the sunlight, looking beyond the buildings to the road. If Billy came along that road, from either direction, he would be visible long before he got to the house.

What alternative was there?

Through the fields? To the south was the pasture that dipped away from the house, but to the north a field with winter wheat rose to a ridge where there was a stand of trees, walnut mainly, that Wallace meant to sell off some day.

The best vantage point was upstairs, the superstructure that might have been a bell tower, four windows looking in the four directions, cold as a bitch in winter, but he sure as hell couldn't be surprised if he kept watch there.

He took a war-surplus carbine, loaded and with an extra clip, a deer rifle he hadn't missed anything with, ever, and a shotgun, .12 gauge. That suggested his hunting jacket, and he put it on. Then, feeling ready for anything, he went upstairs, into the attic and on up into the tower.

The windows were frosted from the cold because some heat would seep up from below. Wallace got seated, leaving his legs on the ladder, got his arsenal up there with him, and with his binoculars looked up the road toward Wyler.

He no longer felt as vulnerable as he had in the kitchen.

TWENTY

Driving down to Wyler, Billy listened to country western, which he preferred and which he heard too little of, except when Carole was on stage. She danced to country western, if you could believe it, and was as sexy as any of the others working with rock.

He liked the rhythm, the lyrics—how many songs were about women who cheated, think of Lucille—and the what-the-hell attitude was just the feeling he wanted now. Maybe that's what Rafe had tried to get from the sauce the day he went out and messed up good.

Snow everywhere, but the road was dry until he was maybe twenty miles from Wyler and it began to come down again. Not heavy, no problem, kind of nice, the fluffy stuff floating down, swirling away from the car, but not accumulating on the Interstate. Billy didn't think of the snow as trouble. It was protection, cover, part of the element of surprise.

Calling the man first was something he would have done even apart from the fact that the lady wanted it. "Call and tell him *Your turn* first." That was all. Billy liked it. He liked it so much he told himself he would have thought of it on his own.

He made the call from the phone at the end of the exit ramp, the same phone he had taken the bum instructions on. He liked that part too, as if he were getting things back in balance. The second touch was taking a room at the Lullaby Motel. He signed the governor's name in the book, looked at the plastic key tag the lady gave him, shook his head and grinned.

"Now if only you had given me my lucky number I'd know this was my day."

"What's your lucky number?" Platinum hair, black roots, false eyelashes that looked like she had lost a bet and had to wear them, her tone probably meant to be vaguely sexy.

"It don't matter."

"No, come on. What is it? Maybe the unit's free."

"Seven, but like I said ..."

"Seven's free! You want seven, it's yours."

He settled in with two cans of Diet Pepsi, turned on the TV, and wondered if they were filming the snowfall. He flipped it to cable and watched a few minutes of a pornographic movie. He switched and got the replay of a Blackhawks game on ESPN. Better.

He would let the man worry a bit. He would wait
until twilight.

On his way to the motel he had driven past the
farm in the rented Merc and got a glimpse of a head
in the tower that jutted from the roof. Understandable but dumb. So the farmer could see. He could
also be seen. And Billy took note of the Olds and
truck in the shed. If they were missing, he would
know the guy was on the run. But where could he
go? Billy had all the time in the world. After he took
care of the farmer, he would cut the deal with the
lawyer, and when he left Wyler it would be with
twenty thousand dollars to go with the four thousand he had left of the down payment.

The Blackhawks lost, but then they had lost the
same game the night before, so it didn't affect their
record. He separated the drapes with two fingers
and saw that the snow was falling more heavily now.
And there was much less light than before. Billy put
on his leather fingertip jacket and grabbed his gloves
and cap. Time to get started.

Wallace was hardly settled in when he saw the
Mercury coming along the road, not too slow, but not
very fast either. He put the glasses on it and Billy's
face leapt up at him. He tracked him and when the
car went on by the house, continuing down the road
and out of sight, he realized he was dripping with
sweat. It ran down the sides of his body, it stood in
beads on his forehead.

When it stopped it was like a fever breaking. Seeing the man, knowing it had started, was almost a relief. Wallace lay the deer rifle across his lap and cradled the carbine in such a way that he could still use the glasses. He had them fixed on the point where the Mercury had gone out of sight, expecting that Billy would turn around and come back, if only for one more pass.

But no Mercury appeared. Outside his glass aerie the snow fell thicker and he welcomed it, seeing it as an obstacle to Billy. Not driving, the roads would not be affected by this kind of snowfall, but it would make approaching the house on foot harder, even by the road, although he would be a damned fool if he thought he could just walk down the road and turn in at the house on foot. Not after calling to say he was on his way.

Why had he done it? Wallace had not expected that kind of warning. It unnerved him to think how many ways Billy could have taken him if he had just picked his own time and place. Calling first and letting Wallace choose his home field for the encounter was for Billy to take two strikes before the game began. Wallace wished he could believe that really gave him an advantage. The fact was it applied a psychological pressure. What it said to him was that Billy was so goddam sure of himself he could give up those two strikes without a worry.

After the snow started, the sun had become a pale disc visible only now and again in the dove gray sky, but now even that was gone. Without the snow it would be dark now. His digital watch gave him 16:40:34, which in winter was late.

He sat there snug in his lofty lookout, listening as much as looking. He didn't want that Mercury rolling down the road with its lights out, maybe on idle, all but noiseless, putting the enemy at the gate without his knowing it. But all he heard was the creak of the house, the steady splat of the snow against the windows, and far off a motor, not a car, maybe a snowmobile, one of the neighbor kids out for a ride in the fresh snow. Dangerous as hell, with buried stumps and, worse, barbed fence wire that more than once had cut up a kid who just goosed the damned thing and let it fly across the fields.

He trained the glasses on the road, moving them from the distant point slowly toward the house, looking to pick up any shape that might be a Mercury creeping along with its lights out.

The window on his right suddenly exploded, sending shards of glass flying everywhere, and even as he fell back and began to scramble down the ladder there was another pop—he realized he had heard one a second before the window went—and a hole was torn in the roof of the tower.

The sonofabitch had arrived.

It didn't matter how. He was there. And Wallace had been sitting up in that tower, visible from four sides, asking for it. And damned near got it. Slivers of glass were stuck in his cheek as if he had met up with a glass porcupine.

His binoculars banged against his chest as he

climbed, half slid, down the ladder, and the deer rifle hit the attic floor. He had the carbine and that was enough. He did not want to be dragging the deer rifle and shotgun around now that it had begun.

Think. Where had the shots come from? Behind the house. Behind! How had the sonofabitch come over the ridge and through that snow-filled field without his seeing? Because he'd had his mind on the road, that's how. The sonofabitch must be out there by the barn, by the shed.

From outside came the sound of a shot. A moment of silence, then another shot. What the hell?

The glasses swung free from his neck as, in a crouch, holding his carbine at port arms, Wallace went down the stairs of his house as if he were an exposed figure on a battlefield. The house had turned into a greenhouse again. The whole damned place was like the tower, exposing him on all sides.

As if to prove this, there was another sound of exploding glass as he came onto the first floor. A volley of shots and the sound of glass and pots and pans and splitting wood filled his ears. Billy was shooting up the kitchen.

But it put him in the same place.

By the shed.

Billy knew he had missed his target with the first shot and that he didn't have a chance with the second.

Disappointing, yeah, but be patient. He had the

farmer pinned up in the house. Renting the snow-mobile and coming as far as those trees, then approaching the back of the barn on foot had been the right idea. In the shed, sitting on the hood of the snowmobile parked there next to the pickup, he had taken careful aim at the glass tower, squeezing the trigger with steady pressure, but the blast had been slightly off and letting go another was a waste. Maybe not. If nothing else he had scared hell out of the farmer, let him know he was there and, with luck, wounded him at least.

Even so it was pique as much as precaution that made him shoot out one tire each on the Olds and the pickup. Now he was going to have to go in after him. Unless he could scare the shit out of him and bring him running outside, where it would be a lot easier to get the job done.

To prompt the farmer, Billy let go at the kitchen windows, sending glass flying through the whipping, shredded curtains and causing one hell of a commotion inside. He figured the man would have gotten downstairs fast, after nearly taking it in the head up there in his glass house.

The whole thing was a glass house.

The silence after the shooting was total. The snow had let up, seemed almost to have stopped, and Billy stood there in the shed, waiting. He wasn't sure what he expected to happen next, but he was ready for it, whatever it would be.

One thing was for sure. There was no way the man could get out of the house without making some kind of noise. And no noises were being made. Billy leaned against the wall the shed shared with the barn. A kerosene lamp hung there. By the smell of it, it was not just an ornament. Billy eased it off its hook and shook it. There was the slosh of fuel. He did not put it back onto the hook.

Fifteen minutes later, Billy figured the hell with it. The farmer wasn't coming out without more persuasion.

Well, that could be provided.

He went to the back of the shed, outside, and started to move slowly around the barn, intending to come upon the house from an unexpected angle.

For maybe a minute he was out of hearing range of the house but when he reached the corner of the barn, he waited half a minute, satisfying himself that his quarry had made no move, then bent over and went very swiftly across the snow toward the house.

Wallace figured there were two ways to look at it. On the one hand, here he was pinned down in his own house and outside was a sonofabitch who had come to kill him and wasn't likely to go away until he had. On the other hand, since this was not likely to end except with one of them dead or severely wounded, being inside the house where Billy had to come for him had its advantages.

Billy might have the advantage of knowing where he was, but he had the advantage of knowing Billy had to come to the house.

Wallace had located himself in the hallway now, where he was not directly exposed to any window and had the protection of walls on three sides. And it was central, as close to the front door as to the back; no matter which entrance Billy chose, Wallace was positioned well to give him a greeting with the carbine.

He had used the carbine only for target practice, but it was his favorite weapon, one he had liked ever since he had first qualified on it years ago, in summer camp with the National Guard. It was even better with the strap binding it to his body, but that was rifle range and bushwhack stuff, not at all what he wanted now. He needed mobility, and the carbine, light as a feather but with the kick of a mule, made him feel more than a match for Billy.

Remember, this was the guy he had conned into shooting Jake Fennel. A smile stretched across Wallace's face. His stomach rumbled then, and he realized he was hungry. Well, he might get a helluva lot hungrier before this was over.

The lamp came through the living room window right after it had been blasted away. Wallace watched it roll, sloshing oil as it did. It stopped, rolled backward, and the spilled oil burst into flame. Wallace let fly with the carbine, going through half a clip, making the lamp dance across the floor, trying to put it out, thinking, my God, the house is on fire, but he only succeeded in moving it to the drapes, and the flames began to lick at the fabric.

The front door was being forced. Wallace came

around the corner, the carbine ready, and put the rest of the clip through the front door.

He had the second clip out of his jacket pocket and was jamming it home as he ran through the house to the kitchen. He lowered his shoulder and protected his face with his arm as he hurtled through the torn-up windows and skidded on the snow-covered deck, but he was balanced enough to hit the ground running.

He made it to the shed without another shot being fired, turned in time to see the back door open and the figure of Billy appear. He shot without aiming but the way Billy dropped back made Wallace sure he had hit the sonofabitch.

Well, he wasn't going to stick around and find out. That was when he saw what Billy had done to the Olds and the pickup. He groped with his ungloved hand around the plastic windshield of the snowmobile and could have yelled with triumph when he felt the ignition key.

He looked back at the house. Billy was coming across the deck, crouched, moving slowly. Wallace aimed this time, squeezing off the shot. Billy straightened, screaming in pain, and lumbered back toward the house.

Wallace, holding the carbine out from his body, started after him, then stopped. How many rounds did he have in the clip? He didn't know. He had squeezed off the last shot, but before that he had let go a burst. Billy was wounded, he was sure of that, but how badly he had no way of knowing. He held

the carbine in his right hand and brought his left to
his face. Sticky. He was bleeding. How much glass
had he taken in the face up in that tower? He was
lucky it hadn't gotten into his eyes. He moved his
hand gingerly upward and came upon needlelike
ends of glass sticking from his flesh not two inches
from his right eye.

He decided to get the hell out of there.

It was not easy pushing the snowmobile off the dry
surface while holding onto the carbine, but he managed to shove it out of the shed onto the snow. He
threw his leg over it and got settled. The house was
quiet. Snow had begun to fall again and it seemed to
be coming thicker all the time. Wallace inhaled,
choked the motor once, very deliberately, then
twisted the key. It started on the first try, but God
what a racket. He grabbed the gearshift just as the
back door opened again and Billy came running out.

Wallace got the snowmobile in gear and took off,
starting toward the house but hanging a left and
heading in the direction of the wheat field and the
far-off stand of walnut trees. He was crouched over
the handlebars, his back tingling with terror.

There was the roar of a shotgun behind him and a
whoosh of pellets to his left. He began to zigzag, and
the shotgun kept going off, but each time he was far-
ther away. He gave the machine maximum accelera-
tion all the way, never even thought of turning on the
light, but he was using his hands to steer and hang
onto the carbine both.

As he neared the ridge, Billy shot again and this

165

time the pellets peppered Wallace's backside, but at that distance they were reduced to the annoyance of BB's.

Just ahead was the ridge and safety. The walnut trees were on his left. Wallace took the ridge at full speed, lifting off the saddle and raising his head as he cleared it. What a sense of escape as he sailed through the air with the lift of the ridge. The carbine slipped free, but he didn't care. He gripped the handlebars more tightly and began to make great sweeping arcs, to the left, to the right, in celebration of having escaped.

His eyes were squinted into the rushing air, alive with snow, and there was a triumphant smile on his face when he went at 45 mph into the barbed-wire fence. The lower strands were snapped by the nose of the snowmobile, but the top wire caught him in the throat and severed his head from his body.

TWENTY-ONE

Julie had a key to the clinic, because she was the first to arrive on Mondays to put on the coffee and lay out the doughnuts and pastry. It seemed fair enough to ask why volunteers were even necessary at the clinic.

"I mean, people go for medical attention, right? It's not like a hospital where you need gray ladies or whatever they're called."

Julie smiled sweetly at Gerald. "Monday is free clinic day. The doors are open to anyone who wants to come. Extra help is needed just to keep things in order."

Gerald nodded. He had not meant to demean what Julie and her friends did. In fact, he was proud of her. What did he himself do for his fellow man, for free, just to be of help? He leaned toward Julie and kissed her on both cheeks.

"The Charles de Gaulle award."

"*Merci, mon ami.*"

"Why don't you show me around the clinic?"

"I thought you were there the other day to have a physical."

"What could I see without my clothes on?"

"Everything?"

"That's what they could see. How about it?"

"Come on Monday and you can help out."

"I was thinking of now."

"Now? It's ten o'clock at night."

"We'll have the place to ourselves."

"You're serious."

He had pulled into the parking lot of the clinic, and that seemed sufficient answer to her question. He said, "I suppose there is some sort of security?"

"Sure. Old Weber."

"Old Weber?"

"You wouldn't know him. He was janitor at the high school for nearly forty years. They made him retire, but your uncle said he could have a job at the clinic as long as he lived."

"He knows you?"

"Of course he knows me."

"I'm dying to meet him."

Old Weber sat at a table in the lobby, a television set with a screen the size of a playing card going in front of him, his hat pulled low over his eyes. He lurched awake after Julie had let them in and, having said his name several times, touched him on the shoulder.

"Morning already?"

"Not quite."

He frowned sleepily at the television, turned up the volume, then turned off the set.

"This is Gerald Rowan, Mr. Weber. Andrew Broom's nephew."

A reverent look crept over Weber's creased face and he snatched his cap from his head, producing a great shock of white hair as if by magic. An arthritic hand was extended to Gerald.

"Your uncle is a great man, son."

Gerald nodded, shaking the hand. It was difficult getting a grip on it, but Old Weber didn't mind.

Julie said, "He wants to be shown around the clinic his uncle built."

It was pretty obvious that Weber was not going to be any problem so far as looking around went. The problem was he wanted to come along, if only to open doors for the nephew of the man he considered his benefactor.

"We wouldn't think of taking you away from your post," Julie said in shocked tones. "I can give him the tour. You stay where you belong."

Put that way, Weber found it difficult to insist, but he watched them go off down the corridor somewhat wistfully, as if he had been deprived of a great opportunity.

"What do you particularly want to see?" Julie asked, hooking her arm through his.

"Records."

"Records!" She shut one eye and looked up at him. "Tell me why you wanted to get in here."

"To check some records."

She shook her head, but pressed his arm more tightly against her side. "Some date."

"I want to be sure I'm pure enough for you."

"You what?"

"Sweetheart, if you ever get herpes it won't be from me."

She tried to pull her arm free but he pinned it to him. "Julie, I'm kidding."

"But you want to see how your physical came out?"

"No."

"Then what?"

"I want to see how my uncle's physical came out."

"Hmmm."

The closed doors along the corridor were identified by signs that stood at right angles to the wall. Medical Records was the last door on the left, across from the office of Dr. Lister. The key that had opened the street door would not open this one. Julie lifted her shoulders. "Sorry."

"Weber?"

"Is it that important?"

"Please."

Waiting wasn't bad since he had the pleasure of watching Julie walk down the corridor and the complementary pleasure of seeing her come back again, accompanied by Weber, who had the look of a man whose sense of self-importance has been restored.

He unlocked the door and pushed it open, reaching inside to flick on the light. Gerald went right in, coming to a stop in the middle of a rectangular room, four walls of which were lined with cabinets five feet high. He shook his head in disapproval.

"The decor?" Julie asked, looking around. The cabinets were beige, the walls orange.

"It's a waste of space. All this should be on computer."

"It is," Julie said. "But Dr. Lister wants the traditional written records as well."

Gerald could approve of this, as a backup, but of course he was in no mood to be critical now. He had moved to the cabinet holding records A–C. He tugged on the appropriate drawer and for a panicky second thought it too was locked. But the drawer gave and then slid nicely open. Julie stood beside him as he ran his hands over the tabs. And then he had it: Broom, Andrew.

"Think you could persuade Weber to leave us alone for a minute?" he whispered.

"I will distract him."

And she did, babbling away about the clinic and what was Dr. Lister's office like, did he think she could see it. Of course she could see it. The two of them left the room, and Gerald pulled his uncle's file.

There were pages of handwritten medical history, but the file built from the back, moving from the past to the present. The lab reports and the EKG of Uncle Andrew's recent physical were at the front of the folder. Gerald studied the results but none of it meant much to him. He would have to get someone to interpret for him. He flipped up his coat and inserted the folder into the back of his trousers, adjusting it so it was not too uncomfortable. He pushed the file drawer closed.

"What is going on here?"

It was the voice of Dr. Lister, from across the hall. Gerald glided across the records room, turned off the light, and eased into the hall, pulling the door shut behind him. The lock clicked.

Directly before him, Dr. Lister stood in the doorway of his office, his hands on the door frame. Beyond him, looking like kids caught in some mischief, were Julie and Old Weber. As Gerald stood there, hoping neither Julie nor Weber would see him and cause Lister to turn around, the doctor went on into his office.

"I asked what is going on?"

Gerald went down the hall on the run, skidded across the lobby where Weber had been seated, and let himself out into the night. There were two cars in the parking lot now, one the Mercedes Gerald had seen at his uncle's the night before. He slid behind the wheel of his own car and started the motor. The file was too uncomfortable, so he slipped it out and slid it under the passenger seat. And waited.

Ten minutes later, three figures emerged from the clinic and came toward his car. Weber shuffled along, Julie was clearly furious, and Lister looked as if he had blown his cork and still didn't know what the hell was going on.

"Tell him," Julie ordered, when she stood beside the car, flanked by Weber and Lister.

"Are you sure?"

"Tell him."

Gerald smiled up at Lister. "We're in love. I thought she wanted it kept a secret, but..."

"Gerald Rowan, tell Dr. Lister what I was doing in the clinic at..." She pulled back her sleeve and held up her arm but she could not get light on the face of her watch. Gerald glanced at his dashboard.

"11:03."

Lister said, "Were you inside the clinic too?"

"Yes, I was. I wanted to see it when it wasn't crowded. Nice place."

"But why..."

"Julie and Mr. Weber were nice enough to give me a little tour. Then, when the phone rang in your office, and they decided it should be answered, I came out here to wait. Who called?" he asked Julie.

She looked over the car, trying to be mad, but the corners of her mouth were threatening to twitch into a smile.

It was Weber who saved the day. "It was a wrong number," he announced. "All that trouble to answer the damned thing and it was a wrong number."

"Why didn't you tell me this before?"

"Because you wouldn't let him," Julie cried, turning on the doctor. "You came screaming in on us as if we were thieves or something, and you didn't give Mr. Weber the chance to tell you what we were doing in your stupid office." She turned to Weber and impulsively kissed his cheek. "Thank you very much, Mr. Weber. It is nice that someone here has some common courtesy."

She flounced around the car. Gerald had the door open for her and she got in and slammed it shut.

"Thanks, Mr. Weber. Good night, Doctor."

As he drove across the lot toward the exit, Julie said between clenched teeth, "I am going to break every bone in your body."

"Is that all you ever think of, my body?"

It was hard to drive while fending off her blows, but he managed to get them to the Roundball Lounge in the basement of the Hoosier Towers without incident. He took her in his arms when he had parked and by the time they went inside, they were good friends again.

TWENTY-TWO

The call from Sheriff Cleary woke Andrew up. He sat on the edge of his bed, his eyes stuck closed, and tried to make sense out of what the sheriff was saying.

"Wallace is dead?"

"As a mackerel. Some wild dogs mangled the body before we got it. A kid out snowmobiling found him. Wallace had been snowmobiling too."

Andrew shook his head to clear it but kept his eyes shut. Until he opened them there was the chance that he could still get back to sleep.

"What time is it, Patrick?"

"7:47."

"That's an airplane."

"Wallace would have been better off on one of those than on a snowmobile."

"You say it was an accident?"

"I do like hell. Someone shot his ass full of buck-shot. Not to mention the house. And it's not clear that everything that happened to his head happened in the accident."

"Accident," Andrew repeated. "Patrick, why are you calling me at this ungodly hour to tell me this? Are you running a goddam news service?"

"Because Agnes Walz particularly insisted that I contact you."

The phone slammed in Andrew's ear, unsticking his eyes. The wall he stared at had a window in it and through the window he could see a fir tree, its branches thick with snow. It was the kind of scene on which the eyes liked to fix before the mind was fully awake. Agnes. Then Andrew thought of Billy. He was completely alert now.

When he shaved his right cheek, he put the fingers of his left hand on his right temple, turning his head as if he were his own barber. He tried not to think of his head being separated from the rest of him. He tried not to think of Wallace. First he wanted a far more coherent account than he had let Cleary give. Then he would think about it.

But he already knew what had happened.

He had activated the assassin.

A shiver of fear and excitement ran through his half-clothed body. He looked deeply into his re-flected eyes.

"I am next," he told himself.

But he could see that he did not believe it. An el-liptical conversation in an Illinois border town, talk of large sums of money being doled out to a killer.

Had he ever really believed he was striking a deal with Billy?

Belief came in the course of the morning. At his office, he read the Wyler *Star*, in which Healy gave full rein to the repressed lyric poet and gothic novelist in himself. "Convicted Wife's Spouse Slain." Andrew also got embellishments from Susannah and the radio.

"I'm going out there."

"Sheriff Cleary did call you ..." Susannah began, as if seeking a justification for his going.

"I should have gone there right away. Where is Gerald?"

"Not in yet."

"Hmmm."

"Would you like me to come with you?"

What an odd suggestion. He looked at Susannah. He looked at her every day, all day, but he had not seen her in years. She was really a very handsome woman. He liked the steady way she looked at him. He said, yes, why don't you come along?

The deputy on duty let them into the farmyard only when he'd radioed the sheriff's office and, after a delay—Cleary was making a point—got an okay.

"He didn't mention the lady," the deputy said.

"He'd better not."

The deputy frowned. "I mean I don't know if I can let her go in there."

"Officer, this is my secretary."

Susannah said to the deputy, "Edwin, for heaven's sake."

"Who's Edwin?" Andrew asked as they walked up

the slippery drive to the house. The deputy could not allow any vehicles into the farmyard.

"He lives several doors up."

"A neighbor of yours?"

"I used to baby-sit for him." Billy's presence was almost palpable inside the house. Susannah justified coming along by taking notes in shorthand, describing the rooms. There had been some kind of fire in the living room, but it had been put out. Edwin joined them.

"I got a call from the sheriff. He said to stay with you."

"There was a fire," Andrew observed.

"Kerosene lamp was taken in for examination. Shot hell out of the place." He pointed at the destroyed window. The kitchen was worse.

Andrew said, "Did anybody turn off the furnace?"

Edwin looked at him. "Good idea. Can't be heating the whole outdoors."

Andrew felt he had done his client a service. Or had he? Would Agnes ever see this house again? Now her husband as well as her boyfriend was gone and her chances of being freed before she was senile were not good. Andrew imagined he would soon be looking into the disposal of this property.

No, he wouldn't. He wouldn't be here. He tried to imagine the white cells eating up the red cells in his bloodstream, he tried to feel poorly, but he just couldn't. It didn't matter. He was going to die. He had received the verdict from the doctor. And he had set in play a plan that would get the thing over with in a way that would make it easier for his wife and nephew and friends.

Such thoughts could sting a tear from his eye, but he was on the back deck now, looking out at the yard, and the breeze coming in across the snow could have explained his damp eyes. Footprints, snowmobile tracks, it was hard to make head or tail of it. Except that Andrew knew it represented Billy's taking out Wallace as he had been hired to do. If it was a messy scene, this was no doubt due to Wallace's lack of cooperation. No reason to blame Billy.

Edwin pointed toward some trees. "It happened just over that ridge."

Andrew nodded. He had seen enough. He no longer doubted that Billy meant business. Susannah put her arm through his as they went back to the car, to steady herself on the slippery drive, and her proximity made Andrew catch his breath. The warmth of another human being. It was the simple things that mattered.

And it was the simple things that could sap his resolution now. He handed Susannah into the car. A glimpse of her calf as she drew her legs in. Another catch of his breath. Impending death made him more than usually susceptible to the joys of this world.

I have had my share, he told himself, as he drove silently back to Wyler. I have had my share.

But Susannah was so different from Dorothy, his curiosity was piqued.

A little late. No, he didn't mean that. He was glad

he had not diddled Susannah and been untrue to Dorothy. He could go out with his chin held high. June? A business matter.

Billy called five minutes after he got back.

"I tried before. Nobody answered."

Andrew signaled to Susannah to close his door. Gerald was still not in.

He said into the phone, "I have been out admiring your handiwork."

Silence.

"I was out at the Walz farm."

"That guy is a sonofabitch."

"Put up quite a struggle?"

"I did my best."

"Well, he's gone."

Silence.

"Billy?"

"Walz is dead?"

"Yes, a kid snowmobiling found the body this morning."

Silence.

"I have not spoken with Agnes yet. I intend to do that very soon. Before lunch. I will let her know that she is in your debt."

"Yeah."

"And then there is the next job."

"You?"

"That's right."

"When?"

He closed his eyes and was beset by the tactile memory of Susannah's arm against his side, by the visual memory of her well-shaped leg. He snapped his eyes open.

"Well, you're in town."

Something like humming came over the phone. "Not today."

Andrew could have shouted with relief. A reprieve from the governor. "Why not?" he asked, his voice calm.

"Last night was a sonofabitch."

"I can believe that."

"Gimme a day."

"I am the one getting the extra day."

"Yeah."

Billy hung up before Andrew could ask where he was staying. Just as well. He didn't want to know. He had no reason to contact Billy.

Talking about how Wallace got it brought a little smile to Agnes's thin lips. She was less happy to hear about the house.

"Would you see about having it repaired?"

"Of course, Agnes. You realize you owe money now?"

She dipped her head and looked at him over her glasses. "Send me a bill."

"I refer to a man from Illinois. Wallace did not die accidentally."

"Oh? That remains to be seen. From what the

sheriff tells me, it looks like an accident. If that is the verdict, well, why should I pay?"

"I'll leave the house the way it is and if you ever get a look at it you will see that someone earned his money."

"You think I should pay?"

"I would advise it."

She thought about it. Clearly it was a great temptation to her not to give Billy the ten thousand dollars, particularly since he could not take back what she had bought.

Andrew said, "He might decide to get you before the state does."

"Nobody is going to get me."

"We can't be sure of that. Of the appeal. But we can be sure that Billy will contact a female associate and have you killed in prison if he doesn't wait to savor the personal pleasure should you get out."

"If I tell you where the money is, you might try to cheat Billy."

"That is very unlikely, Agnes."

"But not impossible."

What a troublesome bitch she was. It was hard to believe that two men were dead because of this woman. "What would you suggest?"

"I've written another note, telling him where the money is."

"I'll see that he gets it. Agnes, don't try to cheat him."

"I hate being in here." She made fists of her hands and closed her eyes very tight. Andrew felt a wave of pity.

"We are trying to get you out."

"Did you read the morning paper?"

Healy. Healy was depicting Agnes as the innocent pawn in the amorous struggle of two men inflamed with love for her. Both had gone down in the struggle, leaving poor Agnes in jail. Healy wanted to know how any jury in Indiana could have found this little lady guilty.

"Has Healy been to see you?"

"Coming this afternoon. What's he like?"

"You read his story."

"What do you mean?"

"He drinks."

Agnes stuck out a small gray tongue at him. He took the little blue envelope and left. As the doors clanged behind him, it occurred to him that this might have been the last time he'd see her. And vice versa. But when he turned there was no sign of her.

TWENTY-THREE

Billy had walked back to town from the Walz farm the night before and by the time he got to the Lullaby Motel that was all he thought about, lullaby. He had underestimated the distance to town, but once he started walking he was stuck with it. But first he looked at his arm. The goddam farmer had hit him with a lucky shot. The round had ripped through his sleeve and grazed his arm and it felt like whatever degree burn is the worst.

Billy rubbed mentholated shaving cream all over the spot and it helped some. He lay in the bed, on his back, stared at the ceiling, and thought of what a mess he had made of the job.

There went the ten thousand. There went twenty thousand. Why would the lawyer go ahead with their deal when he found out about the way the farmer had taken off?

Taken off where?

To the police? That thought had moved Billy, half frozen, along the road to Wyler and out the other side of town to the Lullaby Motel. The platinum blonde was not on duty in the office. At night there was a bald guy who read *Oui* with his eyes bugged out. Billy had called it O-U-I, like a college or something, until Carole corrected him. Not that he read the damned thing. He wanted to look at a woman he would look at a woman. Anyway, the night man had not looked up from his magazine when Billy slipped past the office on his way to Unit 7.

A sleepless night. He thought of calling Carole. He had not said goodbye and maybe now it was a good thing. He did not like to think of going back to Sorrento, but it was a job, and it looked like he was going to need it.

Finally, he did fall asleep, but it was still dark when he woke up, swinging his legs off the bed and flicking on the TV in one motion. Just in time to hear that it was twenty past the hour. Which hour? He had left the bathroom light on, he did not like total darkness, and he got the face of his watch into the light. Seven twenty.

Nothing on the early local news about what had happened at the Walz farm last night.

He tried to believe that he had got Walz with a blast as the farmer zoomed away on that damned snowmobile. The one he had rented was up over that ridge somewhere, but he figured to hell with it.

Going after it would only remind him of the one that got away.

The conversation with the lawyer Broom changed his mood completely. He went into the bathroom and grinned at himself for five minutes. His arm still hurt like a sonofabitch. There were splinters in his body too, his legs and arms, his chest. From the front door, when the guy had shot the hell out of it. But he felt a lot better knowing that Wallace had not gotten away.

Now when he lay on the bed he thought of the best way to do it to the lawyer. His feelings toward the man were friendly and he searched for a friendly way to put him out of his misery. He liked the idea of using the man's car.

That afternoon, he went downtown and checked it out. A Porsche. Parked it in the underground garage of the Hoosier Towers, left it there most of the day. He didn't like the idea of its being indoors, but overcame his misgivings. That is what he would do.

Tomorrow.

After another phone call.

"You talk to the lady about her payment?"

"Yes. The day afterward, you come here to my office and ask my secretary for an envelope addressed to Mr. Sassoon. A. Sassoon. That's you."

"The day after?"

"The day after you earn the balance. I imagine that will be tomorrow. So it will be ready for you the day after tomorrow."

"What was that name again?"

"Sassoon."

Billy repeated it. He felt he should say something else to the man, but he didn't know what. So he hung up.

Tomorrow. Tomorrow it would be. After the man parked his car in the underground garage of the Hoosier Towers, Billy would go down there and put a surprise under the hood, connect it to the starter. One turn of the key and he would have earned his extra ten thousand.

TWENTY-FOUR

He telephoned Dorothy and told her they were going out to dinner.

"Again?" A little laugh. "Andrew, we were out to dinner Tuesday night."

"Humor me."

"Just so it isn't the country club."

"I couldn't agree more."

He did not want to have his last meal in the dining room of the country club, the associations were too powerfully sentimental. Through the windows, under the snow, were the fairways and greens, hazards and traps, designed by Arnold Palmer. The scene of Andrew's many triumphs. But that, along with everything else, must be put behind him.

Tonight was for Dorothy.

They could drive to South Bend and eat at Tippecanoe Place, maybe stay over at the Morris Inn. It would be the opposite of a honeymoon. The last night of their marriage. His hand still clamped over the cradled phone, Andrew felt his lip tremble. He did not want to die.

He got to his feet. Of course he did not want to die. Nobody wanted to die. How would Billy do it? He assumed with a gun. Well, he would much rather be shot than waste away with leukemia. It was a helluva choice, but it was the only one he had.

Gerald had not been in the office all day. Susannah called his apartment and got no answer. Andrew thought of Julie McGough, but pushed the thought out of his mind. When Healy called to ask for an interview, he told him he would meet him in the Roundball and went down to the lounge.

"The wire service picked up my story, Andrew. They want a follow-up."

"I'm not surprised."

"I need more details."

"Why? You're much more interesting when you just make it up."

Healy nodded, taking it as a compliment. Andrew's drink came and they clinked glasses.

"It was the jury I criticized, Andrew, not you."

"I appreciate that."

"Do you think you can get it reversed?"

"Anything is possible. All the evidence was circumstantial."

"And now her husband's suicide."

"Suicide?"

"He figures he's lost her. He thinks she's going to

spend the rest of her life in prison. What can life mean to him now?"

"Have you ever seen Agnes?"

"I interviewed her this afternoon."

"A real knockout, isn't she?"

Healy shook his head, a patient expression on his face. "You're a victim of the plastic age, Andrew. You think love is only for people who have their faces on magazine covers. Look around you. Men and women are attracted to real men and women. Agnes is real."

"I'll grant you that."

"Two men died because of their love for her."

"Tell me about it."

"Did you know her husband and the Fennel guy had been rivals since they were kids?"

"Yes."

"So this has been going on all their lives. This is the culmination. Fennel never gave up. Finally, Agnes's resistance was just worn down. Maybe she felt a little something for him too. Whatever happened, it might have been innocent, the husband is enraged."

"That is why Fennel was over in Sorrento trying to hire a killer to take out Wallace?"

Healy thought about that. "This story has so many angles," he said after a moment, unfazed. "It is inexhaustible. Like love itself."

"Thanks for the drink, Healy."

"Have another."

Andrew looked at his watch. "No. I have a date." He stood up. "With my wife."

"There you go," Healy said, sitting forward at the table. "What did I tell you?"

On that ambiguous note, Andrew returned to the office to find that Gerald had telephoned from Chicago.

"What's he doing in Chicago?"

"He said you would give him a medal when you found out."

"Sure."

"He said to tell you he had good news. Very good news."

"I'm glad to hear it."

"He left a number for you to call, but it's too late. He will have started back."

Andrew was glad. His nephew's enthusiasm was not what he wanted now. Like Healy's imaginative reconstruction of the Agnes/Wallace/Jacob triangle, Gerald's call suggested only that life would go on, hopes and schemes continue to alter human lives. Gerald would have a secure future. Andrew had seen to that. Gerald and Dorothy were the principal beneficiaries of his will, aside from philanthropic bequests, of course. Andrew took very seriously his role as town father of Wyler, Indiana.

But tonight he wanted a sentimental evening with his wife.

Gerald's news could wait.

Gerald's news was that his uncle was in all but perfect health. He had taken Andrew's medical history to a friend who practiced medicine in Evanston. His friend Martin had flipped through the pages, lower lip jutted out, bushy brows lifted above his designer glasses. He slapped it shut and said, "Your uncle is a lucky man."

"What does he have?"

"Very good health for a man his age."

"Nothing wrong with him?"

Martin lifted the cover of the folder, then let it drop. "Nobody is in perfect health. There is always something."

Gerald sat forward. Now it would come. "Like what?"

"He could lose a few pounds, for one thing. He ought to cut out the coffee."

Gerald waited. "Go on."

"Go one where? That's it. What were you expecting?"

"I don't know."

"How did you get hold of his medical records?"

"I stole them."

Martin laughed until he saw that Gerald meant it. He pushed the folder across the desk. "Why?"

Gerald tried to explain his suspicions, but he didn't have to look at Martin to see he was not doing a very good job of it.

"Who is his doctor?"

"A local man. In Wyler, Indiana. Where I live now. He heads the clinic. Lister."

"Theodore Lister?"

"Ted. Yes."

"Theodore Lister is in Wyler, Indiana?"

"My uncle brought him there. My uncle built the clinic and then staffed it. He wanted first-rate medical facilities in Wyler. You've heard of Lister?"

"I have heard of Lister." He pulled the folder toward him again and opened it up. "His name's right there and I didn't think." He read through everything again, and looked at Gerald.

"Your uncle would have received a very reassuring report after this physical. There is no reason why he should be worried."

"Well, he is."

"Then it has nothing to do with his health."

"Martin, I was sure Lister hadn't told him the bad news. But, then, why is Andrew worried? I don't get it."

"Look, do you want me to call Lister?"

"Why do that?"

"I'd like to speak to him." Martin frowned. "But I'd have to lie. I'd have to say your uncle consulted me."

Gerald figured that if Lister hadn't put their conversations at his uncle's and in the parking lot of the clinic together and checked out Uncle Andrew's medical records, he was not the whiz Martin seemed to think he was. He said, "Just tell him I brought those records to you."

"Are they really stolen?"

"If they are, you didn't steal them."

Gerald sat across the desk while Martin put through the call. Martin's deferential tone when he got through to Lister really surprised Gerald. He thought of the wimp in his uncle's den, the nitwit in the parking lot. Of course Martin had never met Lister personally.

"Dr. Lister, this is Dr. Martin Feldman in Evanston, Illinois. You don't know me, but I know and admire your work. Your article on hernias in the *New England Journal of Medicine* is truly a classic. I am calling about a patient of yours, Mr. Andrew Broom."

The smile that had been on Martin's face disappeared. He had been looking at Gerald but now his eyes drifted away.

"Dr. Lister..."

Martin listened and nodded, he tried to smile but it came out a frown or worse. He nodded and listened and looked at the ceiling.

"That is amazing," he said.

The muffled flow went on.

"Of course. I can see how it might have happened. Well, that must be a great relief to your patient."

After Martin put down the phone, he turned his chair ninety degrees and stared at a bookshelf. He turned back to look at Gerald.

"I can't believe that's the same Theodore Lister."

"He's the only one we have. What did he say?"

"It's incredible. No wonder your uncle acted worried. Lister told him, mistakenly, that he has leukemia. I couldn't follow his explanation. Something about a mix-up in the reports from the lab. But these are the lab reports right here."

"He told my uncle he has leukemia?"

"That's what he said."

"My God."

"But he doesn't have it. That's the point."

"No wonder he acted worried."

· "I don't envy Theodore Lister," Martin said.

"My uncle will kill him."

"Or sue him, which is worse."

Gerald was so happy he took Feldman to lunch. It was late afternoon when he called the office in Wyler. His uncle was not in. He left a message.

"Did Dr. Lister call him today?"

"From the clinic? No. Why?"

"Just wondered. Did you miss me?"

"How could I? You weren't here."

They had gone down the driveway and onto the road when Andrew noticed the car in the rearview mirror.

"Who do we know drives a Mercedes?"

Dorothy said, "Why do you ask?"

"One just pulled into the driveway."

"Well, we're not at home."

"I think Lister drives a Mercedes."

"Does he?"

Medallions of veal, a Barolo red from Italy, elegant surroundings in Tippecanoe Place, coffee and brandy, atmosphere. Dorothy was beautiful. They said little. The silence was comfortable. She put both her hands on his right arm as they drove to the Morris Inn.

"We've wasted so much time," he murmured later.

"Why do you say that, Andrew?"

"How long has it been?"

She snuggled against him. "Too long."

Later. "Andrew?"

"Yes."

"How do you feel?"

"Wonderful."

"No. I mean your health."

He said nothing.

She said, "Are you on a diet?"

"Why?"

"You've lost too much weight. I don't like it when you look gaunt."

He held her close. If she could see a change in him already, he was not acting too soon. Earlier he had told himself he should postpone things, take his time. He and Dorothy might have months together still. Now he knew that was nonsense. A good thing, since he had no way of contacting Billy to issue a cancellation.

TWENTY-FIVE

Ten o'clock and still his uncle had not shown up. Gerald had been wanting for hours and hours to tell Andrew the good news, and now he could not sit still. He called the house and there was no answer. Susannah was no help.

"I heard him talking to his wife about going out to dinner."

"Last night? Susannah, it is going on noon."

"It is five after ten. You weren't here at all yesterday."

Whenever the phone rang, Gerald came out of his office and asked Susannah who it was.

"That time it was Dr. Lister."

"What the hell does he want?"

Susannah was surprised. "Did you want to speak to him?"

"No. Maybe Andrew will, but I don't."

"How did your physical go?"

"I haven't heard." He did not add that he would distrust anything Lister had to tell him. Ever since Martin gave him the news, he had alternated between being furious at Lister and wanting to hug him. He did not think Uncle Andrew would want to hug the doctor.

The founder of the firm sauntered in at 10:45 and was surprised when Gerald greeted him at the door wanting to know where he had been.

"I dropped your aunt off at the house on the way in. Why?"

"Uncle Andrew, I have incredibly good news."

He tugged his uncle into the conference room and closed the door. Since leaving Evanston the previous afternoon he had been rehearsing what he would say, but now, alone with his uncle, all Gerald could do was grin. His uncle tried to grin back, then gave it up.

"What is it, Gerald?"

"Your health. Uncle Andrew, you're okay. I know what Lister told you, but I took your records to a man in Evanston and he looked them over and you're all right. There's nothing wrong with you."

"You took my records. How did you get hold of my records?"

"I went to the clinic and stole them. I wanted to see the results of your physical because you'd been acting so down, but I couldn't understand the stuff so I took it to a doctor I know in Evanston."

Uncle Andrew sat down. "Gerald, I don't know what you've been told..."

"He called Dr. Lister. Feldman. The doctor in Evanston. He phoned Lister and Lister told him it was all a mistake. Uncle Andrew, you don't have leukemia. Your health is perfect."

He had to tell him twice. He had to go through the whole thing again, coherently, what he had been told by Dr. Feldman, about the telephone call, everything.

"How could he have made a mistake like that?"

"If it was a mistake," Gerald said.

"What do you mean?"

Gerald thought of Aunt Dorothy taking Lister in her arms. He decided he had done enough reporting for one day.

"I think you ought to call Lister."

"I think you're right."

Uncle Andrew went into his office and Gerald went into the reception room and kissed Susannah. She was flustered but not unpleased.

"What's that for?"

"My uncle."

"Your uncle!" Susannah turned beet red.

A mistake! Andrew Broom could not sit down. A wild elation filled him but was swiftly replaced by rage. A mistake!

How in God's name could any doctor make a mistake like that? Leukemia.

I don't have it. I don't have it. I'm well.

He wanted to sing. He wanted to dance around his

office. He felt even better than he had last night with Dorothy.

But first, Lister.

He picked up the phone. "Susannah, get me Dr. Lister at the clinic."

He replaced the phone and paced up and down his office. A buzz. He picked up the phone.

"Dr. Lister is not in his office today. That's funny, too, because he called you earlier."

"Try him at home."

"Yes, sir."

More pacing and then a minute later another buzz. Andrew inhaled once and picked it up.

Susannah said, "There is no answer at his home."

"Keep trying."

It was not until he sat at his desk that he thought of Billy. Billy! The man he had hired to kill him. Dear God, this was his last day on earth, leukemia or no leukemia, unless he could stop Billy. Where was he?

Who was he? Andrew realized he did not even know the assassin's last name. He could have Susannah call all the hotels and motels in the area, but who could she ask for? Meanwhile, at any moment, Billy might strike.

Andrew looked at the closed door of his office. That door could swing open right now and Billy let go with a shotgun.

He got out of his chair and sidled along the wall of his office. He was perspiring. He had to get out of there. He had to hide.

He opened the door a crack and looked out. His

eyes met Susannah's. She blushed and looked away. What the hell was wrong with her?

"Susannah," he whispered. She turned to him shyly. He gestured. "Come in here."

She came on the run and when he had the door closed threw her arms around him, kissing his face, murmuring incoherently. He took hold of her arms, trying to control her, but she pressed her body against his, eyes closed, head thrown back. What the hell. He kissed her throat.

That is how Dorothy found them, in one another's arms.

"Well," she said, looking around the half-opened door.

Susannah resisted Andrew's efforts to free himself. She had one arm around his middle, one leg between his, a hand on her hip as she looked defiantly at his lawfully wedded wife.

"I've just learned I am in perfect health," Andrew said.

"And the two of you are celebrating?"

Gerald stood in the doorway. "Now, Aunt Dorothy, I wouldn't be so righteous if I were you. I wonder if Uncle Andrew knows about you and Dr. Lister."

"Lister!" Andrew burst free of Susannah.

Gerald said, "He visits your wife when you're away."

"Dorothy, is that true?" The magic of the previous night evaporated as he realized he was not surprised by what Gerald was saying. And then it came to him.

Lister telling him he had leukemia.

Dorothy pretending he looked ill, that he was losing weight. He was a pound or two overweight, if it came to that.

"Dorothy, what do you know about Lister's telling me I had leukemia?"

"Leukemia!" Susannah threw her arms around him as if she meant to protect him from disease and death itself.

"He doesn't have leukemia," Gerald cried. "His health is good."

"Andrew," Dorothy said, "I don't know what you're talking about. I'm sorry I interrupted your celebration. I dropped by to borrow your car. I left mine at the station to get an oil change and I have some errands to run."

Andrew flipped her the keys. "If you run into Lister, tell him I want to see him."

Dorothy looked at him icily, then shrugged and left the office.

Andrew pried himself loose from Susannah.

"When did you guess?" she asked him.

"I had no idea until Gerald told me."

"You!" Susannah said to Gerald, punching his arm as she left the office.

Andrew sat at his desk, his head swimming, wondering what he could do to stop Billy. Gerald was still with him. His nephew's apartment? Maybe he could hide there. There was a muffled sound far below and the building seemed to sway.

"What was that?"

Gerald said, "I don't know. An earthquake?"

"In Indiana?"

Gerald went to the window and Andrew shouted, "Keep away from there! Don't show yourself in the window."

"Uncle Andrew, what's wrong?"

"I need rest."

Gerald put an arm around his shoulders. "I can imagine what you've been through."

"Where is your car?"

"Downstairs. Why?"

"Could I borrow it?"

"Of course, go to my apartment. Sleep."

"I have work to do."

"I'll send Susannah over later."

Andrew went downstairs in the service elevator and when the doors slid open the basement was filled with clouds of smoke and dust.

Three cars besides the Porsche were totaled in the explosion.

TWENTY-SIX

A month after Dr. Theodore Lister was found hanging in the closet of his office in the clinic, Agnes Walz's picture appeared on the cover of *Shoot*, a sensational tabloid sold at the checkout counters of supermarkets from coast to coast.

Actually, only half the picture was Agnes. Her head had been superimposed on the body of a beautiful young woman wearing a bikini. Agnes was referred to as the sexy sexagenarian, the granny over whom two men had fought to the death. "Is sex appeal a crime?" the article asked. Readers who thought Agnes had been unfairly treated by the criminal justice system were asked to send letters and cards and blindfolds to the courthouse in Wyler, Indiana.

Sacks of mail began to arrive within the week, and

before a fortnight had passed they were stacked ten feet high in the boiler room, the lower lobby, and the chambers of Ben Turnip, judge pro tem of the circuit court.

On the strength of this public outcry, Andrew Broom filed his motion for reversal of sentence, and two days later received a favorable verdict. Agnes was released at four in the morning, taken out the back door of the courthouse, and driven in a closed van to her farmhouse.

Repairs had been made, as she had asked. Alone at last, Agnes put water on to boil on her island stove, sat on a stool at the boomerang-shaped breakfast bar, and watched the rising sun send slanting rays across the acres that were now hers alone.

The water came to a boil. Agnes found in a canister a dozen flow-through bags of her favorite tea. She opened the cupboard and stood looking at the shelves, holding the cupboard doors wide, a little smile on her face.

There were her bottles of medicine, just where she had left them. And there was a bottle of her artificial sweetener as well, the brand she had missed so much while she was in custody.

She put a tea bag in a cup, poured scalding water over it, and then, back on her stool, poured a double dose of artificial sweetener into the tea. For luck, she gave it another dose as well.

She had thought Wallace would have thrown out her things, her medicine, her sweetener.

Agnes lifted her cup in a toast to her departed spouse and drank down the tea in three long sips.

TWENTY-SEVEN

It was her first marriage and Susannah by rights could have worn white, but she settled instead on a rose-colored dress with a very full skirt and a scoop neck. For travel, she had a dove gray suit and a black patent leather purse with matching shoes. Her honeymoon nightie was the color of flesh.

On the flight to Montego Bay, they sipped rum drinks and held hands.

"Andrew?"

"Hmmm?"

"Who is Mr. Sassoon?"

"A hairdresser?"

"No." She jabbed a finger into his ribs. "The man who came to pick up an envelope."

"Oh, that Sassoon. He's a special messenger."

Later they lay on the Jamaican beach and Andrew

picked up a fistful of sand and let it run onto her belly, making a mound.

"Odd about Agnes," Susannah said. She had placed her straw hat over her face.

"Yes."

"Is strychnine painful?"

"I never tried it."

"Do you think it was remorse?"

"Do you?"

"You knew her better than I did."

"Not much."

"Two suicides. Dr. Lister and Agnes Walz. I can't imagine how anyone could commit suicide, can you?"

He let another handful of sand form a mound on the mound of Susannah's stomach. At another time he would have been reminded of an hourglass, the grains measuring off inexorably the few precious moments we are granted. Now he found the dusty look of his wife's flesh stimulating. He gave it a kiss.

"No," he said. "I can't."

The End